MW01617319

In Cahoots

with the
Prickly Pear Posse

"Long-time fans of Ann Charles will be thrilled with her latest Jackrabbit Junction mystery, and new readers are sure to fall in love with the Morgan sisters, their daring exploits, and their extended family. Filled with danger, intrigue, snark, raging hormones, and twists galore, IN CAHOOTS WITH THE PRICKLY PEAR POSSE is wicked, can't-turn-the-page-fast-enough fun."
~**Julie Mulhern**, *USA Today* Bestselling Author of the Country Club Murders and the Poppy Fields Adventures

"The Morgan sisters are back in this sexy and screwball mystery series set in the Arizona desert. And for fans of Ms. Charles' Deadwood series—a snarly detective just might make an appearance. You don't want to miss this one!"
~**Kristy McCaffrey**, Author of the Wings of the West Series and The Pathway Adventure Series

"I loved this book and the law dogs on the pages!"
~**Francesca Garcia**, Retired Phoenix Police Detective.

Dear Reader,

One of the things I enjoy about writing multiple book series that take place in one overall story universe is the opportunity to write character crossovers from one series to another. These crossovers can be either a simple mention, like in the Dig Site Mystery series when Quint thinks about his sister, Violet Parker, the star of my Deadwood Mystery series; a cameo for one scene, such as when Claire and Kate Morgan visited Deadwood during Halloween in AN EX TO GRIND IN DEADWOOD; or an actual point-of-view character role … which is what I've done in this book with Natalie Beals from the Deadwood series, aka Violet's best friend and main partner in troublemaking.

I've always wanted to know more about what was happening in Natalie's head. Finally, we discover Natalie's thoughts on life with her rowdy cousins, her feelings about her sabbatical from the dating world, and her struggles with her long-running attraction to a certain Deadwood detective.

This story is character-driven through and through, which is my favorite kind to read and write. It's my first book with four different characters' points of view, which in itself was a fun challenge. Even better, the theme of the book revolves around the craziest character of them all.

I hope you enjoy reading IN CAHOOTS WITH THE PRICKLY PEAR POSSE. I certainly had a blast trying to keep up with all of the wild antics on the page.

Ann Charles
www.anncharles.com

In Cahoots

with the
Prickly Pear Posse

A Jackrabbit Junction Mystery
Book 5

Written by
Ann Charles

Illustrations by C.S. Kunkle

For Kristy McCaffrey

You write what I love.
You read what I write.
You daydream with me.
You make writing more fun.
Thank you for letting me stalk you way back when.
This one is for you!

IN CAHOOTS WITH THE PRICKLY PEAR POSSE

Copyright © 2019 by Ann Charles

Cover Art by C.S. Kunkle
Cover Design by B. Biddles
Editing by Eilis Flynn

Printed in the United States of America
First Printing, 2019
Print ISBN: 978-1-940364-64-3
E-book ISBN: 978-1-940364-63-6

Also by Ann Charles

Acknowledgments

My books are born with the help of many wonderful people. Thank you to:

My husband. You are loving, helpful, and comforting. You help me flesh out stories, smooth out the burrs in my writing, and make my books the best they can be.

My kids, Beaker and Chicken Noodle, for giving me hugs and kisses when I'm chained mentally to the computer for days on end.

My First Draft team: Margo Taylor, Mary Ida Kunkle, Kristy McCaffrey, Jacquie Rogers, Marcia Britton, Paul Franklin, Diane Garland, Vicki Huskey, Lucinda Nelson, Marguerite Phipps, Stephanie Kunkle, and Wendy Gildersleeve. Your patience when I leave you hanging chapter after chapter is the stuff of legends, ha ha ha.

My critique partners, Jacquie Rogers and Kristy McCaffrey, for cheering me on week after week and telling me what works and what doesn't.

My editor, Eilis Flynn, for making the words sparkle.

My WorldKeeper, Diane Garland, for hours of nitpicking and answering my series-related questions.

Francesca Garcia for helping me to make sure the law dogs followed the rules.

My Beta Team for making the Morgan sisters sparkle and shine like diamonds in the desert.

My brother, C.S. Kunkle, for creating illustrations and the cover art pieces that make my stories even more fun.

My graphic artist/cover designer, Mr. Biddles, for your ability to create eye-catching covers that make me say, "Wow!"

My wonderful and amazing readers for your constant support both online and in person. We've had joy and fun! Here's to many more seasons in the sun!

Author Julie Mulhern for your excellent cover quote!

And as usual, Clint (my brother), for giving me the opportunity to be a bossy older sister.

In Cahoots

with the
Prickly Pear Posse

Cast

Claire Alice Morgan (1,2,3,4,4.5,5)—Main heroine of the series, Mac's girlfriend, Harley's granddaughter

MacDonald "Mac" Garner (1,2,3,4,4.5,5)—Main hero of the series, Claire's boyfriend

Kathryn "Kate"/"Katie" Morgan (2,3,4,4.5,5)—Claire's and Ronnie's younger sister, Deborah's youngest daughter

Veronica "Ronnie" Morgan (3,4,4.5,5)—Claire's oldest sister, Deborah's oldest daughter

Natalie Beals (3,4,5)—Claire's cousin from South Dakota, Harley's granddaughter (crossover character from the Deadwood Mystery Series)

Valentine "Butch" Carter (1,2,3,4,4.5,5)—Owner of The Shaft (the only bar in Jackrabbit Junction), Kate's boyfriend

Sheriff Grady Harrison (1,2,3,4,4.5,5)—Sheriff of Cholla County, Ronnie's boyfriend

Chester Thomas (1,2,3,4,4.5,5)—Harley's old Army vet buddy

Harley "Gramps" Ford (1,2,3,4,4.5,5)—Claire's maternal grandfather, Ruby's husband

Henry Ford (1,2,3,4,5)—Harley's beagle/dog

Ruby Ford (previously Ruby Wayne-Martino) (1,2,3,4,4.5,5)—Mac's aunt, owner of the Dancing Winnebagos RV Park, Harley's new wife

Jessica Wayne (1,2,3,4,4.5,5)—Ruby's teenage daughter, Harley's stepdaughter

Manuel "Manny" Carrera (1,2,3,4,4.5,5)—Harley's old Army vet buddy, Deborah's husband

Deborah Ford Carrera (2,3,4,4.5,5)—Claire's mother, Harley's daughter

Detective "Coop" Cooper (5)—Deadwood detective (crossover character from the Deadwood Mystery Series)

Willis Harvey (5)—Detective Cooper's uncle (crossover character from the Deadwood Mystery Series)

Penny (5)—Sheriff Grady Harrison's sister; owner of The Mule Train Diner

Mississippi Brown (3,4,5)—FBI agent responsible for keeping an eye on Ronnie

Joe Martino (1,2,3,4,4.5,5)—Deceased; Ruby's first husband, previous owner of the Dancing Winnebagos RV Park

Deputy "Dipshit" Ernie (1,2,3,4,5)—One of the sheriff's deputies

Aunt Millie (3,4,4.5,5)—Sheriff Harrison's aunt, leader of the library gang

Lyle Jefferson (3,4,5)—Ronnie's ex-husband

Gary (2,3,4,5)—Bartender at The Shaft

Cherry Haywood (4.5,5)—Owner of Dirty Gerties

Elizabeth Harrison (3,4,5)—Grady Harrison's ex-wife

Dick Webber (1,2,4,5)—Old rancher, Butch Carter's neighbor

Tank (5)—Owner of Hummingbird Towing

Mindy Lou Harrison (3)—Sheriff Harrison's niece

Steve Horner (3,4)—Jessica's father, Ruby's ex-lover

Ruth and Greta (3,4)—Members of Aunt Millie's library gang

Chapter One

Jackrabbit Junction, Arizona
Friday, December 28th

Y ou know what sucks about being in jail?" Claire Morgan asked. She stopped pacing the floor inside Cell A at the Cholla County Sheriff's Office to glare at her sister.

"The smell of urine coming from the corner," Kate said. She'd been holding up the concrete block wall since they'd been hauled in by Deputy "Dipshit" Ernie almost an hour ago, refusing to sit on the cot that had been supposedly deloused of late.

"No." Claire crossed her arms. "Being in jail sucks. Period. And it's your fault I'm here, crazy."

Studying her nails, Kate harrumphed. "I'd use an exclamation mark rather than a period after that first sentence to make it more effective."

"I'm going to leave an exclamation mark in the middle of your forehead if you correct my English again, teacher."

"I didn't correct your English. I simply made an editorial suggestion."

Kate looked up from her nail inspection. Her double-wide smile and shifty eyes made Claire cringe. The porch light was on in Kate's head, but nobody was home at the moment. Her sister had been wearing that same manic expression outside of the grocery store earlier right before her nutty train derailed and careened into Claire.

"You need to chill out, Claire," ol' shifty-eyes whispered. She leaned closer. The whole left side of Kate's face twitched. "Gramps will be here soon to spring us."

No he wouldn't, not unless their grandfather had recently developed the ability to read minds across vast distances. "Gramps will not be here soon," Claire whispered back. "I wasn't granted a free call this time, remember? And *you* used your one call to order a freaking pizza."

Kate snort-cackled, returning to her nail inspection. "You shouldn't have tackled a cop." Her voice returned to a normal level. "Even if it was Deputy Dipshit."

"For the millionth time, I didn't tackle him. I was trying to shove him out of the way of your so-called runaway shopping cart and tripped on the front wheels."

"Then how do you explain his bloody nose? Let me guess, your fist accidentally rammed into his face during your heroic attempt to save his life?"

"It was my elbow, not my fist. And yes, it was an accident. If I'd intended to do it on purpose, I'd have given him more than a bloody nose."

Kate sniffed. "Didn't look like an accident from where I stood."

"Yeah, well your head is a big coconut full of funhouse mirrors these days, so your eyewitness report is suspect at best." Claire resumed her pacing. "This is the thanks I get for trying to protect you and your kid. An hour penned in the pokey with you."

"Don't even try to make this about the baby." Kate patted her little round belly, her face morphing into a loving matronly expression.

Just over four months pregnant now, Claire's willowy blond sister had finally begun to show. Sadly though, Claire had looked more pregnant than Kate after Christmas dinner last week, a truth that their mother had made sure to point out in front of everyone during her spontaneous toast with her fourth glass of cognac.

"I don't have to try, Mad Hatter," Claire mumbled.

Getting preggo had rocketed her younger sister's usually grounded brain clear into the thermosphere, where it orbited at the edge of outer space, radioing in for earthly updates once or twice a day.

"I heard that, brat. Next you'll start harping again about my lack of mental stability."

Claire contemplated banging her head on the cell bars until someone came to cart her away in a straitjacket. At least she'd have some peace and quiet locked away in a padded room. "Kate, you were attempting to commit a hit-and-run crime on a deputy of the law with a shopping cart in the grocery store parking lot."

"I told you that I lost control of the cart. Plain and simple. You and Deputy Ernie are making too much out of a minor mishap."

"How could you lose control on a flat stretch of asphalt?"

"The handle was slippery."

That wasn't going to fly in front of a judge. "What about the incident that happened before that?"

"What incident? I don't know what you're talking about. You mean putting groceries in the trunk of my car? Is that illegal now in Yuccaville? It's not like I was trunk-or-treating in a bikini, offering high-mileage lap dances in exchange for a carton of lactose-free milk."

"High-mileage?"

Her sister sighed. "Don't you remember last week when Chester was explaining the difference between high- and low-mileage dances to us during our game of euchre?"

Chester Thomas was their grandfather's old Army buddy who spent way too much time at Dirty Gerties, Yuccaville's only strip club, for a seventy-year-old man. Claire's and Kate's older sister, Ronnie, claimed Chester had the hots for the club's owner. She believed he hung out there trying to land more than a peep show or two, but Claire had her doubts due to the old boy's fondness for bikini mud wrestling.

Claire squeezed her eyes shut, trying to remove all the images from her head that came with Chester and mud and bikinis. "I'm referring to the threat you made."

Kate scoffed. "That wasn't a threat. It was more of a recommendation."

"Wow, that's a serious case of liar-liar-pants-on-fire there.

You threatened to punch Ernie in the mouth for calling you fat."

"That's not true. I merely suggested that someone needed to feed the deputy a knuckle sandwich and I happened to have five meaty fingers on hand."

Boy oh boy, there was no rationalizing with insanity. "Okay, so you were just making a suggestion, I get it. But you do realize that you can't go around ramming people with shopping carts, especially sheriff's deputies, right? If you'd hit Ernie with that cart, he probably would've slapped you with something absurd like an attempted vehicular manslaughter charge."

Kate waved her off. "Once Sheriff Harrison gets here, we'll clear up this little misunderstanding and be on our way home again."

Easy for Kate to say, she wasn't the one facing an attempted battery charge from a Cholla County sheriff's deputy. "What makes you so sure Grady will look the other way this time?"

"Because he's been roughing up the suspect." She gave Claire an exaggerated wink.

"What is that supposed to mean?"

"You know, sinking the two ball in the middle pocket." When Claire continued to frown at her, Kate added, "Paddling up Coochie Creek with our big sister."

Claire recoiled. "Coochie Creek?"

"Rummaging in Ronnie's root cellar."

"Enough, I get it already." Claire shook her head. "Kate, your brain is trying to knit baby booties these days with one damned needle. You have to stop locking horns with Grady's deputy. Ernie is the mayor's son, you know."

Kate's eyes narrowed in a squint that would make Billy the Kid shudder. "I don't care if he's the Grand Poobah of Fred Flintstone's Loyal Order of the Water Balloons."

"It was 'water buffaloes,' not balloons."

Kate pointed at her. "Ronnie's right. You watched too much television as a kid."

"I was educating myself in pop culture."

"This never would've happened if you'd have let me go to the store on my own. I told Ronnie and you before, I don't need a babysitter."

A dog started barking in Kate's yoga pants.

Claire's gaze dipped southward. "Why is your crotch barking at me?"

"It's not my crotch, it's Butch."

Valentine "Butch" Carter was the man responsible for Kate's baby bump. He'd headed to California after Christmas to spend a few days with his family. Kate was supposed to go with Butch, but at the last minute she'd changed her mind and stayed behind to run The Shaft, the bar Butch owned, which happened to be Jackrabbit Junction's only watering hole.

Kate claimed someone had to keep The Shaft running during the busy holiday time, but Claire hadn't just crawled out from under a boulder. Kate was too chicken to meet Butch's family, plain and simple. Claire couldn't blame her. If she'd been in Kate's shoes, she would have hightailed it across the border and hidden in a Mexican mountain village until the baby was due. Commitment and all of the entrapments surrounding it had always given Claire night sweats and hives. Although she had been making progress on staying put in a long-term relationship in spite of these side effects thanks to …

Ruff! Ruff! Ruff!

"Butch is barking in your pants?" Claire asked. That sounded like a punch line in one of Chester's dirty jokes.

Kate stuck her hand down the front of her pants and fished out her cell phone. She grinned at Claire. "Deputy Dipshit should have done a pat down before tossing me in the clink."

"He probably figured you'd have bitten him."

"He'd have figured right." The barking continued. "Here, answer it, but don't tell Butch we're in jail." She held the cell phone toward Claire. "He doesn't need to worry about me while he's visiting his family."

Claire reared back. "I'm not touching that after it's been bumping uglies with your girlie bits."

Kate rolled her eyes. "I'm wearing underwear, doofus. I'm not Ronnie."

Their previously refined older sister, Veronica, had somewhat recently been dragged through hell and back. The culprits? Ronnie's piece of shit ex-husband and a pack of determined Feds trying to humiliate the truth out of her about money laundering, drug deals, and other illegal shenanigans that she'd been clueless about during her five years of marriage. These days, Ronnie lived life on the edge, which included screwing around with Grady Harrison, the sheriff of Cholla County, and not wearing skivvies under her yoga pants, much to her family's discomfort on both counts.

"Take it!" Kate grabbed Claire by the wrist and slapped the phone in her hand.

"Ewww, it's warm."

"Grow up, weenie."

Grimacing, Claire hit the answer button and lifted the phone, holding it a couple of inches away from her ear. "Hello?" she whispered, shooting a worried glance toward the front office at the other end of the hall from the holding cells.

"Kate?" Butch asked.

"No, it's Claire," she continued whispering.

Stop whispering! Kate mouthed.

Claire pointed toward the open door to the sheriff's office where Deputy Dipshit was hanging out, waiting for Sheriff Harrison to show up and smear another layer of law and order all over Kate and her.

"What's going on, Claire?" Butch's tone sounded wary.

Kate's recent temporary insanity plea was his fault and he knew it. It turned out Carter babies spurred hormones that ensured their mothers one-way tickets to Wacko Island until they exited the womb.

"Nothing is going on." Claire faked a cough. "I have a cold and lost my voice."

Kate leaned in close, her hair tickling Claire's cheek as she listened in on the conversation.

"Right." Butch wasn't buying her line. "Where's Kate?"

"Um, she's busy right now."

"Oh, no. What kind of trouble is she in?"

Kate made a slicing motion at her throat.

"She's … uh … slicing some turkey and can't come to the phone because there is … uh … turkey fat on her fingers and in her mouth."

Kate rolled her eyes so hard that her legs almost cartwheeled along with them. Claire flicked her sister on the forehead. If Kate didn't like her excuses, she could shove her phone where the sun didn't shine along with that stupid shopping cart.

There was a moment's pause on the other end of the line filled with Butch's breathing. "Claire, what's going on?"

"Nothing is going on. Everything here is peachy keen."

"Do I need to call Grady?"

Kate shook her head, her expression one big wince.

"No!" Claire shouted. The sound of movement out in the front office made her heartbeat redline. Shit! "I-I … uh … I gotta go … um … g-go help Kate now. I'll have her call you back in a bit." She hung up and shoved the phone toward Kate's pants. "Hide it!"

"Sheesh! Who taught you how to talk? Porky Pig?" Kate tucked the phone down the front of her pants again.

"You can kiss my porky—"

"Keep it down back there," Deputy Dipshit hollered down the hall from the front office.

Claire and Kate sent middle-finger salutes at his back.

Kate returned to her spot holding up the wall.

"So that's how you know Gramps is coming," Claire said. "You texted him."

"Actually, I texted Ronnie. But she has no money for bail, so she'll have to bring Gramps."

In other words, Gramps to the rescue. "Great. He's going to blow a gasket again and lecture us for a month and a day about obeying the law no matter what."

"You should try to be more positive, like me."

"You're not positive. You're just nuts."

"I could whine about not being able to fit in most of my clothes anymore," Kate continued as if Claire hadn't spoken. "Instead I focus on the fact that I'm getting bigger tips for waiting tables at The Shaft now that I have a few more curves."

"Do I need to remind you that the reason we are behind bars currently is because of your sensitivity to comments about your weight?"

She shrugged Claire off as if that was yesterday's news. "But on a positive note, as long as you're behind bars, you're safe from the diamond killer."

"Shhhhh." Claire frowned toward the front office. "The sheriff wants us to keep quiet about that, remember?"

A couple of months ago, Claire and Ronnie had found a stash of glass eyeballs in the undercarriage of a camper at the Dancing Winnebagos RV Park, which was owned by their step-grandmother, Ruby Ford. Inside the eyeballs were diamonds, and inside of the camper were two older ladies acting as "mules" who'd recently sneaked the black market stash over the Mexican border. At least that was Ronnie's theory based off an article she'd found about a mass murder in a border town involving a killer searching for diamonds.

After a series of unfortunate events that started with Claire up to her neck in a water-filled mine shaft and ended with two very dead drug mules, Claire and Ronnie were in a bit of a pickle. First, they had a handful of stolen diamonds. Second, a trail of bread crumbs led to the stupid diamonds. Third, a single-minded bread crumb aficionado was murdering his or her way to the diamonds … and by association, Claire and Ronnie. The latest victim had bought the dead mules' camper from a police auction, but that murder had hit the newspapers six weeks ago.

Six very long weeks of Claire watching over her shoulder and diving for cover every time a car backfired.

Sheriff Harrison had taken the diamonds off their hands after Ronnie had spilled the beans about the whole mess, tucking them away for safekeeping. What Grady had done with the stones, Claire didn't want to know. All she cared about was that he—and the FBI agent in town assigned to keep an eye on Ronnie—kept their firearms handy day and night with their fingers hovering over the triggers.

"Deputy Dipshit can't hear us," Kate said, bringing Claire back to her current snafu. "He has too much baloney jammed between his ears."

She snorted. "That doesn't make sense, Crazy Kate."

"Call me crazy again and so help me, the next time you're sleeping I'll—"

A buzzing sound from the front office announced the arrival

of someone from the world outside, followed by a low rumble of voices. Claire peered out between the bars.

"You think my pizza is here?" Kate joined Claire, sniffing the air. "It doesn't smell like pizza."

Ronnie stepped into view at the end of the hallway, her shoulder-length brown hair corralled by a red and white polka dot headband that matched her dress. It appeared their sister had been visiting the 1950s before coming to their rescue.

Ronnie rushed down the hall to their cell, her bright red heels clomping on the concrete floor. "What the hell is wrong with you two?"

"It's good to see you, too, June Cleaver," Claire said with a grin. "What're Wally and the Beaver up to this morning?"

"It was the deputy," Kate said, her chin lifted. "Ernie was out of line again."

Ronnie growled, lines fanning out from her brown eyes. "Katie, you tried to run the deputy over with a shopping cart for no reason whatsoever."

"That is not an accurate account of what happened," Claire said, defending her loony little sister. "Deputy Dipshit goaded Kate, poking the bear repeatedly."

"And you." Ronnie turned on Claire. "You tackled an officer of the law. What were you thinking?"

"She tripped." Kate looked at Claire. "Someone has been blowing smoke up Ronnie's ying-yang and I'm betting his name rhymes with *lip-spit*."

Claire scowled at their older sister. "You don't really believe what the deputy said after our past experiences with him, right?"

"He's not the one who filled me in on this mess. After I received Katie's text, Grady called. He's stuck at an accident scene and told me to come get you two out of his jail." Her nostrils flared. "Again!"

"Oh, get off your high horse, Ronnie," Kate said. "It's not like we haven't been in jail before."

"Grady was only repeating his deputy's big fish stories," Claire explained.

"Is he letting us off the hook again?" Kate asked.

"For now." Ronnie crossed her arms. "He's going to stop by

the RV park later and take your statements, then make his decision about what to do with you two." Ronnie leaned closer, lowering her voice. "Dang it, Claire. You know better than to let Katie near Ernie. How's this going to look for Grady if he has to keep springing his girlfriend's sisters from jail? The sheriff of Cholla County is an elected position, you know."

"Do you think I wanted to come here today?" Claire asked, glaring through the bars. "Do you think Kate and I woke up this morning and said, 'Let's screw with Ronnie's hoity-toity standing as the sheriff's girlfriend and get thrown in jail,' huh?"

Ronnie sighed, pinching the bridge of her nose. "Katie might have. She's had it in for Ernie for months."

"Hey! He started it," Kate defended.

"This is your doing, Claire. You're the sane one. You need to own up to it when Grady comes by later to keep Katie off the radar for now."

"That's not a bad idea," Kate agreed.

"You both can shove it." Claire gripped the bars to keep from strangling her darling sisters. She glared at Ronnie. "You had to go and get involved with a cop. We are Morgans, remember? We're allergic to badges."

Ronnie's face darkened. "I can't help it. I like Grady."

"He is sort of cute when he's not threatening to handcuff me," Kate said, reaching between the bars to pat Ronnie's arm.

Bahh! Claire growled at the two of them. "You can't keep up this charade."

"What charade?" Kate asked.

"This June Cleaver kiss-ass game Ronnie is playing."

Ronnie's chin jutted. "It's not a charade."

"Come on, Ronnie." Kate pressed her face between the bars and whispered, "You're wearing a dress with polka dots on it."

"So? It's a pretty dress."

Claire scoffed. "It's not your style and you know it. This is a dress meant to impress the local goody two-shoes. You normally wear jeans and T-shirts and boots."

"Not always."

"That's true," Kate told Claire. "Back when Ronnie was trying to be Lyle's perfect, high-gloss wife, she wore fancy dresses and sparkly shoes, remember?"

"What's next?" Claire asked her older sister. "Are you going to dye your hair blond again and start walking around with a hostess tray, asking if anyone would like more *hors d'oeuvres*?"

Ronnie's face looked like someone was pinching her in a tender spot. "You don't understand."

"Oh, we do, don't we, Kate?"

Kate nodded. "You're doing the same thing you did with your ex-husband."

"Trying to be someone you're not in order to impress the rest of the world," Claire added. "I would think that after Lyle's lies and crimes and philandering, *Veronica*, you'd have learned a lesson about the long-term effects of a counterfeit lifestyle for you and your poor family."

Ronnie reached through the cell bars and grabbed a handful of Claire's hair, pulling it. "Take that back!"

"Take what back?" Claire tugged at her wrist. "Let go of me, *Veronica*, or I'll have you arrested for prisoner abuse."

"I'm not letting go until you stop calling me that damned name."

"*Veronica* is your stupid name." Claire yipped while trying to pull free of her sister's grip. "Blame Mom if you don't like it, not me."

Kate slapped Ronnie's wrist, making her let go of Claire's hair. "Stop it, you two. This is not helping the situation." When Claire and Ronnie kept poking and pinching each other through the bars, Kate snarled, "If you don't stop it, I'm going to tell Mom that you guys gave Dad's new girlfriend the cashmere scarf and hat set we originally bought for her."

"What in Sam Hill is going on back here?" Gramps's voice boomed from the other end of the hallway. His Army veteran hat sat crooked on his head, like he'd jammed it on in a hurry.

Ronnie pinned Claire with a hard squint before turning toward Gramps. "I was just playing a game of thumb war with Claire while we waited for the deputy to release her and Katie."

Gramps approached the cell with Deputy Dipshit on his heels. The keys jangled in the deputy's hand, a wad of toilet paper still jammed up one of his nostrils.

"You sure you don't want me to lock all three of them up for the night?" he asked Gramps with a nasally voice. His beady eyes roved down Ronnie's fancy dress, his upper lip wrinkling when his gaze returned northward.

"Tempting, but no," Gramps said, his light blue eyes nailing each of them in turn.

Ronnie stepped aside so the deputy could open the cell door. "Thank you for letting them out, Deputy."

Claire ground her molars at the extra dose of sugar in her sister's tone.

"Yeah, well, Sheriff Harrison gave me an order, and he is the sheriff." Ernie grunted and added, "For now, anyway," under his breath. Deputy Dipshit pulled open the door with an oily smirk. "We wouldn't want anything like this tarnishing that badge of his, now would we? Especially with an election year coming up and all."

Ronnie's cheeks turned bright red, matching her dress. She glared at Claire and then Kate, aiming poisonous darts in their direction.

"Is that some sort of threat, Deputy?" Kate asked, stopping in front of him after exiting the cell.

"No, of course not, Ms. Morgan. Now be sure to take it easy. With that baby coming, you don't want to get in any accidents. Or should I say, any *more* accidents?"

Kate sputtered. Before she could get a handle on her tongue, Ronnie grabbed her by the arm and dragged her along to the front office. Claire followed after an apologetic frown at Gramps and joined Kate at the main desk, collecting her personal belongings from the basket sitting there.

Something on Deputy Dipshit's desk snagged Kate's attention. She took a step toward it.

The front door swung open with a buzz, freezing Kate in her tracks.

"I'm looking for Kate Morgan," a girl carrying a pizza said. When her gaze landed on Kate, she gaped. "Hey, aren't you that substitute teacher we had before Christmas break?"

Kate grabbed the pizza and shoved a wad of bills in the girl's hand. "No, that's another Kate. I'm her twin sister."

"Oh wow, I have a twin sister, too."

Ronnie held open the door. "Everyone out. I'm sure Deputy D—I mean Ernie has a lot of work to do."

The pizza delivery girl led, with Gramps bringing up the rear. At Gramps's car, Claire held the back passenger door for Kate and her box of pizza.

"Be careful with that pizza in the car, Crazy Kate. Gramps doesn't like pizza grease on his white leather seats."

Kate snarled. "I told you to stop calling me that or I'll violate you in the middle of the night."

"Oh yeah, sorry." Claire mimed zipping her lips and shut the door after her sister.

She rounded the back of Mabel, Gramps's 1949 souped-up dark blue Mercury with flames painted down her sides. He'd named his car after his first wife, Claire's grandma, and regarded the piece of steel with almost as much love and care.

"Where's your car, Katie?" Gramps asked as Mabel rumbled to life.

"Still at the grocery store, I think."

"I hope you two learned something from this," he said.

"We sure did," Kate said, sneaking a bite of pizza. She leaned closer to Claire and breathed pepperoni and mozzarella cheese all over her while whispering, "We learned that Deputy Dipshit has a big problem coming his way. That man should not have messed with the Morgan sisters."

Claire sighed, shaking her head. "Kate, I've spent enough quality time with you in jail to last me a lifetime."

Her sister's eyes glittered with a hint of madness as she chewed, looking at least a half bubble off-plumb, if not a whole one. "Don't worry, Claire. Next time, we'll be on the other side of the bars looking in at Ernie."

Claire closed her eyes and groaned. They were going to need to lock Kate in the basement for the next five months.

Chapter Two

I'm standing in the middle of a stampede," Ronnie hollered above the madness of The Shaft's Friday lunch crowd. For a bar and grill located in a lonely valley littered with tumbleweeds and cacti, the dusty pit stop was packed with hungry customers.

Mississippi Brown chalked his pool cue. Dressed in black from head to toe, including cowboy hat and boots, the long-legged FBI agent assigned to keep an eye on Ronnie scouted the bar with his usual squint. "Do you mean a literal or figurative stampede?"

She smirked. "Both. What can I get you to drink?" She flipped through her order pad, looking for a clean sheet.

With Butch home visiting his family, and Claire tearing up the rotting back deck at the RV park where she played handywoman for Gramps and Ruby, Ronnie and Katie were trying to keep up with the busy tables on their own. Too bad their cousin, Natalie, who'd rolled into the park last night after a long drive south from Deadwood, didn't have much experience with waiting tables or pouring drinks. They could have used the extra help. Maybe Ronnie would have to give Natalie a little training session this evening when she showed up for a drink.

"Iced tea," Mississippi said above the din.

"No beer today?"

Mississippi preferred local brews over national brands most days when he was babysitting Ronnie at The Shaft. He'd been assigned to keep an eye on her months ago after the last two FBI buffoons had come swaggering into the bar wearing *Urban Cowboy* costumes with the price tags practically dangling off them.

Claire had sniffed out their fishy fake identities within an hour of their arrival at the bar and had chased them out with plenty of snarling, landing a bite or two in the process. A couple of days later, the buffoons and their black sedan were gone and Mississippi had taken their place with his burly pickup, well-worn pair of shit-kickers, and titanium backbone.

His green-eyed gaze snapped back to her. "I need to stay sharp."

She took a step closer to him so she didn't have to talk so loudly. "Please tell me you have a yearly employee review coming up and this isn't about someone new coming to Jackrabbit Junction to try to kidnap, torture, and kill me for my ex-husband's supposed stash of stolen riches."

"So, you want me to lie, then?" He grinned. "And here I thought you hated it when the FBI blew smoke up your dress." His focus drifted downward. "Nice polka dots, by the way. You trying to be Marilyn Monroe?"

More like Lucille Ball with the way Ronnie's morning was going so far. She'd left the dress on because she planned to work on bookkeeping for Butch today. The fact that Grady might be stopping by the bar later instead of the RV park to deal with her jailbird sisters might've played a *tiny* part in her choice of clothing.

Or maybe not so tiny.

But she switched the high-heeled red shoes for her favorite boots before coming to the bar. There was only so much torture she was willing to endure when it came to trying to convince a man that she could be as polished and compliant as any other wanna-be county sheriff's girlfriend.

"Not quite. I don't have Marilyn's curves or hair color."

"True. You have more of a skinny Jane Russell look, minus the pointy bra."

Ronnie took a step back, pressing her hand to her chest. "Is that an actual compliment, Mr. Brown?"

He shrugged, glancing over her shoulder. "You're nicer than you are ugly, if that counts. And I like your boots."

She laughed at his backward compliment. "And here I thought they didn't program flattery into you FBI robots at the academy."

"They don't. I've gone rogue."

"I guess there's hope for you yet."

"I wouldn't go that far." His eyes creased in the corners. "Most of the time I still can't pass muster, not even with a ten-day head start."

Ronnie jotted down his drink order on her pad. "What do you want for lunch? Your usual? Or does staying sharp mean going hungry?"

"My usual is fine."

Burger and side salad it was. "Do you want it at the bar?" The tables were full, so a bar stool was his only option.

"No. I have a good vantage point here."

Ronnie stuffed her order pad in her apron pocket, taking a moment to scan the room. "What are we watching for today? A mob goon, a hit man, or another black market mule?" she joked, but not really thanks to her ex-husband, who it turned out was never legally her spouse. Apparently, the law allowed him to be married to only one sucker at a time.

Ronnie's five-year marriage to Lyle had transformed from a fairy tale romance to a horror story in a blink. The first few months everything had seemed wonderful, including the lavish vacations and sparkly jewelry Lyle had given her. But then he started traveling for business more and more, which Ronnie found out later were fully paid trips to his clients' high-priced estates. Laundering money, snorting cocaine, screwing blondes, and skimming whatever he could when nobody was looking came next for Lyle in whatever order suited him at the moment.

Fast forward five miserable years to Ronnie sitting in a hard aluminum chair under bright lights. All sorts of authority figures had a bang-up time dragging her through the mud while trying to pry answers from her that she didn't have. The FBI had been especially thorough in their attempts to make her talk. However, much to the Federal Bunch of Incompetent bungholes' disbelief, she was clueless about the piece of shit with whom she'd been sharing a marriage bed—not that they spent much time in that bed together after the first few months of their happily-ever-after life. It turned out that stress, cocaine, and too many loose women left Lyle's penis feeling deflated most nights, unlike his ego. His office couch offered him more privacy than her bed, which he probably needed since any talking in his sleep might give away his dirty secrets.

"All of the above," Mississippi said, cutting through her stumble down memory alley.

She blinked away the nightmare that was her life until a few months ago. The interrogation lights, jail-time threats, and multiple moments of humiliation faded, leaving her neck deep in drink and food orders in a bar filled with bikers, miners, cowboys, and truckers. Not to mention the campers filtering in from the Dancing Winnebagos RV Park located a hop, skip, and jump up the road. The new website that Ruby's sixteen-year-old daughter, Jessica, had created recently for a school project was already paying off with a thirty percent increase in reservations.

"Are you serious?" she said to her FBI pal. Considering Lyle's history, she wouldn't be surprised if every bounty hunter in the galaxy was on the hunt for her.

Mississippi moved even closer to her. "Yes," he said next to her ear. "According to this morning's briefing, your husband's plea deal last month landed several key players from a Dallas crime ring in prison with a likelihood of twenty-plus year sentences for selling AR-15s and AK-47s to a particularly violent Mexican drug cartel across the Texas border."

"AR-15s and AK-47s are …"

"A problem."

"I know that. I was going to confirm that those are illegal in Mexico."

"Definitely. Mexico has some of the strictest gun laws in the world. The cartels down there take advantage of those laws by using illegally obtained weapons to extort businesses, control their territories, and threaten Mexican citizens."

And now Ronnie's lousy ex had gone and pissed off the people who supplied the drug cartels with firearms. Wasn't that just fucking beautiful. "Well. That is sure to make some nasty people real happy with Lyle."

"They're pleased as punch, and even more so since he's basically unreachable at the moment—tucked away all safe and sound in a cushy prison that's more like a spa and sports club for the rich."

The disgust in Mississippi's voice fed the toxic brew bubbling inside of Ronnie's gut. "So how many new problems do your buddies down at the Bureau figure might be coming our way now that the sentencing has been doled out?"

"At least two and as many as five to seven if the cartel decides to join in the fun and games."

"Shit."

Ronnie stared unseeingly at the pool table. As if she didn't have enough of a dust devil swirling around her with some killer hell-bent on finding those damned diamonds, murdering everyone along the path to them. Not to mention the other criminals Lyle had pissed off in the past. Oh, and of course there was the fact that the last two hired hit men—well, one was actually a woman who went by the nickname "the Husky"—also knew about the diamonds, thanks to Katie's big mouth. Those two were in prison now, but convicts were allowed to make phone calls, and that meant there could be even more curious folks interested in those stupid diamonds. Grady was going to want to lock Ronnie in the jail cell with her sisters when he heard this latest news.

"Did they give you any names to help us out like they did the last time?" she asked, blinking away the gloom and doom crowding the edges of her vision.

"Not yet. As soon as I hear something, I'll let you know." He stepped back, glancing over her shoulder again. "And your boyfriend, too."

Grady and Mississippi had tag-teamed to deal with a previous hired killer, figuring out where he was holed up and rushing in with guns at the ready. The FBI knew that whoever came for Ronnie was going to have to go through Grady first, so the sheriff was lucky enough to be included on their newsflashes along with her.

"Sheriff Harrison will be absolutely giddy when he hears your news." She glanced toward the bar and saw the bartender waving to get her attention. She held up her index finger. "I need to get back to work."

"One more thing."

"What's that?"

"Without being obvious, check out the blonde in the blue dress over by the jukebox."

Ronnie slid a glance in that direction. The woman was cute, curvy, and cuddly looking, all of the things Ronnie grumbled about when it came to females these days thanks to Lyle's obsession with the fairer-haired version of her sex.

"What about her?" she asked. Did Mississippi have a thing for blondes, too?

"Do you know who she is?"

"No, why?"

"Because she's been watching you with definite interest since she walked into the bar twenty minutes ago."

Ronnie snuck another glance from under her lashes. Sure enough, the blonde was looking her way. "Maybe she likes my dress."

"Or maybe she likes you."

No, that wasn't a heated look of interest, more of a sizing up. "Well, Mr. FBI, how about you amble over there and work your dark magic to see if I should be worried about her pulling out a handgun and filling me full of bullets."

"From the way that dress is clinging to her, the only thing she could be hiding is a derringer."

Ronnie groaned. "Blah, blah, blonde with big boobs, blah. I need to get back to work."

"I'd advise you to stay put."

"Why's that?"

"Because she's walking this way, and judging from her glare you might want me to act as your backup."

"She's what?" Ronnie turned as the woman joined them. With the sprinkling of freckles covering her cheekbones and her heart-shaped face, she looked even cuter up close.

"Are you Veronica Morgan?" she asked, a scowl pulling down the corners of her mouth.

Mississippi was right. The blonde was clearly not a fan, but Ronnie was damned if she knew what she'd done to piss off the stranger. "Who's asking?"

She crossed her arms. "I'm asking, that's who."

"Yeah, I'm Veronica. Who are you?"

"Elizabeth."

Keeping in mind that she was currently representing The Shaft, Ronnie forced a smile. "Nice to meet you, Elizabeth. Is there something I can get you?" She held up her order pad. "A drink or something for lunch?" Maybe Elizabeth suffered from low blood sugar and was merely frustrated with the current lack of wait staff.

"I'm not here for pleasure."

Ronnie took a step backward, edging closer to Mississippi. He'd better have his gun handy, because something in the broad's eyes made Ronnie wonder if she was about to get stabbed by an ice pick. "Why are you here, then?"

"I wanted to let you know that I've come home."

Had someone elected Ronnie to be the president of the Welcome Wagon's local chapter and forgotten to tell her? "Great, welcome home."

"You don't understand." Elizabeth took a step closer. Her sweet-smelling perfume didn't match her bitter expression. She raised her voice above Dolly Parton, who was singing about slogging from nine to five for a living. "I've come home and I'm going to take back what's mine."

Ronnie shot a frown at Mississippi, wondering if he was making any more sense out of this woman than she was. "What's that have to do with me?"

"You have something that belongs to me and I want it back."

The diamonds? Ronnie's heart stopped beating for a couple of panic-filled moments. "What do I have?"

"My husband."

"Lyle?" Surely the greedy bozo hadn't tried to marry another woman while fake-married to Ronnie and really married to his Wyoming wife.

"No. I'm talking about Grady." Elizabeth's frigid smile gave Ronnie the chills. "You know, Sheriff Harrison, the man you've been screwing for the last month."

Mississippi chuckled behind Ronnie. "Oh, boy."

"You're *that* Elizabeth?"

"Yes, Grady's wife."

Ronnie had heard the story about Elizabeth from both Grady and his aunt Millie, who periodically acted as Ronnie's sidekick when it came to sneaky detective work. Elizabeth had been screwing around on Grady while he was busting his buns to climb through the ranks of the Cholla County Sheriff's Department. While playing hide the pickle with another man, she'd gotten pregnant. But her loverboy didn't have insurance, so she'd pretended the child was Grady's until it was born. After a paternity test proved the real father wasn't Grady, she divorced him and left the state with her child and lover. With Grady being a public servant, Elizabeth's soap opera–style song and dance had been the talk of the county for many, many moons.

The humiliation of it all drove Grady to avoid relationships until Ronnie had come along, tried to bribe her way out of a speeding ticket with fake jewelry, and ended up having hot handcuff sex with the sheriff in The Shaft's supply room. The rest was all flashing cop lights and steamy date nights for the two of them since they'd officially started being a "couple" right before Thanksgiving.

If Elizabeth thought she could squirm back into Grady's life, she had another *think* coming. Ronnie might not be squeaky clean and respectable enough to ever be a county sheriff's wife, but she'd be damned if she'd let this blond bitch screw him over again. "I do believe you divorced him, Elizabeth, according to the stories I've heard."

"Divorce is nothing more than a word on a paper. In our heart of hearts, nothing will come between us other than death."

"Well, isn't that heart-bustin' sweet," Mississippi said, still chuckling.

"That's what we vowed on our wedding day," Elizabeth continued. "And I'm back now to make sure Grady follows through on his promise." With a final scowl at Ronnie, Elizabeth turned and left, flouncing out the door without a backward glance.

Holey underwear! It appeared Katie wasn't the only crazy blonde in town anymore.

"Are you thinking what I'm thinking?" Mississippi asked,

scratching the dark stubble on his jaw.

Ronnie scoffed. "That I have yet another killer keeping me dead center in her sights?"

"Nah, Grady's ex seems borderline deranged, but I don't detect the urge to kill in her."

Apparently he hadn't been looking deep enough into Elizabeth's brown cow eyes, because from Ronnie's front row seat, the woman had plans to bury someone alive without leaving a safety bell to ring for help.

"What are you thinking?" she asked Mississippi.

"That this dusty corner of Arizona is about to have a replay of the O.K. Corral, only this time the Morgan sisters will outshine the Earps as the stars of the show."

* * *

"I'm getting real tired of dealing with old screws," Natalie Beals said, lowering her cordless power drill. She sat back on her heels, growling at the lack of progress she'd made over the last hour this afternoon.

"I think she's talking about you." Chester snickered from his lawn chair in the peanut gallery, elbowing his old Army buddy, Manny Carrera, who was cracking open a beer next to him.

The two troublemakers reminded Natalie of the Odd Couple. Manny was slick and handsome in an older Jimmy Smits sort of way, where Chester was bristly and weathered, like an Army drill sergeant with a steel brush for hair. Both liked women, particularly those that wrestled in mud for a living, and shared way too many details about their younger days with the opposite sex, especially when beer was involved.

Natalie grinned in spite of her aching lower back. "I meant both of you blowhards."

She stood, massaging her sore spots through her lightweight flannel shirt. After the long drive south from South Dakota, her muscles were in dire need of some stretching. Maybe she should join Ronnie tomorrow morning in Ruby's rec room during her yoga routine. Better yet, she could go for a morning walk and enjoy the sun coming up over the Tres Dedos Mountains to the east.

Then again, Gramps had said the temperature was dropping down to the low 30s tonight, which would make for a cold sunrise. Maybe she'd stick to a quick walk from Gramps's Winnebago, where she was camping on the couch, to Ruby's place and watch Ronnie do her yoga while drinking some coffee. That sounded like a winning compromise.

"While I'm over here wearing my fingers to the bone," she told Chester and Manny, "you two wiseacres are talking my ears down to stubs about wild women and wooly times." She lifted the glass of lemonade Ruby had brought out earlier, wetting her whistle with the sweetened drink.

"You mean wooly women for Chester," Manny said. "Old bristle-top here prefers his hot mamas to have a good coating of hair on their legs in the winter."

"Yep." Chester grinned. "Adds more friction and heat. My feet get cold otherwise."

Natalie tried not to visualize any of what they'd said. She'd had too many of their bawdy tales of boozy towns and babes filling her thoughts today. Nightmares were sure to follow.

"Stupid, freaking nails!" Claire kicked a board at the other end of what was left of Ruby's deck. "I swear they're cemented into place, and the damned heads keep popping off those I can manage to get the claw under."

Natalie scowled at the third musketeer sitting quietly, smoking his cigar in the lawn chair to the left of Chester. His bald head gleamed in the sunshine while his blue eyes scrutinized every move Claire and she made. "Gramps, do we really need to worry about salvaging the wood? Half of this shit is dry rotted, and the rest is warped all to hell from the sun and heat."

"Quit your bawling, crybaby," her grandfather said with a quick smile to soften his words. "I can make picture frames out of that wood and sell them to the tourists in the General Store."

Most of Ruby's house was living quarters for her and Gramps and Jessica, Ruby's teenage daughter and Natalie's new but very young aunt. A small portion of the front of the house was the General Store, where campers paid for their spots and could buy odds and ends. Apparently, Gramps had plans to add picture frames to the store's sundries along with the T-shirts Ruby already sold.

"Shelves, too," Chester said. "City folk will pay high dollar for crap like that, especially if you say it's wood from an old barn."

"Some of that wood might make a nice headboard," Manny added, wiggling his salt and pepper eyebrows.

Gramps crushed his empty beer can and tossed it at Manny. "Must you always have your mind in the bedroom, Carrera?"

"What can I say, Ford? Your daughter is a love machine."

Natalie and Claire both groaned while Gramps cursed and Chester pretended to gag.

Last fall, much to everyone's surprise, Manny had ended up in Aunt Deborah's bed after a night of too much cognac and tequila. Their fifteen-plus year age difference hadn't seemed to put a dent in their love life since then. A whirlwind courtship followed by an elopement to Las Vegas meant that Claire, Ronnie, and Kate had gained a stepdad, Gramps's old Army buddy had become his son-in-law, and Natalie had a new uncle.

But that didn't mean any of them wanted to think about Deborah and sex in the same sentence during their lifetime.

Claire looked out toward the row of campers to the west. Under the brim of her Mighty Mouse baseball cap, tension lined her forehead. "Why don't you just give in, Gramps, and let me take the saw to the deck? Then we can wrap up a day of demolition work and get back inside."

Get back inside? That didn't sound like Claire, who usually preferred to work with her hands out under the clear blue sky. "What's up with you?" Natalie asked her cousin.

"Nothing." Claire's brown eyes shifted to her sneakers, avoiding Natalie's gaze.

"Nothing, my ass." Natalie stepped around the pile of two-by-six planks they'd been able to salvage. "You've been watching over your shoulder since we started tearing this sucker apart, not to mention jumping every time a camper door bangs closed."

"The diamond killer has her spooked," Chester muttered around the cigar he was lighting.

"Shhhh!" Claire threatened Chester with her hammer.

"Diamond killer?" Natalie looked from Chester to Manny to Gramps. Each of them nodded, Gramps adding a grimace to his. She turned to Claire. "What are the three *amigos* talking about?"

Claire's expression matched Gramps's. "We have a slight situation we're dealing with down here," she said in a quiet voice.

"More like a shitload of wasps in our outhouse," Chester said and blew out a smoke ring.

"What situation?" Natalie asked, her voice lowering to match Claire's. "Is this something about your dad showing up at Christmas?"

Claire's parents had divorced earlier in the year and Aunt Deborah was still struggling with the aftershocks rocking her world. According to Kate, her mother's hasty marriage to Manny was more of a rebound after learning her ex-husband had moved in with his girlfriend, but Kate assured Natalie that Manny knew what he was getting into with their mother. It turned out the old charmer had married Aunt Deborah for her family as much as for her. He was tired of being a bachelor and craved a big family—even one as crazy as Gramps's.

"I wish it was just about Dad," Claire said, hooking her hammer on her tool belt.

"Is he still here?" Natalie asked.

"No, he headed back to South Dakota right after Christmas."

"Then what's the deal?"

Claire looked at the peanut gallery. "Should I tell her?"

Gramps's grimace spread clear to his ears.

"*Sí*. She's *familia*." Manny winked at Natalie. "We share and share alike."

Chester burped loud enough to scare a couple of ravens from a nearby cottonwood tree. "Does she feel like parachuting into an erupting volcano with the rest of us?"

Claire sent Natalie a raised brow. "Do you?"

Did she? Natalie looked down at her leather gloves. She'd rushed down to Jackrabbit Junction from Deadwood to escape one hell of a sticky mess, wanting to recharge down here in the desert and figure out what she wanted out of life … and who. Or not.

After leaving one clusterfuck, did she want to race into

another one?

A camper door slammed shut across the RV park's gravel drive. Out of the corner of her eye, Natalie saw Claire flinch and frown in the direction of the camper.

Whatever this diamond killer business was, it was giving her cousin a severe case of the heebie-jeebies. No stranger to hair-raising excitement, Natalie couldn't think of a better way to forget about her problem up north than to dig into Claire's *situation* here.

"I'm in. Tell me what's going on."

For the next few minutes, Claire whispered sweet nothings in Natalie's ears. Only the truth was more sour than sweet, and the "nothings" turned out to be a big problem that made Natalie's blood pressure spike.

"Holy shit, Claire." She shook her head. "You should have told me this sooner."

After a glance left and right, Claire tugged off her hat and brushed some loose strands of dark hair out of her face. She stuck the cap back on, pulling it low on her forehead. "Would you have come down if you knew?"

"Hell, yes, and I would've been here a lot sooner, too."

Natalie scanned the surrounding campers, wondering if the killer was already here, waiting for the right moment to strike. It was no wonder Claire was acting like a hen in a coyote den.

"Don't be getting any ideas, Natalie," Gramps said. "With any luck, you'll be on your merry way back to the Black Hills before shit hits the fan. I have enough to worry about with Ronnie and Claire at the moment."

"Don't forget Crazy Kate," Chester said.

Manny chuckled. "The poor *chica* is *muy loca* these days, thanks to that baby."

Natalie had heard all about Kate's temporary insanity due to pregnancy. Claire's trip to jail this morning because of her younger sister was one of many incidents that had been gossiped about by the old guys while watching the deck demolition comedy show.

As troubling as Claire's tale of diamonds and death was, Natalie smiled. "Don't worry, Gramps. This won't be my first rodeo with a killer." She'd had some practice up in Deadwood with sharp-clawed foes and more lately.

Claire did a double take. "Really?"

And here Natalie had thought she was coming south to run from trouble. "You'd be surprised."

She finished her glass of lemonade and picked up her drill again. Back to work. "It sounds like we need to reconnoiter later at The Shaft with Ronnie and come up with a plan to find this killer before he finds either of you."

"Or *she*," Chester said, pointing his cigar at Claire. "We can't rule out the purtier sex. That Husky babe left you with some nasty bruises, if I remember right."

"And one hell of a sore head," Manny added.

Gramps groaned, aiming a glower at Natalie. "Your mother is going to murder me if she finds out what I let Claire drag you into."

"Me?" Claire put her hands on her hips. "You guys are the ones who opened your big mouths about it."

Natalie returned to her end of the deck, her thoughts churning but her heart happy. Her cousins needed her help fixing this mess, and fixing shit was one thing she knew how to do well.

Besides, a game of cat and mouse with a killer would take her mind off the alligators she'd been wading hip-deep in for the last month.

Chapter Three

Mac Garner pulled into The Shaft's parking lot, scoping out the lay of the land under the orange streetlights. Pickups won the popularity contest three to one, most of them local, judging by the license plates. The Shaft's business had grown considerably in the last couple of months, periodically requiring the use of the lot across the street that had belonged to Wheeler's Diner before it went out of business.

Claire's theory for the increase in customers was Butch's new menu specializing in gourmet burgers and local craft beers. Mac suspected the clientele growth had more to do with three unmarried Morgan sisters waiting tables—one of them being his girlfriend, damn it.

He'd like to take Claire entirely off the meat market, but the woman had a history of relationship issues. Kate and Ronnie liked to joke that Claire didn't need to exercise because she stayed in great shape running from commitment. Their grandfather agreed, swearing Mac would have more luck saddling an angry mule than putting a ring on her finger.

Mac steered his truck behind the bar and grill, pulling into a spot between Claire's Jeep and Kate's Volvo. The halogen light Butch had installed outside the back door cast long shadows across the gravel lot.

Hell, these days, he couldn't even get Claire to spend more than a few nights a week in the same bed with him. The part-time handywoman job she had taken at his aunt Ruby's RV park last spring had become a full-time lifestyle for her. No amount of begging or scheming could shoehorn Claire from this dusty corner of the state.

Killing the pickup's engine and lights, Mac sat in the glow from the dash and let the soothing quiet of the desert night loosen his shoulders.

How had it come to this? He rubbed his eyes, weary after the two-hour drive in the dark. How long could he continue working and living in Tucson during the week, going home night after night to an empty house and a lonely bed?

He leaned his head back against the seat rest, closing his eyes. He could still see the road's broken yellow centerline behind his closed eyelids. Something had to give.

But it was Claire.

And her eyes.

The sweet smell of her hair.

That flirty smile.

Those soft lips.

Her curves … Yeah, he really liked her curves.

And then the sex. Sweet Jesus, the amazing sex. If she made him feel any better, he could be arrested.

Somebody knocked on his window.

It turned out to be not just anybody.

Speak of the devil. The sheriff of Cholla County motioned for him to roll down his window.

Grady Harrison stood there in his sheriff's uniform, complete with cowboy hat and jacket. Shadows added more ridges and creases to his face than usual. Mac felt as tired as the sheriff looked.

He rolled down his window. "Evening, Grady. Please tell me Claire's not in jail again."

"She's out for now."

Mac cocked his head to the side. "For now?"

"She didn't tell you?"

"Tell me what?" He sat forward. "I was at a jobsite south of Tucson all day and just rolled into town."

Grady crossed his arms. "This morning at the grocery store in Yuccaville, an altercation occurred involving one of my deputies. He called it into dispatch as an AWDW and took it upon himself to jail the so-called guilty parties."

"AWDW?"

"Assault with a deadly weapon."

"Oh, shit."

"According to my deputy, he made a comment on Kate's weight gain due to pregnancy. Things escalated from there."

"Kate? But you said Claire was in jail."

"By association."

Of course. Claire claimed repeatedly that Kate was the reason for the last several times she'd landed in one cell or another both here in Arizona and back where she'd grown up in South Dakota.

"What was the deadly weapon Kate used?" Mac asked.

"A shopping cart."

"That's a 'deadly weapon'?"

"No. My deputy needs to go through some remedial training on the law and what charges are appropriate."

Mac shook his head. "Well, at least it wasn't her car this time."

"Lucky for my deputy."

"So what was Claire's part in all of this? She didn't play keepaway with your deputy's handcuffs again, did she?"

Months ago, Grady's deputy had tried to handcuff Kate during another altercation. Claire had grabbed the cuffs from him and thrown them into a grassy field. As far as Mac knew, those cuffs were still missing in action.

"No, but she did give him a bloody nose." Grady sighed. "In the paperwork, he claims Kate assaulted him via multiple threats to his person and Claire battered him with her elbow."

Mac cursed under his breath. "Who posted bail?"

"Nobody. I let them out on a promise from Veronica that they'd behave until I could find some time to clear up this mess and convince my deputy to drop the charges."

"Crap. The three musketeers are at it again."

"You heading inside?" Grady asked, thumbing toward the bar.

"Yep." Mac planned on sticking around to help Claire and her sisters close the place up later.

"Good. You can be my backup when it comes to corralling Kate. She gets itchy feet when I'm around."

"I think all three of them are allergic to the law."

"That is the nitty-gritty of the matter right there. Veronica cringes at the sight of my badge like a vampire near a cross." Grady frowned toward the bar. "I'll make a deal with you. Help me get to the bottom of this morning's dispute and I'll buy you a drink."

"It sounds like I owe you a drink for letting my girlfriend out of the slammer for free."

Mac rolled up the window. He grabbed his keys and joined Grady, pulling his coat tight around him. The wind had a definite bite to it tonight. He sniffed in the cold. The aroma of grilled meat in the air woke up his stomach.

They rounded the side of the building. "Does Butch know about Kate's trip to jail today?" Mac asked. The bar owner wasn't supposed to return for another couple of days, if memory served him right.

"No. Veronica asked me not to contact Butch. Kate doesn't want to disturb him while he's with his family."

"I call bullshit. She doesn't want him to find out she's back to her Dr. Jekyll and Mr. Hyde routine." At least that was what Claire and Ronnie liked to call it when Kate acted sane one moment and then flipped into crazy-mode the next.

Grady grunted. "Back? When did she stop? She's been sipping on that madwoman potion since she moved here."

Mac reached the door first. When he opened it, a blast of warm air and Johnny Cash's "Folsom Prison Blues" knocked him back a step. He held the door wide for the sheriff.

The crowd inside The Shaft was so thick Mac couldn't have stirred them with a stick. The smell of burgers was stronger inside, joined by the scent of hops and malted barley. His mouth watered as he searched for Claire.

"I'd like to have his job," Grady said, scowling toward the pool tables.

Mac followed his gaze, seeing a familiar face lining up a shot at the eight ball. Special Agent Brown was on duty tonight, apparently. "You want to work for the FBI?"

"No, but I'd rather spend my day watching Veronica and playing pool than writing up accident reports and busting drug dealers."

"You'd be bored within a week and start harassing the wait staff."

"Harassing?" Grady grinned. "Depending on Veronica's mood, she might call it that." He returned Agent Brown's nod in their direction with a quick wave.

A path cleared to the bar. Mac spotted Claire pouring drinks on the other side. "I see a couple of seats at the bar."

"Lead the way."

They parted the sea of bodies, settling onto the stools at the end of the bar near the swinging batwing doors dividing the kitchen and Butch's office from the rest of the place.

Claire did a double take when she saw him, her flirty smile matching the sparkle in her dark eyes. She finished topping off a glass of beer and then strolled his way, wiping her hands on a towel. "What can I get for you, handsome?"

"Are you talking to me or the sheriff?"

She grabbed Mac's coat collar and pulled him toward her. "I'm talking to the smoking-hot devil who will be sharing my bed later."

Her warm kiss tasted like home sweet home and melted away his chills. Judging by her pink cheeks, rolled-up sleeves, and glistening skin, she was steaming at the moment.

"Be right back." She filled a glass with beer and returned, placing it in front of him.

"Is that the shirt Chester gave you for Christmas?" Mac asked, pointing at her yellow T-shirt sporting a grizzly bear with the words, "WARNING! Will bite if poked."

She nodded. "He should have given it to Kate. She's been a real bear since this morning."

"You mean before or after you two were caged in the Cholla County coop?"

She snapped him with the towel. "That was not my fault." She turned to Grady with a grin. "Would you look at that? All this talk of smoke and bears conjured up the real deal. What'll you have, Sheriff Harrison? An iced tea?"

He took off his hat and set it on the bar. "I'm off duty."

"I'm liking you more by the minute. Pick your poison."

"I'll have the same as Mac, served with a side of truth about the events that took place this morning at the grocery store."

Claire grimaced. "Am I going to regret not having an attorney present?"

"Off the record."

"Promise?"

"Cross my heart."

She grabbed another glass and filled it, setting it down in front of Grady. "Okay, I'll spill. Mac, you're my witness in case the sheriff is crossing his fingers under the bar."

"I have your back, Slugger, but you should know from the get-go that Grady is paying for my drink."

"Son of a cocka-doodle-doo." She hit Mac with a mock glare. "Look at you, cozying up to the law so easily. Breaks my outlaw heart."

"Don't worry," Mac told her with a wink. "You can seduce me back to your *bandido* lair later tonight to cozy up with you instead." He tipped his glass of beer, swallowing several gulps to take the edge off that long, lonely trip from Tucson. The beer tasted good, but Claire tasted better.

Ronnie stepped between Mac's and Grady's bar stools, rattling off an order of drinks to Claire.

"How was the drive in, Mac?" she asked as Claire walked away.

"Long and dark." A glance in her direction turned into a full on stare. "What's with the dress? You heading to a 1950s sock hop with Archie and Jughead after the bar closes, Veronica?"

She wrinkled her nose at him. "Aren't you a crack-up? Don't

give up your day job yet."

Unfortunately, quitting looked to be his only option if he wanted to spend more time with Claire.

Grady caught Ronnie's wrist and tugged her his way. "You look nice tonight."

"Just nice?" she teased, letting him pull her closer.

"Pretty enough to blind me and break my heart with one slow blink."

She tapped a red fingernail on his badge. "Are you still on duty, Sheriff Hardass?"

Grady scowled around her at Mac. "See the sort of disrespect I put up with from these Morgan women?"

"You might as well save yourself time and throw them all in the clink."

Ronnie slugged Mac's on the shoulder. "Bite your tongue, Garner, or I'll tell my new grandmother you're threatening her kinfolk."

Ronnie's grandmother was Mac's aunt Ruby, which made Claire his … something in-law. As glad as he was to see his aunt happy with Claire's grandfather, he would have preferred to keep the limbs of their family trees less tangled. At least there was no DNA shared between them.

"That's actually not a bad idea," Grady said, laughing as Ronnie threatened to wallop him. "Seriously, Veronica. It's a lot safer in jail for Claire and you right now than out at the RV park."

Mac sobered at the reminder of the killer on the hunt for the diamonds Ronnie and Claire had found. Yet another reason he hated being so far away from Jackrabbit Junction. He'd woken up too many times in Tucson covered with sweat thanks to a nightmare involving Claire, a loaded gun, and blood—hers.

No amount of hot air on his part had convinced her to return to Tucson with him where she would be safer. She refused to leave her sisters behind while a killer followed breadcrumbs that led to the RV park.

Claire brought over a tray of drinks, holding it out for her sister to take.

"You sticking around for a while?" Ronnie asked the sheriff, reaching for the tray.

"I'm off duty," he said, his hand sliding over her hip in a sly caress. Mac would have missed it if he hadn't been looking their way. "Maybe I could take you home later, if you're available."

"Whose home?" she asked, shouldering the tray.

"I'm easy. You pick."

"I'll think about it." She blew him a kiss before heading off to deliver the drinks.

"Damned sassy woman," the sheriff said with a grin.

"FYI, Grady," Claire said. "Natalie is staying in Gramps's Winnebago with Ronnie." She left them to deal with a young pup in a Sun Devils cap farther down the bar who was hailing her.

"Who's Natalie again?" he asked Mac.

"Ronnie and Claire's cousin. She's here from South Dakota to help Claire build my aunt a new back deck."

"Right. The cousin. I met her once before. It was here at The Shaft, I'm pretty sure." Grady sipped his beer, looking up at the television in the corner. A Coyotes hockey game was on the screen, the second period almost over. "Is Natalie allergic to the law, too?"

Mac smirked. "Does a one-legged duck swim in circles?"

"Christ." Grady shook his head. "I'm going to worry my hair white by the next full moon because of these women."

"Hey, Mac," Kate said from behind him. "Glad you made it back again in one piece."

Mac and Grady both turned in their seats. Claire's usually well-dressed and polished younger sister looked like she'd been wrung out and hung up to dry. Her hair stuck out every which way, as if someone had rubbed a balloon all over her head and tried to stick her to the wall via static cling. Her eyes were wide, her gaze darting here and there, everywhere but at the sheriff.

"I need to talk to you, Kate," Grady said. His tone was softer than usual, coaxing rather than commanding.

"I know. Ronnie made me come over here."

"Give me the quick version," the sheriff said, leaning back against the bar.

Taking a deep breath, Kate spilled a tale of traded insults and hurt feelings, mixing in a splash of indignation and embarrassment. Her explanation for her actions sounded borderline legit in Mac's opinion, along with her accusation of harassment. Grady seemed to be on the same page as Mac, nodding at her side of the story with a wrinkled brow.

But then the left side of Kate's face twitched several times, and her chin jutted. "Your deputy was lucky I wasn't driving when he said my butt was going to need a 'Wide Load' sign strapped to it before long."

Grady's gaze tightened. "Why's that?"

"Because I would have—"

"Kate!" Claire interrupted from behind them. "Your order is up."

Mac hadn't realized Claire had returned.

"Rudeness!" Kate said to her sister. "You need to learn how to be nicer to the wait staff if you're going to keep playing bartender."

"Yeah? How's this for nicer? Get your ass over to table eight before I call Butch and tell him about your hissy fit this morning."

"It wasn't a hissy fit." She snarled at her sister, bared teeth and all, before taking the tray Claire held out to her. "Grady's deputy needs some schooling when it comes to manners, and I'm just the teacher for the job."

"Go!"

Kate stalked off. Mac could've sworn her hair was sticking out even more.

Grady turned to Claire. "Excellent timing, referee."

"Why, Sheriff, I don't know whatever you might be talking about." She pointed at their glasses. "You two ready for a refill?"

"Not yet," Mac said. He had a feeling he'd need his head on straight tonight. "But I'll take a burger when you have a chance to let the cook know."

"I'm still nursing this," Grady told her. "If you got a minute, how about you give me your account of this morning's showdown?"

After a glance around the bar, Claire nodded. Her story echoed Kate's, only there was less of a defensive edge to it. She, too, blamed Grady's deputy for instigating the whole thing, and then swore that she tripped over the shopping cart's wheel trying to save him from her sister's "runaway cart." The smashed nose had been an accident, no battery intended.

The sheriff waved Claire off when a woman in braids and a flannel shirt called for a pitcher of suds for her and her friends over at the pool tables. Apparently, Special Agent Brown was about to get some company.

"Well, Grady, what's the verdict?" Mac asked after swallowing another gulp of beer. "Are you hauling them back to jail tonight?"

Grady shook his head. "I'll tell you a secret. I stopped at the grocery store earlier and talked with an Air Force vet who works there part-time and happened to witness the ordeal. He told me that my deputy started the whole mess by insulting the 'cute little blond birdie,' as he called Kate. He verified that Claire was trying to referee the match, and really did trip over the shopping cart, falling into my deputy, elbow first."

Claire had skirted the law yet again. "So, now what?"

"I'll talk to my deputy in the morning about keeping his mouth shut and we'll put this mess behind us."

They paused to watch Kate argue with Claire at the other end of the bar. The blond birdie's hands flapped about, her feathers ruffled about something that had Claire's jaw visibly clenching.

"Shit-criminy," Mac said. "Butch's woman is unstable."

"He needs to get his ass home and keep a closer eye on her. That baby of his is causing one hell of a ruckus in my county, and I don't like it one bit. I have enough headaches with Veronica's troubles and all of the black market problems Claire keeps digging up around your aunt's place."

Mac raised his glass. "Hear, hear."

"Long time no see, Mac," a voice said behind him.

He looked over his shoulder, grinning when he saw the apron strapped on Natalie's hips and the order pad in her front pocket. "They put you to work here at The Shaft, too, huh? Building a deck wasn't punishment enough."

"Ronnie calls it on-the-job training, but I call it slave labor." She leaned in and gave him a brief hug, and then held up an order, whistling for Claire. After handing off the piece of paper, she pointed at Grady. "I see you have a law dog at your side. Did you bring him with you, or is he here to rescue us from Crazy Kate?"

Grady raised his glass of beer, holding Natalie's stare. "I'm off duty at the moment."

Natalie held out her hand. "The name's Natalie Beals. We've met before, I believe."

"Grady Harrison." They exchanged a brief shake. "If memory serves me right, Veronica was dealing out junk jewelry the last time I saw you."

"Junk jewelry? No way. Those were high-quality pieces she was using to bribe your aunt for computer time at the library. Ronnie's ex made sure to splurge for the good costume jewelry that looked very real, so she wouldn't figure out he was bonking some other babe on the side." She wrinkled her upper lip. "Men suck. No offense," she added, patting Mac's shoulder.

"Natalie!" Kate called, waving her to the other end of the bar.

"Duty calls … or rather the ol' fishwife, as I prefer to think of the pregnant lunatic these days." She saluted Mac. "Catch up with you later. Nice to meet you again, Sheriff."

Mac finished his drink. "I'm starting to feel like I walked into a dust devil tonight."

"Ha! I've been stuck in the middle of one since the first time I pulled Veronica over for speeding." Grady glanced up at the television screen again. "How's your aunt doing lately?"

"Busy. Jess created a website for the RV park that has reservations pouring in, keeping Ruby hopping."

The sheriff's brow wrinkled. "Is Jess's dad still hanging around giving everyone grief?"

How did Grady know about that piece of shit? "He's renting a room at the Sundown Inn in Yuccaville," Mac answered. "Jess says he's getting the weekly rate."

"Hey, Sheriff Harrison!" A cowboy clapped Grady on the shoulder. "Dirty Dan is playing your song."

The bar quieted, the crowd seeming to take a big breath.

The jukebox lit up. "I shot the sheriff," rang out through the bar, the Eric Clapton version. A group of guys surrounding the jukebox raised their glasses of beer toward Grady and sang along with Clapton, "But I did not shoot the deputy!"

Grady grinned up at the cowboy at his shoulder. "Isn't that sweet of Dan. I'll have to stop by the bank Monday and tell his wife how much I like that new Browning Hell's Canyon Long-Range rifle he bought behind her back."

"Hooo-hoo! You're screwed, Dan!" the cowboy hollered above the crowd. "He's gonna tell your wife about your new gun!" The cowboy lightly punched Grady's shoulder. "Good one, Sheriff! Your next drink is on me." He swaggered back to his buddies, caroling along with them during the next chorus.

"Friends of yours?" Mac asked.

His eyes creased. "I make it a point to be *friends* with everyone I meet." Grady returned to his beer, spinning the glass on the bar. "Is that archaeology team still sorting through old artifacts in your aunt's mine?"

"They took a break for the holidays and returned to the university in Tucson. The lead archaeologist mentioned something about needing to head south to Mexico soon, so another group will be taking his place."

"That reminds me. I ran into Dick Webber at the gas station a few days ago."

Dick Webber was a rancher who owned the chunk of land next to Butch's parcel. Mac had met him and his shotgun two different times because Ruby's Humdigger mine was landlocked in the middle of Dick's ranch. Getting to it required approval from the old guy or risking a backside full of buckshot.

"What's Webber up to these days?" Mac had been heading up to the mine in the dark with Claire the last time he'd talked to the rancher. Webber had tried to convince Claire to leave Mac and take him on instead, offering a fancy new mixer as a bonus.

"Trouble, I'm guessing. He flat out told me that I wasn't allowed to go on his land without a warrant."

Mac frowned. "Why would he tell you that?"

"He seems to have some cockeyed idea that I'm going to go sniffing around a mine located on his land." Grady finished his beer. "You wouldn't happen to know where he got that idea, would you?"

Mac sighed. Unfortunately, he might. "Joe Martino owned a mine surrounded by Dick's land that belongs to Ruby now by default. She found out about it from Joe's ex-wife semi-recently."

"Another mine, huh? Joe Martino sure had his hands in a lot of dirt."

No kidding.

Ruby's departed husband had claimed to be a traveling salesman when he convinced her to marry him way back when. In reality, Joe had been tangled up in the black market, moving stolen goods for big-ticket buyers and storing the pricey pieces in the mines he'd owned around Jackrabbit Junction until the heat cooled.

As if that wasn't bad enough, he'd been pilfering from his black market clients, skimming items here and there over the decades to keep for himself. Shortly after he'd decided to retire from his fake sales job and enjoy his golden years with Ruby, he had a stroke that left him mostly mute as he decayed in a wheelchair. By the time he'd died, Ruby had a shitload of medical bills and no life insurance to help with the debt he'd tallied, or even enough money to bury her husband.

"Joe Martino was one crooked son of a bitch," Mac said, and proceeded to fill in the sheriff with what he'd learned about the Humdigger mine's history. He included what Dick Webber had told him the last time he was out there about the "coyote" den, and then he wrapped up with Claire's theory about the booby traps Joe had set to keep people out.

"Coyotes, huh?" Grady asked. "Does Dick Webber have any proof that the mine is being used by cartels to smuggle drugs and people into the country?"

"He claimed to have noticed signs of trouble around the mine but hadn't actually seen any people. Claire and I found a chamber in the mine with a cot, some canned food, and a few other supplies when we were up there last. We heard some sounds from one of the drifts, too."

"What was back there?"

Mac shrugged. "I didn't want to put Claire at risk, so we got out of there. I've had enough so-called mine accidents lately to make me appreciate fresh air and blue skies more than finding

out who is hiding in a mine."

"I can understand that. Mines give me plenty of pause. I've had too many old-timers tell me tales of ceilings falling and men being buried alive."

Right. Been there, done that, only Joe's ex-wife had been the cause that time, not gravity. The chance of a cave-in happening again grew greater with every passing day, thanks to the Copper Snake Mining Company in Yuccaville being so blast-happy and rattling the earth all over the county.

Mac tapped on his empty glass. "I guess Dick Webber's inflexibility means you can't take a trip with me up to that mine anytime soon."

"It'll take time to get a warrant. I'd need some sort of proof. Something that hints at human or drug trafficking going on up there."

Shit. That meant Mac was going to have to go up to the mine alone.

"In the meantime," Grady said. "I could get you into Joe Martino's condemned house in Yuccaville without much of a problem."

Joe's childhood home? "How did you know about that?"

The sheriff smiled. "The blond birdie's oldest sister mentioned that your girlfriend had cruised by it multiple times over the last couple of weeks. She's concerned with Claire's tendency to obsess about Joe Martino's tarnished treasures."

Damned Claire and her overactive curiosity. She was supposed to wait for him to scout that old house. Mac wondered if she'd broken in already without Ronnie knowing about it.

"I'll take you up on that offer," Mac said, curious about Joe's old home himself. "Let me know if there is something I can do for you in exchange."

Grady grimaced. "Well, there is something."

"What?"

"I need your help with Veronica's mother."

"Oh, God no." He'd rather be dropped in a pit of rattlesnakes than deal with Claire's mom. "What do you need with Deborah?" Mac winced in anticipation of what he might have gotten himself into with this trade deal.

"She doesn't like me."

Mac laughed. "Get in line! She wouldn't pour water on me if I was on fire."

"Really? She seems to treat you okay most of the time."

"Sure, when she's drunk." These days, that happened to be the case more often than not.

According to Claire, her mother was going through some sort of middle-aged crisis, which included a quick rebound marriage to Manny. Having Claire's dad in town for the Christmas holiday had only made Deborah harder to handle for her family. Christmas dinner had been a debacle bursting with tears and angry drunken rants that ended with self-loathing in spades.

"Will you put in a good word for me when you can?" Grady asked.

"You want me to convince Deborah that a representative of the law is a good match for her daughter?" Mac snorted. "You must think I'm some sort of sorcerer."

"It's worth a try." Grady stared down the bar at where Ronnie was showing Claire something on one of her order tabs. "It would make life a little easier for Veronica if her mother didn't hate me so openly."

It would make life easier for all of them if Deborah would listen to her father and move back to South Dakota.

"I can try, Grady," Mac said. "But truth be told, you might be better off stuck in the doghouse when it comes to Ronnie's mom. Deborah's bites tend to be far worse than her barks."

Chapter Four

R onnie tiptoed through the dirt and weeds along the edge of the campground's gravel drive. Gramps's Winnebago loomed up ahead on the other side of Manny's Airstream.

Both campers' windows were dark and quiet, like the pre-dawn world around her.

So far, so good.

She'd asked Grady to drop her off in front of the General Store. Her explanation that walking the short distance to the camper was good for her heart and lungs had been met with a frown, but he'd heeded her request. Truthfully, though, she wanted to avoid being caught by her mother after a night in his bed.

As far as Deborah was concerned, dating the sheriff of Cholla County was akin to sending love letters to Charles Manson. It made no sense to Ronnie why her mother turned all squinty-eyed and snarly when Grady's name was mentioned, let alone when he came around in person.

Claire suspected their mother's dislike stemmed from a handful of blame incited by the amount of times the sheriff had housed her daughters in his jail cells since they'd moved south— especially Katie. Manny claimed it had more to do with Grady getting free milk from one of Deborah's prized cows, which spurred Chester to start telling "udder" jokes about Ronnie's "udder" failures to date. Unfortunately, her past inspired much fuel for laughter.

For the most part, Ronnie didn't give a crap why her mom wasn't a fan of the sheriff. Compared to Lyle and his fake jewelry and big fat lies, Grady was a rare blue diamond. However, for some ridiculous reason, Deborah's disapproval was a burr under *his* saddle. Watching Grady try to win over her mother had Ronnie pulling her hair out.

She stopped under the Winnebago's awning and slipped off her cowboy boots. A glance at her mother and Manny's place found it the same as before—silent. With the stealth of a cat burglar, she fished the spare key from under the RV and unlocked the camper door. Easing inside, she softly shut the door behind her.

Whew! Made it through the gauntlet without a hitch.

A growl sounded at her feet.

She looked down. A certain spoiled beagle sniffed her socks. What was *he* doing here?

"Henry," she whispered to Gramps's dog. "It's me." She scratched between his ears, wincing when his tail thumped several times on the carpet.

With any luck, she could grab some fresh clothes and return to the General Store without waking …

Two loud claps in the darkness made Henry yip.

Ronnie nearly peed her pants.

The lamps bookending the couch came on, lighting up the room.

"Well, well, well," Natalie said from her bed on the couch. "Look who Henry the ferocious guard dog caught. The one and only Veronica Morgan, sneaking in at the butt crack of dawn with her boots and underwear in her hands. It's almost as if I've time-traveled back to our high school days."

Ronnie breathed a sigh of relief. "I'm wearing my underwear, knucklehead. Besides, Claire and Katie were the ones who snuck in after curfew. I was an angel and never broke the rules, remember?"

"Oh, yeah. I'd forgotten how boring you were back then. Time has certainly livened you up."

"You can shove your 'boring' where the sun doesn't shine." She tossed her boots at Natalie's legs, making her cousin dodge and giggle. "I was sneaking in this morning because I didn't want to wake you up."

"Bzzzzt. Wrong answer. You didn't want to wake up your mother and you know it, which is silly considering that you're almost thirty-six years old."

Ronnie walked to the small fridge and grabbed the pitcher of water she kept in it. "You're right. I'm hiding from Mom." She filled a glass and then leaned back against the counter. "I don't know why I'm sneaking around the place. She's probably deep in a drunken sleep again and wouldn't hear a bomb go off next to her window."

"I envy her ability to sleep these days."

What did that mean? Was Natalie up listening to every bump in the night now that she knew about the diamond killer coming for them? Ronnie hadn't been sleeping well for weeks, especially when she was alone in Gramps's RV. Spending the night at Grady's was a relief most nights for more than carnal reasons.

Maybe Natalie was referring to how uncomfortable the couch could be, especially when Henry insisted on sharing it. "I thought you were going to sleep in the queen bed in back since I was staying at Grady's."

"I tried to, but you know how that end of the Winnebago is closer to your mom and Manny's Airstream?" At Ronnie's nod, she grimaced. "I think I heard them having sex last night."

"No!"

"Unfortunately, yes. First, I heard the Bee Gees singing 'How Deep Is Your Love,' then I heard something crash followed by a bunch of loud moaning."

Ronnie shuddered, setting her glass on the counter. "Maybe Mom was drunk and stumbling around again. That could be the crash you heard, and the moaning was her in pain."

Yeah, that was it.

Natalie sat up, pushing the quilt aside. "Listen, oh great and noble Queen of Denial, I know what drunken moaning sounds like, trust me." She straightened the yellow thermal top she wore as pajamas. "What I heard next door was rowdy sex going on between my aunt and new uncle. Even poor Henry was covering his ears. The only way we could make it go away was to come out here and crank up the damned golden oldies on the radio until they finally went to sleep a half-hour later." She crossed her arms. "Your new stepfather is apparently quite a Latin lover."

"Oh, Lord love a duck." Ronnie joined Natalie on the couch. Henry jumped into her lap, circled twice, and then plopped onto his belly. "I wish Mom would stop acting like she's in her raging twenties."

Natalie chuckled. "While I don't love listening to my aunt do the wild thing, I am glad to hear that I could still be enjoying physical relationships when I'm her age."

"Nah, you'll probably be on this silly sabbatical yet."

"No way. One year is the plan, and that's it."

"How long has it been since you broke up with the jerk that instigated this vacation from men?"

"July. Five loooong months, babycakes."

Ronnie smirked. "During the last two years of my marriage to Lyle we had sex three times. I was on sabbatical without even knowing it. How sad is that?"

"Sad enough to bring a tear to a glass eye. But you're making up for it now, right?"

"No. Grady and I are merely good friends, that's all."

Natalie laughed. "Are you practicing for your mom?"

"A normal parent would approve of me being in cahoots with the sheriff of Cholla County."

"Your mother is the polar opposite of normal."

"It doesn't help that Grady is a public servant. She had big hopes for me, you know. A husband with lots of money and prestige."

"You tried that route and look where it got you."

"Penniless with a target on my back." Ronnie groaned, leaning her head on the cushions. "You haven't even heard the latest."

"Latest about Lyle?"

"Yeah. As if I don't have enough trouble with that damned diamond killer business, Loose-lips Lyle has gone and made a bigger mess. He rolled over on some big shot in Dallas to lessen the severity of his sentence."

"Shit-burgers. That can't be good."

She frowned at Natalie. "It's not. Mississippi is on high alert, keeping an eye out for several more troublemakers coming my way."

Natalie scooted closer and leaned her tousled head on Ronnie's shoulder. "What are you going to do?"

"Nothing. I'm sinking like the Titanic after it played chicken with an iceberg. All I can do is try to sink with dignity." Ronnie scratched Henry's back. "To round out my complete list of fucked-up shit, Grady's ex is back in town."

"His ex-*wife?*"

"Yep."

"What's her story?"

Ronnie gave Natalie the quick and ugly version of Elizabeth's infidelity and relocation to Nevada with the kid and real father.

Natalie sat upright, a sneer curling her lip. "Wow! That was some wicked bitchcraft on her part."

"And get this. Yesterday, she showed up at The Shaft and told me she wants Grady back."

"Holy sassy-frassy! What did Grady say about this?"

Ronnie shrugged. "I didn't tell him."

"Why not?"

"I don't want him to think I'm the jealous, insecure type of girlfriend."

"But you are the jealous, insecure type of girlfriend."

She held her fist under Natalie's nose. "You want this up one of your nostrils or both?"

Natalie pushed her hand away. "Seriously, what's really going on inside of here?" She pointed at Ronnie's head.

After a moment of hesitation, Ronnie came clean. "I don't think I'm the right woman for Grady."

"Come again?"

"I'm a Morgan sister."

"And damned proud of it, right?"

Ronnie bit her lower lip.

"Ronnie, you're a fierce warrior and don't take shit from anyone anymore. Be proud of that."

"But Grady is in an elected position. He needs a girlfriend whose history is sparkly clean and doesn't include a tie to a piece of shit who's in prison for money laundering among many other crimes."

Natalie crossed her arms. "Have you considered that this law dog might not be good enough for you?"

She scoffed "Please. After the shit-quake that rocked my world thanks to Lyle, I know my place."

"I don't like the sound of that."

"Natalie, I'm a shiny penny on my good days. Grady needs a polished silver dollar."

"Bullshit. The sheriff is lucky you allow him to grace your side."

"You always were my favorite cousin." Ronnie patted Natalie's knee. "But I wouldn't go that far."

"I'm serious, Ronnie." Natalie caught her hand and squeezed it. "Claire told me that you're dressing to impress again these days, like you used to do for Lyle and his good-for-nothing friends."

"Maybe I like to wear fancy dresses and heels."

"You can't snow the snowman."

"I don't know what that means."

"Yes, you do."

Ronnie sighed. "You don't get it. I'm tired of feeling like a piece of trash that Lyle wadded up and flushed down the toilet."

"Newsflash—if you feel that way, fancy clothing isn't going to fix anything. Take it from a girl who's tried to be someone she's not with each dickhead who has come along. If there's one thing this sabbatical from men has taught me, it's that the only way I can be happy is to be myself both inside and out. If a guy doesn't like what he sees here," she said, circling her hand in front of her, "then I don't need him in my life, sexy gray eyes or not."

"Gray eyes? That's not a very random eye color to throw out in conversation."

"Or blue or green. Whatever. My point is if Grady doesn't like you in jeans and boots, then screw him."

"I am screwing him. That's what got me into this mess."

"Yeah, yeah, yeah." Natalie flopped back onto her pillow. "Everyone is having sex but me, even my crabby aunt. Rub it in."

"So, what do you suggest? I tell Grady that his ex wants him back?"

"Sure. He needs to know about her big plans since he's the prize."

Ronnie fingered the hem of her dress. "What if he likes the sound of that?"

"Then he can go blow a goat for all you care, right?" When Ronnie didn't agree, Natalie poked her in the hip with her big toe. "If Grady wants his ex back, you're history. No amount of red lipstick, pretty dresses, or hot sex will change his mind."

"Oddly enough, you're not making me feel any better."

"Wouldn't it be good to know the truth rather than to keep playing this game with yourself?"

"Maybe. Probably. Yeah."

Natalie grinned. "I mean, look how well pretending to be someone you're not worked out for you with Lyle. "

"You're a brat." Ronnie grabbed a pillow and whopped Natalie with it. "I take it back, you're not my favorite cousin."

"I told you before, you can't snow the snowman."

Ronnie stood and stretched. "I need to get dressed. I told Ruby I'd cover for her at the General Store this morning while she runs errands in Yuccaville."

"Are you going to stretch first? Do some yoga?"

"No, I'm good. I did several yoga poses last night in Grady's bed. He really knows how to work out my kinks."

"Boo! Get out!" Natalie threw the pillow at Ronnie as she ran into the bedroom.

Fifteen minutes later, dressed in her favorite jeans and comfy cardigan sweater, Ronnie pushed open the General Store's door. The air smelled like bacon and eggs—Mac's favorite breakfast. Ruby must be up and spoiling her nephew already this morning.

Behind the store's counter, Claire sat next to the register, frowning down at a piece of paper. Her hair was damp on the ends and wavy, probably finger-combed, knowing Claire. Ronnie caught a whiff of her watermelon shampoo over the store's usual old varnish smell. Paint stains dotted her blue South Dakota Jackrabbits' hoodie.

"What are you looking at?" Ronnie asked as she walked over

to the snack aisle and grabbed a protein bar.

"Reservations for next week."

Ronnie put the bar down on the counter next to the list, looking at the names upside down. "That's a lot of campers."

Claire's frown deepened to a full-on scowl. "I know."

"What's with the sour face? This is a good thing for Ruby and the RV park."

"Depends on your point of view and whether or not you're waiting to be showered with bullets some afternoon while walking out of the tool shed."

"You must have had an extra helping of paranoia for breakfast this morning."

"Kiss my paranoid ass." She pointed at the paper. "See these two names I've circled?" At Ronnie's nod, Claire continued, "The names they've given for the reservation don't match up with what I've found in the online white pages."

She held up the new cell phone their dad had bought her for Christmas. He'd given one to Ronnie as well, including coverage for both of them on his family plan, which made their mother's teeth grind. Katie already had a phone, so he gave her cash instead to help cover the cost of a new pregnancy wardrobe.

"What do you mean the names don't match up?" Ronnie asked. "Are you running some sort of background check on these people?"

"Yeah, and you don't need to get all huffy about it. I'm trying to keep the two of us breathing."

"I know, but it sort of seems like an invasion of their privacy." She leaned over the counter and stuffed the money for the protein bar in the register drawer.

"It's not like I'm scanning their phone records, cheezewhiz. I'm just confirming they are who they say they are and that one of them isn't some cold-blooded murderer hiding behind a fake identity."

Ronnie took a second look at the names Claire had circled. One had listed a home address of Minnesota and the other as Wyoming. Both gave only PO boxes, no street addresses.

"You could check their photo ID when they get here."

"They might have fake IDs."

"If you're really worried," Ronnie said around a bite of chocolate and peanut butter, "I could ask Grady if he'd be willing to run their plates. Given our current up-shit-creek location, he'd probably be happy to help."

"I don't want to involve the cops any more than we have to. Old Dick Webber is right. Once the law sits on your couch and takes off their shoes, there's no kicking them out of your house."

Ronnie glared at Claire. "Grady is not just any cop."

"I know. He's the damned sheriff." Claire lowered the paper, giving Ronnie a once-over. "I saw his pickup out front this morning."

"So? He dropped me off on the way to work."

"Jackrabbit Junction is like twenty miles out of his way to work."

"You know I'm having sex with the sheriff, so why don't you get to the point." She stuffed the last of the bar in her mouth.

"Did you tell him what Mississippi told you yesterday about Lyle?"

She swallowed. "He already knew. Mississippi keeps him in the loop now."

"What about your other visitor?"

"What other visitor?" Ronnie hadn't told Claire or Katie about Elizabeth stopping by yesterday.

"His ex-wife."

Ronnie's mouth fell open. "How do you know about that?"

Claire pointed at her phone. "Natalie texted me."

"I just told her that this morning." Ronnie hadn't made Natalie promise not to tell anyone about Grady's ex, but who'd have figured the news would beat her to the General Store. "Dang, gossip travels fast."

"I'm not sure if you understand how these new phones that Dad bought us work, but there are things called cell phone towers and satellites that help transmit messages at amazing speeds. Certainly faster than your slow butt can walk from the Winnebago to here."

"I'd call you a horse's ass, but that's an insult to the equine population."

Claire chuckled. "Listen, Natalie and I were talking last night at The Shaft after you left with your BB. We had an idea and thought you might be interested."

"My BB? What's that mean? Big Boyfriend?"

"Buddy with Benefits."

"Grady is more than my sex buddy."

"I know, that's why I said *benefits* with an 's,' as in plural." She held up her fingers, ticking them off. "You get sex, food some nights, *and* a get-out-of-jail-free card with unlimited uses for you and your family."

Ronnie glared at her.

"Oh, and a bodyguard when he's not on duty. You really scored with your BB, I tell you."

"Shut up."

"Anyway, Natalie and I decided it's time to reinstate the old gang—minus Kate because she's completely deranged at the moment. With all of this shit coming down on us, we need to watch each other's backs more than ever."

"Old gang? You're not talking about that stupid posse you guys formed with the neighbor when we were kids, are you?"

"It wasn't stupid and you were one of the founding members, if memory serves me right."

"There were five of us, Claire, including Violet Parker. We were all founding members."

"Not true. We voted on allowing Kate to join."

"Oh, yeah." Ronnie smirked. "You didn't want to let her in the posse back then either."

"Only because she was lobbying to paint the treehouse Dad built bright pink. But I was outvoted."

"It was a pretty shade of pink."

Claire shook her head. "The Pink Posse. I still say it was a dumb name." She pretended to gag. "So, what do you say? Are you in or not?"

"In what? The Pink Posse?"

"We changed the name."

"To what?"

"The Prickly Pear Posse."

Ronnie snorted. "Were you two drinking when you came up with that?"

"Maybe a little, but I woke up still liking it. Natalie told me to invite you even though I'm not sure it's a good idea."

Like Ronnie wanted to be part of their silly posse anyway. "Why not?"

Claire rolled her eyes. "Because you're having intimate relations with the sheriff of Cholla County."

"So what? That doesn't mean I'm his lackey."

"You sure? Because that polka dotted getup you wore yesterday told a different tale."

"I'll have you know that I like to wear dresses."

"You don't have to lie to make friends here. I'm your sister, remember?" Claire taped the reservation list on the wall behind her. "And don't feel obligated to join our posse." She turned back to Ronnie with a smile. "Like I said, I'm not sure you should be in it. You seem kind of shifty and cagey these days, and one of our first rules of order is 'no secrets allowed.' "

"Shifty?" Ronnie huffed. "Katie is the one who is shifty right now, not me."

"I agree. I don't think we should let Kate in either."

"Let me in what?" Katie said, parting the curtains hanging between Ruby's private rec room area and the General Store.

"Nothing," Claire said, lining up the cans of chewing tobacco on the shelf behind the counter.

"What are you doing here already?" Ronnie asked.

Katie joined her at the counter. She still wore her uniform shirt from The Shaft. Actually, this one looked clean and didn't smell like last night's beer. "Ruby invited me to come for breakfast. She doesn't like me spending so much time alone at Butch's place while he's out of town." She looked from Claire to Ronnie and back, her gaze narrowing. "What are you two hiding from me?"

"Nothing," Claire said, avoiding eye contact.

Katie focused on Ronnie. "What's going on? Is this about Grady's ex-wife talking to you at the bar yesterday?"

Ronnie gasped. "Crap on a cracker! Did Natalie send out an all-points bulletin?"

"Natalie? No. Gary told me who the blonde was when I saw her talking to you yesterday during the lunch crowd."

"Gary the bartender knows Grady's ex-wife?"

"Yeah. She's his cousin."

Claire leaned her hip against the counter. "You're kidding."

"Don't worry about Gary, though. He said she was always an uppity bitch, especially after she married Grady. He was glad to see her dust trail when she went to Nevada." Katie planted her hands on her hips. "So, what were you two talking about when I walked in here?"

"The weather," Claire said.

"You said no secrets allowed," Ronnie reminded her.

Claire glared at her. "*Ipzay ouryay ipslay*," she said in pig Latin, ending with, "big mouth."

"No secrets allowed in what?" Katie pressed.

"Natalie, Claire, and I are reinstating our old posse gang."

"Yes!" Katie's eyes lit up, her smile a little too toothy for comfort, bordering on manic. "I'm in!" she told Claire, holding out her pinkie. "Who are we going after first?"

Claire looked down at Katie's pinkie finger. "What's that for?"

"Pinkie swear like we used to, remember?"

"We are not pinkie swearing."

Katie held her pinkie toward Ronnie. "Come on, Ronnie. Swear me into the posse."

"Ronnie doesn't have the authority," Claire said.

"Yes, I do. I'm the oldest," Ronnie said, locking pinkies with Katie. "You're in, kid."

Claire's scowl was back. "You are not the oldest. Natalie has you beat."

"Not by much."

"I have an idea," Katie said, grabbing a cherry pastry from the shelf next to the cash register. "We can call ourselves the 'Painted Lady Posse' and wear pink nail polish to show our colors."

Claire glared at Ronnie. "What have you done?"

"Katie, painted ladies are prostitutes in the Old West."

"No shit. I'm the one with the highest IQ here, remember? It's a play on words."

"We are not going to call ourselves the Painted Lady Posse,"

Claire said, clearly disgusted.

"Why not?"

"Because Natalie and I already came up with a name. We're the Prickly Pear Posse."

Katie giggled. "Seriously? Were you drunk when you guys came up with that?"

Claire's lips thinned. "Don't you have a bar to open?"

"That's what you and Natalie were doing last night while Mac and I were cleaning up in the kitchen. I saw your heads together at the bar."

"Yeah, well it seemed like a good idea last night. Now, I'm beginning to have my doubts."

Katie hooked her arm with Ronnie's. "Are you kidding? It's a ridiculous name, but a great idea. We'll all pull together like we used to in the old days."

"You sure you're up to this?" Claire asked Ronnie.

"If you're asking whether I can walk the walk when it comes to Grady, then yes, I'm up to it."

"What's Grady got to do with ..." Katie started. "Oh, right. He wouldn't like this idea at all." She turned back to Claire. "We need to start carrying guns."

"NO!" Ronnie and Claire said at the same time.

"Come on. I told you when I shot your Jeep, it was an accident. It won't happen again."

"It's not my Jeep that I'm worried about."

The door creaked open.

"Oh, look," Natalie said, strolling up to the counter in torn blue jeans and a flannel shirt—her work clothes. "It's the good, the bad, and the ugly. Just the trio of trouble I was hoping to find." She held out an envelope. On the front, cut-out letters that spelled "Veronica" were taped to it.

"What's this?" Ronnie asked, taking it.

"I don't know. It was stuck under the windshield wiper of the Winnebago. I noticed it coming back from the campground shower."

Ronnie tore open the envelope and pulled out a piece of paper. More cut-out letters were taped to it. The message it spelled out made Ronnie gasp.

"What's it say?" Claire asked.

Katie leaned closer. "*You better watch your back,*" she read out loud. She took the paper from Ronnie's loose grip. "The author forgot to use punctuation at the end of the sentence." She held the paper out for Claire to see. "This is another example where an exclamation mark is more suitable than a period."

Claire snatched the paper from Katie's hand. "I'm going to stuff your exclamation marks up your southern sphincter, Crazy Kate."

"Don't call me crazy, Claire."

Natalie took the letter from Claire. "Cut-out letters, that's smart. No handwriting analysis will help with this one." She looked out the door, her gaze thoughtful. "I should try this next time."

"What do you mean, 'Next time'?" Claire took the letter back.

"Never mind." Natalie pointed at the paper. "What do you think? Does this mean your diamond killer is in town? Could it be one of his love letters?"

"Maybe, but it also could be one of Lyle's enemies," Ronnie said, her heart still pounding in her ears. "They would know me by my full name."

"Did those mules who stole the diamonds know you as 'Ronnie' or 'Veronica'?" Claire asked.

Ronnie pondered that. "I don't remember. But if it's the diamond killer, why not include your name, too?"

"Maybe Ronnie is better known in the area, what with her dating the sheriff now," Natalie said. "Claire isn't in the public eye as much."

"But why would a killer warn you?" Claire wondered. "Just to toy with his prey?"

"What are we going to do with this?" Katie asked, taking the paper from Claire.

"I should tell Grady and Mississippi." Hiding behind their guns seemed the safest bet.

Claire crossed her arms. "See, Natalie. This is why I didn't want to have her in the posse. She runs to her BB first thing these days."

"He is not my BB," Ronnie snapped.

"What's a BB?" Katie asked absently while frowning down at the paper. "The letters were cut from a magazine, I'm pretty sure."

" 'Bedroom Buddy,' " Ronnie told her.

" 'Buddy with Benefits,' " Claire corrected.

"BB." Katie giggled. "I like that. Good one, Claire."

"It's stupid," Ronnie said, snatching the letter back. "This needs to be given to the authorities to dust for fingerprints."

"Sure, now that all of ours are on it." Claire took the letter from Ronnie and held it up toward the fluorescent light over their heads.

Crud, that was true. Ronnie sighed.

"Whoever did it was clumsy," Claire said. "The glue got spilled in the left margin."

"I doubt a killer who cuts people into pieces is clumsy," Katie said. "Although the lack of punctuation does indicate a psychotic mindset."

"Are you even aware of what's coming out of your mouth anymore, Kate?" Claire asked.

The door creaked open again.

"What's going on in here?" Chester Thomas waddled inside, closing the door behind him. He looked fresh from his bed in a wrinkly T-shirt and grease-stained jeans. "A hen party?"

Claire stuffed the letter under the counter. "Nothing. We're just figuring out what time we need to be at The Shaft today."

"Really?" He tossed the Tucson newspaper on the counter in front of her. "So this little meeting has nothing to do with the fact that the bodies of a couple of night watchmen at the police auction yard in Tucson were found stuffed into the trunk of an old Cadillac yesterday afternoon?"

"Which police auction yard?" Claire asked.

"The one where a certain diamond-bearing RV was sold months ago to a guy who's now deader than a doornail."

Ronnie spread out the newspaper. All four of them looked down at the article Chester pointed out.

"How did they find the bodies with all of those vehicles there?" Katie leaned closer to the picture of the cars, trucks, and

SUVs lined up for auction.

Chester set a bag of BBQ fried pork rinds on the counter. "According to the police, the K-9 crew sniffed them out. But they had a little help."

"What sort of help?" Claire took his money and crammed it in the register.

"A pool of blood under the trunk." Chester leaned his elbow on the counter, his bristly hair matching his unshaven cheeks. "Ten bucks says those poor guys were left in pieces like the last victim."

Chapter Five

A few minutes later ...

Claire wasted no time trying to rationalize the news about the diamond killer's latest hit and rocketed straight into panic mode. She raced to the kitchen, grabbed Mac in the midst of eating his bacon, and dragged him down to Ruby's basement office. She locked the door behind them, her breath coming fast. Stars dotted the edge of her vision. In her hands, she clutched the rolled-up newspaper with the article about the dead night watchmen in Tucson.

"I have ..." she said in between gasps, "... a last request."

Mac looked at her as if a beanstalk was growing out of the top of her head. "I'm not taking last requests anymore this morning. You missed the window of opportunity." He sat on the edge of the antique, mahogany Queen Anne–style partners desk that had belonged to Joe back before he'd eaten his last greasy potato chip and stroked into the grave. "Unless this request involves sex, then I'm all ears."

Claire bent over to keep from passing out from a lack of oxygen to her brain. She scowled down at the olive shag carpet. "You've had sex on the brain since we woke up."

"No, I've had *you* on the brain since I woke up and found you leaning over me in all of your lovely nakedness."

That was his fault for looking so tempting in the soft morning light with his beard scruff, long lashes, and sexy lips. Not to mention the rigid topography she'd explored under the covers.

When she looked up at him, he was frowning at her with his

head cocked to the side. "Are you okay, Slugger?"

"Probably not, but I'll live. For now. But we'd better get my last request down on paper to be safe."

"What's the request?"

She stood upright and blew out a breath. "I want you to dress up like the grim reaper at my funeral."

One of his eyebrows rose. "Hood and all?"

"Yes, and I want you to stand there with everyone else and not say a single word the whole time."

The other eyebrow inched upward. "Can I hold a scythe, too?"

"Well, yeah. The costume isn't the same without one."

"Can I point the blade at your mother menacingly while I breathe like Darth Vader?"

She scowled, joining him at the desk. "You're not taking this seriously, Mac."

"Of course I'm not." He grabbed her by the hem of her sweatshirt, tugging her closer. "What's with all of this happy talk about the grim reaper this morning?"

She shoved the newspaper at his chest. "The diamond killer has struck again."

He stilled. "Are you serious?"

"Two night watchmen at the police auction yard in Tucson are dead. From what Ronnie and I can figure, Jackrabbit Junction is the next stop on his slice-'em-and-dice-'em tour."

Mac took the newspaper and spread it out on the desktop, bending over to read the article Claire pointed out. When he finished, he cursed under his breath.

"Now is probably as good a time as any to work on my last will and testament along with my burial-with-the-mermaids wishes, don't you think?"

He pulled her into his arms, resting his chin on the crown of her head. "Come home to Tucson with me."

Tucson wasn't home, not for her anyway. Not anymore. There were too many people there and not enough wide-open desert. But she didn't know how to tell him that without making him mad, so she burrowed into the collar of his soft flannel shirt instead, breathing in the scent of him. Mac always smelled like the desert—fresh air, warm sunshine, and hints of sage, mesquite, and something spicy she couldn't put her finger on. Maybe it was just Mac's skin, pure and simple. She wrapped her arms around his waist, wanting to stay down here in the basement with him until the boogeyman went away.

He leaned back and lifted her chin, his hazel eyes searching her face. "Please, Claire. Forget about building Ruby's back porch for now and let me take you somewhere safe. You and Ronnie both need to lay low until the FBI or Grady catch this son of a bitch."

"If I go with you, I leave Ronnie here alone. I can't do that and you know it. Besides, what am I going to do in Tucson? Hide in your house 24/7?"

They both knew she'd start climbing the walls in three days. Tops. As much as she loved Mac and his beautiful house, she needed to be at the RV park, where there were things to do to keep her hands and mind busy.

"*Our* house," he corrected. "I can protect you there."

"Maybe, maybe not. This killer is no fool. It's been six weeks since his last kill. That time lapse tells me he's a planner, not the shoot-from-the-hip type."

"Have you considered that it's all part of a game to keep the police guessing when he'll strike next?"

"I don't think so."

"Claire, you don't even know if it's a man or a woman at this point. How can you be so sure of the reason behind the pause between murders?"

"Fine, you're right, but I do know that leaving the RV park is not the solution. Not with Ronnie and my family here."

He cursed, sitting on the edge of the desk again. "Okay, no Tucson. But if you're staying here, then you have to let me try to protect you."

"I hope you stopped at the army surplus store on your way out of the city last night and picked up an invisibility suit."

"They were all out of their winter collection of desert camouflage, sweetheart," he shot back with a grin. "How do you feel about carrying a gun?"

"Not happening."

"Come on, Claire. You didn't even think about it."

"I didn't need to."

"If this is about what happened last spring with Sophy and her—" he started.

"It has nothing to do with that psycho bitch."

"Then why not?"

"Two words—Crazy Kate." Claire paced in front of him. "Look what happened yesterday morning."

"At the grocery store?"

Claire nodded. "With nothing more than a mere shopping cart in her arsenal, Kate managed to cause a ruckus that landed me in jail. If I'm packing heat, she'll go for my gun and shoot someone, which will probably end up being me by accident, and I don't want to die because that mad pregnant monkey has bananas for brains right now."

He crossed his arms. "All right, you have a point about your sister, but you need some sort of self-defense weapons at your disposal."

"I carry a hammer in my tool belt."

"Claire."

"I'm pretty wicked with a screwdriver."

"Be serious."

She scowled. "Fine, besides a gun, what do you propose?"

"A Kevlar vest."

"Aren't those really bulky?"

"Does it matter?"

It might if she had to escape a killer through tight quarters. "Where are you going to find one in my size around here?"

"Maybe Grady has one somewhere." His gaze dipped to her chest. "I'd like to see you in one of those bulletproof SWAT cat suits."

She stopped in front of him. "Mac, those outfits are pure Hollywood bullshit."

He chuckled. "Pure Hollywood genius is more like it."

"Do you really want to see me squeeze these hips into one of those skintight costumes?"

He stared at the objects in question. "That's a really dumb question, Slugger."

She returned to wearing out the carpet. "What about some of those ninja throwing stars?"

"Who do you think you are? Bruce Lee Jr.?"

"More like Jackie Chan." She did a hand-chopping karate move in front of him, pretending to block and hack at her opponent.

Mac batted her hands away, grabbed her arm, and spun her around so she was facing the desk with him behind her, pressing her into the desk.

"Hey," she said, looking up at him over her shoulder. "Did they teach you that move in geotechnician school?"

"It was one of my electives."

"Really? Babe Wrangling 101?"

"Something like that." He spun her back to face him. "We need to get serious here, Slugger."

She sobered. "I know."

"How about I go to Yuccaville today while you're working on the deck and see what I can find for you to use as self-defense."

"Okay, but don't forget about—"

"Crazy Kate, I know," he finished for her. He caught her hand and laced his fingers through hers. "Will you at least give whatever I come back with a try?"

"For you, MacDonald Abraham Garner, the moon."

He winced. "You remind me of your mother when you use my full name."

"Would you rather I call you 'Sweet Buns' like the old boys do?"

He tugged her close, sliding his hands under her sweatshirt, his warm fingers sliding over her skin. "I'd rather you let me chain you up in our bedroom back home and feed you Moon Pies until this avalanche of shit finishes rolling down the mountainside."

"Claire!" Gramps called from the top of the basement steps. "Get your ass up here."

"Duty calls," Mac said, stealing a kiss.

"I'll be there in a minute!" she hollered back, holding onto Mac's wrists when he tried to pull away. "What are you up to today?"

"Besides building an armory of weapons for my woman?" At her nod, he shrugged. "I was thinking about stopping by Joe's old childhood home."

"What?! You promised you'd wait for me to go inside."

"I'll remind you that *you* promised the same thing."

"And I've waited for you."

His gaze narrowed. "Are you crossing your fingers behind your back?"

She held her hands in front of him, fingers spread wide.

"Then why did your sister mention something to a certain county sheriff about you hanging around that old house a lot recently?"

Damn Ronnie and her big yap-trap. "I wasn't hanging around it."

"You know I can tell when you're lying, right?"

And damn Mac for being able to read her so well. "Okay, so I may have parked in front of the house with Joe's antique spyglass once or twice." Or maybe nine or ten times, but who was counting? "But all I did was look at it, I swear. We agreed to go inside together, so I waited for you."

He searched her face for a couple of seconds. "Last night at The Shaft, Grady offered to provide a police escort into the place."

She gasped. "No way! Really?"

"Do you feel like checking out a spooky old house with me and the local sheriff, Nancy Drew?" He smiled, the dimple in his cheek showing under the beard scruff.

"Yes!" She looped her arms around his neck and kissed him so hard he stumbled backward a step, towing her along with him.

"Damn," he muttered when she came up for air.

"You weren't really going to go without me, were you?"

"I was tempted for safety reasons."

She threatened him with her fist.

He laughed and kissed her knuckles.

"Claire Alice Morgan!" Gramps said, pounding on the basement door. "You two had better not be having sex on the desk again."

Mac winked at her. "He's giving me ideas."

"You're a bad boy." She kissed his dimple, liking the scratchy feel against her lips. "Tell me your ideas."

"Can you hear what they're saying?" she heard Chester ask on the other side of the door.

"No, and I don't want to." Gramps pounded on the wood. "Claire, you need to get up to the kitchen and deal with your mother."

Mac pulled away, grimacing. "And there goes that fantasy."

"What's wrong with my mother?" she called out.

"She's crying."

"Now what!" Claire growled, stepping away from Mac. She grabbed the newspaper from the desk and opened the door.

Gramps stood with a face full of scowl, but Chester was all grins.

"We weren't having sex," she told Gramps. Not this time, anyway. "We were discussing Chester's latest news." She held up the newspaper as proof.

Chester peeked around her. "That's a big desk. Maybe I should bring my next date down here to buff the wood, give 'er a sparkling shine."

"Nobody is buffing any wood down here!"

Mac coughed on a laugh.

Claire rolled her eyes at her grandfather's choice of words. "Why is Mom crying?"

"From what I can understand through her sniveling and sobbing, it has something to do with *your* father and her getting older."

Dear Lord on a surfboard! Not again. "Where are Kate and Ronnie?"

"Kate claimed to have a bout of morning sickness," Chester answered. "She ran off and locked herself in the bathroom."

Gramps's smirk showed what he thought of that lame excuse, which Claire mirrored. "Ronnie is manning the register in the General Store and says she is too stressed about being chopped into pieces to deal with Deborah's theatrical antics today. That leaves you with your multiple college psychology classes. Go put them to some good use for once."

"This is pure horse pucky. All of you!" Claire declared. She pushed past Gramps and Chester, storming upstairs to play shrink yet again.

An hour later, she beat the hell out of a nail that wouldn't let go of a board on the back deck.

"Whoa there, John Henry," Natalie said from the other end of what remained of the deck. "What'd that poor nail ever do to you?"

"It won't come out, so I'm going to pound the damned thing all of the way to Hell."

Natalie laughed as she dropped to her knees between the old, dry-rotted joists that Gramps insisted they try to keep. Their grandfather's hoarding had reached an all-new level when it came to this stupid deck.

Claire picked up the reciprocating saw. She glanced around to make sure none of the old boys had returned from their beer and piss break. The coast was as clear as it was going to be. The saw cut through the stubborn nail like butter. She released the trigger and set the saw aside, blowing out a breath. If only solving the rest of her problems were that easy.

A cool mid-morning breeze ruffled her hair as she scoped out the campground, looking for anything fishy or out of place. The RV park was about two-thirds full, with the majority of campers ringing the edges. Campers were coming and going to the laundry building, restrooms, and General Store. Some Claire recognized, mostly because they'd been here a week or more. Those she didn't, she watched under the lowered brim of her Mighty Mouse baseball cap. Any one of the campers could be the killer, walking around freely, blending in with the crowd.

"What was up with your mom earlier?" Natalie asked from where she knelt between the joists.

"She got an invitation to her high school reunion. The organizers mistakenly included Dad's name on the invite."

"And that turned her into a crying mess?"

More like an alcohol-slinging drunk. "I'm not sure if you've noticed, but Mom and Kate are running neck and neck for top nut around here."

Earlier, Deborah had "fixed" herself by the time Claire had

reached the kitchen, as in used a screwdriver—the orange juice and vodka sort—to loosen up and calm down. When Claire had suggested that her mother seek mental help outside of a liquor bottle, Deborah had scoffed and then hiccupped. "You're one to talk, Miss-Can't-Commit."

What her mother's drinking had to do with Claire's anxieties about possibly one day *maybe* tying the knot with Mac was beyond her, but it had pissed Claire off enough to call her mother a lush under her breath.

Only it had come out louder than she'd meant, and Deborah had heard it. Her mother's response was to walk over, take Claire's hand in hers, and dump the rest of the screwdriver in her palm. "There," she snapped, slamming the glass down on the kitchen counter. "Are you happy now, daughter dearest?"

By that point, Gramps and Chester had managed to get their butts back upstairs and join them in the kitchen, which was good because it took both of them to keep Claire from wrestling her mother to the floor and giving her a big, fat noogie to show her how freaking happy she was at the moment.

"Hey!" Natalie's voice interrupted Claire's daydream involving her knuckles rubbing her mom's drunken head. "You know this junction box you wanted me to check out down here?"

"Yeah, what about it?"

"I think I figured out why the light switch wired to it doesn't work."

"Why's that?" Claire skirted a pile of boards and several exposed joists that jutted out like ribs at the end of the old deck's skeleton. She joined her cousin at the junction box that had been hidden away under the deck boards for at least two decades of sunshine and winter rains, judging from the amount of dry rot.

"Well, for one thing, the wires are capped off."

Why would someone have disconnected the outlet entirely? Had it been a fire hazard? Ruby's place was old enough that the wiring in some parts was still knob-and-tube, a leftover from the 1930s when the main house was built. Claire wouldn't have been surprised if the previous owner had disabled this outer junction box to be safe.

"For another thing," Natalie continued. "There's a camera in here instead of a receptacle."

"A what?"

Natalie held up a small camera, one of those black metal types from the 1970s.

"Let me see that."

She handed it over.

Claire frowned down at the camera. "Why would there be a camera in there?"

"Is there still film in it?"

"As far as I can tell, yes." She handed the camera back to Natalie. "Ah, shit. I hope this isn't another one of Joe's puzzles."

"You mean you don't want to go on another one of his treasure hunts?"

"More like treasure nightmares."

Hunting for Joe's hidden gems was hazardous to Claire's health. Since moving to Jackrabbit Junction and obsessing over one treasure after another, she'd been shot at, nearly drowned, forced down into a mine shaft filled with freezing water, and cold-cocked with the butt of a shotgun. With a brutal killer in her rearview mirror and coming up fast, she wasn't in the mood to experiment with new forms of near-death activities.

"Why would Joe go through such measures to hide treasures around his own property?" Natalie asked. "That seems borderline crazy—not like Kate loony, more like all-out serial killer bonkers."

"What's that y'all said about Joe?" Ruby asked in her soft Oklahoma drawl. Their less-than-a-year-new grandmother stood at the back door, checking out their demolition work. Her curly, reddish-blond hair was pulled back in a ponytail. Her freckle-specked cheeks were smudged here and there with flour, along with her checkered apron as well. "I don't know why Harley wants to salvage any of this darn lumber. It's not worth your time and hard work." She homed in on the camera in Natalie's hands. "What's that?"

"Natalie found it under the deck."

"Well, that sure is an odd place for an ol' camera."

It wasn't the camera that had Claire worrying her lower lip. Ruby didn't know it, but Claire had found some very disturbing pictures under the floor of Ruby's bedroom closet months ago. The photos starred Joe in his birthday suit with various unclothed women, and they weren't playing patty-cake either. Claire hoped this camera didn't have more X-rated pictures on the film in it. She didn't think she could stomach more of Joe's private porn collection.

"You girls interested in some brownies?" Ruby asked.

Red alerts dinged in Claire's head. "Why are you baking? What's my mom doing now?"

Ruby tended to deal with stress by mixing flour, butter, and sugar with other ingredients. When combined and baked, they made Claire's jeans shrink, especially around her hips. With Deborah living in the same RV park as Ruby and Gramps, Ruby baked so much she could have opened her own patisserie in town.

"It's not your mother this time," Ruby said. "I saw that newspaper article." She searched the hills beyond the edge of the campground. "Maybe you gals should come inside for a bit while I make the brownies."

"My butt doesn't need any more brownies." Claire scowled down at the camera. "Ruby, did Joe like to do puzzles?"

Ruby pursed her lips. "Yeah, now that I think about it, he always had a puzzle book in his car when he traveled—ya know, the kind with all sorts of puzzles in it? Except for that last year. After he had the stroke, he just wasn't the same."

"Well, that explains his silly treasure hunts," Natalie said. "The man liked a challenge. I'll take some brownies, Ruby."

When Claire continued to frown at her, Natalie shrugged. "Life's short. Let's eat brownies and be merry."

"Great. I'll have you three belt notches fuller in no time." Ruby stepped back inside.

When the door closed, Claire and Natalie returned to the camera.

"So you think this is Joe's camera?" Natalie asked.

"Maybe." If Claire had to bet, she'd lean toward being all in. "You should take the film to Yuccaville and get it developed."

"Why me?"

"Because if I do it, everyone around here will start harping on me again about being obsessed with Joe and his hidden treasures." Never mind that her obsession was well founded, dang it.

Natalie tapped on the camera's metal casing. "What are you going to do if this holds a clue to another hidden treasure?"

"I don't know." She could hand it over to the sheriff, but Grady had enough on his plate with keeping Ronnie alive and safe most days. He didn't need to deal with another cache of stolen and fenced goods.

"The question is, do I want to know what he's hidden under this particular X on the treasure map?"

"Why wouldn't you?"

"Because Joe's treasures tend to end up with me getting hurt."

An hour and four brownies later, Claire yanked off the final board and tossed it aside, leaving only the joists yet to take apart.

"Good job," Manny said to her from his seat next to Chester and Gramps in their lawn chairs.

"I need a drink."

Chester held up his beer. "Have some of mine, just don't backwash."

"Not that kind of drink." Although drinking away her problems appealed until she thought about her mother's current state.

Claire tightrope-walked across one of the joists and stepped inside the back door. She closed the door behind her and her shoulders lowered an inch. Whew! Waiting for a killer to strike was overrated.

A half hour ago, Natalie and Kate had headed down the road to Yuccaville—Kate to pick up some groceries for The Shaft, Natalie to make sure Kate didn't end up in jail and to see if they could have the film developed at the drugstore in town.

Claire rounded the long oak bar reminiscent of an Old West saloon and opened the mini-fridge behind it where Ruby kept cold drinks. It was packed full of cheap beer and diet soda. Cursing at Chester and her older sister for not restocking the good stuff, she pushed through the curtains dividing the rec room from the General Store.

Ronnie looked over from her post behind the register where she was ringing up a cute sixty-ish woman in a sporty jacket and canvas pants. The lady collected her Dancing Winnebagos RV Park T-shirt and the book on birds of the Southwest, sending Claire a nod before heading out the door.

"I have a bone to pick with you," Claire said after the door closed. She headed down the snack food aisle to the wall cooler at the end full of soda and beer and other refreshments.

"Maybe I don't want to pick bones with you right now."

"Too bad." Claire grabbed a Coke and set it in front of Ronnie, tossing a dollar bill on the counter next to it.

"Listen, if this is about what happened to your Jeep last week, you need to get over it. It still works just fine."

Claire paused in the midst of opening the soda. "What happened to my Jeep?"

"Uhh, nothing."

She growled in her throat. "Ronnie?"

"What's your bone?"

The front door opened.

Claire glanced toward it and did a double take.

"Holy shit!" she said when she picked her lower jaw up off the floor. "What are *you* doing here?"

Chapter Six

"What's your problem?" Kate asked.

Natalie pulled her gaze from the passing scenery of cholla cacti, tumbleweed-choked fences, and the occasional mile marker. She glanced over at her cousin, who appeared to be focusing on the two-lane road in front of her.

"What do you mean?"

Kate shot a frown in her direction. "Why did you come down to Arizona?"

To escape. Natalie returned to the passing scenery. "Claire asked me to come help her with Ruby's back deck."

"That's your story and you're sticking to it, huh?"

"Yeah, pretty much."

She didn't feel like baring her soul on a trip to Yuccaville about what it was back home that had sent her running like hell. That was a conversation best served with tequila and lime with sides of pool tables and classic rock tunes thrown into the mix. Besides, like she'd reminded her wide-eyed self in the middle of the night, she'd come to the desert to clear her thoughts and start the next chapter of her life. Re-reading the last chapter over and over was not helping her on her journey.

"I don't believe that's it," Kate said as they passed the Yuccaville City Limits sign.

"I'm not going to talk about this right now, Kate."

"You're running from something," she said, rolling right through the roadblock Natalie had erected. "You try to act like everything is copacetic in your life since you went on this so-called sabbatical from men, but there's a burr under your saddle."

She scowled at Kate. "Of course there's a burr. I like men. I like how I feel when I'm with a man who likes me. I don't like being lonely, and watching you three with your perfect relationships is like having salt dumped on my wounds."

"Our relationships are not perfect." Kate slowed as they passed in front of the sheriff's office, peering out the side window as they rolled along.

"Close enough."

"Not even." Kate sped up again. "Claire and Mac have a big problem on the horizon with her inability to commit and his job being two hours away."

"That's just logistics. They love each other, that's easy to see."

"Ronnie's love life is an even bigger cock-up." Kate hit the blinker and waited for a van to pass to make a left turn.

" 'Cock-up'? Are you British now?" Or was this one of Kate's new multiple personalities? The one that twitched?

"Ronnie's trying to be the type of woman she thinks Grady wants. In reality, this fake woman is the polar opposite of who she really is, so there's no way she can keep up this shit show for long. And on top of that, Grady's ex is in town and we both know how Ronnie deals with conflict."

"Buries her head in the sand."

"Exactly. Burying her head isn't going to save her ass this time—not with those goons who are hunting her down and certainly not with Grady. He's a damned bulldog, and I should know. She's going to have to stand and fight for once, and even then there's a lot at risk."

Kate turned right into the drugstore parking lot. "And then there's Butch and me."

"What about you two? You seem to be doing okay." Except for Kate's bouts of temporary insanity and growing list of misdemeanors, but those weren't Butch's fault. Well, not entirely. The list had been long prior to Kate getting pregnant. Butch just added a drop of fuel to the bonfire. Explosive fuel. Or maybe it was straight-up TNT.

She parked in front of the store. "Butch and I are okay at this moment in time."

"What's that supposed to mean?"

"Exactly what I said. Relationships are gambles from start to finish. There's no guaranteed happily-ever-after, only sweat, love, and sex."

"Who are you and what have you done with the real Kate?"

"There are two of us in here," she shot back with a grin.

Natalie started to smile back, but then Kate's left eye twitched several times.

"Uhh, right." She grabbed the old camera and her wallet. "I shouldn't be long. Hell, I don't even know if they can develop this kind of film anymore." She stared down at the camera. There was really only a slim chance that anything would come of the film inside of it. Even though it had been tucked away in the junction box, after decades in the summer heat, the film had to be ruined. "You know, Claire thought this was a 1970s-era camera, but I think she's a decade off. I'd place my money on a 1960s model."

"What makes you say that?"

"Remember I was in the photography club in high school? We had a project that required researching older cameras and styles. In the 1970s, they started making more of the camera bodies with plastic to make them lighter to carry." She held up the camera. "But this puppy has a metal body. It's an antique."

"This is so exciting!" Kate's left eye twitched again. "What if the film has pictures of a dead body?" She spoke those last two words in a Vincent Price tone.

Natalie frowned. "I'm not sure I'd call pictures of a corpse exciting."

"If that film contains more naked pictures of Joe, I might lose my bacon and eggs."

"More naked pictures?"

"Never mind that. Claire can tell you later." She pointed at the store. "I have to be at The Shaft in an hour and we need to make one more quick stop after the grocery store, so you'd better get going."

Inside the drugstore, Natalie walked straight to the photo department counter, which bumped shoulders with the pharmacy. The teenager working the counter for the pharmacist came over and took the film from her, but he wasn't sure if they'd be able to develop it or not. He needed to ask the manager, who would be in around noon. After giving him Kate's cell phone number, Natalie returned to the car.

"Well?" Kate asked as she pulled out of the parking lot.

"The manager isn't in and the kid behind the counter thought the camera was an old-fashioned Walkman."

"Kids these days," Kate said, sounding like Gramps and his cronies.

They hit the grocery store and made it back out in fifteen minutes, loaded down with buns, pickles, and several heads of lettuce. They hopped in the car and headed back home. At the edge of Yuccaville, Kate made a U-turn, drove back toward town for several blocks, making a right onto a side street.

"What are you doing?" Natalie asked when she parked illegally, partially blocking a fire hydrant.

"I need to check out something and there are no parking spots." She killed the engine. "Dang library must be having one of their book sales."

"You can't park here."

"We'll only be a few minutes."

"Doing what exactly? Checking out books?"

"Checking out a deputy." The whole left side of Kate's face twitched as she looked in the rearview mirror and tucked some loose hairs behind her ears.

Sirens whooped in Natalie's head. "Kate, are you sure this is a good idea?" She didn't know what her cousin had in mind, but the way Kate's gaze kept shifting between the sheriff's office up the street and the road out of town made Natalie cringe.

"As soon as this pickup drives past us, let's go." Kate reached for the door handle, ducking her head low as the old Chevy rumbled by.

"Go where?" Natalie asked, unlatching her seat belt.

If Kate were going to make a run for it, she'd need to stay on her heels. She couldn't let anything happen to the crazy pregnant woman on her watch or Claire and Ronnie would kill her.

"Now!" Kate said, popping out of the car.

Natalie caught up with her at the corner. "Kate, stop."

Kate turned, her cheeks pink, her eyes too wide for Natalie's comfort. "Hurry up!" She waved Natalie to follow and then continued along the sidewalk, doing a cartoon-like tiptoe act as she neared the cop shop's front door.

Now Natalie understood what Claire had meant about Kate's bouts of insanity. A short time ago, they'd been having a rational discussion in the car. Now they were sneaking along in broad daylight like Elmer Fudd hunting "wabbits."

"What are we doing?" Natalie whispered when she caught up to Kate several steps from the sheriff's front door. "Listen, if you want me to play along with whatever you're about to do, I need to know my part in the show."

"I can't tell you."

"Why not?"

"Because I don't want you to be in on the premeditated part." She took a couple of steps forward and then came back. "Plus, I'm not sure how this is going to go. We're going to have to wing it."

She left Natalie standing on the sidewalk, frowning after her. This might be a good opportunity to walk away and wait for the sirens to come and go.

Kate waved for her to follow and then pulled open the front door of the sheriff's office.

"Ah, hell. Here goes nothing." Natalie jogged over to where Kate was holding the door for her. "Lead the way, Napoleon."

The Cholla County Sheriff's Office smelled a lot like Deadwood's police station—burned coffee, musty paper, and a hint of something chemical—probably a floor cleaner of some type that killed criminal-sized germs. Fluorescent lights hummed overhead, reminding Natalie of the interrogation room back home. Unlike Deadwood, though, there was no door barring visitors from entering the interior office. One tall desk sort of blocked the rest of the room. Natalie figured that was where they were supposed to check in, so she stopped there. Behind it, a few desks were lined up along with one set off perpendicular to them.

Kate, on the other hand, walked around the tall desk, stopping in front of where a round-faced deputy sat with a pen in his hand. His thin moustache appeared to have been drawn on with a fine-point marker. His dark hair was styled with gel and swooped forward from the back, standing straight up in the front as if someone had snowplowed it into an invisible wall.

"Do you need something?" he asked Kate, rising from his chair slowly, like he expected Kate to pull a pistol on him at any second.

"Well, that's a fine hello for ya," Kate said. "Where's Ernie?"

Who was Ernie? And why was Kate waving Natalie closer behind her back? Were they going to gang up on the deputy and … what?

"He's off duty today," the deputy said, his forehead furrowing even deeper as he looked at Natalie, who now stood shoulder to shoulder with her cousin. "Can I leave him a message?"

"Maybe." Kate turned to Natalie. "Take off your shirt."

Natalie froze. Had she heard Kate right? "Come again?"

"Your shirt. Take it off. Now."

Natalie and the deputy exchanged raised brows, then his gaze dipped to her chest for a second … or three. His cheeks turned red and he looked toward the front window.

"Uhhh, no. I'm not taking my shirt off here."

"Maybe I should call the sheriff," the deputy offered, reaching for his desk phone.

"No!"

Natalie and the deputy both flinched.

"This can't wait for Sheriff Harrison," Kate explained at a more normal volume level. She pointed at Natalie. "This woman is being ill-treated and has finally found the courage to come here and file a report."

Ill-treated? By whom? Other than putting up with Chester this morning and his noisy chili con carne de-gassing while she worked, Natalie had been treated the same as always since arriving—like family.

The deputy looked her up and down. "She doesn't appear ill to me."

Kate looked away for a moment to roll her eyes. "I said 'ill-treated,' " she spoke slowly, as if the deputy had trouble hearing her. "She has bruises to show for it." Kate turned back to Natalie. Her twitching face sent a series of frenzied messages that even NASA's rocket scientists would have trouble decoding if given a week to decipher them. "Take off your shirt and show him your bruises."

Natalie took a step backward. "I'm not real comfortable taking off my shirt in front of a stranger."

Kate started to grin, but then appeared to rein it back in. "He's a cop, Natalie." She pointed at his badge. "It's okay to show him the evidence of your pain."

Cop or not, Natalie wasn't taking off her shirt. Not even drunk on a bet.

"Yeah, I'm a … a deputy." He patted his badge. "Deputy Gonzales here to serve and protect, Miss … what was your name?"

Natalie frowned back and forth between Kate and the deputy, unsure what taking off her shirt would do besides make her cheeks burn as hot as the deputy's were at the moment.

"Her name isn't important right now," Kate said. "Maybe you could take my friend in back and have her show you the proof in private." She pointed toward the hall at the other end of the room. "Back by the jail cells where there are fewer windows."

A light flickered on in Natalie's head. Kate wanted to be alone in the front office for some reason. Jeez, if she had just given Natalie a hint of why they'd come here in the first place, they could have avoided this bumbling in front of the deputy.

"I'm good with that," Natalie told Deputy Gonzales. "Lead the way."

Although, there was the small problem—the only thing under her shirt was a bra and two boobs. No evidence of … what had Kate called it? Ill-treatment.

Oh, but she did have a big bruise on her thigh from working on the back porch. That would do in a pinch.

She followed the deputy to the doorway leading down the hall, pausing to wrinkle her nose at Kate, who gave her two big thumbs-up. And a shoulder twitch.

Crazy Kate strikes again!

The deputy turned toward her when they reached the jail cells. "I don't think anyone can see us back here. The windows in the cells are high up and look out over the back alley and parking lot." He glanced around with a worried brow. "You can just lift your shirt some to show me. You don't have to take it all of the way off."

A *thunk* sound came from out front, followed by a small crash. He stepped around Natalie, peering down the hallway. "Everything okay up there?"

"Sure. I bumped one of the waiting room chairs," Kate hollered back.

Liar! Chairs don't crash when bumped.

When Deputy Gonzales focused back on Natalie, she began unbuttoning her jeans. "There's a little problem."

"A problem?" he repeated, looking down as she unzipped her pants. "What problem?"

"The evidence of my ill-treatment is on my thigh. I'm going to have to pull my pants down."

He puffed his cheeks and blew out a breath, focusing on the jail cells. "Okay, let's see it."

She started to wiggle her jeans down over her hips, careful to keep her underwear firmly in place. She was willing to distract the deputy for Kate, but this striptease was only going to make it to first base.

Before she got her jeans over her hips, he held up his hand. "Hold on, let me go get the sheriff's camera."

"Wait!" she grabbed him by the wrist, holding him when he would have returned to the front office. "I'm not sure this is a good idea."

In fact, she knew it wasn't. The less they had officially recorded, the better.

He pulled free. "Why not?"

Another *thunk* sounded from out front.

Deputy Gonzales frowned. "Don't move." He ran out front, skidding to a stop at the other end of the hallway. "What are you doing in there?"

Shit! Natalie raced down the hall after him, zipping and buttoning her jeans as she ran. The jig was up.

"I was looking for a pen," Kate said.

"That's the file drawer. Give that back to me."

Natalie skirted them as Deputy Gonzales tried to tug a

manila folder from Kate's hand. She headed for the front door. "You know, on second thought, I don't feel like reporting any ill-treatment today. Kate, let's go."

"Hold it right there!" the deputy commanded.

Natalie froze. Who knew that the young deputy had such a powerful voice?

"What are you two really doing here today?" he asked.

"Just reporting an ill-treatment situation." Kate's forehead turned bright pink. "We'll just let you go back to your business."

"I don't think so." He snapped his fingers and then pointed at Kate. "I know you! You're one of the Morgan sisters. I'm not letting you walk out of here until the sheriff gets back."

"What? We haven't done anything wrong. You can't hold us here."

"You were trying to steal this." He held up the manila folder.

"I wasn't going to steal it, only read it quick. I was bored waiting for you two."

"I'm no hayseed." He moved, blocking the path to the front door. "You two head in back and get in a jail cell. Now!" he added when they didn't obey.

"On what grounds?" Kate asked.

"Attempted theft."

"Ah, fudgeberries," Natalie said under her breath.

"Hmmm." Kate worried her lower lip. "That could stick."

He pointed toward the hall that led to the jail cells. "Go now or I'll add resisting arrest to the charges."

Kate's fists clenched. "I will not be—"

"Come on," Natalie said, grabbing Kate's arm and tugging her back to the cells.

"Your usual cell," the deputy instructed as Natalie started into Cell B.

Kate dragged Natalie into the other cell.

The deputy closed the cell door behind them. "Hand over your phones and any other paraphernalia. You know the drill."

They both gave up their cell phones and Kate added the car keys.

"I'm going to call the sheriff and see what he wants to do about you two. If he allows you a free phone call, I'll come back and let you choose who gets to make the call."

They watched him walk away. As soon as he was out of earshot, Natalie whirled on Kate. "You know, if you'd have told me your plans before leaving the car, we might not be here right now."

"I was working on the fly."

"What was in that folder that you wanted so bad?"

"Nothing. I just grabbed it quick when I heard the deputy coming back out front."

Natalie crossed her arms. "What the hell, then?"

"I needed to distract him from what I had in my other hand until I could hide it." She peeked out front and then dug in her pants, pulling out a small black rectangle. She held it out to Natalie and whispered, "Here, take this."

After a moment's hesitation, Natalie took the small piece of plastic. It was a flash drive. "What do you think is on it?"

"I'll tell you after I try it out on Butch's laptop when we get to the bar." She made a face. "Shoot! I forgot I need to open the bar. If we get to have a phone call, we need to tell Ronnie to go open for me."

Twenty minutes later, the deputy returned. "Sheriff Harrison was busy," he explained the delay. "He said to tell you two that he's already contacted your sister and someone is on the way here to get you."

"Why doesn't he let us go right now?" Kate asked. "My car is right across the street. We can forget this ever happened." She waved her hand back and forth in front of the deputy's face, as if she had mind powers or something.

He scowled at her hand. "Because your black Volvo was towed about ten minutes ago, so you need a ride."

"What?! Why didn't you stop the tow truck driver?"

"Because I didn't see him until he was driving off with it and passed in front of the window."

He started to walk away and then stopped, adding, "Oh, the sheriff also said to tell you that Veronica will open The Shaft for you, so there is no need for anyone to break any speed limits on your way back to Jackrabbit Junction."

Kate growled at his back as he walked away. "Damned tow

truck driver."

"I told you not to park there."

"I was only partially in front of the hydrant."

They waited another twenty minutes with Kate bitching and cursing the whole time. Natalie stood at the window, staring out into the back lot through the bars, half listening to her cousin's rants. It was just like old times.

The buzz of the front door opening made Natalie wince. If it was Gramps who'd come, there'd be an ass-chewing for both of them all of the way home. She crossed her fingers Ronnie had sent Claire or even Chester.

"It's about time," Kate grumbled, brushing off her work shirt. She looked around the cell with a wrinkled lip. "I'm going to buy Grady some air fresheners for this place. That urinal cake isn't cutting it."

Natalie looked back out the window and sighed. Two days in Arizona and she'd already spent time in jail. That might be a new record for her.

The sound of footfalls on cement drew near—two sets of them.

"Your ride is here, ladies," the deputy said.

Kate let out a small screech. "Galloping Gadzooks!"

Natalie turned from the window and gasped, falling back against the wall.

On the other side of the bars, Detective "Coop" Cooper stared back at her, looking as heartbreaking in his black leather jacket and blue jeans as when she'd left Deadwood mere days ago. His blond hair was wind ruffled, but his face was chiseled smooth where there were usually furrows and ridges.

When she met his gray eyes they searched hers, looking for something—probably the reason why she ran all the way to Arizona to get away from him.

She schooled her expression, trying to pretend her feathers weren't ruffled that he'd tracked her down a thousand-plus miles later. "What are you doing here, Coop?"

Chapter Seven

K atie, you have to at least *try* to stay out of jail, darn it," Ronnie said.

"You promised before we left The Shaft that you wouldn't lecture me on this trip," Katie reminded her.

Ronnie parked Claire's Jeep next to the Hummingbird Towing sign in front of a single-story concrete block building painted bright yellow. According to Claire, this was the same tow truck service that had hauled away the RV in which they'd found the diamonds.

The towing company looked more like a flower shop from the outside with the multitudes of red hummingbird feeders dangling from green plant hangers staked here and there into the desert dirt. The concrete walls were lined with a white picket fence, giving the place a cottage-like air. A long corrugated tin wall branched off to the left of the business. The tin was painted the same bright yellow as the building, giving a happy vibe in spite of the razor wire strung along the top. A rolling gate with spiky posts divided the parking lot from the side and back of the building.

Katie's Volvo was undoubtedly caged on the other side of the barrier. Ronnie just hoped they could free it without having to involve Grady. Lord only knew how much longer he'd want to put up with her family's shenanigans.

"I know what I promised," Ronnie said, shutting off the Jeep. "But—"

"No buts, no coconuts. And for your information, I had a legitimate reason for going to the sheriff's office this morning."

"Really? What was so damned important that you had to

rush in there and get your ass thrown in jail?"

Katie glared across the console at her. "I don't feel like telling you right now because you're just going to be a big, dumb doubting-dolly about it."

Ronnie glared back.

Earlier, upon returning from jail, Katie had shown up at The Shaft a few minutes after they'd opened, grabbed an order pad, and started right to work. Ronnie hadn't had a chance to find out any details about what happened at the sheriff's office beyond what Grady had told her when he called to say someone had to go get her sister out of jail … again.

It had been Claire's bright idea to send that detective from Deadwood to Yuccaville, figuring he was less likely to end up behind bars with Katie and Natalie than Claire was if she were to go get the two jailbirds. She was probably right.

Ronnie had yet to hear Natalie's side of this morning's debacle. She'd only seen her cousin long enough to smile and wave when Claire and Natalie came to cover for them after the lunch crowd petered out. Undoubtedly, her tale of woe would end with "Kate's crazy," same as Claire's story had yesterday.

But back to the problem at hand … "Let's go get your stupid car before you find a way to land me in jail, too." Ronnie pushed open the Jeep's door.

"Maybe I'll lock you in the cell and swallow the key," Katie shot back.

"Nobody swallows keys anymore, Katie. It costs too much money for the necessary X-rays and surgeries to remove them." She hopped to the ground and slammed the door shut on her sister's grumbling.

Katie joined her, frowning at the spiky gate as she straightened her black work shirt. "I hope the groceries I bought this morning are still in my car."

"Where else would they be?"

"The tow truck driver might have popped the locks and eaten them."

"Right, because we have a growing problem in these parts with starving tow truck drivers who like to pillage cars for random food items."

"I forgot to tell you that while I was stuck in jail this morning, I wrote a song especially for you." Katie pulled open the glass front door and waited for Ronnie. "It's called 'Kiss My Ass.' "

"Ahh, you wrote me a love song. How sweet." She stuck her tongue out at her sister as she walked past.

Inside the building, Ronnie paused on the fake grass welcome rug to wipe her boots, eyeing the huge company sign nailed to the wall behind the counter. Bracketing the words "Hummingbird Towing" were paintings of hummingbirds. Only they weren't normal-looking birds, more like a rowdy version of the speedy fliers that would fit in with the likes of Pancho Villa. Dressed in sombreros, bandoleers, boots, and pistols, these hummingbirds hung out on the Wild West branch of the family tree.

But those weren't the only hummingbirds in the office. All along the walls were shelves full of hummingbird replicas made from ceramic, plastic, wire, and more. There were even crocheted hummingbird finger puppets on a mannequin's detached hand that matched the crocheted hat on a foam-shaped head. Oil paintings, pencil drawings, and water colorings of the bird filled the spaces between the shelves. Overhead, hummingbird piñatas strung from the ceiling swayed in the air circulating via the ceiling vents. The place even smelled flowery.

"Obsessed much?" Katie whispered in her ear and then stepped up to the front desk. "Hello?" She rang the little bell sitting on the counter. "Anyone here?"

While they waited for someone to come out to help them, Ronnie circled the room and checked out the decorations some more, admiring the craftsmanship on several of the pieces.

She stopped at one particular picture in a hummingbird frame and looked closer. This one had humans in it instead of birds. Was that Grady? It sure looked like him in one of his typical tan sheriff uniforms, only a decade younger according to the date posted below the picture.

Standing next to Grady was a tall, brawny man who stood several inches above the six-foot-four sheriff. His chest was nearly a Grady-and-a-half wide. His grease-streaked T-shirt clung to his dark skin. His cowboy hat shaded his eyes but left visible a rock-hewn jaw and thick neck that bunched up at his broad shoulders. Ronnie would hate to be at the wrong end of that guy's fists.

"Katie, come check out this picture."

Right then, the door behind the desk opened. Katie was looking Ronnie's way when the same Titan who was in the picture ducked through the doorway and joined them.

Holy Idris Elba! The guy was even more impressive in real life. He wore no cowboy hat today, though, only a pair of raised eyebrows below a high and tight haircut. His square jaw was covered with a layer of black scruff. His grease-stained coveralls stretched tight across his wide shoulders.

His smile lit up his face. "Can I help you ladies?"

Katie turned back to the desk and let out a gasp. "What the planets! You're like Paul Bunyan size." She crooked her neck to gape up at him. "Do you use Babe the Ox to tow cars around for you?"

Oh, God, Katie. Don't piss off the giant.

Ronnie rushed to her sister's side. "Ignore her, she's had a rough day."

He grinned wide, his dark eyes warm and friendly. "You must be the Morgan sisters. I was warned you might be stopping by to pick up the black Volvo."

What did he mean he'd been warned? By whom? Grady? Or did Deputy Dipshit have a hand in this?

"Don't believe everything you hear," Katie said. "Especially if the rumor mongers are wearing stupid, stinkin' badges."

He chuckled, low and deep. Barry White had nothing on this guy. "You're missing someone. I was told there were three of you."

Katie leaned her elbow on the counter, giving him one of her trademark charming grins. "Yeah, well, someone has to stay back at the hideout and reload our pistols." She pointed at the sign on the wall behind him. "Who's nuts about hummingbirds?"

"That'd be me."

"Is this something that's come on with age, or did you pop out of the womb daydreaming about the little winged buzzers?"

He shrugged. "They grew on me after I moved here. I set up a feeder outside and five showed up the first day fighting for the sugar water. So I put up another'n the next day and more flew in to joust and dive-bomb the others. From there, this all spawned." He held his long arms wide. Hell, he could probably wrap them around Katie twice.

"I like it." Katie knocked once on the counter, like a judge with a gavel. "And I like you." She leaned closer and looked at the name stitched in cursive on his coveralls. "Is your name really 'Tank'?"

"No, but that's what I've been called since I played football in college back in Florida."

"Offense or defense?"

"Offense. Center."

"Nice, a protector." She winked at Ronnie. "With all of your problems, we could use the help of a man like Tank, don't you think?"

"Well, I ... I mean, if he ... Uh, I guess, but ..." Ronnie sputtered.

Katie waved her off, turning back to the Titan. "Nice to meet you, Tank. They call me Kate." She went up on her toes and whispered in a stage voice, "But I'm not as crazy as they all think."

Ronnie would beg to differ. "Listen, Mr. Tank. If you could

just tell us how much we owe you for towing Katie's Volvo, we'll get out of your hair."

Tank grabbed a clipboard from the desktop and slid it in front of Katie. "Just sign this," he said.

Katie scanned the paper and then smiled up at him. "Are you a dealing man, Tank?"

Oh no. Here we go. Ronnie winced. She could hear the sirens coming already. Grady was going to drop them off at the county line and tell them not to come back until Katie had the baby.

"What do you have in mind?" Tank asked.

"If you give me a break on the cost of getting my car out of your jail, I'll give you a free meal and drink of your choice at The Shaft over in Jackrabbit Junction." She patted the bar's emblem stitched on her shirt.

"Katie," Ronnie whispered. "That's not how this works. You're going to get us in more trouble."

Katie pointed her thumb at Ronnie. "Ignore her," she told Tank. "She's sleeping with the sheriff and gets all tense about any even slightly shady business that doesn't include dotting i's and crossing t's."

Tank gave Ronnie a once-over, making her wish she'd dressed nicer than jeans and a white tank top under her matching black work shirt. "She's Grady's girlfriend?"

Katie nodded. "Normally, she's not this uptight." She winked at Tank and added, "Hell, she doesn't even wear underwear most days."

Ronnie's cheeks burned. "I do, too!" Well, most of the time. Her yoga pants were made to be worn sans underwear.

Tank laughed, showing off a pair of impressive choppers. "And here I thought Grady was getting back with his ex-wife."

What? "Why would you think that?"

"Because Elizabeth told me so herself just the other day when I ran into her at the gas station."

That little bitch! Ronnie growled in her throat. As if she needed to deal with an overzealous ex-wife right now with all of the other crap raining down on her.

Katie reached out and patted Ronnie's hand. "Now, now. Down, girl." She looked back at Tank. "Between you and me, little Miss Elizabeth is about to realize there's a new version of this fairy tale she's spinning around town."

"You don't say."

"Yep. Morgan sisters don't take kindly to poachers."

"You're a real spitfire." Tank's grin almost reached his ears. "I'll tell you what, Kate Morgan. You give me *three* meals with drinks at The Shaft, and I'll give you back your car for the cost of gas to tow it here."

Katie slapped the counter. "Deal!" She held out her hand.

He looked at it and then back up at her. "Don't you need to ask Butch about this first, bein' it's his bar?"

Of course Tank knew Butch. Everyone here knew everyone else plus their first cousins once removed.

"Nope. I'm sure he'll agree."

Tank's huge hand wrapped around Katie's, making it look like a toddler's. "What makes you so certain?"

"Because I'm having his baby and I said so."

"Well, I'll be. Butch Carter is a lucky man. I'll meet you two out front. Just give me a minute to finish up what I was doing when you showed up." Tank left, ducking back through the same doorway.

As soon as he closed the door behind him, Ronnie punched Katie's shoulder. "What the hell? Why'd you go and blab about Grady's and my relationship?"

Katie scoffed. "Tank doesn't give a ring-a-ding about you playing hide the Ping-Pong paddle with the sheriff, so relax."

"We are not playing hide the … gah!" Ronnie threw up her hands. "You didn't have to bring up my lack of underwear, damn it."

"It makes you more of an interesting character, which you normally are even with your underwear on, when you're not trying to be all goody two-shoes. Besides, we're in Yuccaville, not on Rodeo Drive. Hell, I bet half of the folks around here don't wear underwear either, especially in the summer. It's too dang hot."

"Claire's wrong. You're not crazy. You're frickin' insane."

Katie punched Ronnie back. "Don't call me insane!"

Before she gave in to the urge to twist Katie's arm behind

her back and make her cry "uncle," Ronnie walked away to inspect more of Tank's hummingbird collection while her blood pressure returned to normal.

"Whose bright idea was it to send that dang detective from Deadwood to come get Natalie and me out of jail?" Katie asked, still leaning on the counter.

"Claire's."

"Figures. She probably thought it would be funny."

"Something like that."

"Well, it wasn't. Not for me and especially not for Natalie."

"What's your problem with him? You barely even know the guy, right?" Ronnie picked up a glass hummingbird, admiring the craftsmanship.

"He's a cop."

Ronnie rolled her eyes. "You're starting to sound like Claire."

"*And* he's the reason Natalie ran away from home."

She shot Katie a frown. "What do you mean, she ran away from home?"

"You don't really believe she came down here just to help Claire tear apart the back deck, do you?"

"Well, I sort of did until now. I mean, for that reason and to hang out with her family over the holidays since her mom and dad are visiting her brother."

"She was with family—Violet Parker is like a sister to her, remember?"

That was true. Ronnie set the glass hummingbird down.

Natalie had quickly become best friends with the neighbor kids when they all were young, hanging out at the Parkers' house as often as she did Ronnie's. Violet's family had basically adopted Natalie as one of their own by the time she was a teenager.

"What makes you think Natalie was running away? Is it something she said?" Ronnie flashed back to this morning in Gramps's Winnebago and Natalie's odd comment about gray eyes. The detective had gray eyes—something she'd noticed when she'd handed him the receipt tag to put in his camper window for the week.

"No, not something she said," Katie answered. "Haven't you noticed the way she's been acting?"

"I guess I've been a little too busy freaking out about all of the killers gunning for me." She admired a crystal vase with a flock of hummingbirds etched on it. "Outside of her sabbatical to avoid getting involved with any guys, she seems like the same old Natalie."

"She's sad and lonely."

She glanced Katie's way. "Did she tell you that?"

"She didn't have to. I can see it in the way she frowns toward the horizon when she thinks nobody is watching."

"Maybe she's worried about somebody coming after her, like that detective. I frown at the horizon all of the time, but I'm not sad." On the contrary, Ronnie was scared as hell, yet pissed at the same time. Her piece of shit not-husband had left her in one hell of a predicament.

"And last night at the bar, I mentioned to Natalie that Mississippi is single and probably not looking for any long-term commitments if she felt like hooking up with him to blow off a little steam."

Ronnie wasn't sure Mississippi was human enough to be interested in copulating with a female. Sure, he was good looking in a tall-drink-of-whiskey sort of way, but he was still an FBI agent. Didn't they fit his kind with cyborg parts in the academy? "What did Natalie say to that?"

"That she didn't need any more law dogs messing with her head."

"What makes you so certain this Detective Cooper is the law dog Natalie was talking about last night?"

"Because I had to ride back to Jackrabbit Junction with the two of them today and there was some serious sparking going on in the cab of that pickup."

"Sparking? Are you sure that wasn't your brain short-circuiting?"

"That's it. I'm going to shave your head down the middle while you sleep."

"Okay, okay. I'm sorry." Ronnie crossed her arms. "What did Natalie and the detective talk about on the ride back to Jackrabbit Junction?"

Katie shrugged, brushing some lint off her work shirt. "At

first it was sleep-worthy stuff about the weather and the drive
south. Then Natalie asked about Violet and her boyfriend,
mentioning some other names I didn't recognize who are
probably friends of hers in Deadwood, and he filled her in with
monosyllabic answers for the most part."

"Did she ask the detective why he was down here?"

"She asked that before we even left the jail cell."

"What was his answer?"

"He was all cryptic, telling her he needed a vacation after the
long shifts he'd been pulling at the police station over the holiday
and decided to come down to Arizona after hearing her talk
about how relaxing it is." Katie snorted. "Silly man. That was the
perfect opportunity to tell Natalie that he'd come to see her, but
he chickened out."

"He didn't seem like much of a chicken to me when I
checked him into the RV park."

Something about Detective Cooper reminded Ronnie of
Grady. Maybe it was the way they both stood like they were on
guard, waiting for a criminal to run past them. Or it could be the
take-no-shit attitude implanted in their brains during law dog
training.

"He had another opportunity to come clean a few miles
later," Katie continued. "Natalie asked him if there was anything
he wanted to see while he was down here. He didn't answer right
away, shooting several glances at her instead. I thought for sure
he'd mention wanting to see *her*, but then he looked in the
rearview mirror at me and I could see his face clam up. He threw
out some crapola about being curious where Cochise Stronghold
was located."

"Isn't that south of here?"

"Yeah, it's down by I-10. Mac will tell you all about it and the
geology in the area if you're looking for something to put you to
sleep."

Ronnie didn't need sleep so long as she had Grady by her
with his bedside arsenal. She was looking for more help with
staying alive each day when the sheriff was too busy doing his job
to keep an eye on her.

"What did Natalie say then?" she asked, returning to a less

heart-pounding subject.

"The big bozo told Detective Cooper he should check it out and let her know what he thought. When I suggested Natalie go with him to see it for herself, she mumbled some excuse about needing to help Claire build the deck."

Ronnie returned to the counter, joining Katie again. "Did anything else happen between them?"

Katie shrugged. "I don't know. We'd reached The Shaft by that time and they dropped me off."

"It'd be a shame for this guy to drive all of the way down here from Deadwood and have nothing come of it."

"It'd be more of a shame if Natalie doesn't wake up and realize that he's perfect for her."

"Perfect? What are you talking about? He's a cop. Natalie is like Claire. They're both allergic to law dogs, remember?"

"That doesn't matter. This one is different."

"Different how?"

"I've been around Natalie with other guys she's dated. She acts all flirty and changes into someone else—sort of like you and this silly dress-up game you're playing with Grady."

Ronnie wrinkled her nose at Katie. "It's not a game." With his ex-wife in town telling everyone she'd returned to Yuccaville to get Grady back and Katie making him pull out his hair every day, Ronnie would probably lose if it were a game. The odds were stacking up against her in record speed.

"But today with this detective of hers," Katie continued, "she wasn't putting on any acts. She was plain old Natalie, sans makeup and sex-kitten song and dance. He couldn't stop sneaking peeks at her either. I'm telling you, this could be the real deal with these two if they would both just take a chance."

That was the tricky part of this relationship two-step, wasn't it? Paddling through quicksand seemed less risky some days.

Katie pointed her phone toward the window. Tank parking her Volvo up next to Claire's Jeep.

"Natalie needs to get laid," Katie said, pocketing her phone. "Between you and me, I think I'm going to sabotage her sabbatical." She left Ronnie standing at the counter.

"You can't do that." Ronnie started after her.

Katie turned when she reached the door. Her left cheek twitched. "Wanna bet? And while I'm at it, I'm going to take care of your problem with Grady's ex, too. That bitch will rue the day she messed with my sister."

* * *

"What in the hell were you thinking, sending Coop to come get me out of jail this morning?" Natalie asked Claire as soon as the three old amigos took their late afternoon break from supervising the back deck construction project.

It was the first moment she'd gotten alone with her cousin since Coop had dropped her off at the General Store after springing her from the county pen.

Coop. In the flesh. Here with her in Jackrabbit Junction.

Shit.

He must have showered before coming to get her. She could smell his heady cologne across the cab of the pickup all of the way back to the RV park, making her want to scoot closer and nuzzle his neck.

When she'd mentioned to him after they dropped off Kate that she couldn't hang out this afternoon because she had work to do, he'd shrugged and told her that he needed to sleep after the long drive south. His expression hadn't changed at her addendum that she was helping out at The Shaft tonight, or when she invited him to stop by to eat, drink, and be merry. His parting, "I might see you there," had left her grumbling under her breath about men and why a sabbatical was the smartest thing she'd ever done.

Might see you there.

He'd followed her over a thousand miles to Arizona for his so-called vacation and he "might" see her? The ornery son of a gun was as frustrating on the west side of the Continental Divide as he was on the east.

"You want to know what I was thinking?" Claire said, snapping Natalie back to the present. She lifted one end of a porch joist they'd cleared of nails and screws, waiting for Natalie to take the other end of the board. "I was thinking about ways to

NOT end up in jail with you two. Kate is a black hole these days, sucking everyone into her insane world."

"You're right about that." Natalie hefted the other end of the board. Together, they loaded it into the back of Ruby's old Ford pickup.

Natalie had filled in Claire and the old boys on what happened earlier in Yuccaville with Kate. She'd skipped the part about the flash drive Kate had nabbed from Deputy Dipshit's desk, selling the whole event as just another one of Kate's "crazy" episodes.

Claire moved to the next loosened joist. "So what's the story?"

"Which particular story?" They carried the board to the pickup, dumping it inside next to the other board.

"The one starring a certain Deadwood detective who drove to Arizona to stay at the same RV park as you."

They grabbed another joist. "Oh, that one."

The board clattered in the back of the pickup with the others. A raven squawked at them from a nearby cottonwood tree, apparently unhappy with their racket. Claire flipped it off.

"He claims he needed a vacation." Natalie grabbed another board.

"I heard Tahiti is nice this time of year."

Natalie chuckled as she stepped over a concrete pier, careful not to trip as they carried the board to the truck.

After they loaded another joist, Natalie came clean. "He's the reason I left Deadwood."

"Is he a stalker?" Claire asked.

"No, it's not like that."

They lifted another board.

"Was he giving you trouble back home?"

"Sort of."

"Are we playing twenty questions here?"

They dumped off the joist.

Natalie moved closer to Claire, lowering her voice. "Years ago, we got hot and heavy behind the Purple Door Saloon."

Claire grinned. "You back-alley tramp."

"Not quite. We didn't finish the job."

"Why not?"

"Work called and he ran off to hunt criminals."

"He chose work over sex? What is he, a cyborg assassin sent back from the future?"

Natalie chuckled. "You sound like Vi." Her best friend back in Deadwood often claimed Coop wasn't made of flesh and bone. Natalie knew otherwise, though, after being on the receiving end of those lips and hands. He was no machine, not with the way he kissed.

"I'm surprised Violet didn't tell you he was coming down here," Claire said. "She knows we're allergic to cops."

"She didn't know." A phone call shortly after Coop dropped her off had confirmed Natalie's suspicion—his trip to Arizona had been kept a big secret. Her partner in crime up in Deadwood had sworn up and down that she would have called Natalie and warned her if she'd known Coop was heading south.

"Ahhh, he kept it a secret," Claire said. "Smart move."

They carried another joist to the pickup, dumping it off.

"That's what worries me. He's too smart." Natalie shook her head. "I left Deadwood because I needed to clear my head before I did something stupid."

"Like sleep with him."

"Exactly." They carted another board to the pickup. "Giving in to my whims with him could really screw up a good thing."

"Or just be a good screw thing."

"You're not funny."

Claire grinned. "I sort of am. Besides, you're on sabbatical. Doesn't that make you indifferent to temptations in the form of male flesh or something like that?"

Natalie's bark of laughter echoed across the RV park. "My electromagnetic, anti-men force field has not been working when it comes to Coop for some reason. So, I did what any savvy woman would do in my shoes—packed my duffle bag and fled. I figured a couple weeks of being far, far away from him would give me the time and space needed to take back the reins on my lonely heart."

Another board landed in the pickup. Three to go.

"But now he's here," Claire said.

"Yes, he is." Every sexy inch of him, damn it.

"What are you going to do?"

They carted another joist over to the truck.

"Well, I can't ignore him. That's rude." And truth be told, she enjoyed Coop's company. Over the last few months, they'd built a friendship in between the fun flirting, sharing plenty of grins. Not to mention the other crazy shit they'd experienced together while helping Violet get a grip on her new life in Deadwood.

"You should take a day off and show him around."

"I can't leave you to build the porch alone. Besides, you need my help catching a killer."

"I have the three old biddies here itching to show me all of the things I'm doing wrong on this build. I can last a day without you so long as I have a six-pack at my side." They tossed another board into the pickup bed, returning to grab the last one. "As for the other problem," she said in a quiet voice, glancing toward the hills behind the back fence, "Mac is going to stock me up with some self-defense weapons."

"Like what? A gun?"

"No. Not with Kate throwing bananas around like a mad monkey."

They dumped off the last board.

"Your sister twitched several times while we were at the sheriff's office this morning."

Claire tugged off her leather gloves. "What were you two really doing there? And don't try to blow smoke up my ass. I know my sister. She wouldn't go willingly into a cop shop without a darn good reason."

Natalie lowered her voice. "She wanted to search Deputy Dipshit's desk."

"For what?"

"She didn't say, but she found a flash drive and pocketed it before we were thrown behind bars. She planned to look at what was on it when she got back to The Shaft. I haven't had a chance to talk to her since then to find out more." After Kate had returned to The Shaft from getting her car at the towing company, she'd gone in the kitchen to help prep for the evening dinner rush.

"We'll have to ask her about it when we head over to help with the Saturday night crowd."

"You probably shouldn't mention this to Ronnie until we know what's on the drive," Natalie said. "She's already stressed enough about being the perfect girlfriend for the sheriff."

Claire nodded, frowning toward a pair of older women leaving the laundry building. "If you're not careful, you might end up in the same boat as Ronnie."

"What do you mean?"

She turned back to Natalie. "The law is the law, whether you're having sex with a sheriff or a detective."

"I'm not having sex with Coop."

Claire smirked. "Not yet, anyway. But you and I don't have the greatest track record when it comes to resisting men." She pulled the pickup keys from her pocket.

"I'm not going to sleep with Coop."

Claire chuckled. "Who said anything about sleeping?"

Natalie smacked her on the arm. "I mean it, Claire."

"I'm sure you do, but twenty bucks says otherwise."

"Make it fifty!" a familiar voice said from behind them.

Natalie turned, her heart skipping a beat.

"Who's that?" Claire asked under her breath.

Why didn't Coop say anything earlier about … ?

"Harvey!" Natalie smiled, happy as hell to see Cooper's uncle. Dressed in jeans and a button-up shirt with saguaro suspenders, he smelled fresh as a daisy when she hugged him. "What are you doing down here?"

Willis Harvey's two gold teeth glinted in the sunlight behind his recently trimmed gray whiskers. His salt-and-pepper hair was slicked back; his blue eyes twinkled.

"Taking a vacation from the snow." He glanced around at the other campers, leaning in closer to add, "I hear Arizona is full of pretty birdies this time of year. How about you introduce me to a few with extra-long legs and cute tail feathers?"

Chapter Eight

D on't fear the reaper," Mac sang along with Blue Öyster Cult on the jukebox as he filled another glass with beer from the tap. "Baby, take my hand."

The Shaft was packed tonight—again. Butch's usual bartender had called in sick, which translated into Kate desperate for someone to tend bar. Claire was needed out on the floor with an order pad, so Mac was manning the pumps.

"Someone needs to change this song," Claire said from the wait station at the end of the bar where she lingered while he filled her order. Her black shirt sporting The Shaft's logo hung open over her yellow Dancing Winnebagos RV Park tank top. Her brow was lined yet again as she watched him work.

Mac handed her the beers she'd ordered, singing to her, "Baby, I'm your man."

She put the beers on her tray next to the two tequila sunrises he'd made for her table. "I'm serious, Mac. This damned song is making me want to duck and cover."

"Come home with me to Tucson," he called above the music and din of conversation.

Her mouth thinned. "You know I can't do that."

"You can, but you won't."

She lifted the tray of drinks. "I don't want to get into this right now."

"Neither do I." He nodded at a cowboy who was summoning him from the other end of the bar. "But I have to head back to Tucson in the morning and it would make me a lot happier if you'd come with me."

"What?" She frowned, setting the tray back down on the bar.

"I thought you took vacation next week."

He had, but sometimes work trumped holidays. "There's an emergency at the jobsite south of Tucson."

"What kind of emergency? You build walls for chrissake, not dams. Wait, did Humpty-Dumpty fall off the blasted thing again?"

The cowboy was waving money in his direction. "I need to go settle a bill, Slugger."

He left her to take care of business. He didn't want to leave either, damn it, but last week's big storm caused all kinds of problems on the jobsite, washing out backfill and causing structural cracks in one of the new walls. As project lead he had certain responsibilities, especially with the foreman on vacation in the Bahamas until after the New Year.

He heard his name called while he was giving the cowboy his change. Kate peered out at him through the kitchen window. She was helping prepare orders in back tonight, which Mac figured meant she'd made it past the morning sickness stage of pregnancy. Now, if she could be done with the temporary insanity part, too, her sisters could breathe easier.

Mac stuffed the tip he'd been left in the community tip jar and joined her at the window. The smell of grilled burgers and fries greeted him along with Kate, whose hair was poking out all around her face, looking like her head was unraveling. Her cheeks were extra pink and her nose shiny. This pregnancy business was rough on the poor girl.

"I need you to give Natalie a message for me," she hollered out to him.

"Okay." He glanced toward the pool tables where he'd seen Natalie talking to Ronnie's FBI buddy prior to Claire showing up with her drink order. Natalie was taking an order from two twenty-somethings in Northern Arizona University sweatshirts and jeans.

"Tell her I said the bomb was a dud."

He frowned at Kate. "Come again?"

"The. Bomb. Was. A. Dud!" she enunciated like a kindergarten teacher.

"I heard you the first time."

"Then why did you make me repeat it?"

"Because that doesn't make any sense."

"She'll know what I mean. Just do it, please."

He muttered under his breath about the crazy shit he put up with for Claire.

"If you call me crazy again, Mac," Kate said, pointing a spatula at him, "I'll spray paint a bunch of hearts on your pickup."

"Don't touch my truck, Kate." After nailing her with a hard squint, he turned to find Ronnie waiting for him at the end of the bar. Her polka dot dress from last night had been replaced with a black shirt with laces up the front under her unbuttoned work shirt and black jeans. She seemed to be flip-flopping between June Cleaver and Catwoman. Something about the way her gaze was darting left and right had Mac wondering if the stress of waiting for the hammer to fall had her teetering at the edge of sanity along with her youngest sister.

He almost asked if she was okay, but she shoved her order at him before he could speak. He frowned down at the scrap of paper. "You need to stop scribbling orders in cursive, Ronnie." Her writing seemed to be getting worse as the night wore on, too. What were the outward signs of a panic attack?

"There's nothing wrong with my writing."

"Your letters E, L, and I all look the same; your Q looks like a G; and what the hell is this?" He held the paper out toward her, pointing at the first letter of the last word.

She craned her neck. "That's a capital S."

"It looks more like a dollar sign."

"Wait, it is a dollar sign."

He set the paper down on the bar. "You can't even read your own writing."

She rolled her eyes. "Fine, I'll try to write clearer for you, Mr. Graphologist."

"What's a giraffe-ologist?" Claire asked, joining them at the wait station. "Is that supposed to be an insult?"

"Not giraffe, *graph*. You know, someone who studies handwriting. Sheesh, clean the peanuts out of your ears."

"Keep running your yap-trap, dingleberry, and I'll cram

peanuts up your nose and start calling you Dumbo." Claire took a closer look at Ronnie's scrawls on the order sheet. "Jeez, Ronnie. How is Mac supposed to read this sloppy shit?"

"You're taking his side because he's your boyfriend."

"That's not true. I'm taking his side because I'm having wild and crazy sex with him." Claire winked at Mac, handing him her own order.

"I've had enough 'crazy' tonight," Mac said. "Let's just stick to the wild and wooly fun stuff, Slugger."

"Don't call me crazy!" Kate hollered from the kitchen order window.

"We aren't talking about you!" Claire yelled back.

"How did she even hear that?" Ronnie asked. "Is one of you two wearing a wire? Or has pregnancy made her like that robot chick on *The Six Million Dollar Woman*?"

"You mean Jaime Sommers on *The Bionic Woman*," Claire told her, frowning toward the jukebox, which was now playing Black Sabbath's "Paranoid." "You really need to study up on your pop culture."

"You need to get a new childhood, TV junkie."

"That doesn't even make sense, peanut brain." Claire thumbed over her shoulder. "Did either of you notice who picked the last few songs?"

"No, why?" Ronnie asked, making a weird snort-laugh sound as she peered around the bar. "Are you feeling more paranoid than usual tonight?"

Claire glared at her sister. "That biker babe at table seven is trying to get your attention again."

"My drinks come before Claire's," Ronnie told Mac before diving back into the sea of patrons.

"She's high-strung tonight," Claire said.

"I noticed." Mac searched her face for stress fractures, too. "How are you doing, Slugger?"

"Okay, I guess. It helps having you here." She scanned the dance floor. "I just wish whoever was on this creepy music kick would stop pumping the jukebox full of money."

"I could unplug it and put an out-of-order sign on the glass, if you'd like."

She shook her head, focusing back on him. "So, how long are you going to be gone this time?"

Mac grabbed the cocktail shaker, starting on Ronnie's drink order for a tequila oasis and a bourbon smash.

"I'll try to be back Monday evening."

"New Year's Eve? You'd better be. I have naked plans for ringing in the New Year with you."

Before he could prod her for some naked details, Natalie joined them.

"How's it going back there, Mac?" she asked, leaning on the bar next to Claire.

Something was different about Natalie tonight. Maybe it was her clothes. Instead of a T-shirt and jeans under her bar apron, she had on one of Kate's fancy pink beaded blouses—make that a "tunic." That was what Claire had called it when she'd borrowed it from her sister for a dinner-and-a-movie date with him weeks ago. He searched Natalie's face. Her eyes looked darker, sort of smoky, and her lips were shimmering. Makeup, too?

He was about to ask her what was with the makeover, but then remembered the two times he'd dipped a toe into Kate's feelings and ended up somehow making her cry. Instead, he took the order slip she held out his way: two cosmopolitans and a bottle of sarsaparilla. Ronnie's FBI pal must be on the time clock still. This was his second sarsaparilla tonight.

"Kate has a message for you," he told Natalie while finishing Ronnie's order. "She said to tell you the bomb is a dud, whatever that means."

"It means the cheese has slid completely off Kate's cracker," Claire said, shooting a narrow-eyed glance at the order window.

"I believe she's talking about the flash drive she 'borrowed' this morning from Deputy Dipshit," Natalie told him.

"What are you talking about?" Mac asked, grabbing two glasses for Claire's beer order.

"You know, the reason why we ended up in jail today. Well, that's not the actual reason because the deputy doesn't know about the borrowed drive, which Kate plans to return as soon as she can."

Mac did a double take. "You were in jail today?"

She turned to Claire. "You didn't tell him?"

"He's been gone all day. We haven't had a moment alone … yet," she followed that last bit with a wiggle of her eyebrows in his direction.

Mac winked back at her.

He'd spent the day in Yuccaville. He'd started with a visit to the pawnshop to see what sort of self-defense weapons he could find for Claire that fit her criteria, coming away with a leather sap she could conceal in her back pocket. He figured he'd hit up some stores in Tucson for more non-firearm options before returning on Monday.

Next, he'd grabbed some lunch at The Mule Train Diner. After enjoying a piece of tart cherry pie made by Grady's sister, who owned the joint, he'd headed to the library. Digging through county and state records, newspaper articles on the microfiche reader, and local history books for information about his aunt's Humdigger mine and Joe's childhood home had taken up most of the afternoon. On his way back to the RV park, he'd swung by two of Ruby's other mines, hiking up to the entrances to make sure the barricades Claire's grandpa and he had erected were still in place—and they were, thankfully. They had enough problems to deal with at the moment between the diamond killer and other shadows from Joe's checkered past coming to collect what the bastard had skimmed from them.

He hadn't had time yet to tell Claire about his findings or show her how to use the leather sap since he'd been shanghaied into working as soon as he'd walked through the door of The Shaft.

"What is it with your family and the hoosegow?" He asked both women as he handed Claire her drinks. "Is this some kind of twisted game of jailhouse musical chairs?"

"Maybe it is, smarty-pants," Natalie said.

"Unfortunately, Kate's in charge of stopping the music," Claire said and then left with her order.

"So, why exactly were you in jail?" he asked Natalie.

"That very question has been on my mind all day," Grady Harrison said, taking the vacant seat next to where Natalie waited for her order.

She grimaced at the sheriff. "It wasn't my fault, I swear."

The sheriff let out a low chuckle. "You've been taking lessons from your cousins."

The little bell in the order window dinged several times. When Mac looked over, Kate was giving Natalie the come-hither finger-wag.

"Be right back," Natalie told them and escaped through the swinging doors leading back to the kitchen, supply room, and Butch's office.

"You're playing bartender tonight, huh?" Grady asked while peering around The Shaft. He was dressed in his work clothes still, but his hat was missing along with his badge.

"Butch's usual guy called in sick." Mac grabbed the vodka for Natalie's cosmopolitans. "Ronnie's at table seven next to the jukebox."

"Where did you learn how to tend bar?" Grady asked, turning back to Mac.

"I did it here and there during college to help pay the bills. Turns out I have a good memory when it comes to mixing drinks."

"I heard you paid a visit to the library today."

"You must have talked to your aunt."

Grady's aunt Millie and her rough-and-tough gang of knitting grannies were hanging out near the library's bank of computers and microfiche reader when Mac had been researching Joe's house. She'd recognized him from the Thanksgiving dinner they'd shared here at this very bar, introducing him to her "compadres" when he'd asked if anyone was using the computer. After meeting Millie's "gang," he couldn't understand why Claire and Kate had issues with the old dames. They were very sweet, flirty even, and shared their butterscotch candies with him.

"She stopped by my office before I left. Were you looking into that mine you told me about last night?"

Yuccaville had the best mining library in the state due in part to the Copper Snake Mining Company, which owned some of the deepest open-pit copper mines west of the Rockies. The company headquarters was located at the north end of town amongst multiple huge open pits, bright green settling ponds, and giant trucks and bulldozers.

"That and Joe's old house. I was curious who owns it now."

"J.M. Kessinger, isn't it?"

Mac nodded. He wasn't surprised Grady knew that detail; he was the county sheriff, after all. "I expected it to be owned by the bank. Why would someone pay taxes on that property and yet let the house rot on its foundation?"

Grady shrugged. "Your guess is as good as mine. There are several properties like that around town, leftovers from when Copper Snake was booming and the town was raking in the money. The housing market was tight and people bought high, but then copper prices tanked and the mine started laying off folks. Many walked away from here bankrupt due to being upside down in their mortgages. Others moved on and yet kept their property here, letting buildings turn to dust under the desert sun."

"The mining industry is a fickle son of a bitch that way." Mac poured the cosmopolitans into long-stemmed glasses.

"Yep, same history, different town."

"I have to head back to Tucson tomorrow to deal with something that's come up at a jobsite." He grabbed the bottle of sarsaparilla from the fridge and set it on the tray next to the cosmopolitans. "What are the chances of you taking Claire and me inside that house in the morning?"

Grady rubbed his jaw. "Not good. I'm short two men tomorrow due to the holiday." He shook his head as Mac held up an empty glass next to the taps. "I'll just have an iced tea tonight."

He poured the tea, adding a squeeze of lemon. When he set it down on the bar, Grady added, "Unless you're willing to do the walk-through really early in the morning."

Mac would be working late tonight, which would make getting up early a pain, but he'd take what he could get. "Name the time. Claire and I will meet you there."

"How about six? That'd give me an hour until I have to be at the office."

"Deal."

Ronnie returned to the wait station. "Mac, I need another one of those fancy spritzer drinks you made for table seven. The biker babe loved it and wanted me to give you this as a thank-you for making her night." She handed him a ten-dollar bill. "She also wanted me to get your phone number so she can give you another sort of thank-you when you're off the clock."

Before Mac had a chance to blink, Claire snagged the ten-dollar bill from his fingers and shoved it back at Ronnie. "He's not on the market," she said. "What the hell, Ronnie? You're supposed to have my back."

Ronnie grabbed Mac's hand and put the bill in it again. "You earned that tip," she told him. To her sister, she said, "And I do have your back. I told her that if she was willing to wear a wedding band, she might have a chance with him."

"What?!" Claire's jaw fell open.

"I'm kidding." Ronnie winked at Mac—twice. Or maybe her eye was twitching like Kate's now, he wasn't sure. "I told her he's smitten with my burly sister, but the biker babe is drunk enough not to care."

"Silly drunken floozy." Claire scooped up the tray with Ronnie's earlier order of tequila and bourbon drinks. "I'll take care of these for you, slowpoke," she told her sister before glancing Grady's way. "Sheriff, I'd like you to arrest my sister for being a royal pain in the ass."

"Which sister?" Grady asked with a grin, dodging Ronnie's pinch.

"Both of them. It's Ronnie's turn to sit in jail for once." Claire looked at Mac. "And you stop getting the women all hot and bothered."

He spread his hands wide. "This is all for you, Slugger."

After Claire left, Ronnie turned to face Grady, making a show of batting her eyelashes at him. "How are you this evening, Sheriff Hardass?"

Mac stepped away to give them a moment alone, making Ronnie's clementine spritzer first and then refilling a couple of glasses of beer for some older guys in pocket-covered camouflage vests further up the bar.

He returned as Ronnie walked away with her spritzer order in hand. Grady watched her go. When he turned back, Mac grinned at him. "You're in over your head, Sheriff."

"Is it that obvious?"

"You're wearing the same expression I see in the mirror every morning." Mac took a moment to wash the cocktail shaker cups and set them on the drying rack. He strolled back over with a towel. "Any news on the killer?"

"Which one? Ronnie has them lining up thanks to her ex-husband."

"The one on the hunt for the mules' diamonds."

Grady shook his head, his lined face showing his feelings about the lack of news, too.

"To top it off, there's new trouble on the horizon."

Mac crossed his arms, bracing for another worry-filled tightening in his gut. "What do you mean?"

"Actually, she's old trouble. *My* trouble, but I'm afraid this is going to spread to Veronica's list of problems." He took a drink of tea and then scowled at Mac. "My ex-wife is in town."

Claire had told Mac the story of how Grady's ex had royally fucked him.

"How is that a problem for you?" Mac asked. Grady couldn't still have feelings for a bitch that cold-hearted, could he?

"She paid me a visit at work this afternoon. Brought me some lunch. One of my old favorites."

"Wasn't that sweet of her. Did it include a poisoned apple for dessert?"

The sheriff chuckled. "I didn't eat it. Gave it to my deputies after she left." He stirred his iced tea. "It's not the food that has me cringing, it's what she wrote in the card she included with it."

"A bunch of x's and o's?"

"Close. She wrote, 'Until death do us part.' And then she drew a heart with our names in it." Grady made a pained face. "Does that seem four cents short of a nickel to you, or is it just me?"

"That's the kind of love that makes you want to hop on a plane and flee to South America. Does Ronnie know about any of this?"

Grady shook his head. "I'd rather not tell her, either."

"Why not?"

"She doesn't need to worry about me and my damned ex on top of everything else."

He searched Grady's face. "Is there something still going on between you and your ex? A problem for Ronnie to worry about besides an obsessed old flame?"

One of the sheriff's eyebrows lifted. "Do I have 'sucker' written on my forehead?"

"Yeah, it matches the one on mine and Butch's."

Grady chuckled.

Mac waved at a trucker midway down the bar who was holding up his empty soda glass. "If this gets back to Ronnie and you don't tell her, she'll be pissed."

"Probably, but I can deal with that later. Right now, she needs to focus on keeping an eye out for real problems."

Mac walked over and took care of the trucker's soda. If he were in Grady's shoes, would he come clean with Claire? Maybe. But Ronnie and she both had a lot on their minds with this diamond killer business. He could understand not wanting to worry Ronnie about something as trivial as an ex-wife.

He glanced out over the bar floor, checking on Claire. She and Ronnie were up near the pool tables, talking to Mississippi. The three of them didn't look like they were swapping cookie recipes, not with the shared frowns and the worried glances Ronnie kept shooting in Grady's direction. Now what was wrong?

When he returned to the wait station area, Natalie was back, introducing a guy in a leather jacket who reminded Mac of Daniel Craig to the sheriff. "And this is Mac," she said. "He's trying to convince my cousin, Claire, to give up her wild ways and settle down."

"How's that working for you?" Natalie's friend asked.

"She's a tad skittish."

Natalie laughed. "Only a tad?" She straightened her shirt and combed back a loose strand of hair, shooting a sly glance at her friend before looking up to catch Mac watching her with a raised brow.

She wrinkled her nose at him, but her cheeks darkened.

Ah ha. Now he understood the makeup and fancy duds.

"According to the police report Claire filed," the stranger said, catching Mac's attention, "she's also prone to lead with a right hook."

What police report was he talking about? He looked at Grady. "Does he work for you?" Or was he one of the city of Yuccaville's boys in blue?

The stranger held out his hand. "Nice to meet you, Mac. I'm Detective Cooper of the Deadwood Police Department."

Deadwood? "Are you the guy I spoke to on the phone last Halloween?"

The detective nodded. "And you're the guy who offered to post bail for the two troublemakers."

"Yep. That would be me."

Detective Cooper grinned. "You have a nice bar here. Pretty busy, too. I've heard the food alone is worth the drive south."

It took a second for Mac to realize he meant The Shaft. The detective had him confused for Butch. "The Shaft isn't mine. Butch Carter deserves the compliment, but he's visiting family out of state. I'm just helping out."

"Butch lives with Natalie's cousin, Kate," Grady explained.

"You mean Kathryn Morgan, the five-foot-six blonde known to tackle bartenders and beat them with fake rubber hands?"

Mac grinned at the image the detective painted.

"Claire and Kate ended up in a bar fight up in Deadwood when they were there this last fall," Natalie explained to Grady. "They were dressed as Marcia and Cindy Brady of *The Brady Bunch* at the time."

"Of course they did and were." Grady looked at Detective Cooper. "Did you throw them in jail?"

He shook his head. "Charges were dropped. The bartender admitted he instigated the fight."

"Mac," Natalie said, "will you grab the spare bar stool back there and set Coop up with a drink while I take these over to Ronnie's FBI pal and the two drunk college girls trying to pick him up."

He nodded, handing the stool over the counter. Grady scooted closer to the wait station, making room for the detective.

Detective Cooper stared after Natalie as she walked away. "Did she say FBI?"

"She did," Grady answered. "Veronica is Claire's older sister. She's currently being monitored by the FBI due to her ex-husband's history. He laundered money for several big names in the drug and illegal guns market. After he was caught and sentenced, he started squealing on his old customers to lighten his prison sentence." Grady held up his empty glass to Mac, who nodded and grabbed the pitcher of tea for a refill.

"He sounds like a real winner," the detective said.

"Yeah, he does his damnedest to keep us on our toes down here."

"So, what's a Deadwood cop doing in Jackrabbit Junction, Arizona?" Mac asked, placing a napkin on the bar in front of him. "And what can I get you to drink, Detective Cooper?"

"You can call me 'Coop.' I'm off-duty this week. Enjoying my first real vacation in years." He looked at the shelves of liquor bottles on the wall behind the bar. "I'll just have a whiskey on the rocks, for starters. Maker's 46 will do."

While Mac poured the drink, Grady asked, "So, it's your first vacation in years and you came down to Jackrabbit Junction, huh?"

"Yep." Coop threw out a few bills when Mac set the glass in front of him.

Grady took a drink of tea. "What do you think, Mac?"

Mac shrugged. "You do know about Natalie's so-called sabbatical from men, right?" he said to the detective.

Coop nodded once and then sipped his whiskey.

Mac grinned at Grady. "Well, then I think he's up shit creek, paddling along beside you and me, Sheriff."

"That sounds about right," Grady said. "Tell me something, Coop. Does Natalie get in as much trouble up in Deadwood as she does down here in my county?"

Coop chuckled. "She's allergic to the law."

Grady let out a deep laugh and patted Coop on the shoulder. "I feel your pain, partner."

"What are you planning to do while you're down here on vacation?" Mac asked. "Besides change Natalie's mind."

"My uncle is here with me. He's sort of interested in seeing Cochise Stronghold and Fort Bowie. I was thinking we might take a trip down that way tomorrow."

Mac nodded. "You taking Natalie with you?"

"I'd like to, but she mentioned needing to work."

"I'll print you out a map from Butch's computer when I get a chance tonight," Mac said. "I've been to both of those sites multiple times and can show you some landmarks not listed on most maps."

"I'd appreciate it." Coop glanced toward where Natalie was taking an order at a table near the pool tables. "I'd also welcome any help you can offer with convincing Natalie to come with me."

Mac rubbed his jaw. "She's pretty hard-headed, but let me talk to Claire. She and Natalie are building my aunt's deck together. If anyone can sabotage Natalie's work plans, it's Claire."

Just then Claire returned to the bar with an empty drink tray, still wearing the frown she'd had by the pool tables. She handed Mac an order sheet. "Give that to the nutty broad in the kitchen, will you?"

When Mac returned from the kitchen window, Claire was eyeing the detective and the sheriff, who were talking shop. Her mouth was set in a thin line.

She turned to Mac. "Will you help me out in the supply room for a minute?"

He left Grady to watch the register, following Claire through the batwing doors. In the supply room, she closed the door behind him and leaned against it, her expression full of doom and gloom.

"We have a problem," she told him.

A harsh laugh escaped his throat. "Fuck. Now what?"

Chapter Nine

Sunday, December 30th

Mac woke Claire too freakin' early, damn it. She tried to bury her head under the covers and go back to sleep, but he pulled them down.

"Come on, Slugger." He kissed her forehead. "We have a spooky old house to check out."

Groaning, she sat up and watched him pull on his jeans. "You were amazing last night."

"I'm amazing every night, woman," he shot back, grinning. "Just ask that biker babe from table seven."

She threw a pillow at him. "I meant behind the bar, McStudly." He'd looked calm and at ease back there, even when they'd hit him with multiple orders at once.

He slid his arms into his green flannel shirt, the one that made his eyes look all dreamy. Or was it her eyes the shirt turned dreamy? Ugh. It was too early to form correct sentences. Thank the grammar gods that Kate wasn't here to pick apart her punctuation or Claire would have to stuff a pillow down her sister's throat.

"It wasn't my first time tending bar," he said, buttoning his shirt.

"Yeah, but you were a natural. I half-expected you to start juggling glasses like those fancy bartenders in Vegas."

"I'm full of hidden talents, baby," he said with a wink. "Like the one I showed you last night."

Her laugh sounded groggy. "Is that what you call that? A hidden talent? I thought it was an accident."

He gave her a mock glare. "Bite your tongue, wench, or I'll tie you up and raid your chastity tool belt again."

She went up on her knees, her wrists held out toward him. "Come and take me, my evil and dastardly black knight."

His gaze drifted south over her faded pink Daisy Duke T-shirt and underwear. He sucked air through his teeth. "Damn, Claire. I'm going to hit pause here, but we'll come back to play out this little fantasy another time." He bent down and grabbed her jeans from the floor. "Get dressed and meet me in the kitchen, temptress." He tossed her jeans on the bed at her knees and left the room.

Ten minutes and a tooth brushing later, she joined Mac in the kitchen. He handed her a travel mug full of coffee. "You want some toast?"

She shook her head. "Too early." The coffee was milky and sweet, the way she liked it. She moved in closer and kissed his bristly jaw. "You sure you don't want to go back to bed?"

"No, but I'm sure I'm going to think about you in that see-through T-shirt all day." He finished his coffee and kissed her on the forehead. "Let's go."

Claire yawned in the dark pickup cab almost every other mile on the way to Yuccaville. She rested her temple against the cool window as the tires played a rhythm on the tar-crossed highway. She and Mac had made it home and to bed around two a.m., leaving Natalie and Kate to finish up the last of the mopping since neither of them had to be up at the ass-crack of dawn this morning.

"Your sister needs to tell Grady about this new bullshit move by the FBI," Mac said as they hit Yuccaville's city limits.

Claire leaned forward and turned down Foghat's "Slow Ride" on the radio. She'd like to "take it easy" along with them, but the FBI had managed to crank up her stress level another notch. Being a good girlfriend last night, she'd shared the bad news with Mac in the supply room that Mississippi had given to Ronnie and her, and then buried her nose in his chest until she'd stopped quivering with rage and could return to serving drinks with a smile.

"I told Ronnie that very thing, but she dug in her heels."

"Damn it." He took her hand and squeezed it. "Doesn't she understand that this is not the time to be withholding key information from Grady?"

"She doesn't feel like it changes the overall game much."

"What the hell is wrong with her? How is the FBI trying to tie her ex-husband's suspiciously missing diamond cache to the box of hidden diamonds you two found under that RV not a major fucking change?"

Claire shifted, facing him. "Trust me, Mac. I said the same thing to her last night, only with more cuss words and a couple of snarls thrown in for emphasis. But she made Mississippi and me pinkie-swear we wouldn't say a word to Grady about this latest news."

"She didn't make me swear to silence," he said.

"No, but I did."

He glanced her way twice before sighing and shaking his head. "Yeah, but you cheated on that front, forcing a vow of silence out of me before you'd spill."

"I had to." She lifted his knuckles to her lips. "The posse's rules clearly state that we keep each other's secrets." But Ronnie hadn't said Claire couldn't tell Mac, only Grady. "Besides, as far as I'm concerned, you're in a need-to-know position, especially when it comes to Mississippi's advice about shooting to maim, not kill, if given the opportunity."

Mac cursed under his breath, same as he had when she told him about needing the diamond killer alive to clear Ronnie of any ties to Lyle's missing diamonds mess.

"Those bastards at the Bureau are itching to pin something on Ronnie, damn it." Claire ground her teeth at the panic that she'd seen in her sister's wide eyes when Mississippi had delivered his bomb and blown Ronnie's thin level of calm to smithereens last night. "According to Mississippi, if they can put her in prison along with her ex, they can close this particular case and wrap it in a pretty bow."

"What's his angle on this? Why is he giving you and your sister inside information? Couldn't that get him fired?"

"Maybe, but he likes Ronnie."

"Really?" He frowned at her. "Does Grady know that?"

"Not like-like. He just likes her in general and thinks she's getting screwed on this deal."

"Glad to hear it. And he's right." Mac slowed, keeping the pickup under the speed limit. "But if Grady gets the opportunity to take out the killer, he might." He shot her a hard look. "Hell, I would in a heartbeat if it meant keeping you breathing."

"Which is why I told you about this mess."

Yuccaville's streets were empty besides stray tumbleweeds here and there. They rolled along in silence for a few beats.

"Someone should tell him Ronnie needs this bastard alive to clear her name, Claire." The shadows deepened the scowl lines on his face.

Mac wasn't letting go of this. She didn't blame him, because it made no sense. "Ronnie is mortified at the idea of Grady finding out about this, especially with him coming up on an election year. She wants to keep this all hush-hush as long as possible."

"I don't like it. I don't give a flying fuck about Grady being elected again, and I bet if she'd ask him he doesn't either. What good will it be for him to serve another four years as the county sheriff if she's dead?" His grip tightened on her hand. "Or both of you are?"

She nodded. He'd said pretty much the same thing last night in the supply room after she'd told him about the catch-22 situation, and then he'd whispered it one last time when he pulled her close before they fell asleep.

"Come with me to Tucson today, Slugger. Let me keep you tucked away safe from this shit storm for a night." He circled his thumb on her palm. "I promise to make it worth your while."

"Will you take me with you to the jobsite?"

Both eyebrows were raised when he looked her way. "You want to hang out with me *there*? It could be a few hours while I assess the situation."

"I don't want to sit alone at the house." It would give her too much time to think up new worries.

"Yeah, sure. I'd enjoy your company. I always do."

"Okay, let me think about the ramifications of leaving for a night." She stared out her side window. "It would just be one night, right? I mean, you guys aren't going to work on New Year's, are you?"

He hesitated, but then shook his head. "If you come with me, I'll make sure we don't, whatever it takes."

"Because I'll need to be back tomorrow night to help Kate at The Shaft. New Year's Eve is sure to be a big party there."

"I'll have you back here in time to help with the happy hour rush."

Claire leaned back against the headrest. "If I go to Tucson with you, then I could convince Natalie to take a break from building the porch and go on that trip with Coop to Fort Bowie."

Mac had told her about the detective's request for their help in convincing Natalie to spend time with him. While Claire wasn't thrilled at the idea of her cousin hooking up with a cop, she agreed with Mac that the guy deserved some of Natalie's time after following her clear to this dusty corner of Arizona.

The only snag in heading to Tucson for the night was Kate. Aside from being temporarily insane, could she afford to lose Claire's help at The Shaft? Sundays were the slow nights lately, and Kate had talked about closing early, so maybe Claire wouldn't be missed.

But what about Ronnie and the crap raining down on her? Then again, she did have an FBI agent babysitting her and the sheriff of the whole damned county sleeping next to her.

"Whose idea was it to form this 'Prickly Posse,' anyway?" Mac asked as he parked in front of Joe's boarded-up childhood home. Locked away behind a six-foot-high chain-link fence, the old A-frame, two-story house had seen better days too long ago to remember, judging from the rotting clapboard siding and "Property Condemned" sign on the porch railing.

"It's the 'Prickly Pear Posse,' " she corrected, turning back to him. "Natalie and I came up with it Friday night while you were helping Kate clean the kitchen."

"Weren't you two having a drinking contest that night?"

"Why does everybody think there was alcohol involved with our grand idea?"

He raised one eyebrow. "Who won the contest?"

"She did, but it was still a good idea come morning, so we're sticking to it."

He killed the engine. "What exactly does being in this posse entail besides keeping secrets?"

"Watching each other's backs and going to battle when the situation calls for it."

He crossed his arms. "What else?"

"Helping out when a member is in need, whether you agree or not, and taking turns bailing each other out of jail with no questions asked." Although, given Kate's current mental state, Claire would like to change this rule to allow several questions before rushing to bail her out.

"How come you didn't ask me to be in it?"

"Boys aren't allowed."

"Does that mean I don't have to bail you out of jail next time?"

She sputtered. "I … well … no, you still might have to help me depending on the bail amount."

He grinned. "Do you have matching jackets?"

"Maybe we do, smartass."

"So, if I help you and Ronnie deal with this new FBI bullshit, could I be arrested for being in cahoots with the Prickly Pear Posse?"

"With Kate in the picture, serving time behind bars is always a possibility."

He snorted. "Whose bright idea was it to let Crazy Kate into your club?"

"It's not a club. This is a badass posse."

"It might end up more of a bad-idea posse before this is all over and done."

"For the record, I voted against Kate being included due to her temporary insanity, but Ronnie let her in the door anyway."

Damn Ronnie's weakness when it came to Kate.

"Do Grady and Butch know about this posse, or is this another secret that I have to keep due to my association with a founding member of the posse?"

"You are the only one in the know at this time and it needs to stay that way." She held out her pinkie toward him.

Mac shook his head at her pinkie. "I think you're all suffering from stress-induced temporary insanity, but I'm weak around crazy dames, so I'll keep my mouth shut for now."

She lowered her finger at the sight of the sheriff's pickup pulling up along the opposite side of the street. "Grady's here. I hope he didn't bring Ronnie along."

"Why?"

"For one thing, she's extra bossy when she's low on sleep. For another, she's acting weirder and weirder under the weight of her ex's crap."

"Is that why she was twitching last night?"

"You saw that, too?"

He nodded. "She and Kate are starting to look like they have fleas."

She watched Grady open the door. The dome light shone inside the cab, illuminating his passenger.

"You're out of luck, Slugger."

"Dang it. Remember, Mac, not a word to Grady about Mississippi's news."

"My lips are unhappily sealed."

Ronnie was shivering in the cold desert darkness when Claire joined her on the cracked sidewalk in front of the old house. She'd exchanged her Johnny Cash outfit from last night for a pair of yoga pants and one of Grady's long, thick, flannel jackets. Her hair was bed-tousled, her eyes puffy from sleep—or a lack of it, considering Grady and she had left only an hour before Claire and Mac.

"You should have stayed in his warm bed," Claire whispered as the sheriff pulled out a pair of keys and unlocked the padlock securing the chain-link fence.

"Grady has to go to work and I need a ride back to Jackrabbit Junction."

"Do you want to wait for us in Mac's truck? He can give you the keys so you can run the heater."

"No way. I'd rather be inside with you guys." She leaned closer and lowered her voice. "I can't stop thinking about how they found those night watchmen in the trunk. That story is grade-A nightmare fodder."

Ronnie's fear was understandable. Her enemies seemed to be

growing faster than the cane toad population in Australia.

"You guys ready?" Grady asked, holding open the gate.

Mac led the way through the dead weeds that had taken over what had been a gravel path at one time. Claire and Ronnie followed. Grady closed the gate behind them, joining them on the rickety porch. He stepped carefully around the splintered floorboards, his boots crunching on broken glass. Ronnie frowned at the NO TRESPASSING that had been scrawled onto the siding in big red dripping letters, reaching out to touch the long-dried paint.

The screen door screeched when Grady swung it open.

"How'd you get the house keys?" Claire asked him as he unlocked the padlock securing the sun-faded front door.

"The place has been condemned by the county," he explained. "The sheriff's office is in charge of keeping places like this secured." He popped the padlock and pushed open the door. "Wait here while Mac and I do a cursory inspection to check to see if there are any problems waiting for us inside."

After the guys had disappeared inside Claire stepped closer to Ronnie, bumping shoulders with her. "Did you tell him about what Mississippi told us?"

"No," Ronnie snapped. "Like I said last night, I don't want him to know about that right now."

"But he's the sheriff," Claire whispered, returning to the same argument she'd tried on her sister last night. "It's his county. Sleepover buddy or not, don't you think the man in charge of keeping the county crime-free needs to know that if he shoots to kill in this case, his girlfriend might go to prison?"

"No, I do not, and you pinkie-promised not to tell him either, so keep your big mouth shut or I'll … I'll cut off your pinkie and carry it as a good luck charm."

Claire leaned back, grimacing at her sister. "That's morbid. What's wrong with you? Are you dancing the mad-monkey tango along with Kate?"

"Nothing is wrong with me." Ronnie's right shoulder twitched. "I just need you to go along with me on this, damn it. Posse rules, remember?"

"But what if our silence winds up sending you to prison?"

"I'm not going to prison. The FBI is leaning on me, hoping this will make me squawk about more of Lyle's dirty dealings. They tried it before, using those stupid videotapes of me getting off in the shower and in my bedroom, trying to humiliate me into coughing up answers I don't have. That didn't work for them then, and threatening me with prison now isn't going to work either. Fuck those bullies in their cliché black suits with their files full of lies. And fuck Lyle, too."

Whew! Claire's ears burned from the steam venting out of her sister. "Boy, you're really letting your love fly this morning."

Ronnie glanced at her. "I'm tired of being a victim."

Claire nodded, staring out at the dark street. "Maybe Grady's law dog status will allow him special conjugal privileges when you're behind bars."

"Just do as you promised," Ronnie said with a growl.

"I told Mac you'd be extra bossy," Claire muttered.

Mac joined them on the porch, looking back and forth between them with a narrowed gaze. "Grady says it's all clear."

Claire didn't wait for Ronnie, heading inside first. The sight of a big, metal, space age–looking tube sitting on a stand in the center of the living room made her screech to a stop. Grady was bending down to check out the contraption, shining his flashlight inside the round hole on the end. When he stood up, he snagged his jacket sleeve on the mirror positioned above the hole.

"Holy shit," she whispered, joining him next to the coffin-sized cylinder. She peered inside one of the windows located near the top, but the interior was too dark to see anything. "Is this one of those iron lungs they used for people with polio?"

"I believe so." Grady moved to the opposite side.

"Light up the inside, will you?"

He did as asked. "Do you see something?"

"No, just stained and dusty padding."

"This house reeks of urine," Ronnie said, sidling up next to Grady on the other side of the tube with his flannel coat pulled up over her nose. "Did you know this thing was in here, Grady?"

He shook his head. "I haven't been inside of this place before today."

"There's another iron lung in here," Mac said, standing under an archway leading to the next room. "But it looks like parts are missing from it."

Claire joined him in what appeared to be a dining room. The wallpaper was peeling in large strips, and the overhead chandelier had cobwebs draping so low they touched the top of the partially disassembled iron lung.

This machine had the side panels off with wires sticking out every which way. The top was torn off, too, and leaned against the wall. The padding on the inside was torn, chewed on, and stained with yellow spots—undoubtedly courtesy of the house's rodent population.

Mac directed his flashlight around the room, spotlighting a couple of dust-covered wheelchairs. In the corner was an open cupboard with cardboard boxes half spilling out. Claire borrowed Mac's light and stepped over to the cupboard. Careful not to touch where the rodents had chewed, she tugged the boxes out enough to peer into the open tops. One contained various bandages; another had syringes and empty plastic bottles. A third was half-filled with a mishmash of medical supplies.

She returned to Mac's side. "Why two iron lungs?"

He pointed at what looked like some sort of old-fashioned vacuum attached to a metal suitcase sitting in another corner. "I think that's a portable ventilator from the mid-1900s."

"It's like some sort of creepy medical museum."

"Claire, come check this out," Ronnie said from another archway.

She followed Ronnie into what had been the kitchen at one time. Next to an old standalone porcelain farm-style sink stood a metal hoist with a large canvas sling hanging from cables and pulleys. Several layers of dust coated the whole shindig, but it didn't look as archaic as the iron lungs.

Another wheelchair had been parked facing the wall in the spot where a refrigerator would normally sit. Ronnie started opening a cupboard door.

"I wouldn't do that," Claire said. "Unless you want to chance being infected with the hantavirus."

Ronnie winced and closed the door.

"Grady," Claire called.

The sheriff's shoulders filled the arched entryway. He eyed the hoist. "What?"

"When did Joe's mom die?"

"I don't know. I'd have to look that up. Why?"

"I just wondered if maybe she was handicapped and this was left over from her final days."

"The house is currently owned by a J.W. Kessinger," Mac called from the dining room. "There was no Martino on record for it, although Kessinger could have been her maiden name, I guess."

"Or Joe's family rented it from this Kessinger or someone in his family."

"Or J.W. had some medical issues or a job in the medical industry and stored equipment here," Ronnie said.

"Can we go upstairs or is it too dangerous?" Claire asked Grady.

"We can try. The place was condemned due to foundation failures according to the county records, but the roof looks shot, too. Water damage may have made its way south and rotted the wood flooring upstairs."

"I'll go up and check it out if you'd rather not," Claire volunteered.

"Of course you will," Mac said from behind Grady. He caught up with her at the stairwell. "But you'll follow me up there, Slugger."

"Wait!" Grady called, stopping Mac at the base of the stairwell that was missing the majority of its rail posts. "I should go first. I'm responsible for you being here. Wait until I make it to the top before following me."

He edged past them and started up the stairs. The steps creaked and groaned but held his weight.

When he reached the top Mac started up. Claire followed after he cleared the top step.

"Take it slow, Claire," Grady advised.

"Who was the huge guy wearing the coveralls last night? The guy who joined you at the bar," Mac asked Grady as she climbed.

"That's Tank. He owns Hummingbird Towing."

"Kate had me serve him food and a drink for free."

"I mentioned that I wasn't used to seeing him at The Shaft," Grady said. "He told me Kate had made a deal with him—a few meals in exchange for freeing her car from impound at the cost of the gas it took to tow it to his place."

Claire smirked as she made it to the top. "That sounds like something Kate the wheeler-dealer would do."

"Katie and Tank hit it off when we were at his towing place," Ronnie said from the base of the steps.

"Kate can be quite charming when she's trying to get her way," Claire told them. "Are you coming up, Ronnie?"

"No, I'll wait down here in case you guys fall through the ceiling and need me to call for help."

"That's a comforting thought," Grady said and led them down a narrow hallway. Two doorways opened up off to the left, one to the right; all three were bedrooms. At the end of the hallway Claire could see part of a claw-foot bathtub through an open door.

The bedrooms were empty except for dust bunnies that were aspiring to be tumbleweeds. Pieces of ceiling were falling down in two of the rooms due to the roof leaks Grady had suspected. The floor in the second bedroom creaked something fierce when Grady stepped onto it, making a loud cracking sound that had him backing up lickety-split.

The bathroom was pea green with rusted fixtures and a broken toilet. It reeked of urine more than the rest of the house. Claire heard a thumping sound coming from the packrat debris mound between the tub and toilet. She shined a light on the midden, making out pieces of attic insulation, cardboard riff-raff, and another box of bandages in the pile. The mound shifted as the thumping continued, louder this time.

Back in the hallway, Grady directed his light up at a square panel in the ceiling. "Are you two interested in taking things to the next level?" he asked.

"No," Mac said, shooting a warning look at Claire when he said it. "We've seen enough."

Claire frowned at the square panel, trying to picture what might be up there. She remembered the broken attic window she'd noticed on a prior visit. There were probably lots of pack rats and mice up there along with even more urine and feces. Maybe bats, too. A potential rabies case, for sure.

"Let's go back downstairs," she said, leading the way.

The sheriff brought up the rear, easing down the steps to join them. "Where's Veronica?"

"I think I found something," Ronnie called from a dark open doorway on the other side of the iron lung machine. "Grady, bring your flashlight over here, please."

"What is it?" he asked when he reached her.

Claire was on his heels. She squeezed by his wide shoulders and joined Ronnie as her sister aimed the light toward the back of the small square room.

"What the fuck is that?" Claire whispered.

Chapter Ten

Five hours and one hundred miles later …

A ccording to Claire, Ronnie found an antique electric chair at Joe's old house," Natalie told Coop and his uncle, Harvey, as they bounced along Apache Pass Road on the way to Fort Bowie National Historic Site.

"An electric chair?" Coop glanced at her in the pickup's rearview mirror.

She nodded. "Complete with leather tie-down straps and wires poking out of it."

"Boy howdy," Harvey said from the front passenger seat. "Ya come across that sight on a dark and stormy night and it'd turn yer knees to puddin'."

Natalie smirked. That was sort of the same reaction she'd experienced upon seeing Coop when he showed up to spring her from jail.

She looked out the side window at the passing scrub brush and yucca dotting the Sonoran Desert. The Chiricahua Mountains ran along the horizon to the southeast, adding a blue-brown backdrop to the desert panorama.

What in the hell was she doing here with Coop after what happened last time? He'd rejected her, plain and simple. *I don't date local girls,* he'd told her without even a hint of remorse about leaving her hot and bothered in that alley. If that hadn't been humiliating enough, when she ran into him weeks later at a bar down in Rapid City, he had a blond babe on his arm whose tongue kept trying to take up permanent residence in his mouth.

Coming on this trip with him today was a huge mistake. Thankfully Ol' Man Harvey was playing third wheel, helping to keep the tension between her and Coop at a low simmer. Natalie had called dibs on the backseat at the get-go, claiming she wanted to spread out and be more comfortable. No sooner than the words were out of her mouth she'd regretted how lame they sounded. Who was she trying to fool? The narrow-eyed glance Coop had given her when she'd slid into the backseat made it clear he could see through her smokescreen.

Damn those detective eyes of his.

The journey south from Jackrabbit Junction had included a side trip on a dirt road up to Cochise Stronghold in the Dragoon Mountains. Harvey's four-wheel-drive pickup had easily navigated the winding, rough Forest Service road that wove along granite domes and heart-palpitating cliffs, giving the three of them an idea of the area where the great Apache chief and his people had taken refuge.

Next up was Fort Bowie, the setting for a quarter century of conflict between the Chiricahua Apaches and the US Army. According to Harvey, the fort also sat near the old Butterfield Stage Line and included a cemetery as part of the "viewing attractions."

"Ya think that sparky chair yer cousin found was actually used?" Harvey asked.

"Well," Natalie said, trying to focus on what Claire had said about that chair and not the dust devil of confusion stirred up by the guy sitting behind the steering wheel. "Joe did have a history that could make a working electric chair logical."

She hesitated on explaining further. Claire would already be giving her the zip-it motions if she were there with her. Her cousin's parting words before heading to Tucson with Mac this morning had been to remember that Coop was an officer of the law, first and foremost. There were secrets tucked away at the Dancing Winnebago RV Park that Claire didn't want the law to know to protect both Ruby and the RV park from being dragged through the muck. Joe's criminal past could shut down business for a long time, if not for good.

"What sort of history?" Coop asked, watching her in the rearview mirror.

She held his stare for a moment before returning to her window view. She could always count on Coop the cop to latch onto anything criminally related. "A checkered one."

"Hmmm," he said, but didn't press her for more.

They rolled along in silence for a mile or two. From the stereo, Dwight Yoakam crooned out his hit "A Long Way Home," warning her about the hazards of dragging her heart over rocks for years and years. *Too little, too late, Dwight.* She sang along with him under her breath anyway, trying to focus on letting go of the past and enjoying a day of sightseeing.

Truth be told, she was eager to take a break from Jackrabbit Junction and see more of Arizona. With the sun high in the clear blue sky and the air cool enough for her to need a sweat jacket, it was a perfect day to ramble about at an old fort. Open countryside and glimpses into the past would make for a soothing change from the three stooges critiquing her handiwork … if it weren't for Coop.

"Ya know, I could use more checkers in my past," Harvey said, breaking the silence.

"Your past is checkered enough, Uncle Willis," Coop said.

"Don't go hunting for trouble while we're on vacation."

"Vacation ain't any fun without a li'l side action."

"We're supposed to be relaxing down here, remember?" Coop skirted a patch of washboard in the dirt road. "I've had enough action over the last six months to last me a few years." He aimed a pinched brow at Natalie. "And I'm not talking about women, either."

Natalie lowered her gaze. His business with females was his own. She'd learned her lesson the last time she'd brushed too close to him and ended up with a singed heart.

"I can think of one woman who's given you plenty of action," Natalie said, wondering what sort of trouble her best friend was getting into back in Deadwood while Coop, Harvey, and she were down in the desert.

"Don't remind me of Parker," he said, his voice borderline growly. "She's part of the reason I needed a vacation."

Deadwood had certainly been hopping since Violet moved to town and upset Coop's applecart. Those two usually rammed their horns whenever they shared breathing space, which was another reason for Natalie to keep her distance from Coop. If she were to let herself fall head-over-heels for the boneheaded detective, she'd be stuck in the middle of their arguments.

"I am relaxin' down here," Harvey said. "Besides, I can *relax* horizontally same as I can vertically, if you get my meanin', boy." Harvey slapped Coop's shoulder, wheezing out a chuckle. "Take that hot little dove who strutted in front of our rig this mornin' wearing nothin' but a robe and cowboy boots. My tail feathers are still ruffled about all of that smooth skin."

"I told you, she was wearing peach-colored tights," Coop said.

"We don't know that fer sure."

"You don't, but I do." Coop sent a grin his uncle's way. "Your tail feathers get ruffled at the sight of any woman's legs these days, especially if they're bare."

"That's not true. Yer Aunt Gertrude's legs make me tuck tail and run."

Natalie stared at Coop's profile as he laughed at his uncle's exaggerated display of shuddering and cringing. Who was this guy with the easy chuckle and smiling eyes? She had only seen a glimpse of him once before—the night she'd joined him in the alley behind the bar and let him explore her bare skin both north and south of the border.

Her fingers itched to reach out and explore his skin.

She clenched her fist. Damn Coop for driving clear to Arizona for his so-called vacation. And double damn him for acting like they were just old pals. Not once last night at The Shaft had he tried to touch her, not even when he'd corralled her in the narrow hallway leading to the bathrooms to tell her he was heading back to the RV park to catch some shut-eye.

And that was a good thing, she reminded herself, because she was still taking a break from relationships with the opposite sex.

Right. Taking a break.

She plucked at a loose string in the seam of her jeans. But was having sex once with someone technically called a "relationship"? People had one-night stands all of the time and managed to …

Stop it!

She blew out a breath and leaned her head back against the seat, closing her eyes. It would help her willpower a lot more if she couldn't smell the heady scent of his spicy cologne in the cab. Just breathing brought back flashes of that one freaking night.

Who was she kidding? Hell, she was halfway in a relationship with him already in her heart and there wasn't even any sex in the picture yet.

That was all the more reason not to let it progress any further physically.

Criminy. This week was going to be one long game of tug-of-war between her head and her heart.

A few minutes later, the pickup slowed.

"Accordin' to the map, this is the parkin' lot," Harvey said, paper rustling.

Natalie opened her eyes. There were two other vehicles in the gravel lot parked next to a small restroom—another pickup and an SUV. She looked around at the hillsides. "Where is the fort?"

"Ya gotta hike to it." Harvey held up the map.

"How far?" Coop asked, shutting off the engine.

"A mile and a half each way." He pointed out the window at a large, square signboard with a shingle-roof covering it. "Looks like the trail starts there."

"Let's go check it out," Natalie said, eager to be outside of the cab for a while. She shut her door behind her.

Coop joined her in front of the pickup a moment later, but without Harvey.

"What's he waiting for?" she asked.

"He's not coming."

"What? Why not?"

Coop shrugged. "He said he doesn't feel like hiking."

She stalked over to the half-open passenger side window. "Come on, Harvey. If you can spend the night dancing with all of the dames at the senior center up in Deadwood, you can hike to the fort ruins and back."

He held up a book with a half-naked entwined couple on the cover for her to see. "I'm going to relax like Coop said and read this here informative book I found in the library at the General Store. Maybe I'll take a siesta in between the sex scenes."

Natalie crossed her arms. "You're going to read a romance novel instead of coming to see Fort Bowie with us?"

"I should smile," he shot back.

She turned to Coop. "What's that supposed to mean?"

"It's his new way of saying *yes*," he said with a smirk. "He read that phrase in a Zane Grey book on the trip down and has been driving me nuts with it ever since."

"You two whippersnappers run along and take some pictures for me." Harvey yawned extra big.

Natalie wasn't buying his sleepy act. The old buzzard was playing cupid and she wasn't keen on being hit by any love arrows. "Harvey," she growled.

"Be sure to drag anchor plenty along the way. I have lots of hot sex to keep me busy."

Natalie turned to Coop. "We drove all of the way down here to see the fort and you're going to let him blow it off?"

Coop shrugged. "I can't force him." He started toward the trail, walking backward. "You coming or not?"

After one last scowl at Harvey, who gave her a wink in return, she joined Coop at the trailhead. "Lead the way."

He did, traversing the sandy path at an easy pace, slowing to check out the first set of ruins to their right before moving along. Natalie did her best not to ogle his long legs and narrow hips in his faded jeans as they trekked along. Or his broad shoulders in the dark blue thermal Henley. Or his …

She cursed under her breath and focused on the dried grass, yucca, and scrub brushes fanning out from the trail. The birds in the small trees and bushes lining the dry wash to their left sang along to the beat of their footfalls, throwing in cheerful trills and whistles to punctuate the chorus. The sun warmed her shoulders through her sweat jacket. This place must be an oven come summertime. How did the soldiers stand it way back when, especially if they were wearing wool uniforms with collars and cuffs?

"It smells good out here," Coop said after they'd hiked along for a bit and the trail widened. "Clean and sundried."

She guffawed at his attempt at inane conversation. Coop was never one to stand around and smell the roses back home. His nose was constantly sniffing out crime, his focus on the job 24/7 … even when on the verge of getting it on in a back alley.

He slowed so they were walking side-by-side on the trail. "You don't like the smells of the desert?"

"I think you're playing games today."

"What sort of games?"

She didn't answer for several steps, debating on if she really wanted to keep traveling down this path—the bare-her-soul one, not the trail to Fort Bowie.

After weighing the pros and cons, she continued on course. If Coop had driven all of the way down to Arizona because he thought she'd change her mind about taking their so-called friendship to the next level, she needed to set him straight. Or at least voice her feelings about the matter.

She'd had enough of this flirty game of his that left her breathless and yet pissed at the same time.

"Coop, what are you doing here?" she asked, keeping her focus on the trail in front of them.

"Taking a vacation," he said after a pause.

Bull hockey! "You could have gone anywhere in the world on vacation and yet you came to southeastern Arizona."

"Yep."

She shot him a quick frown. "So you coming down here had nothing to do with me?"

The gravel crunched under their hiking boots for a few beats.

"I didn't say that."

She waited for further explanation, but he didn't offer any, damn it.

They hiked along in silence, tension tightening her chest with every step forward.

"Okay," she said, taking a calming breath before plowing deeper into truth. "What are we doing here?"

"Going to see an old fort."

She scowled at him. "Quit fucking with me, Coop. You didn't drive all the way to Arizona to ask me to come hiking. I want an honest answer from you."

He looked off toward the west, his forehead drawn.

Nothing.

She bared her teeth at him and strode off at a faster pace, needing distance from the maddening man since the thousand-plus miles that she'd already traveled clearly hadn't been enough.

"Natalie, wait," he said minutes later, catching up.

"For what? For you to decide I'm not the flavor of the month again?" She jammed her hands in the pockets of her jacket so that she didn't give in to the urge to pummel him until he told her what she wanted to hear.

What *did* she want to hear?

That was a good question. An actual answer from the non-detective version of Coop would be a good start.

"I'm sorry for what happened before," he said, keeping her pace. "I was an asshole."

Yes, he was. "Sorry for which part?" she pressed. "For kicking me to the curb as soon as duty called and leaving me half-undressed in a back alley like some two-bit floozy, or for shoving that damned bleached-blond bimbo in my face at the bar in Rapid?"

His face lined. "Nothing happened that night with her."

Natalie scoffed. "I wasn't blind. I saw her repeated attempts to lick the back of your throat."

"I know."

"And you let her run those scarlet nails all over you while I watched."

"I did."

She stopped, her face hot, her throat clogged with the same jealous rage that had choked her up that night at the bar. "You no-good son of a bitch."

Dear Lord, it was a relief to quit hiding behind a polite smile and finally say that to his face.

He held up his hands. "Let me explain."

"What's to explain? You're just like all of the other bastards who have fucked me over one way or another—the reason I've sworn off men for now."

He flinched. "Listen, as soon as you left the bar that night in Rapid, I left, too. Alone. The other woman was a tool to keep you away."

"Well, congratulations! It worked like a dream." She started along the trail again, cursing him and all other penis-equipped members of the human race. "And you're a tool for using that girl!" she shouted over her shoulder.

His footfalls on the gravel came closer. "I came to Arizona because I heard you left Deadwood to get away from me."

He'd heard right. Who'd told him that? Violet? Harvey? It didn't matter. "You shouldn't have come here, Coop. I don't know what you hoped to accomplish, but as far as I'm concerned any flames we had burning before are long doused."

"No, they're not." He caught her wrist and tugged her to a stop, forcing her to look up at him. "Your lips say one thing, but your eyes don't lie."

Yeah, well her eyes were traitors. "What in the hell do you hope to accomplish here, Coop? And if your reply includes the word 'vacation' again, I'm going to punch you in the nose."

He held her glare. "I want you, Natalie."

Oh, that was hilarious. He could have had her hook, line, and sinker years ago. Now? He'd have better luck eating pudding with a pitchfork.

She snorted. "I know your type. You only want what you can't have."

He shook his head. "Listen, I fucked up monumentally before. I know that. I also realize that the chance of you giving me another opportunity is slim, but I had to come down here and try."

She searched his eyes while weighing his words. "Why?"

"Why what?"

"Why now? Years later. What's changed?"

"Me." His brow wrinkled. "And you."

"I haven't changed."

"Yes, you have. You know who you are and what you want now."

Maybe he was right on that front. Her sabbatical had cleared her head. Because of that clarity, she'd felt happier and more secure in who she was and the direction she wanted to go. Until now. Once he'd wormed back into the picture as a possible future entanglement, she'd started to flounder.

But enough about her … She crossed her arms. "And how have you changed?"

"I'm not running away from you anymore."

Her laughter rang out in the still air. "You're so full of shit, Coop. Did you read that in some men's magazine article about things to say to pick up women?"

She didn't give him a chance to answer, starting off down the trail again.

"I'm trying to be honest with you," he said from right behind her.

"Okay, then tell me *honestly* what I did to make you want to run away the first time around. Was I too clingy that night at the Purple Door? Because I tried to play it cool so you wouldn't think I was an easy lay." She took a breath and continued before he could respond. "I know it can't have been that phone call later when you told me you don't date local girls, because I didn't whine, beg, or cry when you shut me down without further explanation."

She'd waited until she'd hung up to let the tears of

humiliation and river of swear words flow.

"You scared me," he said.

She'd scared a longtime cop who chased bad guys without hesitating?

"That doesn't make any sense." Up ahead, she saw the stone foundation of what appeared to be the ruins of an old building. "You know what, Coop, let's just drop this subject. I'm sorry I even brought it up."

She jogged ahead, needing to burn through the frustration firing through her veins.

The stone foundation turned out to be what remained of the old Butterfield stage station from the late 1850s, according to the sign. Coop poked around what was left of the walls while she read about the history aloud, trying to pretend their little talk hadn't opened up old wounds and left her raw and bleeding.

When they were on their way again, side by side on the wide trail, Natalie glanced at him under her lashes. His jaw looked taut, his forehead drawn.

Damn. She should have kept her big mouth shut and let things keep rolling along as they'd been. Now there was an awkward tension between them that added dark clouds to what could have been a fun, sunny day.

Up ahead was an old cemetery. Inside the wooden fence were white, round-topped headstones that listed the names of soldiers and their family members, along with Geronimo's two-year-old son, Little Robe, who had died at Fort Bowie.

"See any ghosts?" she asked him when they skirted a prickly pear cactus and paused next to the headstone of one of the soldiers.

Coop had the unusual ability to see wispy folks, something that tended to haunt him up in Deadwood where the dead liked to congregate and stir up trouble.

"Not here," he said, turning back to the trail. "But there was one back along the road into the park where the wagon train massacre happened."

"You sure it wasn't a hiker?"

"He was holding a double-barrel shotgun and wearing nineteenth-century clothes with an arrow sticking out of his chest."

Grimacing, she followed him back to the trail.

They passed more ruins on the left, pausing further along to stare up the hillside at what was left of the first version of the old fort.

"Do you want to hike up there?" she asked.

He glanced at the sky before answering. "I'm not sure we have the time this trip."

This trip? Was he planning on coming back down to Arizona again?

Coop moved along, pausing when they reached Apache Spring to check out the watering hole that had been the setting of many confrontations between the Apache, soldiers, stage riders, and others over the centuries.

They stood in the shade of the gnarled oak trees, listening to several birds in the overhead branches. Claire would be able to tell her the species of the birds after all of her college classes, along with the names of the surrounding plants and their purposes, probably. The water gurgled in the spring, sparkling like diamonds in the shafts of sunlight, making Natalie reach for her water bottle.

"Cochise drank here," she said, and swallowed some warm water.

"So did Geronimo and Bascom and hundreds of other soldiers in charge of patrolling this section of the West."

"It's hard to believe so much fighting happened in such a peaceful place." She offered Coop a drink from her bottle.

He took a swallow and handed it back. "Water was more precious than gold down here."

"Still is." She frowned at him, screwing the cap on her bottle. "I'm not going to have sex with you, Coop."

What the hell? That came out of left field. She pinched her lips together.

One of his eyebrows crept upward. "Do you mean right now next to Apache Spring or later?"

"Both, smartass." She backhanded him in the chest. "You joke, but we need some ground rules down here if we're going to spend a week in each other's company."

"Rules are for fools. Isn't that what you said last month?"

A grin slipped out. "Something like that, law dog."

"Okay, give me your rules. But know this, one of my goals in coming down here was to get away from work and all of the rules and restrictions there. We both know that even when I'm not at the station back home, I have trouble shutting off the detective part of my brain."

"Yes, *we* do. Even when your hands are under my shirt you can't seem to stop thinking about catching criminals."

"Touché." He cringed, but chuckled. "For the record, when my hands were inside your shirt that night, I wasn't thinking about work. Nor was catching criminals on my mind when you unzipped my pants."

She gulped, remembering that moment as if it had happened yesterday. Their hands had been everywhere, exploring, teasing, stroking. It would be so easy to lean forward right now and … *No!*

"I have an idea," she said, fanning her jacket. "How about we put our past aside for a week, along with everything else that's going on up in Deadwood, and enjoy being two friends on vacation together in Arizona?"

He stared at her mouth. "Friends?"

"Yep."

"Does this friendship include kissing?" His gaze drifted upward, his stare heated.

Her heart fluttered in surrender, but she held her ground. "No kissing."

"What about touching?"

She shrugged. "Totally platonic is allowed, of course."

"Of course. Can I hold your hand now and then?"

"That's not very platonic."

His smile bordered on rakish. "I'll hold it as a *friend*."

That could be trouble in the making, but … "Yeah, but only in private."

"Deal." He held out his hand for her to shake.

She hesitated, but then took his hand. Only he didn't shake it. He tugged her back up to the main trail to the fort. Once there, he laced his fingers through hers.

"What are you doing?" she asked as they strolled up the trail hand-in-hand.

"Platonically holding your hand in private."

For several steps, her mind was obsessed with the feel of his calloused palm against hers, her thoughts flashing back to the feel of those fingers on her skin so long ago. But then he pointed out some ruins off the side of the trail and she relaxed, enjoying the blue sky and this mellow version of Coop.

They reached the ruins of Fort Bowie a short time later and started exploring what was left, reading the markers at each building site, sharing ideas about what it had been like when it was running strong back in the nineteenth century. Only one other couple had been there when they arrived. They'd headed back down the trail soon after that, leaving Coop and her alone in the warm sunshine and whispering breezes.

"You realize that this fort was up and running strong about the same time Deadwood was just getting rolling," he said from inside the rubble-strewn foundation of one of the officers' quarters, returning to where she stood reading the information sign.

"I wonder if any of the soldiers from here went up to Deadwood or the reverse."

"I wouldn't be surprised. People traveled by horseback and stage more often and farther than most realize, although some folks settled into one spot and built a life there." He took her hand again. "Come on, let's go look at the barracks."

An hour passed quickly as they traipsed around through the patches of grass, yucca, cacti, and fort ruins, exploring the evidence of history that time and Mother Nature were tearing down. By the time they made their way toward the visitor center, taking Coop's hand seemed natural ... well, mostly. The small thrill that came with touching him so freely made her grin wider and laugh quicker.

This relaxed version of Coop was surreal, so different from the hard-ass detective persona she was used to up in Deadwood. When he looked at her with those gray eyes and smiled, her body warmed and her knees turned to jelly.

He climbed the steps to the visitor center with her in tow.

On the wraparound covered porch, they stopped to look out over the old fort, leaning their elbows on the railing.

"Tell me about Joe's checkered past," he said after a bit.

She frowned at him. "Has that been eating at you since I brought it up back in the pickup?"

"No, but you're hiding something from me, and *that* is bothering me."

"I hide a lot of things from you."

He gave her a mock squint. "I know, and I'm going to enjoy interrogating you about each one of those secrets."

She raised one eyebrow. "Will you be using thumbscrews to drag the truth out of me?"

The side of his face pinched. "That's a little too rough for my tastes."

"Really? I always had you pegged for a fan of the rough stuff."

"You did?" He turned toward her. "Would you like your interrogation to be rough, Miss Beals?"

A spark of lust ratcheted up the heat in her core. She glanced around, making sure there weren't any park employees within hearing distance. "I'm not going to be easy to crack."

His gaze dipped to her chest. "I've heard that nipple clamps can really make a suspect squirm."

She winced, crossing her arms over her chest. "I used to work with a girl who got her nipples pierced with loops and liked to wear a rhinestone-studded chain draped between them. That always made me nervous. I mean, what if she caught that chain on a door handle or coat hook."

His laughter rolled out over the grassy ruins. "Why would she be walking around half naked with her chain hanging loose?"

"I don't know. You've seen the shit that goes down during the Sturgis Motorcycle Rally. The idea of piercings and chains isn't so far-fetched for some of those biker babes, is it?"

He laughed again. "Along with some of the guys, too." He looked back out toward the ruins. "Tell me about this Joe your step-grandmother used to be married to, and why your cousins looked worried at The Shaft last night."

He'd noticed that? Of course he had, he was a cop. "Are you

going to switch back into Detective Cooper mode on me if I come clean?"

"How's that different from what I am now?"

"Coop the tourist is playful and fuzzy."

"I'm not fuzzy."

She gave in to the urge that had tempted her off and on since they'd left Jackrabbit Junction and ran her fingers along his jaw, the stubble scraping her skin. "You're right. Playful and bristly, then."

He caught her hand before she could pull it back and tucked it through his arm, drawing her so close their shoulders touched as they stared at the fort's ruins.

When he looked her way, his smile creased his eyes. "Trust me."

Oh, boy. That was like crossing the Grand Canyon on a tight wire. She focused on the flapping US flag in the center of the parade ground. "Okay, but you have to promise not to say anything to any other law enforcement members if I do." She held her pinkie out for him to seal the deal.

He wrapped his own around hers. "Cross my heart."

She leaned closer to him and in a quiet voice spilled what she knew about Joe's history in a rush of run-on sentences.

"Holy fuck," he said, frowning at her after she finished.

"That's not the worst of it."

"What do you mean?"

In another breath, she filled him in on the diamond killer and her cousins' current worrisome position while waiting for the hammer to fall. "Remember, you have to keep quiet about all of this. If Claire finds out I told you, she'll tear me a new ass."

He nodded, his forehead drawn. "Mum's the word, but this is some serious shit."

"I know."

"And you're right in the thick of this mess with them now that you're here."

She shrugged. "They're my family."

"How do you feel about carrying a gun?"

She laughed.

"What's so funny?"

"Mac asked Claire the same thing lately."

"Is she carrying?"

"Not with Crazy Kate running around throwing poo at anyone who looks at her wrong." Natalie explained the situation with Kate and her pregnancy-induced temporary insanity.

"Sweet Jesus," he muttered when she finished. "Your family really knows how to keep life exciting, huh?"

She chuckled. "Are you regretting vacationing down here now?"

He stared down at where her hand rested on his arm. "Not even a little." His gaze lifted to hers and held for several breaths. "I'm sorry."

"For what?"

"Hurting you."

She jerked as if she'd been burned. "Don't, Coop." She tried to pull free, but he held her in place. "Let's not go there again." She was having too nice of a time to return to all of that pent-up pain.

"I know you're angry at me still and I don't expect those feelings to go away without some time, but I need to clear the air." When she didn't say anything, he continued. "You messed with my head that night at the Purple Door Saloon."

She thought back. "But I didn't do anything." Well, besides almost having sex with him, which broke all of her rules about first dates—not that what happened between them was even close to a date.

"You're right. You didn't. You were just being yourself, and that was the problem. We were supposed to be having a little fun, but I lost control somewhere along the line. That was new for me." His gaze slipped to their hands. "I've never lost control around a woman before, but you had this way of kissing me that turned me inside out."

Her pulse pounded. "Coop, stop," she whispered.

"No. You need to understand why I acted as stupid as I did after that night. You scared the shit out of me, Natalie." He looked up and gave her a crooked smile. "Hell, you still do. All you have to do is look at me and my hands get clammy and I can't remember my name. That's some powerful trouble. These feelings … they're new to me. It's unsettling to say the least, yet addictive as hell."

She leaned toward him, unable to stop herself. Maybe just one kiss … "Coop," she whispered.

His focus lowered to her mouth.

"Howdy doody, tutti-fruttis!" Harvey's voice called out behind them, splashing ice-cold water on the moment. The screen door to the visitor center whapped closed behind them. "What's going on out here?"

She pulled free of Coop's hold. Her cheeks baked as she stared blindly out at the juniper- and yucca-dotted hillside behind the ruins.

"I thought you weren't up to hiking," Coop said, facing his uncle.

"I wasn't. Ranger Phil stopped by to see how I was doing and we got to talkin'. He invited me to follow him up here on the service road so he could show me around. He's inside yammerin' on the phone right now, but I'll introduce ya as soon as he joins us."

Harvey sidled up next to Natalie at the railing. "How was your stroll around the fort? Did you learn anything enlightenin'?"

She glanced his way. The old goat had seen Coop and her holding hands, she could see it in the way his blue eyes twinkled and his gold teeth shone in his banana-wide grin.

"It was certainly educational," she admitted.

"Educational, huh?" He snickered. "Is that what you kids call it these days?"

Chapter Eleven

T his plan is going to work about as well as Hitler's attempt to ice skate through Russia," Chester told Ronnie as he drove his truck into the lot at the Dirty Gerties.

Ronnie rolled her eyes. "Quit being such a fuddy-duddy. I know what I'm doing."

He guffawed. "I bet Custer told his second in command the same thing before he rode west out of the Black Hills toward Little Bighorn." He parked and turned to her. "There's still time to change your mind, you know."

"You sound like Katie."

Her sister had tried to talk Ronnie out of following the instructions in the voice message that had been left for her this morning on Katie's phone by Lyle's lawyer. Ronnie had thought she'd clipped all ties to her ex-dickhead non-husband, but she'd overlooked one loophole—Katie still had the same phone number as she had before Ronnie's world imploded.

"No shit," Chester said. "I'd have figured Crazy Kate was the mastermind behind this buggy notion of yours." He glanced out the window as a black pickup eased past them and exited the parking lot. "I bet if you call the sheriff right now, he'd be here in five minutes to join us."

"I don't want the sheriff here for this."

"But have you thought about—"

"Damn it, Chester." She glared at him. "Don't you get it? This is my mess, not Grady's."

He pulled the keys from the ignition. "A man likes to help his woman, and you have plenty of holes in your chicken fence in need of mending between your ex-husband's phony baloney and this diamond killer swinging for you."

"Maybe I don't want *my man's* help with this particular hole in my fence." She crossed her arms. "I'm getting real tired of everyone thinking I can't take care of myself. I'm the one who married Lyle's greedy ass, and I'm the one who has to get myself untangled from his criminal fuckups. Besides, Grady is *only* my boyfriend, not my husband, not even my fiancé. He does not get to put his nose in every dark corner of my screwed-up life just because I'm having sex with him on a regular basis."

"Okay, okay. Remove your teeth from my keister." Chester held up his hands. "Chalk up my comments as concern for you in an uncle sort of way."

She huffed. "I appreciate that, Chester. I really do. But people keep telling me that I need to quit trying to be the perfect little woman for Grady, yet as soon as life starts swatting me with frying pans, they expect me to go running to him. If I'm going to solve my own damned problems from now on, I need to pull up my big-girl panties and walk the walk—alone. Besides, leaning on a man during my marriage is what got me into this stinking situation."

"Fine, I won't bring up your bed buddy again." He raised his bushy gray eyebrows. "Out of curiosity, exactly how often is a 'regular basis' when it comes to the sheriff greasin' your chassis?"

She opened her door instead of answering that. "Get your ass inside and ask Cherry if we can use her office for the next thirty minutes. I want to get this phone call to that lying, cheating, no-good shitbag ex of mine done so we can find out why in the hell he's knocking on my door again."

The strip club was the ideal location for her to call Lyle without drawing suspicion from her family or risking anyone overhearing their conversation. The last thing she needed right now was Grady finding out she was in contact with her ex. Besides the fact that he was already hip-deep in her problems, the lawman in him would badger her for every single detail of the call, and there were mortifying parts of her past that Lyle might bring up. Private R-rated stuff she wasn't comfy sharing with her current lover.

"All righty then." Chester stepped to the ground. "Let's get to it."

As they crossed the parking lot, she glanced around to make sure there were no Cholla County Sheriff's Department vehicles cruising by. She had no doubt that Deputy Dipshit would race to tattle to Grady if he saw Ronnie walking into Dirty Gerties. Anything to add more smudges to her blemished "jailbird" reputation.

Chester grinned as he held the door for her. "Does good ol' Grady handcuff you during this 'regular-basis' sex? I've heard tell that some of those guys on the pokey patrol are really into the kinky stuff."

She jabbed him in the ribs as she passed. "My sex life with the sheriff of Cholla County is none of your beeswax."

"Now who's being the fuddy-duddy?"

The dark interior of Dirty Gerties throbbed with a loud, steady bass beat that made her teeth bounce. The underlying smell of lemons and pine lent a clean feel to the dirty dancing happening front and center. According to Chester, the strip joint was spick and span compared to most, and he would know after all of his years of mud wrestling in the ring with bikini babes. Although nowadays his trick hip tended to slow him down.

The mud pit in the middle of the wide-open room was covered with boards today, turning it into a large stage surrounded by shiny brass rails. Three of the four stripper poles at the corners were in use to entertain the Sunday afternoon crowd that partially filled the black leather booths hugging the walls.

Ronnie scanned the shadows as they made their way to the bar, looking for a familiar face and coming up with a match in a corner booth—the man she'd called after receiving Lyle's lawyer's message and arranged to meet here so he could listen in on the phone call along with Chester.

Mississippi nodded his head at her one-minute gesture before returning his attention to the red-haired, long-legged cowgirl in chaps and tassels who was busy wrapping herself around one of the brass poles like a red stripe on a candy cane.

Cherry Haywood, the club's owner, was topping off a mug of beer when they sidled up to the bar. Her platinum blond hair was pulled back in two pigtails. Her impressive rack bulged under a tiny tight tank top with "Dirty Gerties" scrawled across the front of it. In the rose-colored lighting she looked half her age.

"Howdy, Sugarbear," she said to Chester.

Sugarbear? That was a new-to-Ronnie nickname.

"You're looking rough-and-tumble good with that bristle lining your jaw," Cherry added with a wink of her long, fake eyelashes. Her smile shifted to Ronnie. "Hey, Stretch. You here to dance around a pole with those long legs of yours and make some extra cash? I pay well."

Cherry was known for running a top-notch strip joint. She not only compensated her girls with good money but also included benefits like health insurance and vacation.

"Cherry, if I ever consider removing my clothes for a living, your club will be my first stop on the job hunt."

Chester snickered, elbowing Ronnie. "Rubbing up and down a pole would surely make your sheriff stand up and salute."

Ronnie elbowed the wiseacre back. "Remember why we're here, *Sugarbear*."

"Fine, spoilsport." He waved Cherry over after she slid the mug of beer to a beefy middle-aged guy in a Diamondbacks baseball cap and flannel shirt.

"What can I get you two?" she asked.

"We need a favor," Chester said. "We need to borrow your office for about a half hour to make a top-secret phone call."

Her eyes creased. "Ohhh, that sounds sexy."

"I have to call a loser from my past," Ronnie explained.

Cherry's smile flipped into a grimace. "That's not very sexy at all." She dug into her cleavage and pulled out a key, holding it toward Chester. "You're welcome to it. I'm covering here today. My bartender takes Sundays off."

He palmed the key, ogling Cherry's chest. "What else you storing in there?"

She blew him a kiss. "Take me to dinner sometime and maybe I'll whisper the answer in your ear afterward."

Chester's cheeks darkened as he watched her walk away.

"Are you going to take her up on that?" Ronnie asked, sliding off the bar stool.

"Probably not."

"Why not?"

He grimaced. "That's a lot of woman there for one man to handle."

Ronnie waved for Mississippi to join them and followed Chester down the hallway past the restrooms and payphone to Cherry's office.

"Wow!" she said after Chester hit the lights.

Cherry's office was a mass of primary colors, from the custom red leather couch to the blue carpet and yellow plush office chair behind an all-glass desk. Silver stars swirled together with loops of golden rope to decorate the cream-colored walls.

"Cherry is a Wonder Woman nut," Chester explained.

"Yeah, I can see that." Behind Cherry's desk was a painting of Wonder Woman looking more sexy than badass. A fitting tribute to the brunette bombshell being they were in a strip club.

Mississippi stepped into the room, dressed in his usual black shirt, jeans, and boots attire, and closed the door behind him. He turned around, his eyes widening as he took in the décor. When his gaze snagged on the painting behind Cherry's chair, he let out a low whistle. "Holy golden lasso!" He skirted the glass desk and gaped at Wonder Woman. "Damn."

Chester plopped down on the leather couch, making himself comfortable. "She's something, ain't she?"

"Are we talking about Cherry or Wonder Woman?" Ronnie asked, pulling a piece of paper from her pocket. Katie had drawn an unhappy face with an arrow through its forehead above the phone number Lyle's lawyer had rattled off on the voice message.

"Both," Chester said and let out a husky laugh. "What'd ya think of Cinnamin the Cowgirl's pole-dancing act, Mr. FBI?"

"A pretty girl dancing half-naked in chaps and cowboy boots?" Mississippi sat on the edge of the glass desk. "What's not to like?" He handed a small cell phone to Ronnie. "One anonymous burner phone, as requested."

Ronnie took it and dropped into Cherry's office chair, her knees wobbly all of a sudden.

"Are you ready?" she asked her two witnesses. Her hand trembled as she punched in the phone number, screwing up twice in the process.

It had been months since she'd talked to Lyle, and that last time had been through a Plexiglas window with holes. After all of his grand fuckeries that she'd learned about since then, not including the first wife he'd never divorced, she was a tad concerned that the mere sound of his voice alone would make her head explode.

She took a calming breath—in through her nose, out through her mouth—drawing on all of her yoga and *namaste* meditation hocus-pocus.

"You sure you want to do this?" Mississippi asked. His forehead had developed a series of horizontal lines since entering the office.

"She's sure," Chester answered for her. "And before you ask, she doesn't want her sheriff boyfriend to know about it either. Trust me on this before trying to talk her into it. I'm still walking bowlegged from the ass-reaming she gave me out in my pickup."

Ronnie wrinkled her nose at the bowlegged blowhard. "Could you refrain from using words like 'ass' and 'reaming' while we're in the back office of a strip club?"

He waved her off. "Cherry doesn't allow any of that S&M fun stuff here."

Ronnie took another breath and then hit the call button. Before it started ringing, she put it on speakerphone for Mississippi and Chester to hear.

One ring.

The cell phone slipped from her clammy hands and clattered onto the desk.

Two rings.

Mississippi picked it up and handed it back to her, his green eyes searching her face.

Three rings.

She took the phone back and attempted a smile.

He winced at her expression.

"Veronica?" said a smooth voice from her sordid past through the phone.

"Hello, Lyle." Her words came out creaky sounding, like she was choking on a frog. Or maybe it was the wrecking ball of rage clogging her throat.

"It's wonderful to hear your voice again, *darling*."

She cringed at the intimacy inferred in that one word. She opened her mouth to tell the prick where he could shove his smarmy endearment but Mississippi held out his hand to stop her. He mimed taking another breath.

She followed suit before saying, "Don't bore me with pleasantries, Lyle."

"Oh, feeling feisty are we?" He lowered his voice. "Are you wearing any panties?"

She gasped, her cheeks catching fire at Mississippi's frown. Jeez, what was it with everyone's interest in her damned underwear lately? "Wh— I— You— Why?"

"I think about you often, *darling*, especially at night in the dark." His breathing grew louder in the phone. "Remember that trip we took to London and France when you didn't wear any underpants?"

A muffled snort came from the bristle-topped jackass sitting on Cherry's couch.

Ronnie squeezed her temples. Yes, she did remember that trip. What Lyle was forgetting to mention was that in her excitement to travel to Europe for the first time in her life she'd forgotten to pack any extra bras or underwear. The horny idiot on the other end of the line had thrown away the only panties she'd had while she slept that first night. He'd refused to let her go shopping for more until they'd reached Paris because he got off on her going commando through the streets of London.

And this underwear mention was one of the reasons why she hadn't wanted Grady here. It was bad enough to have Chester and Mississippi listening to this episode of *The History of Ronnie's Foolish Follies*. She'd sooner jump into a swamp full of gators than look into Grady's amber eyes right now.

"Tell me, Lyle," she said in a tight voice. "Do you think about your Wyoming wife late at night, too?"

"Now, *darling*, let's not be catty. We have only a few minutes to talk and I'd rather not fight this time. How is Deborah doing? Is she as lovely as always?"

Chester's horrified expression at Lyle's words about her

mother would have been comical if Ronnie wasn't so busy grinding her teeth down to nubs to keep from calling Lyle every name she could think of at the moment.

Mississippi gave her the motion to keep Lyle talking. She didn't know why that mattered since they weren't tracing the call.

"Mom is fine," she answered, lowering the phone onto the desk.

"Is she still gracing the Rapid City society pages? I thought I heard something through my attorney that she'd divorced your father due to an extramarital affair."

What had he been smoking in prison? Her mother had been in the society pages maybe once or twice, and that was only due to being seen at one of the hoity-toity parties Ronnie had hosted for Lyle's so-called business partners.

"Mom is remarried now and lives elsewhere." Deborah still had Ronnie's childhood home in Rapid City, but she couldn't see how her mother's life was Lyle's business anymore.

"Remarried already?" His laughter sounded canned. "She didn't waste time finding another sugar daddy. What about you, *darling*?"

If he called her "darling" one more time, she was going to hire a prison guard to jam a riot stick up his patronizing ass. "What about me?"

"Is there someone else keeping your bed warm now?"

Why did he care if she was screwing anyone or not? He'd been too busy bonking his bimbos over the last few years of their marriage to share Ronnie's sheets.

She took another yoga breath. "Why did you want me to call you, Lyle? And don't waste my time trying to tell me it was to catch up, because I don't believe for a damned minute that you give a flying fuck about me and my family."

Mississippi crossed his arms, scowling down at her.

She flipped him off with both middle fingers.

"I need a favor," Lyle said.

Was he freaking kidding? After he'd shredded her dignity to pieces and then thrown the remaining scraps of her self-respect to the FBI sharks for further frenzied feeding all the while hiding behind his lying lawyer, the jerk wanted a favor from *her*?

Mississippi shook his head, apparently able to read her thoughts about reaching through the line and castrating the cocksucking, monkey-fucking bastard with her bare hands.

This time she took two yoga breaths. "And what favor would that be, Lyle?"

* * *

"You mean you actually called that sleazeball?" Natalie asked Ronnie several hours later at The Shaft while waiting for Gary the bartender to fill their drink orders.

Crudnuggets, she'd left Jackrabbit Junction for half a day and in that short time her cousin had joined Kate's crazy train. Why on earth would Ronnie bother returning that cheating bastard's call when he had done nothing but screw her six ways from Sunday at every turn since she'd married him?

"Shhhhh," Ronnie said, leaning closer. "I don't want anyone else to know about this besides Katie and you."

"And Chester," Natalie added. "I can't believe you took that gossip queen with you. He'll have it on the front page of the *Yuccaville Yodeler* tomorrow morning."

"No, he won't. He promised me he'd keep his lips sealed about this. Besides, I needed his help getting Cherry to let us use her office."

"Why couldn't you talk to Lyle here in Butch's office?"

"Because I needed Mississippi to be there with me." Ronnie's cheek twitched several times. "I didn't want anyone else I know to get suspicious, and the FBI is like a big red elephant in our family."

"Red elephant?" Natalie repeated, scratching her neck. "I don't think that's an actual saying."

"Whatever. You know what I mean." Ronnie's hand trembled as she tucked a strand of hair behind her ear.

Natalie shifted gears. "So, Chester is good friends with the owner of Dirty Gerties, huh?"

Ronnie tittered like Aunt Deborah, a surefire warning sign that her cousin was skidding out of control. "I think she wants to be more than friends, but Chester is too nervous to sleep with her."

Chester Thomas was nervous about sleeping with a woman? Was the world coming to an end?

"Did you tell Grady about this phone call?"

"Of course not, and you can't either." She held up her closed fist. "Posse promise?"

Natalie frowned, but bumped fists anyway. The secrets were piling up down here in the desert.

"It was humiliating enough to have Chester and Mississippi listening in on that phone conversation. If Grady had been there, I would have keeled over."

"Why? What did Lyle say?"

"He sort of brought up our sex life."

Natalie pretended to gag. "I hope you disinfected your vagina before you started sleeping with Grady."

Ronnie wrinkled her nose in reply. "You're one to talk after screwing around with a Mr. Clean lookalike who was banging that tattooed titty-tassel tart behind your back."

She couldn't help but laugh at Ronnie's alliterative description of the tramp who'd inspired many rants after Natalie had broken up with the cockroach they'd both been screwing. That whole mess, which had seeded the sabbatical idea in her head, seemed like another lifetime.

After Natalie stopped laughing, she told Ronnie, "You should probably give Grady the short and clean version of the call, though."

When Grady eventually found out, and Natalie had little doubt that he would somehow being that he was the sheriff, this call might cause some friction between Ronnie and him.

"What is with you and Chester and Katie all wanting me to bow at Grady's knees and kiss his feet?"

"Uhhh, I wouldn't go that far."

"Just because we're swapping bodily fluids doesn't make him the king of my universe." The corner of her mouth twitched several times too fast to count.

Natalie frowned at Ronnie, wondering who was driving in her head, because there seemed to be some gear-grinding going on during the downshifts.

Was this what her own future would be like if she took the next step with Coop and started sharing his bed? She'd certainly contemplated a legs-entwined fantasy all of the way home from Fort Bowie, sneaking peeks at him, remembering the feel of his skin under her hands as though the alley scene had happened last night instead of years ago.

If she were to give in to her feelings, would she start dressing differently? Would she struggle to keep from losing her own identity? Would her newfound self-confidence go down the toilet? How long before she started hiding things from Coop, like Ronnie was with Grady and this phone call to Lyle? Coop was a cop inside and out, and while she wasn't a hard-core criminal, Natalie bucked the rules more often than not.

She shook off her Coop worries and returned to Ronnie's problems. "I just think Grady would be interested in hearing that you talked to the douche-noggin who bent you over backward for five years while he was snorting cocaine off various bimbos' bare asses."

"Shhhh." Ronnie glanced around, her eyes wide. "How do you know about Lyle doing that?"

"You told me one night when we were drinking, remember?"

She chewed on her lower lip. "No."

"You should probably lay off the gin and tonics for a while." Natalie took the margaritas Gary the bartender held out for her and set them on her tray. "So what was this favor the pigeon-livered flapdoodle wanted from you?"

"He wants me to contact his mother."

That seemed left of center. "Why?"

"She has something she wants to send me but doesn't know where to send it."

"Are you going to do it?"

"She was a sweet lady."

"Yeah, but your ex–devil spawn came from *her* womb."

Ronnie blinked both eyes rapidly, like her eyelids were stuck on fast-shutter-speed mode. "Mississippi wants me to do it. He's curious what she has to send me. I am, too."

"What address are you going to use?"

"A post office box the FBI tracks in Tucson, compliments of

the pool ball wizard in back."

Natalie glanced back toward the pool tables where the FBI agent was shooting pool again tonight in between barroom scans. "Does he think this mysterious gift of hers has to do with those stolen diamonds the FBI is trying to pin on you?"

Ronnie let out a loud squawk. "How do you know about those?"

"Claire told me all about it before she left for Tucson."

"I told her not to tell anyone!"

"You told her not to tell Grady, and she didn't. But I'm part of the posse, remember?" Natalie held up her fist for another fist bump.

Ronnie obliged, frowning.

"Order up!" Kate called from the kitchen window.

The order was Natalie's, judging by the bleu cheese and bacon burger in the center of the plate.

The feel of cool air on her back made her glance toward the door for the umpteenth time. Coop had said he and Harvey would be stopping by later, but he hadn't said when.

The sight of a blue-eyed, reddish-blond haired man standing in the doorway made her do a double take.

"Hey!" She patted Ronnie's arm. "Look who's back."

Ronnie glanced up from checking her order pad as Valentine "Butch" Carter stepped up to the bar. His face was lined and weary, but his smile was warm and wide.

"Butch!" Ronnie rushed over to give him a hug. "You're back early."

"There was a snowstorm in the forecast back home and I didn't want to get stuck there for the New Year, so I left a day early." He glanced around the bar. "Where's Kate?"

"She's working in the kitchen," Natalie said.

"Hi, Natalie," he said, glancing down at the shirt she was wearing with The Shaft emblem on it. "What's with the waitress getup? Did you lose a bet to Ronnie or Kate?"

"Both," she joked. "The place has been hopping lately and your baby mama needs to take breaks whether she likes it or not, so here I am."

He nodded. "Thank you for that. Kate tends to forget she's

pregnant when she's at work." He looked at Ronnie. "You're paying Natalie, right?"

"I tried, but she won't take the money."

At Butch's wrinkled brow, Natalie shrugged. "You're family. Besides, Kate lets me eat and drink for free."

"Order up, Natalie!" Kate barked, peering out the window. "Ronnie! What in Sam Hill is taking Natalie so …" Her focus shifted, her eyes widening at the sight of Butch.

A loud screech came through the window.

A second later, the swinging batwing doors slammed open and Kate leapt into Butch's arms, knocking him back a step. Her mouth collided with his, her arms wrapping around his neck, her legs circling his hips.

Natalie turned away. A spasm of envy throbbed in her chest for a moment at the look of pure joy she'd seen on Kate's face when she'd burst through the doors.

Sweet sassafras, she missed being with a man.

Damn Coop for stoking the fires in her heart today. Before he showed up in Jackrabbit Junction, she had been lonely, but it was nothing like the gut-aching misery she felt tonight.

She cast another glance at Kate and Butch, who were whispering to each other in between kisses. Kate's love for Butch showed bright and clear in her glowing face.

Would letting Coop into her heart turn her into a smitten kitten like Kate? Would she greet him at the door when he finally got home from the station with kisses and wicked promises of what she'd do to him as soon as she'd stripped him naked?

"Kate's crazy," Ronnie said in her ear. "But Butch loves her anyway." There was a wistful note in Ronnie's tone.

When Natalie looked around, Ronnie was weaving her way through the tables with her full drink tray held high.

Sighing, Natalie grabbed her burger plate from the order window, set it on her tray next to the drinks, and followed Ronnie's lead.

She glanced back at the bar after dropping off her order, watching as Butch led Kate by the hand back through the swinging doors. The spasm twanged in her chest again, making her wince.

Dang it, she was happy for Kate. Truly. Her cousin had been a mess the last time Natalie was in town—pregnant by accident without any hope that Butch would want the child, let alone the woman carrying his kid. Natalie had whooped and danced weeks later when Claire had called to tell her that Butch and Kate had patched things up and were back together arguing about what color to paint the nursery.

And baby makes three …

Meanwhile, Natalie's own chances of having a family were shrinking by the day. Another few years and she'd be reaching the upper ages of safe baby-carrying. Sure, she could have a kid with a sperm donor or adopt, but watching her best friend raise her twins on her own had shown her the hard life of single parenting. Natalie would much rather have someone there with whom to share the highs and lows of family life.

But Coop wasn't that "someone." He was married to his job. Hell, most days he didn't have time for a girlfriend, let alone a kid. All that the future held with him was sex.

Good sex, though.

Possibly *really* good sex if she went by the taste she'd had that night behind the Purple Door Saloon.

But sex wasn't everything. There were the rest of the hours in a day to consider, and that was when Coop would be gone, out risking his life to keep Deadwood's streets safe.

Her best bet was to play it cool and keep things mellow with Coop.

Just friends. Groaning at how boring that sounded, she grabbed her order pad and headed for a table filled with a handful of dusty cowboys who looked fresh from the range.

As she made her way back to the bar with their orders, a pair of gray eyes watched her approach.

Her heart swooned, the fickle organ.

When had Coop arrived? She dragged her gaze from his and noticed another familiar face on the next bar stool over. Grady was missing his uniform tonight. He must have gotten off early enough to go home and change.

Where was Ronnie?

Natalie found her cousin back near Mississippi. So had

Grady, and judging from his pinched brow, he wasn't thrilled about it either.

"Howdy, boys." She handed off her order to the bartender. "How are my favorite law dogs this evening?"

Chapter Twelve

W ho's the undercover cop?" Mississippi asked Ronnie.
"What undercover cop?" She picked up his empty
sarsaparilla bottle and set it on her tray with the other
used beer mugs and martini glasses.

Cops didn't concern her much these days, undercover or not.
She had bigger problems.

"The one your cousin is flirting with at the bar. He's sitting
next to the sheriff."

Grady was here? She looked over her shoulder and ran
smack into his hard stare.

She smiled at him, trying to be sunny in spite of the shit
storm swirling around her tonight.

Grady frowned back, all dark clouds and thunder.

Great, there were more squalls and rain on the horizon.
Wasn't that just her damned luck lately?

"Your boyfriend looks like he's drinking a glass of bitter
beer," Mississippi said, chalking his pool cue.

"Yep." She dragged her gaze away from Grady, turning her
back to him. She blew out a breath of defeat. "I wonder what in
the hell I did now."

Between the diamond killer, Lyle, and now Grady, she
couldn't seem to catch a break. This damned-if-she-did and
damned-if-she-didn't teeter-totter ride was nauseating her.

"Maybe you should've included him today." Mississippi set
the chalk on the edge of the pool table. "You still can, you
know."

"Sure, I could." She grabbed the empty plate from his table.
"But I don't want to." Not yet, anyway.

The phone call today with Lyle had stirred the bubbling brew of fury and humiliation in her core to a boil again, spurring heated blasts of cursing and streams of acidic tears at random. She needed to keep her distance from Grady until her emotions had settled back into a low simmer so she didn't open her mouth and burn him to a crisp with a fireball of rage.

"Stubborn much?" Mississippi lined up a shot at the seven ball.

"Kiss my ass, FBI." She passed behind him to grab an empty glass from a shelf on the wall cue rack and bumped his pool cue, screwing up his shot. "Oops."

His gaze hardened. "Your fangs are showing."

She scowled back. "You can thank the rat bastard who kept calling me 'darling' today for that."

"You didn't answer me about the undercover cop."

Ronnie chanced a glance toward the bar again. Grady's back was to her now thanks to Butch, who'd taken Gary the bartender's place. From the looks of the situation, Grady was introducing Coop to Butch. Natalie was missing from the scene. She must have gone in back to help Katie or paid a visit to the ladies' room.

"The cop is a friend of Natalie's from South Dakota who's down here on vacation this week."

"Judging from the way he watches your cousin when she's not looking, I'd say he's daydreaming about strip searches and handcuffs, and not necessarily in that order."

"Maybe, but Natalie's on sabbatical from men."

"No shit?"

"No shit."

"With those lips of hers, that's a damned shame."

Ronnie had a feeling Coop the cop would drink to that.

"You're being flagged." Mississippi pointed toward a table with five college-aged girls.

"No, I believe they're waving at you to join them." Their smooth faces and eager grins looked younger than the twenty-one years their driver's licenses had indicated when she checked them. "They're here to celebrate the cute little redhead's birthday. Another margarita for her, Mr. FBI, and I bet you could get her to unwrap you later in your pickup."

He grunted and lined up another shot. "Way too young and green for me. I like riper versions with softer curves."

She watched him sink the seven ball. "Riper often means they come with bruises." Ronnie was covered with them at the moment.

He looked her way, his forehead lining at what he saw on her face. "Bruises build character." His focus shifted, landing on something behind her. His frown deepened. "I'm thinking the peach rubbing all over your boyfriend is rotten at her core, though."

"What?" Ronnie spun around.

A blonde in a tight pink dress and white cowboy boots had her arms looped around Grady's neck from behind, whispering in his ear. Or maybe she was sucking on his ear. It was hard to tell from her vantage point.

The woman turned to smile at Butch.

Elizabeth!

Ronnie gasped. She shoved her tray of dirty plates and glasses at Mississippi.

"Ronnie, don't," he called after her as she stalked toward the bar.

Don't what? Drag the heart-breaking strumpet out back by the hair, dip her headfirst into the grease bin, and then stake her to the ground next to a fire ant hill until dawn?

Mississippi was right. That might land Ronnie in deeper trouble than what she was bobbing up and down in already. She'd settle with serving Grady's ex a super-sized wedgie with a side of Ronnie's boot up her ass.

By the time Ronnie reached the bar, Grady had managed to extricate himself from his ex-wife's version of the sleeper-hold. The frown he'd shot Ronnie earlier was downright friendly compared to the glower he was giving Elizabeth.

"… to go home," she heard him say when she drew within earshot.

Elizabeth crossed her arms, pushing her hooters higher so that they almost winked at everyone over her dress's skimpy neckline. "I waited for you there like you told me to, but you didn't show.''

"Say what now?" Ronnie said, dragging her eyes from Elizabeth's ample bazookas. Grady had told his ex to meet him at his house? When had this previous conversation gone down? More important, how long had he been talking to the hussy and why hadn't he mentioned it to Ronnie?

Grady growled. "When I said to go home, I meant your mom's place, not my house."

"But your home is my home."

"Not any more, remember?"

Elizabeth noticed Ronnie standing on the sidelines. Her face twisted into a snarl that would have made a lion tamer drop his chair and run. She aimed her snarl at Grady. "It's still *our* home, even though you brought this trailer park tramp into our bed."

The trailer park was fitting since Ronnie was currently living at an RV park, but she chafed at the tramp bit. "That's downright funny coming from a gutter whore like you. You were the one who got knocked up with another man's child while you were married to Grady."

"Oh, you stupid … Shut up!" Elizabeth grabbed the full mug in front of Grady. With the flick of her wrist, she plastered Ronnie's neck and work shirt with beer.

The barflies around them quieted.

Ronnie gaped down at her soaked shirt, shivering as the cold beer trickled down her stomach and soaked the waistline of her jeans. Something cracked in her ears. It might have been the camel's spine under the weight of that final piece of straw.

When she looked up at Grady's ex, she saw red—literally. There was a big red splotch on Elizabeth's left breast. As Ronnie stared at it, the thick red goop slid south and dripped onto the top of the bitch's white cowboy boot.

"What did you do?!" Elizabeth squawked, her mouth wide in horror as she stared down at her red boob.

"Oops," said a voice from the other side of the bar.

Ronnie and Elizabeth turned at the same time. Katie smiled, the red ketchup bottle in her hand still aimed at Grady's ex. "I guess I got a little excited and squeezed prematurely in the heat of the moment."

Elizabeth gurgled with rage. She scooped up a handful of peanuts from a bowl on the bar and threw them at Katie, who ducked.

When Katie popped back up, her eyes were wide with her crazed Mr. Hyde look. "Are you nuts?" she yelled.

"You stained my dress!"

"Darn, you're right. Let me help you with that."

Katie drew the soda water gun from its holster behind the bar and aimed it at Elizabeth, spraying her in the chin and neck. "Sorry about that, my aim was off." She lowered the nozzle and blasted the front of Elizabeth's dress while Grady's ex screeched. "There we go," Katie said. "I think we got the worst of it off."

Wolf whistles rang out down the length of the bar, followed by hoots and claps.

Elizabeth raised her hands, claws extended, and tried to climb over the bar. She howled like a banshee, slashing out at Katie with her fingernails. Katie stepped back with the spray gun still in hand, cackling like a mad witch while she squirted Elizabeth in the face.

Then Grady was there, grabbing Elizabeth by the waist. He pulled her back down to the floor while getting sprayed in the face several times in the process. At the same time, Butch was taking casualties to the other side of the bar while trying to grab the soda nozzle away from Katie, who refused to let up on the spray.

Ronnie would have laughed at the clown act if it weren't her pregnant sister and sheriff boyfriend co-starring in the show. She covered her mouth. What had she done now? She'd jinxed them all.

A spray of water splashed her already soaked chest. "That's it! I'm done," she shouted above the racket. She untied her waitress apron and tossed it at Coop, who was watching the wrestling match with his drink paused halfway to his mouth.

Pushing through the batwing doors, Ronnie unbuttoned her soaked shirt as she walked. She dumped the shirt on the floor, slipped Claire's spare flannel jacket over her wet bra, grabbed the Jeep keys along with her purse, and exited stage left out the back door.

The Jeep rumbled to life without a problem, thankfully. She cranked up the stereo and shifted into gear. As she gunned it past the front door, she caught sight of Natalie running outside.

Ronnie didn't take the turn toward the Dancing Winnebagos RV Park. Instead, she barreled down the road toward Tucson, singing at the top of her lungs about "dancing the night away" along with Van Halen while leaving Jackrabbit Junction and all of its dust devils in her rearview mirror.

Almost thirty minutes later, she skidded to a stop on the dark empty road, her headlights shining on a sign that said she was leaving Cholla County.

This was it, the end of Grady's tether. If she kept going, she and her problems would be out of his hands. He'd get his county back and she'd get … sad. Very sad. And lonely. Heartbroken probably. Miserable definitely. Not to mention that she'd miss her family. And Aunt Millie. Chester, too. Maybe even Mississippi a little. Probably her mother a little … or not.

"Fuck! Fuck! Fuck!" she yelled, pounding her fist on the steering wheel with each curse.

Running away was not the answer. Running away would only hurt the people she loved.

She let out one last curse and then turned around in the middle of the road, heading back to the hot mess she'd left behind.

The closer she got to Jackrabbit Junction, the more her chest ached. She needed more time to come down from today's heaping plate of shit-aroni, but where could she go where nobody would be able to find her? Sleeping with the head of the sheriff's department made disappearing a challenge worthy of a magician's hat and wand.

She sped past The Shaft and continued on toward Yuccaville, trying to think of an empty lot where she could park for an hour or two without being disturbed. Unfortunately, Claire's Jeep was as well known among Grady's men as Katie's Volvo, so Yuccaville was out.

A crossroads sign up ahead sparked a memory—and then an idea. She slowed and turned off on the dirt road Grady had taken her down months ago.

She bumped along slowly, trying to remember where the second turnoff was. There. Up ahead. She turned and drove for a few minutes until she reached the spot he'd taken her to the night he told her he wanted to make their relationship more public—his new house.

Technically, it was only the location where his new house was going to be built later this year. Right now, all that was there were stakes topped with white or red flags.

She parked between two flags and killed the engine. Silence filled her world, interrupted only by sporadic gusts of wind.

"Honey, I'm home," she whispered, and then the dam burst behind her eyes. "Stupid tears!"

It took her a couple of minutes to empty her tank, the weight of her worries leaking out through her tear ducts—Lyle's bullshit, Elizabeth's games, the diamond killer's threats, Mississippi's warnings, Grady's frowns, her mother's scorn, Claire's obsessions, Katie's craziness, Chester's ... what? Her tears stopped. Apparently, that was all she'd been storing up for the time being.

Whew! The ache in her chest had finally eased. She mopped up her cheeks with Claire's flannel jacket and rested her arms on the steering wheel. Outside the windows, the desert breathed in short bursts, making the Jeep shudder, cholla cacti and greasewood bushes shake, and the tumbleweeds roll.

She killed the lights, breathing easier in the silvery light of the moon. She leaned her head on her arms and closed her eyes. Returning to her yoga schooling, she focused inward and released breath after breath of tension and frustration until she fell asleep ...

A tapping sound made her jerk upright. Her heart fluttered in her throat. What was that?

She looked out the passenger-side window.

Grady stood on the other side, his stony profile lit by his pickup's headlights. He pointed at the lock. "Open up, Veronica."

Jumping Jehoshaphat. She couldn't escape the law in this county no matter how hard she tried. With a tired sigh, she unlocked the door and sat back in the seat. She felt too spent to be angry or embarrassed at being found in her hiding spot.

He opened the door but hesitated. "Mind if I join you? It's cold out here."

It was chilly in the Jeep's cab, too. How long had she been asleep?

She motioned him inside. "It's your future house." She started the Jeep to warm up the cab again.

He slid the bucket seat back as far as it would go and settled in next to her, his knees bumping up against the handle on the dashboard. Then he stared out the windshield.

She waited for the lecture to start from his side of the cab. When it didn't, she followed his lead and stared out the window, too, enjoying sitting in the dark next to him.

"It smells like beer in here," he said finally.

No surprise there. The front of her bra had been soaked as much as her shirt. "You want to give me an old-fashioned Breathalyzer test, Sheriff?" she teased, making kissing noises.

He chuckled. "For starters, yeah. Then I want to take you home and to bed."

"You do have a nice bed." Very soft and full of him sans the badge, but before she let her thoughts wander any farther down that road, she was curious about something. "How did you find me out here? Do you have some sort of tracking device on Claire's Jeep?"

It wouldn't surprise her if Mac had installed something to protect Claire. Or maybe Mississippi had planted a bug on it without Claire's knowledge. The FBI might deem it as a necessary precaution to monitor all of Ronnie's family. Damned busybody government spooks.

"It's not on the vehicle, it's on your phone."

She scowled. "You're tracking my phone? Listen, Grady, just because I'm sleeping in your bed doesn't give you the right to monitor me twenty-four hours of the day."

He leaned the seat back as far as it would go and put his arms behind his head. "It wasn't me tracking you."

"Then how is it that *you* are the one here with me?"

"I drew the short straw," he joked. "Kate is monitoring both you and Claire. She set it up on your phones at Christmas when you two weren't looking. She came clean about it tonight after everyone calmed down and Natalie told us that you'd bailed, heading down the road toward Tucson."

"Why on earth?"

"She figured you two were going to continue hiding stuff from her because she's pregnant and she wanted to be able to track you down when needed." He unzipped his coat and yawned. "I don't agree with invading your privacy on that level, but it certainly came in handy tonight when you hightailed it out of there." He looked her way, the glow of the dashboard lights glittering in his eyes. "Now, are you ready to tell me what's going on?"

Not really, but she was tired of hiding and running and worrying. "What did you do with your wife?"

His eyes narrowed. "Your FBI boyfriend drove her home."

Poor Mississippi. Then again, he did like women with curves, and Elizabeth had plenty to spare. "He's not my boyfriend, Grady."

"She's not my wife, Veronica."

Silence filled the cab again. The heater whirred, taking the edge off the cold. She sniffed inside Claire's flannel jacket. He was right, she did smell like beer.

"If he's not your boyfriend," Grady said, his voice almost hesitant, which wasn't like him, "do you mind filling me in on what you were doing with him in Cherry Harwood's office today for a half hour?"

She cursed under her breath. "When Cherry tattled on me, did she mention that there was a third party in her office with us?"

"Cherry didn't tattle. Elizabeth did. Her cousin was there and called her."

"Gary the bartender?" Ronnie thought he didn't like Elizabeth much. Why would he tell on her?

"Another cousin, not Gary. Yuccaville is a small town and you and your sisters have a way of standing out from the locals like porcupines at a nudist colony."

She grimaced. That probably wasn't a good thing. "So, Elizabeth has her spies watching me now, huh?"

"You and me both, not that I give a damn about her thoughts on my actions." The disgust in his voice was clear. "However, I am curious about that office meeting. And the third attendee."

"Curious as the sheriff of Cholla County?" In other words, was she going to get an ass-chewing about following the law again? Because that would ruin the mellow buzz she had going at the moment.

He closed his eyes, shifting in the seat so his knees didn't rub the dashboard. "Curious as the man who has enticed you into his bed and wishes you were there with him now instead of out here in the middle of the cold desert."

She leaned her seat all of the way back to match his and turned on her side, staring at him in the semi-darkness. "Grady, I have problems."

He shrugged. "Who doesn't?"

"You, for one."

He scoffed. "What do you call an ex-wife in town who appears to be delusional about why we divorced, shows up at my workplace with home-cooked meals for me, and wants to return to the life we had before she ran off with her lover and his baby?"

The bitch was cooking for him, too? Ronnie filed that away for a future teeth-grinding moment. "Okay, you have something there, but this particular problem of mine involves potential prison time."

His eyes opened. "What?"

"And with you up for reelection this year, I don't know that I should be sharing your bed anymore. I could ruin your career."

He looked her way, his forehead lined. "What happened in Cherry's office today?"

"The third party was Chester."

"Chester Thomas?"

"The one and only. He was acting as one of my witnesses. Mississippi was the other."

"Why did you need witnesses?"

"I called Lyle."

"Your ex-husband?"

"Well, officially he and I were never—"

"Veronica, cut to the chase."

"Lyle had his lawyer contact me via Katie's phone, whose number his lawyer still had on file. Lyle wanted me to call him."

"And you raced to do his bidding?"

"No, I didn't race to do Lyle's bidding, damn it. I needed to talk to him because of the impending prison situation I mentioned a moment ago."

He looked up at the Jeep's hardtop, squeezing the bridge of his nose. "Explain this prison business, please."

Ronnie did as he requested, telling him about the FBI's new match game that tied the diamonds found under the mules' camper to those Lyle had hid who-knew-where.

After Grady finished cursing about the FBI's bullshit move, she explained what happened during the phone call to Lyle, leaving out all of those icky "darling" endearments and the bit about her lack of underpants in England.

"You should have told me about this sooner, Veronica," he said after she finished, still staring upward.

"Why? So you could remind me about how stupid I was to stay married to my ex-husband for all of those years?"

Because if that was why, she was going to cram her beer-smelling bra down his throat. She knew her screwups well, both past and present. She didn't need Grady's help feeling like a big dumb dope.

"No, damn it."

"Then why?"

"Because I'm in love with you, woman."

Everything inside her went still, except for her pulse, which was pounding so loud the citizens of Yuccaville probably heard it. Grady had flooded her with compliments over the last month, especially after sex, but the L-word had not come forth prior to this moment.

"Come again?" she said.

"You heard me, Veronica," he said to the roof.

Yeah, but why would he … "Is this a new interrogation tactic, Sheriff?"

"Christ!" He glared at her. "You're so damned hard-headed

sometimes. Contrary to what you seem to believe, there's a plain old guy underneath my badge and uniform, and he's over the moon about you."

Her heart soared for a moment, but then reality lassoed it and hauled it back to earth. "You shouldn't love me. I'm going to mess up your perfect life."

He growled and focused back on the hardtop. "Too late. I already do, so let's move on to the next point—what can we do to keep you from being the FBI's fall guy?"

She grimaced. "You're not going to like the answer Mississippi gave me to that question."

"Try me anyway."

"We have to capture the diamond killer alive. His confession could clear my name."

Grady snorted. "Oh, good. I thought it was going to be something difficult. I'm glad to hear it's merely capturing an extremely violent serial killer by hand. Maybe we can use licorice ropes to string him up."

She stared at his lined profile for several beats before giggling. "Licorice ropes, really?"

His gaze shifted to her, one eyebrow raised. "Would you rather I use homemade dandelion-stem handcuffs?"

She giggled harder. He watched her, his face relaxing into a smile. He reached out and caught her hand, resting it on his chest.

When she quieted, his expression sobered, too.

"I'm fucked, Grady," she whispered.

"*We* are fucked, Veronica, but together we stand a better chance than you alone."

She slid her fingers inside the buttons on his shirt, making contact with his warm skin. "I don't want to drag you down with me."

"Wherever you go, baby, I'm following. Get used to that idea."

"With your lights flashing?"

"Whatever it takes." He hit her with a hard look. "But you have to stop hiding shit from me."

She sighed, thinking of her many secrets, some awkward,

others full-on humiliating. "But your career is—"

"My career isn't who I am." His palm covered hers, stilling her fingers. "Being a sheriff is only a role."

"Yeah, but it's an important role. People need you."

"Still, it's just a role. I have other roles, too."

"Like what?"

He shrugged. "Muscle car aficionado."

Grady and Butch and Mac made a tight trio on that one. "What else?"

"Nephew of the leader of an old-lady library gang."

She grinned about Aunt Millie, Ronnie's spunky partner in crime. "What else?"

"World's best lover." He wiggled his eyebrows at her.

She wiggled her eyebrows back. "Best? I'm not sure about that last one. You might have to prove it to me."

His eyelids lowered, his focus dipping to her mouth. "Climb over here, sassy woman."

"This cab is a little tight for us. Wouldn't you rather go home to your bed?"

"We'll manage. Besides, you parked in my future master bedroom. We'll have to improvise without the walls and mattress."

Ronnie shut off the engine. She scrambled over the gearshift, hitting her shoulder on the passenger-side window before kneeling astride him.

He grabbed her hips, pulling her even closer. "There. That's better."

She unbuttoned her flannel jacket. "Now what?"

His hands moved northward. "Your bra is in the way."

"So are my pants." She moved over him, her knee bumping the door panel. "And yours."

"We'll get to those in a bit." He pulled her down, kissing her while he popped the clasp on her bra. "I've been thinking," he whispered against her cheek as his palms explored her chest.

She shifted her hips a little, her boot heel getting caught on the Jeep's dashboard handle for a second. "About what?"

"Licking the beer off your skin." He hauled her along his body so he could do just that.

She shivered at the heat of his mouth on her cool flesh. "I like your tongue, but ... ohh God, Grady. Yes." She pressed against him, banging her elbow on the doorjamb.

"But what?" he said and then did that thing where he flicked, circled, and sucked until she moaned.

The toe of her boot got lodged somehow under the dash. She shifted to maneuver it free. "But this cab is too small for us."

He reached down and unbuttoned her jeans. "I thought you Morgan girls liked to be daring and adventurous."

"We do, but ..." She paused as he slid his hand down inside of her pants, her breath fluttery at his touch. "But it's Claire's Jeep. She'll be pissed if we have sex in here."

"I don't care about your sister's feelings at the moment." He growled at the thin barrier her underwear posed. "Why are you wearing underwear tonight?"

Ha! If only he knew how much that subject was the talk of the town these days. She frowned. Wait, maybe it was better he didn't know.

She tried to lift up to make more room for his hand and hit her head on the roof. "Hold on. Just let me ... there."

He groaned in her ear as his fingers hit pay dirt.

Her left hip started to cramp, but she breathed through the slight pain, not wanting him to stop. She bent down and slid her teeth over his earlobe.

"Veronica?" He turned his head to give her better access as she nibbled her way down his neck.

Her toes tingled from lack of blood flow. "What?"

"Say it." His fingers worked their magic.

Say what? It was hard to think in this damned sardine can. "I want you inside of me."

"That's not what I meant."

There was no time for chatter right now, damn it. Her hip cramp was growing into a full-on charley horse. She shifted, trying to ease it back down to an ache. "Uhhh, you're the world's best lover."

He chuckled. "Nice try, but no. And next time try to pretend you're not reading your lines."

Easy for him to say. All he had to do was lie back while she contorted over him.

He drew her mouth down for a kiss, lacing his fingers through her hair as he caressed her tongue with his. He tasted a little like beer and a lot like Grady, savory as hell with a heart-pounding dollop of virile. She moaned into his mouth, her body humming faster and faster under his touch. Oh, sweet mother of pearl, she was so close to …

Pain zapped hot and sharp from her hip down to her knee. Stupid charley horse! She tried to adjust to relieve the cramp but her knee got jammed between the seat and door.

She pulled away from his mouth with a yowl, tugged his hand out of her pants, and shoved open the Jeep door, stumbling outside into the cold.

"Son of a billy goat troll!" she yelled at the wind and walked in a circle, stretching her hip while massaging away the pain. "That Jeep is too damned tight for us to screw around in," she told Grady when he joined her wearing a big grin on his face.

"Come here, hot mess." He wrapped her in his coat and rubbed her hip for her.

She looked up at him. "So this is your future bedroom."

"Actually, we're now standing in the master bath."

She wrapped her arms around his neck, leaning into him as he continued to work out her kinks. "Do you want to take a shower with me, big boy?"

"Hell no. It's too cold here right now."

She kissed his chin. "I love you, too, Sheriff Hardass."

He stopped massaging, his eyes holding hers. "Okay, you win. We can pretend we're in the shower while we have sex out here, but I'm keeping my coat on the whole time."

His phone rang while she was unbuttoning his jeans.

She stilled. "You want to answer that?"

"No, I'd rather have freezing cold sex with you."

The phone kept ringing.

"Yeah, but it's like two o'clock in the morning." Who would be calling him this late?

He tipped her chin up, closing in on her mouth. "It will go to voicemail."

She pulled back. "What if it's an emergency?"

He sighed. "Fine, spoilsport." He pulled out his phone and frowned at the number. "It's work. One of my deputies."

"Take it."

He answered with, "Harrison here."

Ronnie leaned closer, trying to listen in and hearing the sound of sirens coming through the line.

"Is he alive?" he asked.

She frowned at the pain she saw pass over Grady's face.

"Okay, I'm about fifteen minutes out. Keep me posted." He hung up. "We gotta go."

"What's wrong?"

"I think the diamond killer has struck again."

She gasped. "What? Who did he …" She couldn't finish. She gulped. "Please, not …"

He took her by the shoulders, steadying her. "Your family is safe. The killer moved on to the next one in line."

"What do you mean? I thought Claire and I were next."

"You forgot about someone."

She thought for a moment, going down the line from the start of the hunt.

Oh no!

"The tow truck driver who removed the camper from the RV park?" At his nod, she clutched his coat. "Not Tank."

He nodded again, his expression grim. "Come on, we'll take my pickup."

Chapter Thirteen

Monday, New Year's Eve—Too Damned Early O'clock

*Y*ou mess with my head," Coop whispered, his breath tickling her ear as he leaned in close.

Natalie shivered. "Coop, stop." She pushed away from him.

The Purple Door Saloon throbbed around them, a loud pounding beat playing on the jukebox while faceless patrons talked and tipped back drinks at the bar and tables. Natalie and Coop had the pool table area in back to themselves, the lighting even more shadowed than usual tonight, far too intimate for Natalie's common sense to see clearly.

She walked around the pool table, using it as a barrier between them. "Is it my turn?"

"Yes." He leaned his hip against the table, chalking up his pool cue as he undressed her with his eyes. His T-shirt hugged his chest, his forearm muscles rippling as he turned the chalk back and forth in slow motion.

She dragged her gaze away from the long and lean temptation across the table and tried to make sense of the arrangement of the pool balls on the green felt. "Three ball in the corner pocket."

Before she could bend over to take the shot, he was behind her, brushing up against her. "All you have to do is look at me and my hands get clammy," he said, his words making her blood pulse in her fingertips.

She leaned back into him. His lips grazed the side of her neck as his hand trailed down her bare arms. Goose bumps spread in the wake of his touch.

She shouldn't be letting him touch her. She needed to make him stop, but he felt too good.

The song on the jukebox grew louder, the beat pounding, blocking out the sound of everyone in the bar except for Coop and his heated whispers.

"You're powerful trouble," he said.

Boom, boom, boom.

"Just friends, law dog," she reminded him over her shoulder.

"Take off your shirt," he ordered, his fingers sliding under the hem of her camisole.

Boom! Boom! Boom!

The beat was louder now, making her whole body throb. Or maybe it was Coop's fingers sliding up her ribcage that had her heart pounding. Or the way he was licking the shell of her ear.

"I'm losing control," he said and growled in her other ear.

Maybe just one kiss.

He tipped her head back, leaned in close, and barked at her.

BOOM! BOOM! BOOM! BOOM!

Natalie jerked awake, her heart hammering along with whoever was knocking on the bedroom door in Gramps's Winnebago.

Another bark sounded next to her. Henry nudged her arm with his cold nose and then licked her palm, which was coated with dog slobber.

She grimaced and wiped the slobber off on her camisole. Claire had warned her about letting Gramps's dog sleep in the bed with her. Next time she went to bed lonely, she'd … her dream version of Coop popped into her head … well, she'd just go to bed lonely.

"Natalie!" Kate called from the other side of the bedroom door, her voice higher than normal. "If you don't unlock this freaking door I'm going to chop it down."

Her and what ax? Kate always closed her eyes when swinging any weapons—bats, shovels, broomsticks. She'd be lucky to hit the broad side of a barn most days.

"Calm down, gangster!" Natalie grumbled, scrambling out from under the covers. Blinking the sleep out of her eyes, she unlocked the door and yanked it open. "Sheesh, Kate. Where's the damned fire?"

Henry raced past Kate and headed for the door.

"I'll tell you in a bit." Kate rushed into the room, sniffing. "Gross. It smells like dog in here. You shouldn't sleep with Henry if you're going to close the bedroom door. His bladder can only hold so much for so long, you know." She opened the built-in dresser drawer and grabbed some clothes.

Natalie waved her off about the dang dog.

"I'm going to let Henry out. Hurry up and get dressed," Kate said. She opened the closet and pulled out a black bag before heading back out toward the front of the RV.

"What time is it?" Natalie hollered, peering out the bedroom window at the dark sky.

"Early," Kate said from out front. "Henry, come back here. You need a leash." Natalie heard the steps creak and then the door slam.

Too damned early according to Natalie's foggy brain, especially after a late night helping Kate and Butch close and clean up the bar. And why was Kate here already? Didn't she know pregnant women needed a lot of rest, especially after whooping it up in a barroom brawl?

Natalie grabbed a pair of jeans, replaying the madness from the night before as she dressed ...

She'd been refilling the toilet paper in the ladies' restroom, trying to jimmy open the stuck lock on the toilet paper holder, when the hooting and howling had started. Figuring someone had turned the television channel to a local game, she popped the lock, replenished the toilet paper supply, and washed her hands before heading out to pick up her order at the bar.

A spray of water shot through the air above a crowd hovering around the bar.

She frowned and pushed through the front of the group to see what was going on. When she reached the front row, her eyeballs did one of those cartoon popping-out of-her-head expressions—at least they did in her mind.

John Wayne would have been proud of Kate. Four months pregnant and she still dodged Butch's attempts to corral her like a wild mustang. Poor Grady was taking the brunt of Kate's dousing as he tried to secure his caterwauling ex-wife and stop her frenzied clawing at Kate.

Someone bumped into Natalie from behind, snapping her into action. She rushed the scene, trying to figure out how she could join in the fun. Before she could get a leg up on the bar, Coop grabbed her by the wrist and tugged her aside, holding tight when she tried to pull free.

"Stand down, bruiser," he shouted above the ruckus. "The sheriff and Butch don't need your help in the ring."

Elizabeth elbowed Grady in the breadbox and wiggled free, lunging at Kate again. "You could have fooled me."

They both ducked a stream of soda spray.

"Your family likes to stir up hell with a long spoon."

Natalie grinned. "We shot out of the womb roadhouse rowdy." Speaking of her posse, someone was missing. "Where's Ronnie?" She had to yell over the screams and cheers as Kate nailed Elizabeth in the chin with a blast of soda water.

"I think she left." Coop handed her a waitstaff apron. "She threw this at me and said something about being done with this shit." He pointed at the batwing doors. "She took off that way."

What?! "And you let her go?"

Coop shrugged. "I left my handcuffs at home."

She ran in back, but Ronnie was gone.

"Shit!" Natalie picked up a soaked work shirt from the floor. It smelled like beer. Returning to the front, she raced out the front door in time to catch sight of the Jeep's taillights. "Ronnie! Wait!" she shouted, her words disappearing into the dark desert night.

On the way back inside The Shaft, she held the door for Grady, who was carrying his kicking and screaming ex-wife out the door with Mississippi on his heels. "You're going home!" Grady said over Elizabeth's angry cries. "And if I see you back here again, I'm having Butch file a restraining order to keep you away, you hear me, Liz?"

Natalie didn't wait for Elizabeth's answer, closing the door behind her. Butch and Kate were nowhere to be found, but Coop and Gary the bartender were mopping up the pools of water on the bar with rags. Throughout the rest of the bar, conversation had returned to normal, life moving on as if catfights were normal on a Sunday evening in Jackrabbit Junction. Natalie grabbed an order pad and started making her rounds, returning to normal life along with everyone else.

… Blinking back to the present, Natalie slid her arms into a faded flannel shirt. Why was Kate in such a rush for her to get dressed, anyway? Did she need help at the bar? Hadn't Butch said last night that he wasn't opening The Shaft until late afternoon since it was New Year's Eve? Natalie figured the late start would give her plenty of time to set piers for the back porch before Claire returned.

She walked out front to grab her work boots. Kate was back, pouring yesterday's coffee dregs into a mug. "Who put you in charge of wakeup crew this morning?" Natalie asked. She took the cup of coffee Kate offered with a grimace. "And why must I drink my coffee cold?"

"Because we're going to Yuccaville and I need you firing on all plugs."

"You mean cylinders. Plugs *spark*, that's why they're called 'spark plugs.' "

Kate rolled her eyes. "Whatever, Claire Jr."

"Officially, I'm older than Claire." Natalie took a gulp of the day-old coffee, grimacing at the stale bitterness. "Why am I going to Yuccaville? I have a porch to build."

"Ruby's porch can wait." Kate tossed Natalie her coat. "We have a code red situation."

Code red, huh? Natalie squinted at Kate. "Says the crazy soda-gunslinger."

Kate stuck her index finger in Natalie's face. "Don't call me crazy."

"Okay, okay." She knocked Kate's finger away. "But if this is some kind of retaliation mission to hunt down Elizabeth and shave her head, I'm dragging anchor. I think you won the most rounds in the fight last night and should just wear your championship belt with pride as you walk away from the ring."

"It's not a retaliation mission. More like one of those murder mystery parties with a twist. Finish your coffee. The clock is ticking."

A twist of what? Kate the sleuth was almost as nerve-wracking as Kate the brawler. As much as Natalie would rather have headed to the General Store for a quick breakfast and then get to work on the porch, she couldn't let Kate go to Yuccaville alone. There were too many opportunities for the whack-a-loon to wind up behind bars again.

"Instead of playing Nancy Drew, maybe you could take up knitting." Natalie swallowed the last of the coffee. No, wait—those knitting needles could be deadly in a mentally unstable, pregnant woman's hands. "On second thought, have you considered sculpting with Play-Doh? I bet you could make some amazing Michelangelo re-creations."

"If I take up any hobby, it's going to be knife throwing."

Natalie started to laugh, but then realized Kate was serious. The sound that came out of her mouth was more like a gasping hiccup. "Are you planning to join the circus or something?"

"Or something," Kate answered with a wink. Or was that an eye twitch?

Bananapants! "Does Butch know you're loose?"

"I left him chained to the bed. Come on, we have Prickly Pear Posse work to do." She held open the door, motioning for Natalie to hurry up.

Damn it, where was Ronnie? And how come Butch hadn't locked Kate in the basement after last night's wet-n-wild floorshow?

After grabbing her phone and wallet from the counter, along with the spare key, Natalie followed Kate outside into the cold morning. The sun was peeking above the Tres Dedos Mountains to the east—at least Natalie thought that was the name Mac had called them the other day.

She watched Kate lock the Winnebago door and pocket the key before grabbing Henry's leash and tugging on the dog to follow her.

"Hold up!" Natalie checked her pocket and the hiding spot under the wheel well. Both keys were still there. "Where'd you get that key to Gramps's Winnebago? I thought there were only two."

"That's not important." Kate grabbed Natalie by the wrist and dragged her over to the gravel drive. "We have a job to do."

Natalie yawned. "What's the damned rush and who put you in charge of playing drill instructor?"

"I'll explain when we're safe from eavesdroppers."

What eavesdroppers? The RVs all around them were dark. Hell, the birds were just stumbling out of their nests, the sleep still blurring their eyes.

As they passed the restroom building, a copper-haired dame with long colt-like legs rushed out of the men's bathroom door wearing nothing but a short satin robe and high-heeled slippers.

A little cold for lingerie this morning, wasn't it? Natalie smiled and nodded. The poor woman must have forgotten her reading glasses along with her flannel pajamas.

Seconds later, the men's room door opened again. Old Man Harvey stepped out, wearing jeans, yellow suspenders over his half-tucked in shirt, and a randy grin.

"Mornin', sidewinders," he said. "What has your tails shakin' this early?"

"Harvey!" Natalie slid to a stop, glancing back to make sure the hubba-hubba was out of earshot. "What were you doing in there?"

He walked over to her. "Givin' sexy Red some guitar lessons on the sly." He wiggled his bushy eyebrows.

Natalie scowled at him. "Jeez! In a public bathroom?"

Kate waited a few feet ahead of them. "What does that mean?"

"I'll tell you later." Natalie frowned at the horny old goat. "What were you thinking?"

"I was enjoyin' the music." He wrapped his thumbs in his suspenders and rocked back on his heels. "Red plays one hell of a flute solo."

"I thought you said guitar lessons," Kate said.

Natalie groaned. "This is a family-friendly campground. Next time, enjoy your horizontal polka dancing in the privacy of your fifth wheel."

"Polka is more fun when you're vertical, although my left knee will go on me if I'm not careful. Besides, I'm banned from my own barracks."

"By whom?"

"Coop said he'd shoot me if I had hip relations in the camper this week."

"And you believed him?"

"The boy is spoonin' with his Colt .45 on the pullout couch. There's no sneakin' past that law dog when he's guardin' the door."

Lucky Coop. Better a Colt .45 than Gramps's slobbery dog. Then again, squeezing Henry in her sleep wouldn't leave her with a bullet hole.

"Natalie, we have to go." Kate grabbed Natalie's elbow, propelling her along.

Harvey rushed along with them toward the General Store. "What's all the hustle and bustle about this mornin'? You two tryin' to catch yesterday?"

Natalie thumbed in her cousin's direction. "Kate has some nutty wild hair."

"Don't call me crazy!" Kate snapped.

"Officially, I didn't say the C-word, so can it, Star-Kist." She glanced at Harvey. "What are you and Coop planning to do today?" She tried to sound curious instead of obsessed, pretending the image of Coop sprawled out on the couch bed wasn't burnt into her brain now.

What was he sleeping in these days, anyway? Months ago, Coop had been "babysitting" Violet when she'd been put on his version of house arrest. Natalie had stayed over one night, too, finding him in the kitchen the next morning in nothing but a pair of gray sweatpants and bare skin. Well, bare under all of his scars. Coop seemed to be a magnet for sharp and pointy weapons, along with bullets.

Harvey shrugged. "Well, bein' it's New Year's Eve, I'm thinkin' on headin' into town to get some liquor to celebrate, maybe checkin' on Red later to see if she wants to blow my horn." He snickered at her loud groan. "What about you?"

"Since Kate here is dragging me to Yuccaville at this ungodly hour for some mysterious reason, I'm thinking I might be spending the day in jail *again*."

"We are not going to end up in jail," Kate said. "Not this time." She looked away and mumbled something.

"Did you just add 'I hope' to the end of that?"

"Of course not."

"Her fingers are crossed," Harvey pointed out with a laugh.

"Ya want some help not ending up in jail? I could use a ride to the liquor store."

Good idea, Natalie thought. If Harvey were with them, she'd have bait to lure Coop to come spring them again.

"You're on. You need to grab anything back at the camper?"

"Let's see. Spectacles, testicles, wallet, watch," he chanted as he patted his forehead, then pants zipper, and then the right side of his chest and left. When he finished his routine, he nodded. "I'm ready to go to town."

"It sounds like you already did back in the bathroom," Kate said, pulling her car keys from her pocket.

"I thought you didn't know what guitar lessons were," Natalie said.

"I didn't, but your friend's zipper is unzipped," she shot back. "And there's lipstick on his chin."

Harvey let out a hoot, tugging up his zipper before wiping off his face. "I like Kate. She's a spunky monkey."

"You don't know the half of it." Natalie looked at her cousin. "You mind more company?"

"Nope. We could use a lookout."

Natalie frowned. That didn't bode well. "For what?"

"You'll see soon enough."

As they neared the General Store, Henry tugged on the leash until Kate let him go free. The beagle raced up onto the porch, ducking inside the doggie door Gramps had installed while Natalie was home in South Dakota.

"Hold up there, Crazy Kate," Chester called from the porch swing.

Kate pointed her car keys at him, switching to rabid dog mode in a blink. "Call me that again, Chester, and I'll castrate you with a butter knife!"

"Whoa there, pelvis puncher." He raised his arms in defense. "I apologize, Porn Star. I forgot about your 'nut' allergy."

Harvey leaned closer to Natalie. "Your cousin's banjo seems to be strung a little tight this mornin'."

"Yeah. She's thinking about joining the circus."

"Really? Sword swallowin'?"

"Knife throwing."

Harvey winced. "Remind me to wear my metal codpiece around her."

Natalie raised one eyebrow. "You have a metal codpiece?"

He nodded once. "Well, I should smile."

She actually did smile. "What do you wear it with?"

"My birthday suit. It makes for fun knock-knock games with the ladies."

Before Natalie could groan, Kate ordered, "Let's go, you two. In the car. Now!"

"She's bossy, too," Harvey said, grinning at Natalie. "I have a weakness for bossy women."

"You have a weakness for women, period." She pulled open the passenger-side door.

"Where you off to in such a rush?" Chester asked, hurrying down the porch steps.

"Yuccaville," Kate said, climbing inside.

Chester blocked her door from shutting. "You thinking of serving more jail time?"

Kate glared up at him. "What if I am?"

Natalie buckled her seat belt. "Kate, I don't have time to sit in jail today."

"We're goin' to the hoosegow for New Year's Eve," Harvey sang from the backseat, rubbing his hands together. "Sounds like I'll be startin' the new year down where the pancake tree grows beside the honey pond."

Natalie frowned back at Harvey. "We are *not* going to jail." She turned back to Kate. "Are we?"

"That depends."

"On what?" Chester asked, still standing between Kate and the door handle.

"If we get caught."

Chester scowled into the morning sunshine, which now lit the desert in a golden glow. "Well, if you're going to do some troublemaking, I'm coming along." He smirked. "Jail sounds more fun than the lovefest going on inside."

What was going on in the house? Natalie peered out the windshield at the General Store. She hoped Aunt Deborah and Manny were keeping their love romps to their camper, because she had a deck to build today and didn't feel like listening to their love cooing again.

"If you're coming along, Chester, get your ass in back. We need to move this train out of the station." Kate shoved him out of the way and pulled her door closed. She waited for Chester to crawl in behind her before shifting into gear.

After Natalie introduced Chester and Harvey, she turned back to Kate. "Okay, Ms. Mysterious, now that you have us all captive, what in the hell is going on?"

Kate shot Natalie a worried look. "You remember Tank from the other night?"

"Who's Tank?" Harvey butted in.

"A giant ex-college football player who runs a tow truck service in Yuccaville," Kate told him.

"What about Tank?" Natalie asked, remembering Tank well. A good-looking man of his size with a smile to match was hard to forget.

"Ronnie called me early this morning." Kate hesitated.

Natalie huffed. "From where? A beach in South America?"

Last she'd heard, Kate's phone tracking device seemed to have worked. Ronnie was sitting in the desert somewhere between Jackrabbit Junction and Yuccaville—at least her cell phone was. Natalie hadn't heard back from anyone if Grady had actually found Ronnie or Claire's Jeep. She'd tossed and turned in bed for a bit, cursing Ronnie for driving off one minute and making her worry the next. Eventually, exhaustion had stepped in and shut her down.

"She called from the hospital in Yuccaville," Kate said, the lines on her forehead deepening. "The diamond killer blindsided Tank last night."

"Oh, God," Natalie whispered.

It was one thing to hear about a murder happening far away to someone she didn't know. But she'd served Tank a double bacon burger and mozzarella-topped sliced tomatoes on the side, and he'd had her hold the caramelized onions because they always gave him a "whoppin' case of heartburn." Tank wasn't just another faceless victim. Finally, the weight of the danger Ronnie and Claire were in plopped down on her chest.

"Did she say diamond *killer*?" Natalie heard Harvey ask Chester.

"Yep. Ronnie and Claire have managed to get themselves into a bit of a pickle over somebody else's stolen diamonds."

"A bit?" Natalie laughed without humor. "Why Tank?"

Kate stopped at the U.S. Route 191 junction. To their left, Butch's red pickup sat in the parking lot of The Shaft. Kate touched the window, a small smile forming on her lips for a moment. Then it faded.

She turned toward Yuccaville and then hit the gas. "The camper where Ronnie and Claire found the diamonds sat in Tank's tow yard until the investigation wrapped up and the feds took it away. The killer must have thought Tank might have found and stashed the diamonds, so he was next on the hit list."

Natalie was afraid to hear Kate's answer to her next question, but she asked anyway. "Is Tank okay?"

The killer hadn't left anyone alive to date, but there was always a chance.

Kate took too damned long to answer.

"Kate!" Natalie growled. "Enough with the pregnant pause."

"I can't help it. I am pregnant. And no, Tank's not okay. Now if you want to know if he's alive, then yes, he is. At the moment, anyway. He's in critical condition, but he's strong and the doctors are hopeful."

Natalie blew out a breath, relief trickling through her limbs. If Tank lived, maybe he could help them with identifying the killer before he struck again. "What happened?"

Kate turned down the heat, directing the vents toward the back seat. "When Ronnie called this morning, I was still half asleep, but I'll tell you what I can remember. Keep in mind that Ronnie rattled off the quick and dirty version, hurrying because Grady wanted her to hang up so he could take her somewhere safe where she could sleep while he continued his investigation."

It was times like this that having a law dog for a boyfriend paid off. Would it be the same for Natalie with Coop?

"Grady Harrison is the sheriff of the county," Chester explained to Harvey in the back. "He's also mattress dancing with Ronnie, Kate's sister."

"The tango or foxtrot?" Harvey shot back.

"That probably depends if Ronnie remembers to wear underwear or not," Chester said, snorting with laughter.

"Chester," Natalie scolded.

"What? Everyone knows she's allergic to underwear."

Harvey snickered. "I'd like to meet Ronnie. How old is this cousin?" he asked Natalie.

"Too young for you, horny toad." She looked back at Kate. "Did Ronnie tell you anything else about Tank and how the attack happened?"

She nodded. "Tank was working late last night, wrapping up some paperwork since New Year's Eve tends to be one of his busiest nights of the year. He told the officers who were the first to show up on scene that he heard something crash out behind where he stores towed vehicles. Said it sounded like someone broke a windshield. When he went out back to investigate, someone shot him in the neck with a tranquilizer dart. He pulled it out, but before he could get back to the safety of the office, he passed out."

"That'd be like taking down a rhino," Chester said.

"How do you know Tank?" Natalie asked Chester.

"He's a card-carrying member at Dirty Gerties. Cherry introduced us a couple of years ago. I took my old Ford pickup to him once when she was belching smoke. He fixed her up real quick and only charged me half price because I'm Cherry's friend."

"When Tank woke up," Kate continued, "he'd been tied to the lifting thingamajig in his garage."

"The hydraulic hoist?" Natalie asked.

"Does that lift up the cars?"

"Yeah."

"Then, yes, that thing. The killer had tied Tank's wrists far apart and raised the lift high, so that Tank's toes were barely touching the floor."

"Smart move," Harvey said. "Hard to get any leverage when yer spread out like that, even for a big fella."

"Then what?" Natalie pressed Kate.

Kate sniffed, swiping at her nose. "The killer started hitting

Tank with a hose. Grady told Ronnie it had been filled with sand. The killer asked where the diamonds were, but Tank had no idea, of course. The poor guy was caught in the middle of this mess, like all of the other victims before him." A muscle in Kate's jaw twitched. "Tank had no idea how many hits he took from the bastard, but Ronnie said she heard the ER doctor tell Grady that Tank's back looked like a Jackson Pollock abstract painting."

Natalie sucked in air between her teeth. "Christ."

"How did Tank get away?" Chester asked. "The bastard hasn't let anyone else live."

"He underestimated Tank," Kate said. "Grady told Ronnie that the hoist thingie had been leaking hydraulic fluid off and on for a while out of a lift hose."

She slowed as they neared the Yuccaville city limits.

"In the midst of torturing Tank, the killer's phone rang. When he stepped outside to take the call, Tank wiggled the leaky hose so that hydraulic fluid ran down the rope tying his wrist, making his skin slippery. By the time the killer returned, Tank had both hands free and was in the process of untying his ankles."

"Then what?" Natalie asked.

"The killer pulled out a gun and shot at Tank as he turned to run."

"Holy shit."

"Just shot *at* Tank?" Harvey asked. "Or actually put a bullet in him?"

"He shot Tank in the back."

"Damn. Beaten and shot."

"But that didn't stop Tank."

"I have a feelin' he was given that name fer good reason," Harvey said.

"They should have called him Sherman," Chester said.

"Tank grabbed some tool and threw it at the killer," Kate continued.

"A hammer?" Natalie asked.

"More likely to have been a wrench in a garage like his," Chester said.

"It doesn't matter," Kate said in a growly voice. "Do you

want to hear the rest of the story or not?"

Natalie crossed her arms. "Go on."

"Tank threw an unspecified tool and knocked the gun out of the killer's hand. It landed under a worktable. The killer bent over, trying to grab the gun. At that moment, Tank got up and charged, slamming him into the workbench covered with tools." She shot Natalie a frown. "All sorts of tools that will not be named."

Natalie scoffed and then waved for Kate to keep going.

"Tank tried to reach the gun, but the killer pulled a knife and stabbed Tank in the back of the leg."

Son of a bitch! Poor Tank—beaten, shot, *and* stabbed.

"By the time Tank recovered and got the gun, the killer had run off into the darkness. Tank shot off a few rounds, but he doesn't know if he hit the guy at all."

Harvey grunted. "It's hard to hit a runnin' target under the noonday sun, let alone with a bullet in yer back and a knife wound in yer leg."

"Unless you have a shotgun full of buckshot," Chester said.

"Someone down the street heard the gunshots and called the cops," Kate said. "When the Yuccaville police showed up, they found Tank slouched in his office chair. He'd dragged himself inside and locked the door, intending to call the police only to find out that his phone lines had been sliced."

The killer was very thorough—except for realizing the hoist had a hydraulic fluid leak.

"Ronnie said she heard Tank had bled out quite a bit and was going in and out of consciousness when they hauled him away in the ambulance. By the time Grady and she arrived at the ER, Tank had been stabilized enough to be able to fly him to Phoenix. Grady was able to get a few minutes with Tank before they took off. Last Ronnie knew, Tank lived through the flight and was headed to surgery to remove that bullet. It was lodged too close to his spine, requiring a specialized surgeon. There's a risk of partial paralysis from the waist down if they aren't careful when they dig it out."

Natalie shivered even though the car was plenty warm. "The killer is still in Yuccaville." She stared out at the buildings and vehicles as they cruised into town, wondering where the son of a bitch was hiding.

"Did Tank get a look at the killer?" Chester asked.

"Yes, but the guy was wearing a mask the whole time." She grimaced at Chester in the rearview mirror. "Get this. It was a mask of John Denver."

"The country singer?" Harvey asked.

Kate nodded. "Here's something even creepier. Tank told the cops that the killer kept whistling 'Sunshine on My Shoulders' while he was beating Tank with the hose."

"Hmmm," Harvey said. "I've always preferred 'Thank God I'm a Country Boy,' myself."

"Me, too," Chester said. "But that would be harder to whistle."

"Yeah. I'd want to clap, too, or at least smack my knee."

Chester grunted in agreement. "Probably makes it hard to torture someone when you're happy clapping."

Natalie scowled at Chester.

"What? It's important to analyze personality traits when trying to find a killer. We need to know if he's calculating or just plain crazy, like Kate."

Kate reached behind her, trying to pinch Chester's leg as she swerved across the centerline.

Natalie grabbed the wheel. "Kate, knock it off." When Kate turned back forward, Natalie leaned back and pinched Chester's leg herself.

"What's that for?" He rubbed where she'd pinched.

"Don't call her crazy!"

Harvey grinned. "Yer cousin reminds me of Sparky—all pinches and pokes."

"Sparky" was his nickname for Violet up in Deadwood. And he was right, except that Violet's brain wasn't on leave due to temporary insanity.

"Speaking of pokes," Chester said, "how about we swing by Dirty Gerties before heading home."

"Isn't it a little early for a strip club?" Natalie asked.

"It's never too early for a strip club," Harvey said. "Or a poke."

Chester raised an invisible glass in a toast. "Where have you been all of my life, Willis Harvey?"

"Chasin' skirts."

"Dear Lord," Kate said. "You've managed to clone Chester."

"Who knew there were two?" Natalie settled back in her seat, ducking a little as Kate drove by Grady's office. "So, Ronnie is somewhere tucked away and Claire is still in Tucson. I guess for the moment, we can breathe easy."

"Maybe," Kate said.

"What do you mean, 'maybe'?" Chester asked.

"The killer is going to wait us out. The Prickly Pear Posse needs to take the offensive now."

Harvey leaned forward. "Did you just say prickly hair pus—"

"Prickly pear *posse*!" Natalie interrupted, emphasizing the last word. She squinted at Kate. "What do you mean, take the offensive? Where are you taking us this morning, Kate?"

"Well, for starters, Ronnie wanted me to drop off a fresh set of clothes at her current hideout and pick up Claire's Jeep keys."

"What about after that?"

Kate smiled—the wild-eyed version. Then she pulled what looked like a snub-nosed black and yellow pistol from her coat pocket. "The posse is going hunting."

Chapter Fourteen

Six hours later …

I leave this place for one damned day," Claire muttered as she strapped on her tool belt. "And my sisters go full-goose bozo on me."

Claire had woken up this morning to a slew of voicemails and text messages, most of them from Kate, none of them making much sense. When she'd texted Ronnie to get some answers, she'd gotten crickets. It wasn't until Butch called Mac an hour later to see if he could help behind the bar at The Shaft tonight that she'd been able to clear things up about Kate, Ronnie, and the diamond killer's latest victim.

Mac and she had wasted no time packing up and heading back to ground zero. Death threat or not, this was her family. He didn't question her need to return to the nest in spite of the dangers it posed.

"Kate is definitely flirting with the lunatic fringe these days," Natalie said. Her cowboy hat shielded her eyes from the noonday sun as she looked up from mixing a wheelbarrow full of cement. "Her common sense has a Gone Fishin' sign posted on the door. But Ronnie isn't cuckoo. Not yet, anyway."

"What do you call parking alone in the desert in the middle of the night when a killer is on the loose?"

"Unraveling at the seams."

"Six of one," Claire said with a shrug.

She took a moment to check out what her cousin had accomplished so far on the back deck project. Five of the twelve piers were already in the ground with the cement starting to cure.

Natalie had made good progress, along with her "helper."

Claire smirked. Detective Cooper sure didn't look like he was on vacation with the way he was shoveling away to make room for the eighth pier. Were those bullet holes in his T-shirt? Behind him, in the shade of a cottonwood tree, Chester and Cooper's uncle were tossing back beers and smoking cigars while enjoying the show.

"Who told you about Ronnie's adventures last night?" Natalie asked, setting aside the hoe she was using to stir.

"Butch called." Claire pulled on her gloves and stepped over to hold the concrete tube form in the hole while Natalie poured the cement into the hollow center.

When the wheelbarrow was empty, Natalie stood back with her hands on her hips. Her flannel shirt and jeans were torn, dusty, and splashed with cement. "So you heard about the scuffle between Kate and Grady's ex?"

A guffaw rang out from the hole digging crew. "That was no mere scuffle, Beals." Coop paused to look their way, leaning on the shovel. Sunlight glittered on the beads of sweat lining his forehead. "Assault charges could be filed on both of them." He lifted the hem of his T-shirt and used it to wipe his face.

She wasn't surprised one iota by Coop's comment. Kate seemed to live from one potential assault charge to the next these days. Claire was, however, a tad stunned by the number of scars visible on Coop's stomach and ribs. Snips and snails! Had someone rolled him up in barbed wire and left him out to dangle in the wind? If those scars and the holes in his T-shirt were anything to go by, he must have really crappy luck.

She looked toward Natalie. Her cousin was ogling the detective in plain sight. From Claire's vantage point, it appeared the walls of Natalie's sabbatical were crumbling all around her. She bumped Natalie's shoulder as she walked past, nudging her back to work before the girl openly drooled and looked the fool.

"Who drove my Jeep home?" Claire asked, picking up a forty-pound bag of dry concrete and lugging it over to the wheelbarrow.

"I did," Chester said, cracking open a can of beer. "And I don't think your sister was 'parking' alone out there in the middle of nowhere, if you get my gist."

Claire aimed a glare at him. "What do you mean?"

"When I climbed behind the wheel, the passenger seat was lying all the way back, there were boot scuffs on the dash, and handprints going every which way on your passenger-side window."

Harvey snickered. "Sounds like somebody was runnin' the bases in the passenger seat. Could ya tell if they hit a home run?"

"Nope, but it didn't smell like sex, only coconut, thanks to the air freshener."

"Oh jeez." Claire scowled at Natalie. "If Ronnie and Grady had sex in my Jeep I'm going to smother her with a pillow and save the diamond killer the trouble."

"You really think the sheriff of Cholla County would play back seat bingo in your Jeep?" Natalie asked.

"Make that front seat bingo," Chester corrected.

"Well, I should smile," Harvey said.

Chester hooted and toasted beers with Harvey.

" 'I should smile'? What does that even mean?" Claire asked the two clowns.

"Don't ask," Coop said, taking a swig of water.

"Did you tell Claire what happened this morning?" Chester asked Natalie.

"You've been sitting there on your keister since she walked outside. Have you heard me tell her?"

"Careful, Coop," Harvey called to his nephew. "Natalie's gettin' bucksnortin' mean as the day wears on. Get too close and she might tear you a new one."

Coop lowered the bottle of water, eyeing Natalie. "You think I should take the bull by the horns, Uncle Willis?"

"I'll take you by the horns," Natalie mumbled, turning away with pink cheeks. She sliced open the bag of concrete Claire had delivered and dumped it into the wheelbarrow.

"There's a whole lotta horniness going on around here," Chester said and elbowed Harvey. "We need to get in on some of it."

The two chuckleheads cackled and snorted.

Claire groaned. There were some things she hadn't missed

while she was in Tucson with Mac. The peanut gallery was one of them. Her mother was the other.

She walked over to the pile of gravel that had been delivered last week and started filling the other wheelbarrow with it. "What happened this morning?" she asked Natalie as she shoveled.

"Kate dragged me out of bed at the crack of dawn and made me go to Yuccaville with her."

"Us, too," Chester said.

"You two volunteered," Natalie reminded him.

"I was misinformed and told we were going on a liquor run," Harvey said.

"Did you or did you not come back with a big bottle of bourbon?"

Chester crushed his empty beer can. "It's the least Kate could do after shooting poor Harvey with her Taser gun."

Claire lowered the shovel. "She shot you?"

"Woo-wee, did she!" Harvey hooted. "I haven't felt so much juice flowin' through me since I spent a weekend in Reno with a workin' girl named Dr. Anesthesia."

"Don't you mean 'Anastasia'?" Natalie asked.

"Here we go," Coop said, jamming his shovel in the dirt.

"That mighta been her real name," Harvey said. "But when she was on the clock, she liked to play doctor and hook these little electrode doodads onto yer pointy parts to jumpstart ya into action, if ya know what I mean." He winked.

"Harvey," Natalie said, mixing a groan in with his name. "I swear, you should write a book about your past."

"Don't encourage him," Coop said.

Claire rolled the wheelbarrow of gravel past her cousin. "Why did Kate shoot Harvey? Was he poking fun at blondes?"

Kate's tolerance level for blonde jokes these days was hovering between Extremely Unstable and Downright Explosive.

"It was an accident," Chester said between cigar puffs.

"Kate was showing the boys her new Taser gun while we were sitting at a red light," Natalie explained. "When the light turned green, the jerk in the pickup behind us laid on his horn. Kate jumped, accidentally squeezing the trigger."

"Why did she have her Taser gun out in the first place?"

Claire dumped the gravel in the hole.

Natalie scoffed. "Because the light in her brain keeps shorting out."

"She wanted us to go hunting," Chester said.

"She did?" Harvey huffed. "I don't remember that."

"Well, she shot you right after she said it," Natalie told him, stirring water into the concrete mix.

"I remember talkin' 'bout Dirty Gerties and the tale about Tank," he said. "But then I have a scratch in my vinyl record and skip to the diner part."

Natalie shot Claire a worried glance. "You heard about Tank, right?"

Claire nodded, setting the concrete tube form in the hole. Kate's voicemails had been wordy on that subject.

"Where's Ronnie this afternoon?" The airwaves had been silent on her older sister's whereabouts.

"Last we knew, she was sleeping in the back office at The Mule Train Diner," Natalie said.

"Grady's sister's joint?"

Natalie nodded. "Grady didn't want her staying alone at his place while he helped with the investigation, and she was exhausted after being up all night."

"Poor Grady, he must be dead on his feet, too."

"Probably, but cops never sleep." Natalie's lips thinned. "Isn't that right, Coop?"

He didn't look up from digging. "Not unless we're given orders to get some bed rest."

"Or on vacation," Harvey added.

Natalie stopped stirring. "Which means you're not supposed to be out here digging holes, Mr. Tourist."

Coop grinned, still shoveling. "A man can only sit back and watch a woman struggle to do a job for so long."

Natalie laughed and gave him the bird. "I was not struggling, Johnny Law."

Claire thumbed in the direction of the cottonwood tree. "Those two don't seem to have a problem with sitting back."

"We're supervising," Chester said, puffing on his cigar.

"So, what exactly was Kate planning to do with her Taser

gun?" Claire added another splash of water to the concrete mix for Natalie. "Hunt down the killer and immobilize him for ten minutes?"

"I guess."

"Does she have some inside information the cops don't know about?"

"I don't know. Before Harvey recovered from being Tasered, she wanted to swing by Tank's tow yard."

"Did you?"

"No. We ate breakfast at The Mule Train Diner instead. The nurturer overruled the nutter in Kate. She felt bad about what she did to Harvey and took him out to breakfast to make up for it."

"And she bought me a bottle of bourbon at the liquor store." Harvey smiled at Natalie. "I like that girl. When she gets all lathered up, she reminds me of Sparky."

"Who's Sparky?" Claire asked.

"Violet. Harvey is her self-appointed bodyguard."

"Leave Sparky Parker out of this," Coop said. "I'm on vacation, remember?"

"Violet and Coop lock horns at nearly every turn," Natalie told Claire.

Claire chuckled. "That must make it interesting."

If Natalie's best friend and her boyfriend were constantly battling, whose side would Natalie take?

"What's that supposed to mean?" Natalie asked.

Claire just shrugged. "How was Fort Bowie?"

Natalie's cheeks darkened. "Interesting." She pointed at the wheelbarrow. "You dump, I'll smooth."

After the concrete was poured, Claire asked, "Interesting in a historical re-enactment sort of way?"

Such as a replay of that night in the alley behind the Purple Door Saloon?

Her cousin's gaze shifted to Coop for a second. "There were no re-enactments going on, just explanations about what happened long ago."

Oh, a lot of hot air then. "That sounds a little boring."

"Actually, it was nice. I enjoyed it."

Hmmmm. "So, are the *walls* still in place?" As in the sabbatical ones Natalie was hiding behind.

Natalie shot a frown in Coop's direction. "There's a bit of crumbling, but the foundations are still there."

"Bah," Claire whispered. "Like I said, boring."

Natalie wrinkled her upper lip in a mock snarl. "Go get me another bag of concrete, Jezebel."

The three of them finished the remaining piers over the next couple of hours, taking turns digging, shoveling, and stirring. They were taking a break in the shade next to Chester and Harvey when Claire's phone rang.

"It's Ronnie," she told the others and walked over next to the gravel pile to take the call. "Well, well, well," Claire said in the phone. "If it isn't the belle of the assassin's ball."

"Don't be jealous now, evil stepsister Drizella. I'll let you wear the glass slippers if it'll make you feel prettier." Ronnie's voice sounded husky. Sleepy maybe. "What are you doing?"

Claire harrumphed. "I'll tell you what I'm not doing—I'm not having sex in my Jeep, unlike you and the sheriff."

"We did not have sex in your stupid Jeep."

"Then why are there boot scuff marks on my dash and handprints all over my passenger window?"

There was a pause on the other end of the line. "Okay, Sherlock. We *tried* to have sex in your Jeep, but there wasn't enough room to pull it off."

"I could have told you that."

She and Mac had given it a whirl themselves one night on the back road near Ruby's Lucky Monk mine. It had been a bit like playing Twister during an earthquake, leaving both of them bruised and sore the next day.

"Next time, have sex in somebody else's vehicle, head cheerleader. It's bad enough I can still smell sour milk every now and then from the pie fiasco at Thanksgiving."

"Get over it, you big baby. Now, if you're done chewing on me, I need a ride home."

"Where's Grady?"

"Sleeping, I'm told, and I don't want to wake him, either. He was up all night and most of the morning."

Mac was sleeping, too. He'd worked late so that they could come back early today, not knowing at the time that they'd need to rush back here for reasons other than the New Year's Eve party at The Shaft.

"I'll send someone to come get you," Claire said. "Natalie and I have more work to do, and according to the message Mac got from Grady, you and I are not supposed to be alone together anywhere. It's too risky."

"He's worried," Ronnie said, her tone apologetic.

"So am I." Claire sat on the gravel pile, shifting until the stones didn't poke through her jeans. "Aren't you?"

Ronnie blew out a breath. "Yes and no."

"What do you mean 'and no'?"

"I'm tired of running."

"What about the stunt you pulled last night?"

"Who told you about that? Grady?" Ronnie asked.

"Kate texted me."

"Yeah, well, I sort of snapped when Elizabeth and Katie got into it, which was my fault. Katie was protecting me." The line went quiet for a moment, and then Ronnie added, "I think I'm screwing up everyone's life here."

"Shut up, Ronnie."

"I'm serious."

"So am I." Claire scooped up a handful of gravel, letting the rocks clatter back onto the pile. "I've said it before and I'll say it again, you and I and Kate are all in this together, come hell, deranged killers, bounty hunters, or Mom. Besides, I need you more than ever."

"Why's that?"

"Because Kate's brain is still taking a vacation in the Bermuda Triangle. She's our monkey and this is our circus."

Ronnie chuckled. "You know, when Butch first told us that Carter babies make women crazy, I didn't believe him. Not really. But we're only four months into this pregnancy, and our sister is swinging from chandeliers and throwing bananas at passersby on a daily basis now."

It couldn't get any worse, could it? Claire hoped not.

"Natalie said that Kate dragged her out of bed and drove her to Yuccaville this morning," Claire said. "She wanted to hunt down the killer. Kate was even carrying a Taser gun."

Ronnie swore under her breath. "How did Natalie stop her?"

"She didn't. Kate Tasered Harvey by accident."

"Harvey is Coop's uncle, right?"

"Yep. After Harvey recovered, Kate snapped back to normal."

"Lord love a duck! Butch needs to handcuff himself to her before she really hurts somebody."

"Handcuffs wouldn't hold her. Kate would dislocate her thumb and slip free." Claire scooped up another handful of gravel, looking over at where the others sat drinking and talking, sharing laughs. There was a time when Ronnie, Kate, and she were like that—no threats lingering over their heads every damned day. She missed those days. "I've been thinking, Ronnie."

"Uh oh."

"Kate is onto something."

"You mean by carrying a Taser gun?"

Claire dumped the handful of gravel. "I mean by going after the killer."

Silence filled the line. "That's probably a bad idea," Ronnie said in a low voice.

"I know."

Another pause came and went.

"But I like it." Ronnie sighed. "I'm so tired of being hunted. Ruby slammed a kitchen cupboard door the other morning and I nearly peed my pants."

Claire snorted. "I can't walk around this place without feeling like I'm being watched through the crosshairs of a sniper's rifle."

"Going on the hunt will be dangerous," Ronnie said.

"Yep." Claire picked up a piece of gravel with quartz in it, turning it so it sparkled in the sunlight. "One of us could get hurt, maybe even killed."

"How is that different than the position we're in now?"

Ronnie was right. Better to go down shooting than running away with her tail between her legs.

Claire tossed the piece of gravel into the air, catching it as it came back down. "Mac and Grady aren't going to like this idea at all."

"They're putting themselves in the line of fire for us and I don't like that." Ronnie groaned. "I feel so guilty about Tank, and the others who've lost their lives. This is my fault, Claire. I'm the one who kept the mules' diamonds. What in the fuck was I thinking?"

"You kept them, but I was the one who found them and showed them to you. Like I said before, we're in this together."

Ronnie sniffed. "Okay, but we can't let Katie and Natalie get in the middle of this, posse rules be damned."

"I agree."

"So what now?"

"We get your ass home. Tonight, we'll help at The Shaft and bring in the New Year like normal. Tomorrow, when we sober up, we turn the tables and start hunting the hunter."

* * *

Ronnie said good-bye to her sister and pocketed her cell phone. She leaned back on the couch where she'd crashed after spending most of the night at the hospital with Grady as bits and pieces of Tank's story came together.

Afternoon sunshine made the small frosted window opposite her glow, bathing the office in a warm light. Grady's sister was kind enough to let Ronnie take over her office for the morning. The smell of baked bread had made her dreams happy instead of terror-filled. Pharmaceutical companies should take note—instead of sleeping pills, create air fresheners in scents of baking sourdough and whole wheat.

She looked around the room, trying to make connections between the décor and Grady's sister, Penelope. Although, he said, she preferred to go by the name "Penny."

Ronnie had expected the mule knickknacks and wall art in the diner to extend to Penny's office, but instead the room was filled with framed pictures of the Sonoran Desert. She walked over to a trio of cholla cacti pictures next to the door—diamond, teddy-bear, and chain-fruit cacti. The photographer had used a magnifying lens, picking up details on the cacti's spines and flesh, including a tiny beetle clinging to the tip of one of the sharp needles.

Ronnie smirked, feeling like the beetle at the moment. Life was nothing but a series of sharp points. The risk of her and her loved ones being impaled grew greater each day. Even now, she was putting Penny's life at risk just by being here.

Claire was right. It was time to take control of her life, one hunter at a time. She stared down at her palms, wondering if she could kill someone if the situation required it.

Months ago, Ronnie had taken on a bounty hunter in the parking lot at The Shaft, but there'd been no intent to kill then, only disable. This could be different, even if they intended to maim. Going head to head with a serial killer could end in a kill-or-be-killed scenario, FBI bullshit be damned. Could she pull the trigger if it came down to it?

She didn't doubt Claire could kill when backed into a corner. Her track record was rock solid.

Claire had taken on Joe's first wife and then that lying slickster who'd come looking for one of Joe's treasures. Both times she'd come out on top. Ronnie just hoped she could be as brave as Claire if the time came.

Someone knocked softly on the office door.

"Come in," Ronnie called.

Grady's sister stepped inside the office, bringing in the smell of pan-fried meat and potatoes with her. She closed the door behind her.

"How are you doing?" Penny asked, crossing to lean against her desk.

With hair as black as Grady's and long legs to match, she stood about an inch taller than Ronnie. They sure grew 'em tall like the saguaros down here in southeastern Arizona. Penny shared her brother's amber-colored eyes, too, but where Grady's face was rigid and craggy, Penelope's was soft and round, with a smile that lit up her whole face.

Ronnie had liked Grady's sister at first sight this morning, but that could have been because she was holding a freshly baked cherry pie straight from the oven when Grady had led Ronnie into the kitchen via the diner's back door. It was hard not to like someone with a warm smile and hot pie.

"I'm good," Ronnie said, rubbing her arms. She'd be even better when she got back to Jackrabbit Junction and had a hot shower. She could still smell beer on her skin when she stuck her nose down in her shirt, even though Katie had dropped off a clean one earlier.

"Can I get you anything to drink?"

Ronnie shook her head. "Thanks for letting me crash here." She pointed at the empty plate on Penelope's desk. "The sandwich was delicious and your lemon meringue pie is to die for. Where did you learn to bake like that?"

"Thanks. I went to culinary school in San Francisco."

"Then what are you doing in Yuccaville?"

"Shortly after I graduated, my mom fell and hurt her hip, so I came home to help."

"Where was Grady at the time?"

"In hell. It was right after Elizabeth pulled him through the wringer backward and then left him strung out to dry in front of the rest of the town."

There was no love in Penny's tone, making Ronnie like her even more.

"I had big pastry chef dreams at first, but over the last few years I've come to realize that being here with my family makes me happy. I'd have missed them after a while. And now I have this place and get to bake whatever I want each day. What more could I ask for?"

"You're lucky." Ronnie would love to switch places with Penny. Although she couldn't bake for shit and would probably eat all of the profits. "Grady has nothing but kind things to say about you."

"He better not say anything mean," Penny said with a grin. "Or I'll give him a rose garden on his arm that will make him cry like a little girl." She looked Ronnie up and down. "How come my brother hasn't brought you around to meet our mom or any other family members yet?"

That was Ronnie's fault. She'd resisted his invitations to meet his family every time, telling him that she was happy to get to know his aunt Millie and would prefer to ease into the rest. In reality, she hadn't figured she'd last long enough to merit a family visit, what with Ronnie's sordid past bubbling up into Grady's life like acid indigestion every week or so. She'd guarded her heart as much as she could, but the foolish organ had still fallen head over heels for him.

"I sort of have a not-so-clean-and-shiny history," Ronnie said, grimacing.

"So what."

"I wasn't sure how your family would take to Grady dating someone with a tattered past."

And a threadbare present.

And a frayed future.

Penny crossed her arms. "We're not perfect, you know."

"Yeah, but—"

"You've met Aunt Millie."

"Sure, but underneath the white collar crime ring she wears is a big ol' sweetheart."

Penny laughed. "Oh boy, it's no wonder Aunt Millie crows at the sun about you. I'm sure you've heard about our niece, Mindy Lou, too."

Yeah, and then some. The last Ronnie knew, Mindy Lou was having kinky motel sex with Ruby's ex. Small town drama had Hollywood beat by far. "Mindy is just looking for someone to fill the hole in her heart."

"That's one way of looking at it. Unfortunately, the rest of this town doesn't agree with your point of view."

"Screw what other people think." As far as she was concerned, Mindy Lou wasn't in much of a different situation than Ronnie. They'd both been hurt by ex-lovers and were trying to figure out who they were these days.

"Our family has plenty of dirty laundry, too," Penny said. "To be blunt, I'm happy that Grady's finally quit the monkhood life. I thought he'd given up on the female sex entirely after Elizabeth's bullshit."

Ronnie thought of the nights she'd spent in Grady's bed. He was actually quite far from monkhood these days.

"I'm nuts about your brother," she told Penny.

"Why do I hear a 'but' in there?"

"But your brother deserves a woman who will make the community proud."

"No, my brother deserves a woman who will love him through thick and thin, and not try to manipulate him at every turn."

"I'm not into running anyone else's life," Ronnie said. "Hell, I have trouble handling my own most days."

Penny laughed. "I like you, Veronica. I've noticed a change in my brother since he's started dating you. A good change. You make him happy."

If Penny knew how much baggage Ronnie carried into the relationship that Grady was now shouldering, too, she might feel different.

She smiled in spite of her misgivings. "I hope so. And please, call me Ronnie. Grady's the only one who insists on using my full name." Well, Grady and Lyle, the sleazebag.

"Tell me something, Ronnie." Penny crossed her arms, her eyes taking on that same intense stare her brother used during his informal interrogations both in and out of the bedroom.

"What?"

"Now that you're sleeping with the sheriff of Cholla County, why do you have a damned FBI spook haunting you day and night, too?"

Chapter Fifteen

Claire was up to no good. Mac could tell by the way she wouldn't hold his stare tonight, as if he might see something in her eyes that answered the question in his.

He stood behind the bar at The Shaft while the din of conversation, clink of glasses, howls of laughter, and throbs of classic rock ebbed and flowed around him. In the midst of pouring drinks and chatting with Coop, he kept an eye on Claire. He would rather have stayed home with her tonight, locked up safe and sound, but she would have none of that.

"Is this place always busy or is it just the holidays?" Coop asked him, finishing off his whiskey.

"It's pretty hectic most nights. Butch has built up quite a clientele, especially since he expanded the menu. The upsurge over at the RV park has helped, too."

Butch had closed the kitchen around nine, but most of the partiers were sticking around to bring in the New Year anyway, keeping Mac hopping most of the time. Claire, Ronnie, Kate, and Natalie were all making sure glasses stayed full while Butch bussed the tables and visited with locals.

"Where's your uncle?" Mac asked.

"He's back at the campground playing cards with Chester and Natalie's grandparents, and I think Claire's mom."

Right, the big euchre tournament Mac had caught wind of before heading to The Shaft. "You ready for a refill?"

Coop held out his glass. "Make it another neat, please."

While Mac refilled Coop's whiskey, he scouted the bar, looking for trouble. He found her lickety-split, barging through the sea of bodies, coming right for him with her sister in tow.

After both Ronnie and Claire had given him their drink orders, Claire leaned her elbows on the bar at the wait station and scowled at her sister. "What makes you think you can just go around inviting any Tom, Dick, or Harry to join our posse?"

Oh, jeez. Not this posse business again. Mac filled a mug of beer from the tap.

"Penny is not just anybody." Ronnie took the beer Mac handed her. "She's Grady's sister."

Claire smacked her forehead. "That's even worse, Rufus McDoofus. What in the hell is it with you snuggling up to the law? You have some kind of fetish for badges?"

Mac aimed a wrinkled brow at Claire, who seemed to have forgotten that an off-duty cop was sitting next to her.

"We don't need no stinkin' badges!" Natalie said, leaning on the bar on the other side of Coop. "Two mojitos and a Moscow mule, please, Mac." She turned to Coop. "Hey, digger. How do you feel about playing a game of pool with me in about ten minutes? Butch is going to spell me for the rest of the night."

Coop raised one eyebrow. "You looking to get schooled tonight, little girl?"

Natalie hooted. "Hey, Claire, did you hear that? Coop thinks he can beat me at pool."

Claire grinned. "I'll bet Ronnie's tips from tonight that you bury him the first game and plant flowers over top of him the second."

"Bet Katie the preggo monster's tips instead of mine," Ronnie said. "That will guarantee Natalie doesn't feel sorry for Coop midway through and let him win."

Kate's tip jar had the words *Baby Clothes* written on it, which she told Mac might help keep tips coming in even though she was slowly blowing up into a "hot air balloon," as she put it.

Ronnie took the second beer Mac handed her. "For your information, Claire, Penny is a lot different than Grady."

Claire scoffed. "Oh, yeah? How? And having a uterus doesn't count."

"Well, for one thing, she's not as bossy as Sheriff Hardass."

"Cops are not bossy," Coop said, defending his band of brothers and sisters in blue. "We're trained to take control of a situation."

Natalie snorted. "Please. You're bossy as hell, Coop."

"What are you talking about, woman? I let you tell me what to do all morning and afternoon today."

"And you were a big help, Coop," Claire said. "But I'm not buying that you're not bossy. I saw you in action at the bar in Deadwood, remember? There was definitely some barking going on when you broke up the fight."

"That was your sister doing the barking, not me."

Mac chuckled. "Kate could give a German shepherd a run for its money."

Ronnie took the third beer from Mac, saying to Claire, "Penny needs to be in the posse. She'll make a good spy, trust me. She can grill her customers, plus she's better at telling a stranger from a local than any of us."

Claire pursed her lips. "We could use an ear on the ground."

"Why?" Mac glanced her way while filling the last of Ronnie's order. "What are you guys planning?"

"Nothing," Claire and Ronnie said at the same time.

Bullshit. He handed Ronnie the last drink.

"You can check out Penny for yourself," Ronnie said. "She'll be here any minute. Grady is bringing her."

"What?" Claire glared at Ronnie's back as her sister walked away with her tray of drinks held high. She turned back to Mac, grumbling, "That's Ronnie for you. Drop a bomb and then walk away."

"Why do you need an ear to the ground, Slugger?"

Claire glanced at Coop and Natalie, who were both watching her with wrinkled brows.

"No reason. It's probably a good idea, is all." She smiled too wide. "How's it going back there tonight?"

"You are such a lousy liar." He grabbed the drink mixer cup and poured a shot of tequila into it. "I'll have to torture you for the truth later."

Claire wiggled her eyebrows. "I'm a sucker for your kind of pain."

"I hear electric shocks are quite titillating." Coop lifted his glass of whiskey. "You could give that a whirl."

"I thought you were into thumb screws," Natalie said, flirting.

Coop smiled at her over the rim of his glass. "Sure. Among other types of screws." Then he took a slow sip, watching her the whole time.

"Snakes alive!" Natalie's chuckle sounded nervous. "Who are you and what have you done with Detective Cooper?"

"When the walls come tumblin' down," Claire sang John Mellencamp's "Crumblin' Down" lyrics out of the blue.

While he was mixing margaritas, Mac saw Natalie elbow Claire in the ribs and shoot her a knock-it-off glare.

"I wonder if that song is on the jukebox," Claire said, laughing, rubbing her side. "I'll have to check later."

"Hey, Mac," Kate said, sliding into the space Ronnie had left. "There's a hottie at one of my tables who wants your number."

Claire gaped, spinning around to frown out over the bar. "That's it! I'm getting tired of drunk broads hitting on my man. Which one?"

"I'm not telling you, because you'll go start a fight and Butch said there was no monkey business allowed tonight."

"I'll start a fight? What about you, Queen Kong?" Claire turned back to her sister. "Did you tell the harlot that Mac is taken?"

"Not yet. I'm trying to get him a good tip, dang it. Excuse me for looking out for your man's best interest."

Mac chuckled. He handed Claire the margaritas and grabbed the vodka from the shelf behind him. "Tell the drunk hottie I'm not interested," he said to Kate while looking at Claire. "I'm too busy trying to convince my girlfriend to make an honest man of me these days."

Claire batted her eyelashes at him. "But you're so sexy when you're corrupt."

"And don't you forget it, gorgeous." He added a splash of vermouth and a few olives and handed it to her. "Off you go, minx."

She purred and left with her drinks.

"How are you feeling tonight, Kate?" Mac asked as he grabbed the bottle of white rum.

She harrumphed. "Why does everyone keep asking me that?"

Probably because Butch had told them to watch for telltale signs of Mr. Hyde trying to surface.

"Because you're pregnant and unstable as hell," Natalie answered. She covered her mouth. "Sorry, that's the shot of tequila Mac slipped me earlier speaking."

"I'm not unstable."

"Uhhh, you shot Coop's uncle with a Taser gun this morning, remember?"

"Come on! How many times are you going to throw that in my face? I bought him breakfast and bourbon to make up for it. Besides, Harvey is fine with the jolt. He told me that I remind him of a pretty doctor named Ana-something from Nevada."

Coop coughed on a laugh, looking away with a grin.

Natalie patted his back, chuckling.

Mac wondered what the joke was. He'd have to ask one of them about it later. He finished the mojitos for Natalie and handed them to her.

"Where does Butch keep the ginger beer?" he asked Kate.

She came around the bar and grabbed it from the fridge for him. When they turned back to the masses, Butch was standing at the wait station, his brows drawn.

"Honey," he said to Kate, "what are you doing back there with Mac?" His gaze shifted to the soda water gun for a split second and then back to Kate.

"Relax, Valentine." She returned to the other side of the bar. "I was helping Mac find something." She patted Butch's chest, smiling up at him. "You worry too much."

He pointed at the colorful bruise on his cheek. "I'm still black-and-blue from last night's throwdown."

She rolled her eyes. "You need to lighten up. Be more like Coop's uncle."

"Why?" Butch's gaze narrowed. "What did you do to him?"

"She Tasered him," Natalie tattled.

Kate whirled on her cousin, her eyes wide, her rabid dog side showing. "Zip your lips or I'm going to come for you in your nightmares."

Natalie gaped at Mac and then Butch. "Did you guys see

that?" She nudged Coop, who was still grinning into his glass of whiskey. "Stop laughing."

"See what?" Mac asked, setting the Moscow mule on Natalie's tray.

"Kate's head spun around and a red-eyed banshee shrieked at me for a split second."

"Oh, stuff it, stool pigeon." Kate handed Natalie her tray of drinks. "Shoofly pie-face, you're bothering me."

"Kiss my grits, crazy train." Natalie headed back into the crowd.

"Don't call me crazy," Kate shouted after her.

"Now you did it, sweetheart," Butch said, looking toward the door. "Somebody called the sheriff to come take you away."

Kate followed his gaze and let out a screech. "I need to go to the bathroom." She ducked down and scampered off.

Mac exchanged nods with Grady as he joined them, noticing the dark circles under the sheriff's eyes and the slow way he moved, as if each footstep took a conscious effort.

The tall, dark-haired woman behind him had to be the sister Ronnie was telling Claire about earlier. She shared her brother's eye color, along with his hair color and height, but her features were much softer. Her smile was easy to look at, along with the rest of her.

"Happy almost New Year," Grady said, and then introduced his sister all around.

Coop stood to offer Penny his seat.

"You don't have to do that," she said, giving Coop a once-over. Her face gave away nothing on what she saw.

"It's no problem." He grabbed his glass. "I need to go warm up at the pool tables. There's a big game starting soon that I don't want to miss." He headed off into the crowd.

Penny took Coop's bar stool while Grady lowered himself onto the one next to her.

"What can I get you two?" Mac asked.

She tapped her fingers on the bar. "I'm driving home later, so I'll stick with something virgin."

Grady smirked at her. "That will be a first for you."

She wrinkled her nose back at him. "Some brother you are.

You're supposed to defend my honor, not paint me red and hang me out to dry."

"I owe you for that low blow about my ex on the ride here." He pointed toward Mac. "Let him get you something with some fire in it. I can have one of the boys come pick you up, if needed."

Penny shrugged. "Maybe later. Besides, your guys are going to be busy tonight watching for drunk drivers. Let's start with a Shirley Temple for now," she said to Mac.

Grady ordered a beer.

While Mac poured their drinks, Butch asked Grady, "Did you hear from your ex at all today?"

"Nope. Mississippi was at Tank's place this morning with me. He said Elizabeth pouted all of the way back to Yuccaville last night."

"How is Tank?" Butch asked.

"The surgery went well. They're keeping him in ICU for the night, but they expect him to make a full recovery."

Mac set Grady's beer in front of him. "Did you learn anything from the crime scene that might help you locate the killer?"

Grady scowled, shaking his head. "Tank got his gun, but the guy was wearing gloves, so the prints on it will most likely belong to Tank. The gun is registered to a bogus name—some eighty-year-old widow from Amarillo named Ida Lou something or other."

Butch crossed his arms. "What about security cameras?"

"Two of the cameras were spray painted over before the attack. The third showed a shadow pass at the edge of the screen, but nothing else."

"Did Tank notice anything about the guy that stands out?" Penny asked.

Grady shook his head. "Average height. Blond hair. Good shape physically. Strong enough to drag Tank around, and we all know he's no string bean. But due to the John Denver mask, long sleeves, and turtleneck, that's all we have to go on at this time. No distinguishing tattoos or birthmarks that Tank could see at the time."

"Did he have an accent?" Mac set the Shirley Temple in front of Penny. He went to work finishing Kate's order so it'd be ready when she scampered back to face Grady.

"Tank said his voice was on the nasally side, but there was something the killer said that made Tank think he was a southerner."

"What's that?"

"It was some saying like, 'Me 'n you are gonna mix, boy,' or something along those lines. Tank said he hadn't heard anyone say that since he'd moved west."

"So possibly a southern drawl," Penny said, as if taking notes in her head.

"There's something else," Grady told them. "Tank tackled this guy, ramming him into a worktable with tools on it. He said the guy was limping as he ran off."

"Which leg?" Penny asked.

Mac glanced at Grady's sister. Was this penchant for sniffing out criminals a family trait?

"Left." Grady took a sip of his beer.

Butch grinned. "Don't mess with Tank."

"Don't mess with Yuccaville," Penny said, raising her glass in a mock toast.

Grady cast a tired smile her way. "Don't get cocky. We haven't caught the son of a bitch yet."

"Someone will." She shrugged at Grady's raised brow. "Either your crew or the local police will find him, especially since you put out an APB to keep an eye out for Tank's attacker and reminded everyone about the Silent Witness hotline. Local folks are going to be pissed about Tank getting hurt. Everyone loves Tank."

"She's right," Grady told Mac. "Several folks stopped by Tank's place and volunteered to keep the business going for him while he's on the mend. We took names to give him when he's coherent enough to respond to the offers."

"I hope you're right about the killer being caught soon," Mac said to Penny.

Grady pointed his glass of beer at Mac and told her, "His girlfriend is Veronica's sister."

"Claire?"

Mac paused. How did she know … oh yeah, she was Grady's sister.

Grady nodded. "Butch is dating the youngest sister."

"Kate, the pregnant one." Penny returned, again as if reading from invisible notes. She smiled at Butch. "You should have brought her around the diner before now. She stopped by with some friends and her cousin this morning for some breakfast. She's a real sweetheart."

Grady guffawed. "When she's not wielding a soda water gun."

Or threatening to spray paint Mac's pickup or shooting holes in Claire's Jeep or Tasering old guys or … Mac chuckled to himself, finishing Kate's order and setting it on the tray she'd left.

"Where is Kate tonight?" Grady asked, looking around. "I have a bone to pick with her about something I heard come over the radio earlier today." His gaze paused on Ronnie, who was talking to Coop and Mississippi back by the pool tables.

"She's around here somewhere. Is Kate's order ready to go?" Butch asked. When Mac nodded, he picked it up. "I'll take care of it for her. If she shows up, tell her to come find me."

"Will do."

Momentarily caught up on orders, Mac checked on the rest of the folks sitting at the bar. Then he poured himself a Coke and added a splash of Jack Daniels whiskey to it. He stared out at the partiers, locating Claire and then breathing a sigh of relief. The Jack and Coke went down easy, sweet and smooth.

Back in Tucson last night, he'd busted his ass dealing with the crack in the new wall. The temporary fix had forced him to work until early this morning with a small crew earning triple-time pay. Being leaned on by upper management hadn't helped his stress level.

At one point, he'd stepped aside to take a quick assessment of what needed to be done yet and wondered what in the hell he was doing—with his life, not the wall. The allure of his job had faded over the last six months, in part because he'd opted out of the promotion he'd been working hard to land prior to meeting Claire. That promotion would have included traveling—a lot of traveling—and while Claire had said she'd be willing to go with him, he knew better. Her family was here in Jackrabbit Junction, along with her heart.

Now his future seemed bleak career-wise. It wasn't because he didn't take that promotion, though. It was because Claire didn't really want to be part of the life he'd built in Tucson, which meant spending a lot of days and nights away from her.

As he'd stood there on the jobsite, squinting under the bright halogen work lights, he tried to envision his future with the company and came up empty. There was no future for him there, not if it didn't include coming home to Claire each evening.

Mac took another drink of his Jack and Coke, watching Claire move from table to table, grabbing empty glasses, talking with the partiers.

Damn. Before she'd crashed into his world, his career was his life. If someone had told him a year ago that a woman would flip his dreams upside down, he'd have laughed.

He blew out a breath. Of all places, why Jackrabbit Junction?

He thought of the view from the front porch of the General Store. Could he handle waking up each day and watching the sunrise over the Tres Dedos Mountains? Would it get old? Mundane?

Claire looked his way, catching him watching her. She smiled and blew him a kiss.

He raised his glass in return, thinking about her in his bed. He'd get to spend night after night with her warm curves pressed up against him under the covers, smelling her skin and the sweet mix of fruity shampoo and honeysuckle blossoms that was Claire. *That* wouldn't get old. Neither would sharing meals and moments throughout the day with her.

His gaze drifted to where Butch and Kate were standing over by the jukebox, taking a moment to slow dance together while Bob Seger sang about running against the wind. A cheer over by the pool tables caught his attention. He watched Natalie do the limbo under a pool cue Ronnie was holding out while Coop and Mississippi grinned and clapped.

Life wasn't about where he lived, it was about the life happening around him. If Claire were here, along with Butch,

Grady, and the rest—well, minus Deborah, then Jackrabbit Junction would do just fine for him.

Solving where to live was all good and fine, but what in the hell did a geotechnician do in this dusty pit stop to make money? He couldn't tend bar the rest of his life, could he?

"Hey, Mac!" Ronnie's voice pulled him out of his reverie. She jogged up to the bar, her face flushed from either the limbo fun or the gin and tonic he'd made her a half hour ago. "Can I get a pitcher of the local brew for the guys over in the corner?"

He grabbed a pitcher and started filling it, checking the crowd for Claire again. There she was, up with Natalie, talking to her cousin while she chalked her pool cue. Butch was there, too, showing something on his phone to Coop.

Mac focused on the foam in the pitcher as it rose. How was he going to keep Claire safe until this damned killer was found?

He glanced toward Grady with a grin. "Have you thought any more about locking Ronnie and Claire up in your jail until you find the killer?" He was only partly kidding. If the two trouble magnets sat in jail, they'd be much safer than anywhere else around here.

"Real funny, Mac," Ronnie said, sidling up next to Grady. "Don't listen to him, Sheriff Hardass."

Grady put his arm around Ronnie's waist, pulling her closer. He smiled up at her. "It's a good idea, Ms. Morgan."

Ronnie squinted back. "Watch it, boy, or I'll handcuff you to the bed again."

"Again?" Penny asked, her gaze bouncing between Ronnie and her brother.

Grady grumbled something into his beer that Mac couldn't hear.

Ronnie laughed. "He was showing me how handcuffs work and forgot he'd left the key in his other pants."

"Wait until I tell Aunt Millie," Penny said.

"Don't even think about it, Penelope Sue."

Penny glanced toward the pool tables and did a double take, her smile fading. Mac followed her gaze, watching Coop rack the balls while Natalie pretended to stretch, her expression cocky and taunting. Mississippi sat at a nearby table, drinking his iced tea as he looked out over the bar.

"I see your FBI pal is here," she said to Ronnie as Mac was handing over the pitcher.

"Leave it alone, Penny," Grady growled.

Mac waited until Ronnie had walked away to ask Grady, "Are they bringing in more FBI agents to help catch the diamond killer?"

Grady shook his head. "According to Mississippi, the FBI is still set on tying this diamond mess to Veronica's ex and his cache of missing stones. They don't see any reason to send backup agents until the killer attempts some sort of action directly against Veronica; otherwise they are wasting resources. They figure the killer might sit for another stretch of time before making a move. They have one guy here. In their opinion, that's enough."

"Assholes," Mac muttered, realizing Ronnie must have finally told Grady about the FBI's newest screw job and the need to catch the killer alive to save her bacon.

"Mississippi tried to tell me that the FBI's faith in my department's ability to protect Veronica is a compliment—but he couldn't say it with a straight face."

Mac took another drink of Jack and Coke to wash down the bitterness that the FBI's decision left in his mouth.

"What kind of a name is 'Mississippi'?" Penny asked with a curled upper lip.

Grady shrugged. "I don't know. If it perturbs you so much, why don't you go ask him yourself, hotshot?"

"Maybe I will." She picked up her Shirley Temple and took off in the direction of the pool tables.

Mac chuckled. "Your sister reminds me of Ronnie and Claire when it comes to the FBI. Did she have a run-in with them at some point in the past?"

"You could say that. She was engaged to an agent when she lived in San Francisco."

"What happened?"

"She seems to suffer the same fate as me—ending up on the shitty side of infidelity." He grinned. "When she found out what he'd been up to, she chased him around his apartment with a hotshot. That sort of became her nickname in the family."

"You mean a cattle prod?" When Grady nodded, Mac laughed. "Why did he have a cattle prod in his apartment?"

Grady groaned. "Don't ask."

"Mississippi better watch out." Mac finished his Jack and Coke, setting the glass off to the side for a refill later. "Then again, maybe he'd like being zapped." Same as Coop's uncle.

"Penny has a sharp tongue. I'm just glad she's sparring with him tonight and not me."

"So, how's Ronnie doing after what happened to Tank?" Mac hadn't really had a chance to talk to anyone other than Claire. He'd slept most of the afternoon and been busy pouring drinks since walking into The Shaft.

"Your guess is as good as mine. When I talked to her earlier on the phone, she said she was ready to deal with what was coming her way." Grady shook his head, his forehead lined. "I'm worried about what that means. Has Claire said anything that sounded the alarms in your head since she found out about Tank this morning?"

Mac chuckled. "She says stuff constantly that makes my alarms ring." He thought back to their conversation earlier after she'd come in from working on the deck to hit the shower. "But she hasn't said anything out of the ordinary."

Now that he thought about it, she'd had a grim look on her face when she was brushing her hair in the mirror after her shower. Her smile had seemed forced on the way to The Shaft, too, but he'd just figured she was tired. "Something is different, though. I just can't put my finger on it."

Grady scratched his jaw. "Maybe it's stress."

"Could be. Being on a hit list can't be easy on the nerves. Tank is a big guy and look how he ended up. Claire has one hell of a swing, but ..." Mac grimaced, not liking the direction his thoughts were headed.

"I'm going to find him," Grady said.

Mac wasn't sure if he was offering comfort or trying to convince himself, but he hoped Grady was right.

Butch made his way through a group of girls hip-bumping to Queen's "Another One Bites the Dust." He held two empty pitchers and set them on the counter. "What did you say to Kate?" he asked Grady.

"Nothing, I haven't even seen her yet. Why?"

"She asked me to come over here and get refills for her tables. I think she's worried about the hose-down she gave you last night."

"She should be," Grady deadpanned. "Tell her I'm considering arresting her for assaulting an off-duty officer and having her celebrate the New Year from behind bars."

Mac took the pitchers and set them in the sink, grabbing two clean ones from the shelves. "She might believe you, Grady," he said over his shoulder. "And make a run for the border, giving Butch one hell of a chase."

Butch laughed. "Speaking of the border, I have tomorrow morning open, Mac."

"Open for what?" Grady asked.

"Mac wants me to go up to Humdigger mine with him so that ol' Dick Webber doesn't take a shot at him for trespassing."

Grady rubbed his jaw. "You want me to send one of my newer deputies with you in plain clothes? I don't think Dick knows this kid—he's fresh out of the academy."

"Nah," Butch said. "We're taking someone with a lot more sleuthing experience."

"We are?" Mac asked. "Who?"

Butch pointed over his shoulder. "A vacationing detective from South Dakota who's about to get schooled at pool—at least that's Kate's prediction. Which reminds me. I need a bottle of tequila and two shot glasses for the pool tournament participants. Things are about to get exciting back there."

Chapter Sixteen

Not quite midnight …

Ten bucks says Natalie's dry spell ends tonight," Claire said to Kate, who was feeding money into the jukebox.

"What are you talking about?" her sister asked, sliding another dollar bill into the slot.

"Look up by the pool tables."

Kate turned, her brow wrinkling. "Oh, no! I didn't realize she was wearing my zipper shirt under her work shirt."

"And she changed into your miniskirt." The jeans Natalie had been wearing earlier were gone, but the cowboy boots were still the same.

"What is she thinking?" Kate crossed her arms. "That's my 'get it on' outfit."

"More like 'tear it off,' if you ask me."

Kate scowled at her. "It's better than your see-through T-shirts and those Daisy Duke shorts."

"Better? Nah. And my T-shirts aren't see-through. They just hug the girls nicely. That outfit," Claire said, pointing at Natalie, who was chalking up a pool cue while chatting with Coop, "is much more accessible than any of my outfits."

Kate smirked. "She doesn't look like a woman on a sabbatical from the male sex."

"Sabbatical or not, she's got Coop on the brain."

"Maybe she's just going to torture him a little. Natalie has a wicked streak in her and he stung her pretty bad before."

That was true, and Natalie could hold a grudge like the Hatfields and the McCoys. "She is the queen of revenge."

"She told me earlier tonight that she wants to stay 'just friends' with Coop," Kate said. "Anything more could mess up the dynamics of their group of friends up in Deadwood."

Claire scoffed. "That is not a 'just friends' outfit. Those are sex-in-a-back-alley duds, all the way."

"Hey!" Kate punched Claire's arm. "I paid good money for those labels."

"And I'm sure Butch has appreciated them appropriately."

Kate's smile was enough of an answer for Claire.

She turned back to the jukebox. "Let's play some of Natalie's favorite sexy songs," Claire said. Thanks to Kate's money, they had six songs to choose. "Here we go." She punched in the letter-number combination.

" 'Start Me Up'? You think that's sexy?" Kate asked.

"Are you kidding? The Rolling Stones are all about sex, baby mama." Claire scanned the list. "Here's another."

" 'You Shook Me All Night Long,' " Kate read aloud the AC/DC title as Claire added the song to the playlist. "Are you trying to sabotage Natalie?"

"Of course. Oh, this one is great." She typed in the keys for "Magic Man" by Heart.

"Yeah, I always liked that song, too," Kate said. "Why are *you* sabotaging Natalie?" She pointed at the screen. "Play that one."

"Dancing in the Dark" by Springsteen? Claire hesitated—that wasn't her favorite song by "The Boss"—but it was sexy and Natalie always liked to dance to it. "Natalie's coiled too tight, especially since a certain law dog showed up. She's spent enough time patching up her inner self. It's time to return to the fun stuff in life, like a relaxing roll in the hay, and the perfect guy to help her unwind is right in front of her."

"Mississippi?"

Claire looked over her shoulder. Natalie had moved and was now pouring tequila into a shot glass next to where Mississippi was sitting. She set the full shot glass in front of the FBI agent and then filled another shot glass for herself.

That would be Natalie's second shot of tequila tonight. Claire grinned. Tequila was a sure-fire ingredient for some slap-and-tickle fun in the dark.

"Not Mississippi, bird brain," Claire said, turning back to the jukebox.

"Don't call me bird brain, wiener wonder." Kate leaned closer to Claire. "Who's the black-haired babe sitting at the table with Mississippi? She looks familiar but I can't get a good look at her face."

Claire punched in the letter-number combination for "Feel Like Makin' Love" by Bad Company. That one should get things sparking in somebody's pants. "What babe?"

"The one who looks like she's ruffling Mississippi's feath … oh, that's Grady's sister. The one who owns The Mule Train Diner. Damn, I wish I had curves like her."

Claire glanced over in time to see Penny steal Mississippi's shot of tequila and drink it. She set the shot glass back on the table with attitude and flipped off Mississippi. Then Penny stood and tapped the table in front of him with her index finger, emphasizing some point from the looks of it before walking away. Mississippi watched her go, a smile curving his lips. After one last glance at Natalie and Coop, he grabbed his drink and followed Penny into the crowd.

"What was that about?" Kate asked.

"Who knows?" Claire turned back to choose the final song. "Maybe she doesn't like the way he discards his cigarettes, like another monkey I know who goes ape-shit about littering."

She felt Kate's glare on her. "Lit cigarette butts start fires every year, cheese-dick. And for your information, Mississippi is trying to quit smoking."

"No shit?" That wasn't an easy habit to break. Claire still craved cigarettes periodically, especially when she had a violent killer hunting her for some diamonds that she wished she'd never found. So much for bumming a cigarette from Mississippi later when she was drunk and looking to sneak a quick hit.

"Help me pick the last song, Fire Marshal Kate." Claire hooked her arm through Kate's.

Kate scanned the songs, giggling. "Natalie's going to kill us for doing this."

"I know." Claire chuckled.

"Oh!" Kate touched the glass. "How about this one?"

"Perfect!" Claire punched in "Fire" by the Pointer Sisters. "Mark my words, Natalie is going down tonight."

"Are we still talking about that O-ring zipper on my shirt or something else?" Kate pretended to hold a cigar and wiggled her eyebrows, looking like a mix of Groucho Marx and Chester.

Claire laughed. "You're a bad influence, Porn Star."

"Takes one to know one, Daisy Duke."

* * *

"Heads or tails?" Natalie asked Coop, flipping a quarter in the air. She caught it and smacked it onto the back of her hand, hiding the coin under her palm as she waited for his call.

He stared at her across the pool table, his gray eyes hooded in the dim light. Dressed in jeans, boots, and a black shirt, he looked like a fatal case of heartbreak in one hot-to-the-touch package. A rush of lust rolled through her, making her skin steam.

Hell's bells! They hadn't even started playing yet and she was already melting.

You're on sabbatical, the left side of her brain reminded her. *Don't play with fire.*

Right. Don't touch. She needed another shot of tequila.

No, bad idea. Tequila made clothes fall off.

The jukebox kicked to life. Mick Jagger belted out "Start Me Up." Natalie shot a frown toward the dance floor. Even the Rolling Stones were working against her tonight.

"Lady's choice," Coop said, trailing his fingers along the edge of the corner pocket as he rounded the pool table.

"Stop being a gentleman and call it." Natalie's pulse revved as he closed the distance between them. "Tonight we're going to play a square game from start to finish." She gave him a mock squint. "No letting me win this time so you might get some back alley action."

"I didn't let you win that time."

"You sank the eight ball in the wrong pocket on purpose."

"That wasn't on purpose. You distracted me." He leaned on the table's side rail, his body only inches away.

Dear Lord, he smelled like sex and spice and everything nice. *Really, brain? Nursery rhymes about sex?* She snorted. She probably shouldn't have had that shot of tequila. Or the one before that. History had shown that mixing alcohol and Coop made a highly combustible fuel that rocketed her common sense to Jupiter.

She swayed to the Stones' beat, playing it cool, pretending she wasn't fighting the urge to lean forward and lick Coop's neck. "I don't remember doing any such thing."

His gaze dipped to the O-ring zipper at her chest. "You bent over the table in my line of sight when I was trying to shoot. I could see down your shirt clear to your navel."

Natalie pursed her lips. Okay, that was entirely possible, especially with tequila playing puppet master. But … "I was wearing a bra that night."

"I remember. It was black lace with a pink polka dot satin edge and a little pink bow right here." He pointed to a spot below the O-ring.

"You remember that?"

Coop bent closer, whispering in her ear, "Your panties matched." His breath warmed her neck, and his words made her unmentionables smolder.

A delicious shiver rippled down her back, leaving goose bumps in its wake. "Wow." She tried to laugh, but it came out raspy. "Well, at least I made sure to coordinate that night." Most mornings she threw on whatever was clean and called it good.

Coop leaned back, one eyebrow raised as his gaze moved over her, dipping clear to her boots. "I'm curious."

"About what?" she asked. What she was wearing under her clothes tonight? A flare of heat burned its way up her neck. Sweet Jane almighty, he could flirt the bloomers off a preacher's wife.

"About what's under your hand." He cocked his head to the side. "I call tails."

She tried to ignore the deep throb going on in her southern hemisphere and lifted her palm. "Tails it is. Name your game."

"Nine ball." He took the quarter from where it sat on the back of her hand, his fingers lingering on her skin. "And this time, don't let me win to try to soften me up so that I won't arrest you for vandalizing a vehicle."

The second time they'd played, she'd been doing her best to distract Cooper. He'd caught her red-handed with the windshield wipers—blades and all—from the Jaguar belonging to the asshole sperm donor who'd impregnated her best friend a decade ago … and then scuttled away from all child-rearing responsibilities.

She shrugged. "A girl's gotta do what a girl's gotta do. Besides, if memory serves me right, you called that game a draw."

He shrugged back at her. "A guy's gotta do what a guy's gotta do. Rack 'em, Beals."

Natalie grabbed the ball rack from the wall and set up the game. She could feel his eyes on her and did her best to keep her hands steady, trying not to let him see how much he was flustering her.

She lifted the ball rack. "Have at it, Five-O."

He looked up from placing the cue ball for the break shot. "Five-O?"

"Like the TV show, *Hawaii Five-O*."

He smirked.

"What? You don't like nicknames, Sexy Two-Shoes?" she joked, grinning at the wrinkled brow he sent her.

He bent over the table. "If you're trying to distract me, name calling won't work." He took his shot, sending the one ball into the side pocket.

"What will?" she asked as he moved closer to her for his next shot.

He glanced down at the O-ring zipper. "Playing dirty."

* * *

When Ronnie returned from a quick visit to Butch's office, Claire and Katie were pouring drinks behind the bar. Mac had switched sides, holding down the bar stool where Grady had been sitting minutes ago while Butch occupied the seat next to him.

Ronnie did a double take at the change-up. What the hell? All she'd done was refresh her lip gloss, run a brush through her hair, shuck her work shirt for something more comfortable, and spritz her neck with perfume.

She stepped up to the wait station, leaning on the bar next to Mac. "Where's Grady?" If he got called into work because of some emergency, or something to do with the damned diamond killer, she was going to order a huge gin and tonic to dunk her head in for the rest of the night.

"He's over at the corner table talking to some guys who work for the county," Butch said. "Nice shirt."

Ronnie glanced down at the Tijuana Toads T-shirt. She'd been too lazy to walk to the Winnebago earlier and raided Claire's drawer instead. "Thanks, it's one of Claire's."

Mac looked over and grinned. "One of my favorites."

"*Ay yi yi,*" Claire said and trilled her tongue at Mac. "*Te amo, mi corazón.*" She set a full glass of beer in front of Butch. "Actually," she told Ronnie, "I just saw Grady drag his sister over to the *Big Buck Hunter* video game, and she didn't look very happy about it."

Ronnie glanced in the direction of the video game. Penny had her arms crossed as she listened to whatever her brother was saying. She shook her head while pinching her lips together.

What was going on over there? Family business, or something to do with a certain FBI agent Penny had been visiting with by the pool tables before Ronnie went in back to change?

"What's your bet, Ronnie?" Claire asked, pulling her focus back to the bar.

"My bet for what?"

"Natalie and Coop."

Ronnie's gaze shifted to where their cousin was playing pool with the detective. At the moment, Natalie was watching while Coop took a shot. Ronnie saw him sink the ball in the side pocket and then stand upright, smiling in Natalie's direction.

"Natalie will win in the end. She always does." Although Coop appeared to be a hotshot, too.

AC/DC's famous opening guitar riffs rang out across the bar. "You Shook Me All Night Long" beat to life loud and clear. Had someone cranked up the jukebox louder than usual?

Ronnie watched her cousin. Natalie scowled in the direction of the jukebox and poured herself a shot of tequila. She lifted the glass to her mouth, but then hesitated and set it down on the table.

Hmmm. Maybe Natalie had found her match in more ways than one.

"We're not talking about the pool game," Katie said above the music.

After another check on Grady and Penny, Ronnie turned back to her sisters. "What then?"

"Natalie's sabbatical. We're all betting on whether Coop will run her off the rails tonight and when and how. We've each thrown ten in the pot." Katie placed a beer pitcher partly filled with money in front of Ronnie.

Ronnie scoffed. "You guys are betting ten bucks on whether our cousin will have sex or not? What is wrong with you guys?" She reached into her back pocket and pulled out a wad of tip money. "I'll see your measly ten and raise each of you another ten." She stuffed twenty dollars in the pitcher. "My money is on Natalie instigating sex by twelve-thirty in Coop's truck."

"Are we playing *Clue* now?" Mac asked.

"Yeah." Claire leaned on the bar across from him. "The perverse, small-town bar version."

"What makes you so sure Natalie will take the lead?" Butch asked Ronnie.

She held up her hand, ticking off her fingers. "For one, she's drinking tequila. Two, she's wearing Katie's quick-access zipper top. Three, somebody—and I'm assuming it's Claire—has the jukebox playing some of Natalie's favorite songs extra loud. And four, she likes Coop way more than this 'just friends' phony baloney she keeps telling everyone."

Claire laughed and stuffed another ten in the pitcher. "I say twelve-oh-five, Natalie at the helm, and in the storage room."

"Christ." Butch grimaced. "Why does everybody like to screw around in my storage room? After catching Ronnie and Grady in there, I wince when I have to get supplies."

"I can't believe you two have no faith in Natalie," Katie said. She added a ten to the pitcher. "I'm going to bet the Don't Pass Bar in this Craps game and say Coop will try to bust down Natalie's wall with a kiss or two, but she'll resist him and wake up still wearing her underwear in the morning." She looked toward the pool tables with a wrinkled brow. "Although if she keeps hitting that tequila bottle, she'll have one hell of a headache."

"Boring," Claire sang.

Ronnie laughed and held out her hand for a fist bump. "Natalie has little willpower when it comes to hot guys."

Katie harrumphed. "Resisting a man is not boring, you two-bit tramps. It's sort of old-school romantic. Besides, Natalie is different now thanks to her sabbatical. She's stronger and has a lot more self-control. When her sabbatical truly goes down in flames, there won't be any liquor involved."

"What do you know about resistance and self-control, you pregnant unmarried hypocrite?" Claire asked, laughing.

Butch laughed, too, until Katie tried to snap him with a bar towel. Then he hid behind his glass of beer and chuckled some more.

"What's your bet, Butch?" Ronnie asked him. It would be interesting to hear a guy's point of view on how this might turn out for Natalie.

He added money to the pitcher. "Your cousin is bullheaded. I'm with Kate. Natalie will hold out, but not before Coop makes it to second base. Maybe even third. With that bottle of tequila in the mix, though, I'm going to predict that come morning her underwear is MIA."

Ronnie snorted. "Tequila really warps her mind."

"Mac's turn," Katie said.

All eyes turned to Mac. He looked toward the pool tables, his expression thoughtful. Then he pulled a twenty-dollar bill out and shoved it in the pitcher. "My money is on Coop."

"What do you mean?" Claire asked.

"Natalie will try to seduce him, but he's not going to go through with it tonight. Kissing may or may not be involved, though."

"So you think her sabbatical will still be in place at morning light?" Katie confirmed.

"Yes, but only because Coop resists her."

"You're nuts," Claire said. "He drove all of the way down here for her."

"Exactly, and that's why he's going to resist her. He's not

going to blow it on some quick drunken moment of weakness. He's going to want it to count when it happens."

The romantic in Ronnie liked the sound of that. Claire liked it, too, judging by her sister's dreamy expression as she smiled at Mac.

"But what if tonight is his only opportunity?" Ronnie asked.

Mac shrugged. "If he plays his cards right, it won't be."

Grady wove his way through the crowd toward them, his amber gaze locked onto Ronnie as he approached. Where was Penny and what had they been talking about so seriously?

"Nice T-shirt, *bandida*," he said when he reached her side. "You come here often?" He stole a kiss and then looked at the pitcher full of money. "What's with that?"

Ronnie slipped her arm around his waist, smiling up at him. "We've started a friendly, *totally legal* pool among family and friends on whether Natalie and Coop will do the wild thing tonight," she explained. "It costs twenty bucks to play if you feel like weighing in."

Grady scoffed. "For real?"

"Yes, for real." Claire crossed her arms. "We live in the sticks and Crazy Kate broke the dartboard when she got mad at Mom last week, so this is all we have to do for fun."

"Call me crazy again, Claire, and we'll have a wet T-shirt contest." Katie drew the soda water gun and aimed it at Claire to emphasize her point.

Grady pointed at Katie. "Drop the weapon, woman." After she obliged, he pulled out his wallet and stuffed a couple of bills in the pitcher.

"What's your bet?" Ronnie asked.

"I always bet on cops."

Ronnie laughed. "Where and when, Sheriff Hardass?"

"The storage room before midnight."

Butch cursed under his breath.

* * *

Just friends.

Natalie downed the shot of tequila she'd been toying with for the last ten minutes, needing something to numb her body and stop the tingles of awareness running riot under her skin. The liquor burned all of the way down.

"*He's a magic man,*" Ann Wilson sang from the jukebox in her haunting voice.

Damn it. What were the chances of three of her favorite drinking songs playing one right after another tonight? She glanced at the bar, frowning at the sight of her cousins all grouped together around it staring at her. Claire raised her beer toward Natalie in a toast.

Natalie nodded at them once and then turned back to the game.

"Eight ball in the corner pocket," Coop said, bending over to line up the shot.

Natalie watched the pool cue move back and forth between his long fingers. Talented fingers. Fingers that knew just where to …

"Grawwwk." The sound creaked from her throat before she could stop it.

He glanced up at her. "What'd you say?"

"Crock … of crap. You making that shot, I mean." She bit her lower lip to block anything else stupid from leaking out between her lips. "Sorry. Take your shot."

He raised his brows. "You sure?"

"Yeah. But I'm going to chalk up, because I have a feeling it's going to be my turn to shoot pretty quick."

"Oh, yeah?" He cocked his head. "I'll make a bet with you."

She hesitated, the chalk in her hand. "What's the bet?"

"If I make this shot, you don't drink any more tequila tonight."

"You don't like me drinking?"

"I want to win while you're sober so you can't use the excuse later that you lost because you were drunk."

She tipped her head to the side. "And if you miss?"

"I'll do a shot with you."

"Okay." She chalked the pool cue. "I'll take the bet."

He aimed, shot, and missed.

Natalie set the chalk down, staring at him, trying to judge if he screwed up that shot on purpose. He was too hard to read.

She poured tequila in the shot glass she'd been using. "You want me to get you a clean one?"

He joined her, standing too dang close. "No. My germs think your germs are sexy."

She tried to laugh, but it sounded too husky to be believable. He tossed back the tequila, chasing it with a sip from his whiskey glass. "I don't know how you can drink that stuff." He took the tequila bottle and refilled the shot, holding it out to her. "Bottoms up, Beals."

The tequila slid down her throat with less heat. Or maybe the three previous shots she'd had tonight had scorched a path south.

She set the glass down and smiled at him. "My toes are numb," she announced, and then wished she hadn't.

"Have you lost feeling anywhere else?"

She thought about it for a second. "My lips are halfway there."

He leaned closer. "Halfway where?"

Staring too long into his gray eyes was trouble, so she really should stop. "I don't remember."

His mouth lowered, his lips just a hop, skip, and drunken stumble away. "Natalie."

The heat from his breath tickled her chin. Apparently, that part of her wasn't numb yet. "Yeah?"

"It's your turn."

To kiss him? "Shoot."

"Correct. Unless you want to forfeit the game already."

She blinked out of her agave-fueled stupor. "Balls! I mean, shoot. Pool balls. Arghhh! It's my turn."

Her cheeks hot, she sidestepped him and floated to the table, giving herself a pep talk as she lined up her shot. "Eight ball in the side."

He stood right where she was aiming, filling her view with parts of him better left naked in the bedroom. The big cheater.

She hit the cue ball and landed the shot. When she stood upright, her head cleared. Her mind shifted into pool ace mode, thank the tequila gods.

"Nine ball in the far corner." She sank the ball for the win and raised her arms in victory.

Springsteen's "Dancing in the Dark" started up on the jukebox. Natalie's victory smile flipped upside down. She turned to her audience over at the bar, her gaze sliding from Kate to Claire to Ronnie … and then to the beer pitcher full of money on the counter next to them.

No, they didn't.

Kate gave Natalie a cheesy smile and two thumbs-up.

Oh, hell. They did.

"Next game is eight ball," she told Coop. "Rack 'em up. I'll be right back."

"Where are you going?"

"To kick some Morgan ass." She leaned her pool cue against the wall and headed for the bar.

* * *

"Uh oh," Claire said. "Here she comes. I think we've been made. Everybody act normal."

Everyone besides Claire stared at Natalie as she stormed the bar like a frothing tidal wave.

Claire remembered the pitcher of money one second too late.

"What in the hell is this?" Natalie held up the pitcher.

Utter silence was her answer. Crickets didn't even chirp. Mac, Butch, and Grady looked everywhere but at Natalie, while Kate and Ronnie were frozen with slack-jawed expressions on their faces.

Claire rolled her eyes. "It's money," she answered, being purposely obtuse.

"Funny, Claire." Natalie looked at each of them in turn, ending at the weakest link. "What's the bet, Kate?"

"You. Sex. Coop. Tonight."

Claire groaned. "Really, Kate? Did your brain just telegraph that via Morse code? That's it. I'm kicking you out of …" Claire remembered the sheriff was sitting there with them at the last minute and didn't know about their posse. "Out of the *group.*"

Kate flicked her arm. "You can't kick me out. It takes a group vote."

"Fine." Claire looked at Ronnie. "What do you say we send Kate packing?"

Ronnie shrugged. "Sure."

"Ronnie!" Kate gaped at her sister.

"I say Kate stays." Natalie weighed in, scooping out the money and cramming it in her skirt pocket. "That makes the vote tied."

"What group?" Grady asked, looking to Ronnie.

"Just family stuff," Ronnie replied, patting his arm.

"What are you doing with our money?" Claire asked, laughing when her cousin stuck out her tongue at her.

"I'm taking it."

"What?!" Ronnie stepped forward, reaching for the pitcher. "That's a lot of cash."

Natalie leaned over the bar and grabbed the soda water gun from the holster, aiming it all around. "Listen, you gaggle of smartasses. It's my sabbatical, so I win the bet. And when I find out who rigged the damned jukebox in your favor, there'll be hell to pay."

She holstered the soda water gun and headed back to the pool tables.

"Wait!" Claire called after her.

"What?" Natalie stopped and turned around.

She smiled at her cousin's flushed face. "Tell Coop I'm rooting for him."

Natalie raised her hand and pretended to wind up her middle finger. "Root for this, turkey gumbo!"

* * *

Almost midnight …

Natalie really shouldn't have had that shot of tequila when she returned from threatening her cousins. But she had, because … why did she do it?

Oh, yeah, she was mad because Claire had been right all along. Natalie was going to give in and have sex with Coop, and she'd probably like it. A lot. Too much.

But first, she was hot.

"Don't drink mad," she muttered to herself as she made her way to the restroom, pinballing through the crowd.

The bathroom was nice and muffled, cozy almost after the noise and commotion on the other side of the door.

"It smells good in here, too," she told her reflection in the mirror. "Like vanilla cake." She leaned forward and pulled her lower eyelids down. "Yep, pink."

Wait, what color were they usually? She couldn't remember, but pink seemed normal.

She bounced off the wall and stumbled into a stall, remembering to lock the door behind her.

"What am I doing?" she asked the stall door as she stood next to the toilet. She didn't have to use the bathroom. "Must be a habit."

Giggling, she returned to the sink.

Her purpose for coming in here resurfaced. "You're going to splash water on your face, remember?"

Right. She needed to sober up so she could play the third game against Mr. Sexy Detective. He'd won the second game, landing shot after shot with a finesse that made her even warmer for his form, and now it was time to see who was the best at pool.

She splashed her face, getting dribbles of water on the neckline of Kate's shirt. Oops.

Back in the mirror, she stared at the girl with the messy hair. She finger-combed it into less of a mess. This was nothing compared to Violet's wild curls. A pang of sadness washed over her. She hadn't talked to her best friend in too long. Maybe she should call her now and wish her a Happy New Year. It was almost that time.

Wait, what time was it anyway?

Natalie felt her pockets for her phone, but then remembered it was sitting in Butch's office.

Oh, well. "Let's go kick some cop ass," she told her reflection.

The girl in the mirror gave her a thumbs-up, like Kate had earlier.

"Stupid gamblers," she muttered as she pulled open the ladies' room door.

A blast of shouts and hollering made her wince. What was with all of the ...

Someone grabbed her by the wrist and tugged her outside through the patio door.

The cold washed over her, but the tequila's heat kept her warm on the inside.

"Happy New Year, Natalie." Coop's voice penetrated the thick fog in her brain.

She stared up at him in the dark. Slivers of light leaked through the patio doors, highlighting his rugged face. "Did I miss it?"

"Not really."

It was so dark out here, but the view above was incredible. "Look, Coop. Lucy in the sky with diamonds. Have you ever seen so many stars?"

"I don't give a damn about the stars right now." He backed her against the wall. "I've been wanting to kiss you all night."

She hiccupped. "Okay." She looped her arms around his neck and raised her mouth to his. There was no fighting this.

"You don't want to try to stop me?"

She laughed at the idea. "Nope."

"If I start, I'm not sure I can stop."

"Good."

He groaned, his hands spanning her hips. "Natalie, we shouldn't do this. Not now, not here."

She placed her finger over his lips. "Stop talking, Coop, and unzip this silly shirt."

"But it's cold out here."

"I'm burning up for you." She pressed against him, sharing her heat.

"Oh, hell, Nat—"

She shut him up with her mouth, tasting the whiskey on his lips, wanting more of Coop. One kiss turned into another and then another and then Natalie lost count. Frenzied touching followed, zippers slid down, fingers explored, thumbs flicked. Her head spun from the rush of feelings, or tequila, or both.

"Holy wow," she gasped, staring up at the stars sparkling in the dark, plush sky as Coop kissed his way down her neck. Was this really finally happening? It'd been so long since the last time they'd played this game. She'd dreamed about it too many times, aching to feel him touch her, showing her how much he wanted her.

His palms explored the backs of her thighs and higher as his mouth teased her through her bra. She clung to his shoulders as the world tilted and turned around her. A delicious ache grew within her, throbbing in all of the right places. She moaned, craving more of him.

Coop's lips climbed back northward, his hips pressing into hers. "Tell me to stop," he whispered in a ragged voice and then licked the shell of her ear.

"I don't want to." She lifted her leg and wrapped it around his thigh.

His hands cupped her hips, pulling her tighter against him as his mouth skimmed her collarbone, nipping and sucking as he went. "I can't resist you," he murmured against her skin. "Your lips, your body, your smell. You make me ache every night."

"I can fix that for you." She moved her hips, teasing him, inviting more intimate touches.

He groaned. His mouth returned to hers, his tongue flirting until she growled and kissed him fully, making slow love to him with her mouth.

When they came up for air, he put his hands on the wall on each side of her head. "We have to stop."

She covered her eyes. "Oh, God! Are you going to leave me hot and panting against a wall in the dark again?"

"No." He pulled her hand down. "But we're not going to do this tonight." He grabbed the O-ring zipper on her shirt and tugged it up. "Not like this. Not while we're drunk."

"I'm not drunk."

"You stumbled out of the bathroom."

"Okay, maybe I'm a little toasted, but I want you," she said as he adjusted his jeans.

"The feeling is more than mutual, but this is wrong."

She frowned. "Because I'm a local girl?"

He stilled. "No, Natalie. It's wrong because I'm crazy about you. When we do this for the first time, it's not going to be drunken sex behind a bar."

"What if I change my mind about saying 'yes' in the morning light?"

"You won't."

"I might."

He leaned closer and ran his thumb along her lower lip. "I want to be cold sober when I strip you naked, local girl. I want to remember kissing every single inch of you with total clarity."

"Oh." She gulped. "What else do you want?"

"I want you to be tequila free, so that you remember not only giving yourself to me, but also feeling every single movement when I'm making you mine."

Heat filled her.

Words left her.

Her heart fainted.

She nodded, trying to kick start her brain back to life.

"Now, how about some New Year's champagne?" he offered, taking her hand. "Your cousins were filling glasses when I left the pool table to find you."

"Don't we have another game of pool to play?"

"Not tonight. I'll finish schooling you some other time."

"You'll finish schooling me?" she guffawed. "You only won the second game because I drank too much tequila."

"Ah, hell." He held the door open for her. "See, I knew you'd use that excuse."

Chapter Seventeen

Tuesday Morning, New Year's Day

W hat's the story on this mine?" Coop asked as Mac eased Claire's Jeep through a dry wash at the bottom of a shallow ravine on the road to the Humdigger mine.

Mac glanced at Coop, who was sitting in the passenger seat. "My aunt Ruby owns it."

He dropped into a lower gear as he climbed up the other side of the ravine, the tires spinning a little in the loose sand and gravel. This glorified deer trail hadn't improved since the last time he and Claire had visited the mine, but the Jeep's four-wheel drive was taking it in stride.

"Has Natalie told you about Ruby's husband?" Butch asked Coop from the backseat. "The one she was married to before Natalie's grandpa?"

Mac glanced at Butch in the rearview mirror, wondering how much show and tell was a good idea when it came to the Deadwood detective.

If Claire were along for the ride, she'd be covering their mouths at this point, but she was probably still sprawled out in their bed after last night's revelry at the bar. She'd downed her fair share of beers, stumbling out to the Jeep with Mac's help around two in the morning. She'd conked out on the short drive to the RV park, so plastered that he'd had to carry her inside and undress her. When he'd joined her under the covers, she muttered something about "Crazy Kate" and burrowed into his side, returning to her drunken slumber. Those naked plans for New Year's that she'd mentioned before had been drowned out by alcohol … for some reason. Mac wondered if it had to do with the diamond killer or Ronnie, who'd been acting odd last night as well. Maybe both.

"Do you mean Joe Martino?" Coop asked.

"Bingo." Mac skirted deep tire ruts in the road. "Now the question is what have you heard about Joe?"

"Natalie mentioned he had a checkered past." Coop shifted in his seat, glancing Mac's way. "She also told me about the other problem you're dealing with down here."

Butch guffawed. "Which one? We're flush with trouble most days, especially since baby hormones took over Kate's brain and she morphed into a modern-day Pancho Villa, leading her sisters in a rebellion against law and order."

Mac chuckled. "We should call her *Panch-ita Bandida*."

"I like that," Butch said. "Rolls off the tongue easy and sounds sexy, like 'Testarossa' or 'Maserati.' "

"You have cars on the brain." Mac slowed to ease over a rough patch of road.

"I know, and that's another problem."

What problem was that? Something to do with Kate? The baby? Something else? As far as he knew from Claire, Kate had no issues with Butch's newest business venture.

"I've always been partial to AC Cobras myself," Coop said. "Natalie did mention that Kate isn't usually this … uhh, spirited."

Coop appeared to be choosing his words carefully. Mac checked the mirror to see how Coop's statement went over with Kate's other half.

Butch was grinning. "Spirited? That's one way of putting it."

"How would you say it?" Mac asked.

Butch shrugged. "She's a bad mama jama."

" 'Just as fine as she can be,' " Mac finished the chorus to Carl Carlton's classic R&B hit. "Now I'm going to be singing that song all of the way up to the mine, damn it."

Butch laughed. "Don't sing it in front of Kate. She might hurt you. She keeps threatening to remove my baby-making tackle if I don't stop."

They bumped along for a moment listening to Deep Purple sing "Hush" on the stereo.

Mac tapped his fingers on the steering wheel to the beat, his thoughts returning to Claire and this crazy posse matter. He didn't entirely believe her comment the other day that the posse was just some nostalgic fun, a flashback of a club they'd formed as kids. Mac knew her too well. She wasn't one to sit back and wait for trouble to come to her. That was more Ronnie's style. Although lately, Ronnie was acting differently, more aggressive, snapping her teeth at the end of her chain rather than cowering in her doghouse.

Something was up, and with Natalie in the mix, Mac wondered what the three might be scheming on the side. Kate was their distraction, sidetracking Grady and Butch with her bouts of temporary insanity while the rest of the posse worked behind the scenes. But to what end?

He looked Coop's way, remembering what he'd said earlier. "What other problem did Natalie tell you about?"

"This diamond killer business."

Mac slowed over a teeth-rattling patch of washboard road. "How much did she tell you?"

Had Natalie spilled about the whole sordid mess, from Claire finding those glass eyeballs to all of the dead bodies left in the killer's wake? Well, all except for Tank, who managed to live to tell the tale.

"Enough to know Claire and her sister are in deep shit, especially after what Grady mentioned last night about the attempt on the tow truck driver's life in Yuccaville."

A volley of curses came from the back seat. "Kate is set on finding the damned killer before her sisters are crossed off his hit list." Butch leaned forward. "You know, I've tossed around the idea of paying Grady to lock up Kate in a jail cell to keep her out of trouble until they catch that asshole. Her tendency to ride tornadoes bareback these days keeps making my heart redline. It's only a matter of time before my engine seizes."

Mac smirked. "I suggested the same thing to Grady recently for Claire and Ronnie, too."

"Are there really diamonds?" Coop asked.

Mac and Butch's gazes locked in the rearview mirror. There were, and they were currently stored in the safe in Butch's house because that was one of the securest places in the county thanks to Butch's state of the art alarm system.

A deep V formed on Butch's forehead. "There are."

"Locked up safe in 'evidence' somewhere?"

"More or less," Butch answered.

According to Grady, until the killer was caught and the case wrapped up, he had to follow procedure when it came to what to do with the diamonds, whatever that meant.

"Sounds like Grady has his hands full." Coop's grim expression reflected Mac's feelings on the whole problem.

"You could say that," Butch said. "He'd tell you that since the Morgan sisters moved to town, he's developed a heart condition."

Considering the messes Grady continued to have to deal with thanks to Ronnie's ex-husband, Mac figured a "heart condition" was putting it nicely.

"You didn't answer my question," Coop said.

Mac sent him a raised brow as he eased through another dry wash that cut through the road.

"What's the story with your aunt's mine?"

"Joe kept it a secret from her for some reason." Mac scowled. Not for the first time, he wondered how many secrets Joe had taken to the grave with him, and if his aunt would ever be free of the dead man's web of deceit. "We found out about this mine recently only because Joe's first wife told my aunt about it."

Butch gripped the seat as Mac maneuvered over a rocky section in the road. "Joe's first wife, Sophy, is in prison south of Tucson for killing Joe's cousin years ago," he told Coop. "And for attempting to kill Claire."

Coop turned to Mac. "Your Claire?"

Mac nodded. "Last spring, Claire figured out Sophy was up to something shady and refused to remove her teeth from Sophy's ass."

Butch chuckled. "Claire's a badger. She'll fight at the drop of a hat. Kate aspires to be like her."

Mac groaned. "One Claire Morgan is enough for these parts."

"Now you sound like Grady."

"What happened between Claire and Joe's ex?" Coop pressed.

"Claire started hounding Sophy, stepping over the legal line now and then." For Claire's sake, Mac didn't want to tell the detective about the breaking and entering bit, in which he participated, albeit sort of unwillingly. "Sophy threatened bodily harm and Claire still refused to back down. Things came to a head when Sophy caught Claire trespassing and tried to blow her to pieces with a shotgun. Luckily, Claire limped away from that battle, bruised and bleeding, but still breathing."

"Jesus," Coop shook his head. "So, Natalie's tendency to rush Hell with a bucket of water is genetic."

"That and her allergic reaction to cops," Mac said.

"By the way, Coop …" Butch grinned at Mac in the mirror. "How were Natalie's allergies last night?"

Coop turned in his seat, looking from Mac to Butch with one raised eyebrow. "Who did you two put your money on?"

Natalie must have told Coop about the bet that was going on at the bar while the two were playing pool.

"Good ol' Mac was behind you all of the way last night," Butch said. "Figuring you for a gentleman."

"What about you?" Coop shot back.

"Natalie is stubborn as hell and hard to tear down. I put my money on her strength."

"I can't fault you for that."

"No hard feelings on the bet," Mac told Coop. "Claire started the whole game to have fun with Natalie. Besides, she was on your side."

"Really?"

"Claire's been in your corner since you blew into town."

"I'll remember that the next time she comes to Deadwood and ends up in the back of a police car. What about you? Whose corner are you in today?"

"I'm not picking corners. I have my own broken fence to fix."

Butch leaned forward. "What broken fence are you talking about?"

"I'm tired of the commute between Tucson and Jackrabbit Junction."

"That is a hell of a drive to do too often. Claire isn't willing to meet you halfway?"

"Yes, but that's not a long-term solution. To be honest, I'm not sure I want what Tucson has to offer anymore."

There. He'd finally said it aloud. It felt good to get it off his chest.

In the mirror, Butch's brows drew together. "What *do* you want?"

"Something with lasting potential." Including Claire and a wedding ring, but one hurdle at a time.

"What do you do in Tucson?" Coop asked.

Mac gave Coop the quick version of his job, ending with, "I can't push for Claire to come to Tucson permanently because she will."

"I don't understand the problem then."

"Claire has already told me that if I asked her to, she'd put my job in front of her family and her happiness here."

"That's no good over time," Butch said.

"Right." Claire would end up resenting him.

Mac steered over another section of washboard-like rutted road, waiting until it smoothed out to continue. "I have a decision to make. Do I walk away from my career after six years of college and a decade and a half of employment with the same company for a woman who suffers from commitment phobia? Do I give up good money and a nice house in Tucson for an uncertain future and a spare room in my aunt's place in Jackrabbit Junction?"

"That's a lot of blood, sweat, and years invested in a career," Coop said.

"But you'd have Claire," Butch threw in.

"Maybe. That commitment phobia issue offers no guarantees."

The three of them were quiet for a moment looking out at the desert.

"I had a similar decision to make years ago," Butch said. "Only there was no woman. Should I leave a prosperous business with my brother in the city for a rundown bar in the middle of the desert? In the end, the need to escape to a place where life seemed easier won."

Mac chewed on that. "Now look at you, Mr. Easy Street. A busy bar and a kid on the way."

"Don't forget the 'bad mama jama' keeping me on my toes," Butch added with a grin.

They rounded a bend in the road and for a short time Mac could see the opening for the mine in the hillside. He slowed and pointed it out. Butch had been up to the mine with Mac before, but they'd gone through the booby-trapped front entrance that time, and Mac had paid the price with a dislocated shoulder.

"You really think Joe was keeping this mine a secret?" Coop asked. "Or was it just a dud property not worth the work to try to sell it?"

Mac shrugged, hitting the gas again. "If we find something hidden in the mine today, then I'll lean toward the secret theory."

"Joe has a history of hiding stolen goods in his mines," Butch explained.

"What sort of stolen goods?"

Mac told Coop the abbreviated version of Joe's history, focusing on the items tied to the mines that Joe had owned, the same mines that now belonged to Ruby. Mac skipped over the additional pinched pieces Claire had found stashed around the campground, keeping in mind her paranoia about the law barging in and making life hell for his aunt.

"And you think something might be up there?" Coop asked.

"Maybe. Or it could be just a human coyote hideout."

"If that's the case," Butch said, "we'll need to find some sort of evidence of human trafficking. According to Grady, Dick Webber won't allow the law to cross his property without a search warrant."

Grady must have told Butch about his run-in recently with Dick at the gas station. The old rancher was hard core that way. He'd snuck up on Claire and Mac the last time they'd come out this way, catching them on the way up to the mine. Lucky for them, Dick had taken a shine to Claire and ended up helping out by showing them the "other" entrance—the one Mac was headed toward today.

He started watching for the grove of mesquite where Dick had told him to park last time. It had been dark during that visit, though, so everything looked different in the light of day. They'd have to hike the remaining distance up to the mine, but it was only another few hundred yards or so.

"No matter the case," Mac told Coop, "I need to evaluate if the mine is worth keeping or if it's a liability for my aunt."

Coop scratched his jaw. "Seems odd to purchase a mine that sits in the middle of someone else's land."

"I agree," Mac said. "Was it a good deal that fell in Joe's lap? Or did he buy it on purpose, knowing Webber was paranoid and wouldn't let the law on his land?"

Butch nodded at Mac in the mirror. "Insurance."

"Exactly."

"I understand now the *what* and *who* behind today's trip," Coop said. "But why did you bring me along?"

"Because the last time Claire and Mac were up to the mine, they heard something inside," Butch answered.

"What sort of something?"

Mac grimaced. "The sort that might require the assistance of someone who knows how to handle a firearm."

"But I left my Colt .45 back at the camper."

"Not a problem," Butch said. "Mac brought his aunt's shotgun for you."

Coop snorted. "Well, that was neighborly of you."

"I'm all about taking precautions these days," Mac told him. "I've come close to dying too many damned times in the mines around here." He didn't know how many of his nine lives were left, but he really wanted to make it back to Jackrabbit Junction in one piece this morning, if possible.

He rounded another bend and saw the mesquite grove. Pulling off the side of the road, he killed the engine. "We go on foot from here." He crawled out of the Jeep.

The sun was high in the cloudless sky, adding a hint of warmth to the crisp air. The temperature had dropped close to freezing last night, but it was supposed to climb back up to a high of sixty-three degrees by this afternoon. It was a good day to hike up to an abandoned mine and figure out what was hiding inside.

The mesquite trees were full of sparrows, chattering and cheeping away. Mac walked to the back of the Jeep, where he'd stowed his aunt's gun and his backpack full of equipment. Something moved under the creosote bushes nearby, making the branches rattle. Probably a rabbit or more birds.

Butch and Coop joined him as he lifted his pack that bulged with supplies and safety gear. He'd already double-checked the battery life on his flashlights, portable gas detector, and other "toys," as Claire liked to call his rather expensive equipment.

The rumble of an engine approaching made the three of them turn. A beat-up 1967 Chevy pickup pulled in behind them, parking about twenty feet away. The driver's side door creaked open.

"Who's that?" Coop asked.

"Dick Webber." Mac remembered the old rancher's truck from the last time.

"So that's Webber. Did you tell him we were coming?"

"Didn't have to," Butch said. "Dick watches over his property like a hawk." He raised his hand in a wave as Dick eased to the ground. "Hey, Dick!" Butch walked over and shook the older man's hand.

Dick pulled a cane from his pickup cab, along with his trusty shotgun, which Mac had also met before.

"Is that a Remington 12-gauge pump-action shotgun?" Coop asked, squinting at the two men as they made their way closer.

"Yep." Mac slid his arms through his backpack, adjusting the straps. Coop apparently knew his firearms by sight alone. "Howdy, Dick," he said when they drew near.

Dick nodded hello to Mac, his long white beard blowing in the slight breeze. "Where's your woman?"

"Sleeping off our New Year's party."

His dusty, sweat-stained cowboy hat tipped to the side. "She marry you yet?"

"Nope. Her feet are still too cold."

"I got a solution for that."

"Oh, yeah?" What was it? The double-wide, jetted tub he'd talked about last time while trying to lure Claire away from Mac?

Or a shotgun wedding compliments of a certain 12-gauge, maybe?

"Offer to keep her feet warm until death do ya part."

Mac chuckled. If only it were as simple as keeping Claire's closet full of slippers.

The old rancher eyed Coop, a scowl spreading up his face. He raised his shotgun several inches. "Who's this? He stands like a law dog."

"He's a friend," Butch said. "He's visiting from South Dakota with his uncle."

Dick's gaze tightened as he sized up Coop. "What do you have to say for yerself?"

"I like the antique cannon in your hand. Hard to find one in good shape. Where'd you get it?"

Dick's hard expression cracked, a big grin spreading from cheek to cheek. "It was my pa's. I treat 'er better than I did my last two wives."

"You'd like my uncle's double-barreled beauty. He calls her 'Bessie,' and sleeps with her most nights."

"Still using the cane, I see," Butch said to Dick.

"Yeah. Ever since that damned fall I took, my knee gives out when I step wrong." Dick leaned over and spit a wad of tobacco in the dirt. "I hear you got a bun in the oven, Butch."

"Yep. It's halfway baked."

The rancher pulled a can of tobacco from his back pocket. "How you gonna run a bar with a baby hangin' around?"

"That's a predicament I've been struggling with for some time now. You want to buy my bar, Dick?"

"No, thanks. That's too much people work. Ranching is more my style. Cattle don't bitch and whine about their feelin's day and night."

"What would you do if you sold it?" Coop asked Butch.

Dick snorted. "He'd play with his old cars all day long."

"The bar was supposed to be a hobby of sorts," Butch explained to Coop, "after I unloaded my half of the business I owned with my brother."

"It ain't no hobby no more," Dick said, stuffing a wad of chew between his cheek and gum. "Businesses are like women.

At first they seem all sparkly and excitin', but then they start nagging ya day and night, never happy with what you give 'em."

Mac chuckled under his breath. Claire was sure missing out on a golden opportunity by shooting down Dick's marriage offer.

Butch nodded, grinning. "You're spot-on there, Dick. The Shaft has gotten too busy lately. It's taking everything Kate and I will give it and always needs more."

"You could delegate more of the responsibilities." Mac closed up the back of the Jeep, handing off Ruby's shotgun and some shells to Coop. "Hire a manager, maybe." He'd run his fair share of projects over the years that took as much time as he could fit in each day, having to delegate to subcontractors in order to finish the job on deadline.

"I've thought about that." Butch rubbed the back of his neck. "But I'm no good at delegating. I like to do things myself. That was part of why I had to leave the business I had with my brother. I was working too much, and the stress was eating me alive. The hands-on part is what I love about the car restoration gig."

"Sure would be nice to have all the free beer you could drink, though," Dick said, aiming his shotgun at whatever was moving under the creosote bushes. "And plenty of women when ya want 'em, too."

The bushes stilled and Dick lowered his gun.

"Hey, Dick, I have a question for you," Mac said. "Back when Joe Martino was alive, did he come up to his mine much?"

"Sure. He paid me what I called a monthly 'trespassin' fee,' so he could come up here whenever he wanted." Dick rested the shotgun on his shoulder. "That there was some of the easiest money I ever made."

"You mean like rent money?" Mac pressed.

"Sure, if ya want to call it that."

A bribe was probably more accurate, knowing Joe. Mac frowned in the direction of the mine. What in the hell was Joe up to out here? With the asshole dead, there was only one way to find out.

"Well, Dick, it was good to see you again." Butch must have picked up on Mac's itch to get moving. "Good luck with your coprolite search today."

Coop let out a strangled coughing sound and turned away to clear his throat.

"Thanks. Be careful this mornin'." Dick pointed his shotgun toward the mine. "I'd hate for something to happen to any of you due to some fishy business goin' on up there."

As Dick lumbered back to his pickup with his cane and shotgun, Coop and Butch grabbed some water and hats for the hike.

"I'll lead the way," Mac said when the three of them stood at the back of the Jeep again. He started toward the trail.

"Shit. Hold on," Butch said. "I left my phone in the backseat." He disappeared around the side of the vehicle.

Mac paused, looking over at Coop, who still stood at the back of the Jeep while he stared down at a handful of shotgun shells in his palm.

Behind them, Dick's pickup door creaked open.

"Coop." Mac took a step toward the Jeep. "Do you—"

A loud *BANG* thundered across the desert, silencing the sparrows. What sounded like a rain of hailstones plinked against the back of the Jeep, leaving dents in the metal and shattering a tail light.

Coop grunted, stumbling forward.

"What in the hell was that?" Butch came around the side, frowning toward where Dick Webber now lay on the ground by his open door, trying to sit up.

"Dick?" Butch called, starting toward the old rancher.

Dents in the metal ... shattered tail light ... Coop grunted ...

He turned back to the detective, whose face was pale and lined with pain.

"Holy shit!" Mac shucked his pack. "Coop's been shot!"

Chapter Eighteen

C laire pocketed her cell phone. "Coop's been shot," she hollered over the whining sound of the hammer drill while pulling on her work gloves.

Natalie looked up from where she was drilling holes in the house's foundation for the header board. The drill stopped. She frowned at Claire, pushing up her safety glasses and pulling out her earplugs. "What did you just say?"

"She said Coop's been shot," Chester answered from his supervisor's chair under the shade of the cottonwood tree. He turned to his newest partner in debauchery, Harvey. "You want to do anything about that? I can drive, if you need to go somewhere."

"You cannot drive," Claire said. "You've had three beers already today."

"What are you? My ex-wife?"

"Is Coop gonna live?" Harvey asked Claire.

Natalie stood, her face lined under her cowboy hat with either worry or fury, maybe both. "What the hell happened? Is Coop okay? I'm going to kick someone's ass if he's—"

"Calm down, John Wick, nobody killed your puppy," Claire told her. "Mac said they're at the ER in Yuccaville having the birdshot extracted from Coop's back. When the doctor is finished, the nurse will patch him up and send him home."

"Who shot him?" Natalie asked, her tone still high and tight, as if her heart had a death grip on her windpipe.

"Dick Webber did by accident. He fell and pulled the shotgun trigger when he hit the ground. Coop and my Jeep both took a hit."

Chester snickered. "I'm beginning to think people have it out for your Jeep. First Crazy Kate shoots a hole in it and now ol' Dick Webber peppers it with birdshot."

"Never mind the damned Jeep," Natalie said, her hands on her hips. "You're sure Coop is okay?"

Claire shrugged. Mac would have told her if they should drop everything and rush to the hospital. "According to Mac, Coop suffered several flesh wounds and bled a bit on the bumpy ride to Yuccaville, but he's refusing any heavy-duty drugs and should be able to return to most normal activities tomorrow."

"Fuck me." Natalie leaned against the side of the house, her shoulders hunched. "Now he has another holey shirt."

Claire picked up the cordless drill. She'd been securing the second beam to the posts bolted into the piers they'd set yesterday when her cell phone had started vibrating in her pocket. Trying to lighten Natalie's mood, she added, "Mac also mentioned that Coop has an impressive vocabulary of swear words."

"Well, he is a cop." Natalie looked at Harvey. "You're not worried about your nephew?"

Harvey hooked his thumbs in his suspenders, crossing his ankles. "Nope. If he's still breathin', he'll be fine. Coop's tough. He's made of rawhide wrapped with steel cable and coated with a thick layer of polyurethane."

"Yeah, but …"

"You've seen how scarred up he is, girlie," Harvey said. "He didn't come by those wounds from rollin' around in a meadow full of daisies."

Natalie nodded, frowning down at her boots.

"Mac expects them to be home within the hour," Claire said, taking off her Mighty Mouse cap and brushing several strands of hair out of her face.

She winced at the bright sunlight, still suffering from too much drinking last night. The pounding in her head had dulled thanks to some painkillers, but bending over repeatedly and working with loud power tools was reminding her why she needed not to overindulge with alcohol. She couldn't even think about food yet. The smell of Gramps frying onions and eggs this morning for Ruby's omelet had sent her rushing from the kitchen, spilling her black coffee on her faded La Diabla she-devil T-shirt.

"What did they find at the mine?" Chester asked.

"They didn't make it up there. Coop got shot before they hit the trail."

While Claire wasn't happy Coop got hurt, she was relieved that they hadn't been able to go up to the mine. She'd been jittery since waking up and learning from Chester that Mac, Butch, and Coop had headed up there this morning. Somebody had booby-trapped Humdigger mine for a reason. Who and why were questions she wanted to help Mac find the answer to someday soon—together.

While she was relieved none of the guys were seriously injured today, she had a bone to pick with Mac. Why hadn't he woken her up and taken her along? He knew she wanted to go up there with him when he went next. He could have at least told her he was going. After all, she'd waited for him to check out Joe's childhood home, dang it.

When they were in Tucson, he'd made her promise she'd include him in any of the posse plans, which she had technically so far, being that they hadn't made any definite plans yet. If this long-term, long-distance relationship business was going to work for them, the open lines of communication needed to run both ways.

Claire looked over at Natalie, who was still staring at her boots like they were crystal balls giving her glimpses of doom and gloom. "What's rattling around in your brain bucket, Natalie?"

Her cousin glanced her way, her expression troubled. "He's a cop."

Ohhh. Claire had a feeling Natalie was looking into the future and realizing the possibility of more bullet holes.

"So what if he is?" She jammed her hat back on her head. "Grady is, too. Besides, I've met plenty of retired cops who were still in one piece." Although there were a few scars on them—some mental and others physical.

"But what if Coop is some kind of magnet for danger?"

"Life's one big crap shoot," Chester piped up.

Harvey grunted in agreement. "It's like I told Sparky back home, ya never can tell which way a mule will jump." He grabbed a beer from the cooler at his feet. "And if ya could, where's the fun in that?"

Speaking of Deadwood, Claire asked, "Have you talked to Violet about your cop problem?"

"Not really. We've texted a few times about her kids and aunt, but that's it."

That was odd. Natalie and Violet were like sisters, usually sharing everything under the sun. "What's up with that?"

Natalie rubbed her neck. "I don't know. She's been busy with life, I guess, and I haven't had a lot of free time."

"Bullshit. Quit playing dodgeball with me."

Half of Natalie's face pinched into a grimace. "Fuck, Claire. I'm flirting with disaster down here, and I don't know that I want her to know about it."

Claire's bark of laughter echoed across the campground. "Sheez, Natalie. It's not as if Coop is the grim reaper." Unlike the killer knocking on Claire and Ronnie's back door. After a quick scan of the hillside behind Natalie for the umpteenth time this morning, she focused back on her cousin. "Enjoy the moment, have some fun, and quit making this more than what it is."

"What is it, though?"

"Hanky-panky with a side of spanky," Harvey cut in.

"*Sex*tracurricular activity," Chester added.

Grinning, Harvey threw out, "A bit of grope-and-hope without the slap-and-nope."

Chester wheezed. "A *sex*essful vacation-ship."

Claire took off her hat and threw it at them. "Knock it off, Tweedledee and Tweedledum." She turned back to Natalie. "I don't know what 'it' is between you and Coop, but whatever 'it' is, you can't seem to squelch it. So stop trying. It's only making you more miserable and distracted, which is making working with you dangerous to my health."

"Please, I'm not *that* distracted."

"You screwed your glove to the beam earlier," Chester reminded her.

"It was a tight fit in that crevice," Natalie defended.

"And then you dropped the hammer drill on Claire's foot," Harvey added.

"My hands were sweaty."

Claire snorted. The top of her foot still throbbed from that damned drill. "You've lost your tape measure three times so far this morning."

Natalie crossed her arms. "You guys keep hiding it from me, I just know it."

"Face it, Natalie. You're a hot mess because of that cop."

"I'm not hot."

Claire walked over by the old boys and retrieved her hat, dusting it off before pulling it on. "How did things go last night, anyway? Did you invite Coop inside the Winnebago for a nightcap?" And then some.

"I don't want to talk about it."

"Ah ha!" Chester said, cracking open a beer. "You owe me a ten-spot," he told Harvey. "The Winnebago of Love was rockin' and rollin' from the horizontal boogie blues."

"There was no 'ah ha' or boogie blues to be had, nosy nellies," Natalie said. "Coop was a complete gentleman. He saw me safely inside and then left. Nothing else happened."

The red blotches on Natalie's cheeks were hard to read. Did they mean she was telling the truth and unhappy with Coop's actions—or lack of actions, or did they mean she was hiding something from Claire and the peanut gallery about what really happened last night? Inquiring minds and snooping gamblers wanted to know. She'd have to catch Natalie alone later and press her for more details.

"Well, where's the fun in that?" Chester asked. "Even Willis here got some hokey pokey-ing in last night after the euchre tournament in Ford's rec room, didn't ya?"

"Sure did, and a fine dance it was. She turned herself around and I showed her what it's all about."

The two dirty birds broke into another fit of wheezes and snorts, clinking their beer cans together.

Claire shook her head, and then winced as a bolt of pain shot through it. She was getting too old to over-imbibe like she had last night. Her attempt to escape the stress of the diamond killer's hunt via drowning in the bottom of a bottle had worked temporarily, but she was paying for it and then some today.

"Come on, Natalie." Claire pointed her drill at the ledger board. "Let's get this done so we can get the joists into place before we head over to The Shaft."

Natalie nodded, wiping her face with her shirtsleeve.

"Later," Claire continued as she pulled a couple of wood screws from the pouch of her tool belt, "you can tell me what really happened last night between you and Romeo when you two disappeared at midnight."

Natalie hit Claire with a scowl. "You're not getting your money back."

"Fine. You're buying dinner tonight with *our* money."

"Deal." Natalie stuck the hammer drill bit into the shallow hole she'd been pre-drilling earlier. "Have you heard from Ronnie or Kate this morning?"

"Yeah. Kate texted that she was going to go pick up Ronnie at Grady's place and then run some errands before opening the bar."

Natalie looked up, her gaze wary. "What sort of errands?"

"I don't know." Claire winced. "Honestly, with Kate's fluctuating level of insanity, I was afraid to ask."

* * *

"I thought you said we were going to run some errands," Ronnie said to Katie as she parked her Volvo in front of The Mule Train Diner in Yuccaville.

"We are, but there's something we need to do first."

Ronnie leaned closer to Katie. "Did your cheek just twitch?"

"It itched." Katie shoved Ronnie back to her side of the car. "Stay out of my face and I'll be just fine."

"Yeah, you say that, but then you do something cr—"

"Don't say the C-word!"

"I was going to say 'creative,' you loony." She dodged Katie's pinching fingers, giggling. "Seriously, I'm not hungry." Especially after last night's binging on gin, tonic, and more gin. "What are we doing here? Did you order some pies for the games today?"

In the past, Penny had made pies for The Shaft for different occasions. According to Katie, Butch planned to have the bowl games on the television screen throughout the afternoon and evening for locals who wanted to stop by for food and drinks.

"We're having a meeting." Katie looked around, scanning the street. "Do you see any of Grady's deputies?"

Ronnie checked. "No. Why would they be following us? What did you do on the way to pick me up?"

"Nothing, but there was one parked outside of Grady's place when I came to get you. He drove off when you opened the front door for me. I suspected Grady was worried about you being alone at his house and keeping extra eyes on you. Guard law dogs, you know." Katie opened her door. "That or he's having you followed day and night."

She followed her sister outside, checking again for a Cholla County Sheriff's Department vehicle, but finding none. If Katie was right with her guard dog theory, Ronnie had mixed feelings about being babysat by Grady's crew—cocooned yet under a microscope.

She stepped up next to Katie. "What kind of meeting are we having? A pie-meeting?"

"You'll see. And you have pie on the brain."

When they reached the front door, it was locked. The lights were off in the front part of the diner. Ronnie pointed at the closed sign. "You sure you have the right day and time for this clandestine meeting?"

Katie knocked on the glass. "I'm positive."

Penny stepped out from the kitchen, waving at them through the glass. She unlocked the door and held it wide, closing and locking it again behind them.

"Sorry we're late," Katie said to her. "Ronnie has a hangover. I had trouble dragging her ass out of your brother's big bed."

Ronnie gaped at her sister's back as Katie followed Penny to her office. "Hold on a second!" She caught up with them. "If you'd have told me we were going to some 'secret' meeting with Grady's sister, I would have moved quicker."

"No worries," Penny said. "Besides, you timed it perfectly. Grady stopped by a short time ago on his lunch break and made himself a sandwich in the kitchen. If you'd been here earlier, he'd have a bunch of questions for us now and we'd be up shit creek."

"Does he do that often?" Ronnie asked, curious to know more about the family man side of Grady. "Stop and eat here, I mean?" She'd run into him here eating lunch one day when she was dodging the FBI, back before they'd started dating.

"Sure." Penny answered her question. "I make sure he eats healthy. Otherwise he'd skip meals and the stress of his job would be extra hard on him." She looked back at Ronnie as they passed through the kitchen. "When Elizabeth finished raking him over the coals years ago, he was skinny as a rail from barely eating at all." Penny's mouth tightened. "And now the cheating bitch has the gall to return to town like nothing happened, leaving her lover's kid back in Nevada for whatever reason."

Spoken like a true-blue pissed-off sister, Ronnie thought with a smile. She looked around at the darkened kitchen, focusing on the prep counter, picturing Grady standing there. She could almost smell his bay rum cologne in the air.

Wait. She lifted the collar of her shirt and sniffed. Oh, his scent was on her since Katie had rushed her so much this morning that she hadn't taken a shower yet.

"Someone needs to shove Elizabeth's head in the toilet and flush repeatedly," Katie said, jumping on Penny's bandwagon.

Penny laughed. "Kate, you're my kind of woman—the show no mercy, head-on-a-spike brand of spitfire."

"Please don't encourage her," Ronnie said, grimacing. "She's already been in your brother's jail multiple times over the last month."

Katie whacked Ronnie's arm. "Shush it, or I'll lock you up in Grady's jail and run away with the key."

Ronnie believed her.

For the second time in twenty-four hours, she found herself in Penny's office admiring the cacti photos on the walls. The recessed lights were on today, making the southwestern décor look even homier.

"So what's this secret meeting about?" she asked Katie and Penny while admiring a black-and-white shot of a giant saguaro.

"Your problem," Penny answered. "We'll get started in a

minute. I invited someone else this morning who will be in charge of ground patrol. She's in the bathroom."

Ground patrol? Ronnie frowned toward Grady's sister. "Are we building an army?"

"Sort of." She moved to the door. "Here she comes."

Ronnie heard the familiar squeak and creak of a walker. The sight of Grady's aunt Millie filling the doorway along with her infamous cherry red walker lined with dingle balls made Ronnie grimace and wince at the same time.

"That's not a nice face to greet me with on the first day of a new year," Millie said, smiling at Ronnie.

Ronnie moved over and gave Grady's aunt a hug. "It's not you, Millie. It's what Grady will do to me if he finds out I'm meeting on the sly with not only his sister but his aunt, too."

"Pshaw," Millie said, sitting on the couch Ronnie had crashed on yesterday. "That boy needs to loosen his tie. You're good for him." She pointed at Katie. "Her? Not so much."

Katie and Millie had a history that included whispered threats to do bodily harm and a possible smashed toe—Katie's, thanks to Millie's walker. They'd agreed at Thanksgiving to let bygones and hurt toes be a part of their past, but Katie still got her feathers ruffled when Millie shared breathing space with her.

Katie flipped off Millie. "Good to see you, too, dingle-ball bully." She scowled at Penny. "You're putting Mad Dog Millie, the ring leader of dancing-with-the-oldies gang, in charge of ground patrol?"

"It was 'Sweatin' to the Oldies,' " Ronnie corrected.

"I know that, Claire Jr.," Katie snapped.

"Yes, I am," Penny said. "Between Aunt Millie and her library friends, they'll be able to cover a lot of ground."

"You mean her library lynching buddies," Katie grumbled.

Millie cackled. "Ronnie, I'm liking your little sister more and more. She's got some spark in her bloomers."

"You might want to be careful around her," Ronnie said. "Pregnancy has made Katie's teeth sharper."

Katie blew a raspberry at Ronnie.

Penny chuckled, shaking her head. "I think this diamond killer of yours is going to regret the day he came to Yuccaville hunting up trouble."

Frowning, Ronnie leaned against Penny's desk. "I'm worried about Millie and her friends and you getting hurt."

"What about me?" Katie asked.

"You're Butch's problem. He's the one who knocked you up and sent you careening over Insanity Falls in a wooden barrel."

"Wow. Your love is so warm these days, like a scratchy wool blanket infected with smallpox."

"Don't worry about me and the girls," Millie told Ronnie. "We pick our teeth with barbed wire."

"So, what's the plan?" Ronnie asked Penny. "How do we find a killer who could be hiding in any of Yuccaville's many nooks and crannies?" That was assuming he was still lying low in town and hadn't pulled up stakes until things cooled down.

"Aunt Millie and her crew will canvass the streets, paying visits to hotels and motels, asking if anyone has caught sight of a John Denver wanna-be with a left-legged limp." Penny pointed at her aunt. "Try to be discreet about it, Aunt Millie. We don't want the sheriff's department or the local cops to get distracted from keeping an eye out for the killer. The end goal is for somebody to find the killer before he comes for Ronnie or Claire."

"What are you going to do?" Millie asked her niece.

"I'm going to hit some of the businesses where a killer might pass through, like Dirty Gerties and the gas stations. I'll talk to the owners, give them my number, have them act as extra sets of eyes."

"Good." Katie crossed her arms, her small baby bump showing under her blue flannel shirt. "I'm going to get hold of Tank if I can. I'll pick his brain, see what other clues he might have but doesn't realize." She looked at Ronnie. "You need to talk to Mississippi."

"Why?"

"Because he was there with Grady and might have learned something your sugar daddy isn't telling you."

"Grady isn't my sugar daddy."

"Are you sleeping under his roof and eating his food?"

Ronnie sighed. "Well, sometimes, but that doesn't make him a sugar daddy."

"Did he buy you those boots?" She pointed at Ronnie's new silver cowboy boots.

"For Christmas."

"And those earrings?"

"Shut up," Ronnie said. "I bought him things, too."

"Yeah, right."

"I could meet with Mr. FBI Agent," Penny offered, her expression hard, her eyes narrow. "I could make Mississippi howl like a bluetick hound dog for us."

"What's the deal with you and Mississippi?" Katie asked. "I saw you two butting heads a couple of times last night before you and I had our pre-planning meeting in the bathroom. How do you know him?"

"I didn't. Not until last night."

"You'll have to excuse Penny," Millie told them. "She used to have mad monkey sex with an FBI agent she lived with in San Francisco until he started investigating other women's vaginas with his rather rambunctious penis."

Penny squeezed the bridge of her nose. "You could have just said he screwed around on me, Aunt Millie."

"Yes, I could have, but 'screwed' is such a vulgar word."

So maybe Penny's animosity to Mississippi was what had Grady talking to her over by the *Big Buck Hunter* video game last night, and why she hadn't looked happy about whatever her brother was saying.

Katie snorted. "Penny, your FBI jerk sounds like Ronnie's ex-husband."

"Does he still live back in South Dakota?" Penny asked.

"Sort of." Ronnie cringed at her sordid, crime-laced history.

"He lives in prison," Katie blabbed. "Although it's one of the fancier resort-style lock-ups, we're told."

Ronnie growled at her sister. "While you're busy giving your tell-all about my past, why don't you spill about your ex-criminal boyfriends?"

Katie chuckled. "I'd rather tell them about your aversion to wearing underwear."

Millie cackled again. "It's no wonder Grady gets all googly-eyed when you're around."

"The sheriff of Cholla County does not get googly-eyed," Ronnie said. Although he did get very handsy when they were alone, which tended to make her get lippy back. "And I don't have an aversion to them. I skip wearing underwear because my yoga pants have a built-in crotch."

"Don't we all." Katie giggled. "And mine currently has a baby in it."

"That's enough with you, Mr. Hyde. Let Dr. Jekyll come back out to play."

"As you wish." Katie ran her hand down her face, smiling innocently at Ronnie when she was finished.

"That's creepy," Ronnie told her.

She shrugged. "What about Claire and Natalie?"

"What about them?"

"We need to give them a job to do."

"They have their hands full building Ruby's back deck in the day and working at The Shaft at night."

"That's true. Besides, Claire needs to keep Mac distracted."

"Why's that?"

"Because he's onto us," Katie said. "I can tell by the way he's watching us when he's working behind the bar."

Hmmm. Mac was very clever that way. "I'll talk to her." Ronnie looked at Penny and then Millie. "So, are we done here? Because I need to go back to Ruby's and shower before I head to work."

Penny nodded. "We should exchange phone numbers before you two leave so that we can keep in touch. Otherwise, we each have our assignments."

"Listen, I can't thank you two enough for helping Claire and me like this," Ronnie said. "You're putting yourselves in danger and don't think that I'm oblivious to that. If there is anything I can do in return, don't hesitate to let me know."

"There is one thing," Penny said as she lowered herself onto the arm of the couch next to her aunt.

"What's that?"

"My mom wants to meet you. Come to her birthday party with Grady."

Ronnie gulped. No! Not the mother. That was the real-relationship-deal stuff. "Is there anything *else* that I could do instead?"

Millie snickered. "Don't be such a puss. My sister just wants to sniff around you a bit. I promise she doesn't bite."

"Not usually, anyway," Penny added, and then the two of them laughed and laughed.

Chapter Nineteen

Mac climbed the porch steps to the General Store, pausing at the top to look to the east. The greens of Jackrabbit Creek's riparian vegetation snaked through the alluvial valley, which stretched wide as it sloped upward from the RV park to the purplish-blue Tres Dedos Mountains in the distance. Overhead, the vast blue sky made him want to lie on the sandy ground with his hands behind his head and soak up the fresh desert air.

It was a nice view.

It was a new year.

"It's time to shake things up," he said under his breath, feeling the certainty in the notion with a rush that made him eager to return to Tucson and set changes in motion.

But first, he needed to clear a landing strip on this end.

His aunt, the very person he needed to talk to, was leaning on the counter next to the cash register in the General Store, reading a magazine.

Kismet? Maybe so.

"Morning, darlin'," Ruby called out.

"I thought Harley and you were heading to Tucson today," Mac said as he walked to the back of the store and grabbed a bottle of iced tea from the cooler. He picked up a bag of trail mix on his way to the counter.

Ruby's curly red hair was pulled back in a ponytail today, her denim shirt rolled up at the sleeves. "We are, but not for another hour or so. We're fixin' to spend the night. Which reminds me, can we camp at your place if we do?"

"Of course." He set the tea and trail mix on the counter.

"You know you don't even need to ask."

She looked up from the magazine. Her green-eyed gaze searched his face, her freckled forehead lining at whatever she saw there. "What's going on with you, hon?"

Mac decided to ease into the truth. "I tried to go up to the mine this morning."

"Which one?"

"Humdigger." He threw a few dollar bills on the counter.

She pushed his money away. "You don't need to pay."

"We've had this discussion before." He pushed it back toward her.

With a sigh, she took his money and put it in the cash drawer. "What do you mean, 'tried' to go up to the mine?"

"Natalie's friend Coop was with me. He got shot before we could hit the trail."

Her green eyes widened. "What?!"

Mac explained what had happened, including the hour wait at the ER while Coop was being patched up, and ended with dropping the detective off at his camper a few minutes ago. Coop had told Mac he planned to clean up, change his clothes, and maybe sleep for a couple of hours after their late-night partying and early morning shoot-'em-up fun.

"Does Natalie know about this?" Ruby asked, her hand on her chest.

"Probably. I called Claire from the ER. I'm assuming she told her cousin."

"Holy smokes. I'm sure glad that boy is okay." She sat on the stool behind the counter. "Maybe you should just stay out of that mine, darlin'. First you end up in the ER with a dislocated shoulder and bruised ribs because of it, and now this."

His aunt didn't know about the odd sounds Claire and he had heard when they went inside the mine's back entrance last time, nor the cavern with the cots and other evidence of possible human trafficking, and she didn't need to as far as Mac was concerned.

"That isn't going to happen." He tore open the bag of trail mix. "You need to know what you have up there mineral-wise, and I want to know why Joe kept its existence a secret."

She puffed her cheeks and blew out a breath. "Some days I wonder if the best thing for us would be to sell this place and be rid of its peccadillos, once and for all."

"I don't think Claire would like to hear you say that." He poured several pieces of dried fruit and peanuts into his palm. "Her heart is tied to this place now."

His aunt eyed him for a moment, her gaze narrowing. "Tell me what's goin' on with you, Mac."

"What do you mean?" He tossed the handful of trail mix into his mouth, crunching on the sweet and salty blend.

"The last few times ya been here, you've had a rain cloud followin' you around."

It was no surprise Ruby had picked up on signs of his mental struggle. Since Mac's mom died almost twenty years ago, his aunt had been filling in for her sister and mothering him whenever she had the chance.

"Maybe you're just picking up Claire's mom on the radar," he said with a grin. Deborah did tend to hover over him like a dark, menacing thunderstorm cloud when she was on one of her "take-better-care-of-my-daughter" rampages.

"You joke, smartypants, but I'm serious. Tell me what's really goin' on in your noggin'."

Before Mac could answer, the curtain leading to the rec room opened and Claire's grandpa strode through. "Ruby, where did you put my—" Harley stopped when he noticed the two of them standing at the counter. "Am I interrupting something?"

"No," Mac said, opening his bottle of tea.

"Yes." Ruby's focus returned to Mac. "My nephew was fixin' to tell me what's been bothering him."

Harley grimaced. "I'll come back later."

"Wait," Mac said, surprising Harley and himself. He toyed with the bottle cap, wondering how to broach his decision to shake up his life. He waded into it. "Ruby's right. I've been struggling with a problem lately, and I've finally come to a decision that affects the two of you as well as Claire."

"Are you going to ask Claire to marry you?" Harley asked. "If so, I should install shackles in the basement to hold her steady before you pop the big question."

Mac smirked. Harley knew his granddaughter too well. "Not yet."

Truth be told, though, Mac had bought Claire a ring before Christmas. Nothing fancy, just a garnet shaped into a heart. Something simple that he thought a girl who doesn't wear a lot of jewelry might like. But he'd chickened out and tucked the ring away, worried a proposal would send her scurrying back to the Black Hills.

"I'm tired of commuting back and forth to Tucson," he said and took a drink of cold tea.

Harley joined his wife behind the counter. "I don't blame you. That's a long drive to make as often as you do."

"And dangerous, too, especially as tired as you often are when you make the drive after a day on the job." Ruby's forehead lined. "Have you talked to Claire about this?"

"More or less." He sprinkled more trail mix into his palm. "She's offered to spend three nights a week in Tucson with me and share the long commute, but I don't think that's going to cut it."

Harley put his hand on Ruby's back. "What will?"

"That's what I've been trying to figure out for the last few weeks. I've come to the conclusion that the career track I was on no longer appeals."

His aunt leaned her elbows on the counter. "Is this about that promotion you passed up back in November?"

"Partly." He tossed the snack mix into his mouth. He'd been aiming for that particular job for years. When that no longer became a goal, he'd started floundering, asking bigger-picture questions without being able to see the answers anymore.

Harley harrumphed. "Claire should have pushed you to take the promotion."

"She did," Mac told him. "She even agreed to leave this place and travel with me wherever I went, but in the end I passed on the job." He wanted Claire by his side, but he didn't want her to sacrifice her happiness for him.

"So, what's the problem then?" Ruby asked. "Have you changed your mind now about taking that promotion?"

"Actually, no." He fiddled with the bottle cap. "I'm leaning in the opposite direction now."

"Opposite how?" Harley pressed.

Mac laid his cards face-up on the table. "I'm going to quit my job."

His aunt's jaw dropped. "But honey, you love your job."

"I used to."

"Ah, hell." Harley crossed his arms. "Claire's gone and done it. She's rubbed off on you with her dandelion-seed-in-the-wind ways."

Mac chuckled. "Not quite. My feet are still touching the ground. They're just turned in a different direction now."

"What are you going to do if you quit?" Ruby asked. "What about your house? Your plans to travel overseas? Your—"

"I don't have any answers yet," Mac interrupted. "I'm still feeling my way through this, but I can tell you that the idea of continuing on my current path doesn't hold my interest anymore."

Ruby's ponytail bobbed as she nodded. "Okay then, what can we do to help?"

He looked at Claire's grandfather. "For starters, I may need to rent your Winnebago until I can find a more permanent place to live." Although if he did move into Harley's RV, he was relocating it to another spot in the campground. There was no way he could handle living next door to Claire's mother.

"Phooey on that," his aunt said. "You'll stay in the spare room with Claire for free. She works hard around here, earning room and board and then some for both of you."

"I don't want to crowd you two."

Ruby waved him off. "We've been fixin' to spend more time up north at Harley's place in the hills. Maybe bouncing back and forth every so often with Jessica if she's willin', especially come summer when it's so darn hot down here."

"What are you going to do for a job?" Harley asked.

"Honey!" Ruby frowned at her husband. "Give the boy a chance to breathe before leanin' on him about work."

"Okay, okay." Harley held up his hands. "But you know your nephew. Mac's not one to sit around for long. He's going to go stir crazy here if he doesn't have a job to do."

"Harley's right," Mac said. "I don't know what I'm going to do yet, but I'll find something. I could probably try to get in with the county, but that could take a few months."

Or years, most likely, but Mac didn't want to wait until a job came open to move on with his life now that he'd started the ball rolling. He and Claire could live on his rainy day savings for a long time, especially if he sold his house.

Speaking of Claire, he looked at them in turn. "Listen, I still need to talk to Claire about this, so keep it under your hats until I give you the thumbs-up. I wanted to run my plans by you two first, because after I quit you'll be seeing a lot more of me here."

His aunt reached over the counter and squeezed his arm. "Darlin', whatever you decide to do, you know I'm behind you one hundred percent."

"Thanks."

"*And* if you need financial help for anything, you know I have the money set aside that we found in the basement office last spring."

Mac shook his head. "That's Jess's college fund."

"We have enough money to cover her college without touching that." Harley eyed Mac, his forehead drawn. "Have you considered buying and running your own business?"

"What the planets are you talkin' about, Harley?" Ruby beat Mac to the punch.

Harley shrugged. "Mac has plenty of on-the-job experience running projects from start to finish, including budgeting and more, right?"

They both looked at Mac with raised brows.

"Sure, I guess."

"Do ya have somethin' in mind for him?" Ruby asked.

Harley shook his head. "Not at the moment, but running a business isn't much different than running a large project at a jobsite. You need to wear multiple hats and keep your crew working toward a common goal, all while keeping your spending in check and your costs down."

"Except that yer the boss," Ruby said. "If you succeed or fail, it's all on you."

His aunt had nearly failed with the RV park, coming within

days of losing it to the bank thanks to the medical bills Joe ran up before he died.

While Harley and his aunt figured out his future, Mac tipped the rest of the bag of snack mix into his mouth. Now that they were behind him moving to Jackrabbit Junction he needed to break the news to Claire. Would she be happy about him being there day after day? Or would living with him 24/7 feel too much like a commitment without the marriage certificate?

"I think you'd be good at running your own show, Mac," Harley said, bringing him back into the discussion. "I'd even be willing to go so far as to back you financially if you decide to buy a business and give ownership a try."

Mac blinked. A few months ago, Harley had been irritated whenever Mac came around, muttering about him being Ruby's white knight. After a few tense discussions, they'd come to an understanding about their roles in his aunt's life. Did Harley's offer mean he didn't see Mac as an adversary anymore?

"Thanks, I'll keep that in mind as I move forward," he told Harley. "And thank you both for being accepting when it comes to me moving here."

"Honey, you've helped me so much over the years since your momma died," Ruby said, patting his arm. "Don't hesitate to let me know how I can return the favor."

The front door creaked open, and Ronnie walked inside with Kate on her heels. Ronnie paused when she saw the three of them standing at the counter. "What's going on?"

Before anyone could answer, Kate closed the door. "Ruby, can I buy two gallons of milk for The Shaft?" she asked as she headed toward the coolers. "We're running low and I forgot to grab some at the grocery store while Ronnie and I were running errands in Yuccaville."

"Sure thing, honey."

"Where have you been all morning?" Harley asked Ronnie as she joined Mac at the counter.

"Uhhh, I crashed at Grady's place last night." She scratched at a spot on the counter where the varnish was flaking off, avoiding eye contact with her grandfather.

"She had too much gin with her tonic," Mac said, chuckling.

She wrinkled her nose at him. "Zip your lip, loverboy." She glanced back at Kate, who was lugging the gallons of milk toward the counter. "How was the euchre tournament last night?"

Mac rushed over and took the milk from Kate, setting them on the counter.

"Your mother drank too much again," Harley said, his mouth tight.

"But it was still fun." Ruby rang up the milk.

Harley scowled at Mac. "Not fun. Chester's new drinking buddy stole my wife's heart."

"He did not." Ruby laughed, swatting Harley's arm. She winked at Mac. "But that ol' boy sure can crank up the charm. Turns out I'm real partial to most South Dakota folks."

"You and me both," Mac said.

"If that's true," Ronnie said to Mac, "you need to stop giving me so much trouble about my handwriting when you're bartending."

"She said *most* South Dakota folks," he shot back with a grin. "Maybe you're not on my 'most' list yet, Ronnie."

He chuckled as she threatened him with her fist, stepping back to watch as Harley gave his granddaughters a hard time for fun.

This would be his new life from now on—family, and lots of it, with all of the chaotic highs and lows swirled into the mix. He'd always enjoyed his solitude, even preferred it at times. After he moved here, privacy would be a thing of the past—at least for a while.

Was he really ready for a life in Jackrabbit Junction?

* * *

"Slugger?" Claire heard Mac call for her. Footfalls crunching on the gravel outside the tool shed came closer.

Relief poured through her at the sound of his voice.

"In here," she hollered and scrambled to her feet. She pulled the pry bar free from the inside door handles, leaning it against the wall in the corner.

She moved to the workbench—and the piece of paper she'd

left lying on it. Frowning down at the words glued to the paper, she dropped onto the stool, her knees still a little shaky. Why couldn't all of this diamond killer shit just blow away in the wind like the rest of the tumbleweeds around here?

The sitting-duck reality of her situation had hit Claire on what was supposed to be a quick trip to the tool shed to grab another set of clamps. When she'd caught sight of the envelope stuck under the windshield wiper of Gramps's Winnebago, her head had started pounding again for a whole new reason. After she'd read what was inside the envelope, her heart had copycatted her head, thumping hard in her chest as the world closed in around her, making it hard to breathe.

She'd raced to the tool shed and shut herself inside, sliding a pry bar through the handles to be safe. Then she'd slid to the floor in the corner next to the workbench, panic squeezing her lungs as she stared at the doors, waiting for the killer to huff and puff and blow her tool shed down.

After a blur of moments with the only sounds outside of the shed coming in the form of throaty gurgles from a pair of ravens, calm and reason had returned to the helm and made the screaming broad who'd pirated her brain walk the plank. Claire's breathing had returned to normal. The pounding in her head had eased, too, along with that of her heart. But she hadn't reached the level of composure necessary to unbar the doors and step outside, returning to her role as sitting duck under the wide-open sky.

Now Mac was here, though. He'd make her feel better, and he'd know what to do about the damned note.

The hinges squeaked as one of the doors opened. Mac stepped inside, his brow creasing as he crossed the floor. "What are you doing in here with the doors shut?"

She held up the piece of paper. "Someone sent us another note."

"Another?" Mac took the paper from her. "*I have my eye on you,*" he said, reading aloud the cut-out magazine letters. "Hmmm. Nice touch here." He pointed at the picture of an actual person's blue eye that was used in place of the word *eye*.

"Yeah, that visual ups the creepiness factor to a solid ten-point-oh in my book."

She looked at him standing there in his khaki pants and a long-sleeve T-shirt that matched his hazel eyes. Earthy, level-headed, and rational, Mac was her rock island in the maelstrom of her life. What in the hell was she thinking, living two hours away from him day after day? She should have made him take that promotion, packed her bags, and gotten the hell out of Dodge.

And leave her family?

Maybe.

"What do you mean, *another* note?" Mac asked, frowning at her.

Claire sighed. "We got an anonymous letter like this one on Saturday. It was stuck under the Winnebago's windshield wiper in an envelope with Ronnie's name on it, just like this one was—only there was no name on the envelope this time."

"What did the previous note say?"

"It read: *You better watch your back.*" She pointed at the paper in his hand. "The letters were also cut out from a magazine, just like this one, but there were no freaky pictures on it."

"Christ, Claire." He set the paper down on the workbench. "Why didn't you tell me about the first one?"

She thought back to the day Natalie had brought them the envelope with Ronnie's name on it. They'd been in the General Store talking about … "I forgot about it because Chester came into the store with that newspaper article about the diamond killer leaving those two night watchmen in the trunk of a car in Tucson."

Mac searched her face for several seconds. Then he cursed under his breath. "Come here." He pulled her into his arms. "You're trembling. Tell me the truth," he said as his lips brushed her temple. "Were you hiding in here?"

"Yes." She buried her nose in the collar of his shirt, breathing in his warm desert scent that always helped to calm her. "The letter made me feel like the killer was here at the campground, toying with me. A fly trapped in his web."

"Oh, Slugger." He leaned back and cupped her face. "How do you feel about me borrowing Grady's handcuffs and keeping you chained to me from now on?"

Her laugh was low and husky. "God, Mac. I'm so tired of waking up each day and wondering if it will be my last on earth."

His hands slid to her shoulders, squeezing them. "You're going to make it through this in one piece, Claire, especially now that Grady and his men have something of a description of the killer, thanks to Tank. Everyone is on high alert, including your family. Why do you think Chester or your grandfather sit and watch you work?"

"Because they're bored and like to give me trouble."

"Well, partly yes, but also because everyone is keeping an eye on you and Ronnie. Grady doesn't want either of you two to be left alone, if possible. We're all working together to stand guard until the threat of the killer is gone." He kissed her forehead. "You aren't even supposed to come back here alone."

"Natalie went inside the house to get something to drink," she explained. "I decided to make a quick trip to the tool shed in the golf cart while she was gone."

"Where was Chester?"

"He and Coop's uncle went in search of more cigars."

"Are you carrying the mace I bought you?"

Claire nodded. "And the leather sap."

"Good. Keep them in your tool belt at all times."

Claire wrapped her arms around his neck. "I love you."

"Of course you do," he said, smiling. "I'm quite irresistible according to the ladies at The Shaft."

She poked his ribs, making him grunt and laugh at the same time. "Maybe we should get some handcuffs. Being cuffed to me might keep you from running off to the Humdigger mine without me in the future."

He had the grace to cringe. "I'm sorry, Slugger, but Butch told me only last night that he was available this morning."

"And you couldn't have mentioned it to me?"

"You were drinking."

"I would have stopped had I been given the opportunity to join you guys."

He looked off to the side, scowling. "Honestly, I didn't want to take you up there."

"Why not?"

"It's too dangerous. Look what happened to Coop."

She scoffed. "Coop's injury had nothing to do with exploring the mine. That was a freak accident." Although, judging from the number of scars on Coop's torso, he seemed to attract such calamities.

"It could've been you who was shot if you'd been there with me."

"Instead, it was just my Jeep."

"Exactly. The Jeep's replaceable. You're not." He tucked a strand of hair behind her ear. "I can't lose you."

The intensity of his gaze warmed away the last of her chills. "Mac, I don't want to lose you either, and you have bad luck in mines. Next time you go, take me along. Please. We're in this together, remember?"

"Okay. When I go up there again, you'll be right beside me. Dick Webber will appreciate you tagging along more than Coop, I'm sure." He glanced at her mouth, leaning toward her. "But given the choice I'd rather leave you safe and naked in our bed."

She pulled him closer. "By the way, who took off my clothes last night?"

His mouth curved upward. "They looked very restrictive and uncomfortable."

"Even my underwear?"

"You know how elastic can bind. By the way, how's your head feeling?"

"It and my heart are much better now that you're back from that mine, safe and sound. Kiss me already, damn it."

He did. She closed her eyes, sinking into the spell he wove around her, and slid her hands around his back.

When he pulled back, she sighed. "Did you come looking for me for some particular reason this afternoon, or were you just missing me?"

Mac leaned against the workbench and settled her between his long legs, his hands resting on her hips. "Actually, I need to talk to you about something."

Footfalls sounded on the gravel outside.

"Claire?" Natalie called.

Claire peeked out the shed window. She could see her cousin standing next to the golf cart in the drive. "I'm in the shed with Mac," she hollered.

Natalie paused outside the doors. "Are you decent?"

Claire rolled her eyes. "Yes."

"For now," Mac added with a wink.

"Good." Natalie pushed open the door. "Because I need you to get your asses in that golf cart. We have a problem up at the house."

"What now?" Claire folded the anonymous note and stuffed it back into the envelope to show the posse later. She grabbed the clamps that had spurred her journey to the tool shed and took Mac by the hand, following Natalie outside.

"Your sister is freaking out," Natalie said, climbing behind the wheel of the golf cart. "Hurry up and get in."

"Which sister?" Mac asked as Claire locked up behind them.

"My money is on Kate." Claire shoved him into the passenger seat of the golf cart, squeezing onto his lap.

"Actually, it's Ronnie." Natalie hit the gas pedal. "She got a call from Mississippi."

"Uh oh," Mac said.

"Somebody stabbed her ex while he was working at the prison laundry, stuffed him into one of those industrial dryers, and turned it on. One of the other inmates found him. He heard the sound of Lyle banging around in there."

Claire shuddered at the image that put in her head. "Holy hell. Is he dead?"

"Not yet." Natalie glanced her way. "But the new year is just getting started."

Chapter Twenty

Natalie hadn't seen Coop all day. As a matter of fact, she'd pretty much avoided him, working on the back deck alone late into the afternoon so that she had an excuse for not checking on him before hurrying to The Shaft to help wait tables.

It wasn't that she had trouble handling the sight of blood or playing nurse. Her avoidance issue had roots stretching much deeper—clear to her daft heart that couldn't seem to stop pining over the damned man.

The last thing she needed right now was to get involved with a guy who risked getting shot for a living. Falling for a cop was a younger woman's game. Natalie was too old to stomach the constant worries that came with his job. A daily diet of stress and ulcers held no appeal, even if it came with a sexy dessert like Coop.

Time and again as she leveled and secured the deck joists to the header board and piers, her logical brain presented various reasons why sticking with friendship when it came to Coop was the smart plan for her future.

Yet just the thought of him left her breathless with sweaty palms, which resulted in the drill slipping from her grip and landing on her own toes not once, but twice.

Gah! Why did he have to follow her to Arizona?

"Earth to Natalie." Mac's voice cut into her thoughts. "This is Houston calling. Come in, Natalie." He set two bottles of Corona on her drink tray next to the three shots of tequila and a small bowl of lime wedges.

Natalie blinked back to Earth, taking stock of her order.

"What about the cosmopolitan?"

"That was part of your last order, remember?"

"Oh, yeah." She sighed. "I'm a little distracted tonight."

One of Mac's eyebrows lifted. "Have you talked to your *distraction* since he was patched up at the ER this morning?"

She shook her head. "Coop doesn't like anyone fussing over him." She knew that from a previous experience when he'd refused to go to the hospital for possible broken ribs, snarling at her when she'd tried to talk sense into him.

"Maybe he'll stop by later." Mac looked toward the main door.

Natalie followed his gaze, her heart shooting out of the starting gate only to screech to a halt when it landed on a trucker with a freight company logo on his cap. He waved at Mac before heading out into the cold desert night.

"Friend of yours?" she asked.

Mac shrugged. "I asked about his custom-painted Peterbilt parked outside in the lot, and he told me *all* about his vindictive ex-wife, including their vicious custody battle for their two prized Pomeranians."

Huh. Real life was stranger than fiction some days. "And thus we have a shining example of the glamorous life of a bartender counselor. Do you charge by the hour for your liquid therapy sessions?"

"Remove thy drinks from my bar, mouthy serving wench," he said with a smile, threatening to spray her with the soda water gun.

She delivered the tray of drinks to a table full of retirees staying at the RV park while on their annual birding vacation. As soon as Natalie had dropped off the drink order, Kate swooped in and grabbed her by the wrist, pulling her off to the side.

"We have a problem," Kate said, her gaze darting back and forth between the bar and Natalie.

Uh oh. Kate's left cheek was twitching again.

Natalie crossed her arms, bracing herself for another wild ride with Crazy Kate. "What's going on?"

"It's Mac."

"Mac?"

"Yes, Mac."

Natalie grinned at Kate's gunslinger squint aimed at the man of the moment. "You mean our 'Mac,' who is currently tending bar?"

Kate's glare swung her way. "Natalie, don't make me shave your eyebrows while you sleep."

Something flickered in Kate's eyes in between the twitches. Natalie took a step back to be safe. "Keep your razor holstered, Cactus Kate. What about Mac?"

"He's spying on me."

Natalie tried to keep a straight face. "Why would Mac be spying on you, Kate?"

"Because the sheriff put him up to it. Grady somehow knows what our posse is up to. There must be an infiltrator in our ranks. It's probably that batty aunt of his. She could easily play the double agent part."

Holy huckleberries! "What in the hell are you talking about, Kate? What's the posse up to now?"

"You know." Kate twirled around, fluttering her hands in the air, looking like a butterfly caught in a dust devil.

"What are you doing?"

"Trying to throw Mac off our scent."

Natalie glanced toward the bar. Mac was staring their way with a perplexed expression on his face that probably mirrored her own. "I don't think he's spying on you, Kate." She turned back to her cousin. "I was just there talking to him. He's too busy making drinks and chatting with customers to spy on you tonight."

"You underestimate Mac and his big science brain. I'm telling you, he's onto our plans to catch the killer."

"What plans? Did I miss a meeting?"

Kate waved her off. "Don't you worry your pretty head about things. You just do what Ronnie and I say and you won't be eating bugs anytime soon."

What? Natalie shook her head slowly. "Kate, I think your rudder is broken. Or your hull is cracked and you're taking on water. Either way, maybe you should lie down in Butch's office and try to focus on fixing your leaky brain."

A loud cackle of laughter came from Kate. She stopped laughing as quickly as she'd started. After a frown aimed at the jukebox, Kate leaned closer and whispered, "I have to go now."

Without further madness, Kate scurried away.

Shaking off that brush with insanity in the pregnancy form, Natalie cleared an empty table and carried the dirty glasses and mugs to the bar.

Mac "the spy" brought over the dish tub so Natalie could empty her arms and hands. Then he filled a glass with ice water, dropped a lemon slice into it, and set it in front of her. "You look thirsty."

"I am, thanks."

He nodded toward the jukebox. "What's up with Kate tonight?"

Natalie lowered the glass, watching him closely in case there was a grain of truth in Kate's loony ramblings. "Why do you ask?"

"The left side of her face keeps twitching whenever she hands off her drink orders."

"She's overstressed tonight."

"I keep catching her watching me like it's high noon and she's ready to draw and shoot."

"She's pregnant."

"Pregnant with a touch of paranoia seems more like it."

He nailed it. "I think she's catching downdrafts from the shit storm pummeling Ronnie's world."

"Could be. I should warn Claire to steer clear of her tonight so they don't end up in jail again before sunup."

Natalie snorted. "Kate does have a way of sucking her family into her maelstrom."

"Order up!" Claire said from the kitchen order window.

Mac walked over and grabbed the burger and onion rings, delivering the dish to a cowboy at the other end of the bar.

When he returned, Natalie asked, "Why is Claire working in the kitchen tonight?" Serving drinks was much more Claire's style, but since Natalie had arrived at The Shaft her cousin had been helping Butch prep food orders.

Mac glanced toward the order window, his brow lined. "That

letter she found today on the windshield of the Winnebago really knocked her sideways. Kate agreed to switch with her tonight and let Claire hide in the kitchen."

Claire wasn't the only one hiding tonight. Ronnie wasn't faring much better than her sister after learning about the attempted murder on her ex-husband. It wasn't that there were any lasting feelings for Lyle on Ronnie's part, more that someone had been able to get to Lyle, who was safely tucked away in prison. By comparison, Ronnie was an easy target. So, when the opportunity came to stay back at the RV park with Chester, Harvey, Jess, Manny, and even Deborah, Ronnie took it.

Natalie shook her head. "This is no good, Mac. Claire has a hard shell, but she's starting to crack along with Ronnie."

Kate was overzealous about many things, but she was right. The killer needed to be found before Claire or Ronnie had a full meltdown.

Butch stepped out through the batwing doors, joining Mac behind the bar. "We're winding down," he said, filling a glass with soda pop. "I think I'll close early and take Kate home. She's looking more frazzled than usual tonight."

Frazzled? That was one way of putting it. Natalie noticed one of her customers hailing her and headed off to see what the lady needed. While she was taking her order, the jukebox started blasting "Thank God I'm a Country Boy."

Natalie looked up sharply at the sound of John Denver's voice. Over by the bar Claire stared out through the order window, her eyes wide.

"Mac," Natalie said, waving to get his attention. She pointed toward the kitchen window.

He nodded and set down the glass of beer he'd been filling, moving to the order window. As Natalie watched, Claire pulled her hands down her face, nodding at whatever he was saying.

"Do you see anyone acting funny?" Kate was back at Natalie's elbow.

Frazzled didn't cut it. Kate's hair was a mess, sticking out around her face like she'd been recently electrified. Add that to her twitchy cheek and darting gaze, and Kate was one top hat with a "10/6" style tag away from joining the Mad Hatter's tea party.

"Funny how?" Natalie asked.

"I'm trying to see if the diamond killer is here tonight."

Natalie frowned. "You mean you played that song?"

Kate nodded. "When I talked to Tank today, he reiterated how much the killer was into John Denver. He even wore those big goofy glasses over his John Denver mask. That gave me the idea to play some of Denver's music on the jukebox and flush him out."

"You should have warned Claire about your plan."

"Why?"

"Because of the note."

"Which note?"

Behind Kate, Natalie saw The Shaft's front door open. Coop walked inside and paused, scanning the room. His gaze locked onto Natalie. There was no mistaking the heat in his gray eyes as he unzipped his leather coat.

John Denver's voice faded under the rush of blood in her ears. Her heart slammed against her ribs, trying to break free so it could dance around Coop's feet, the foolish organ.

"Natalie?" Kate pressed.

Natalie shook off Coop's spell. "Talk to your sister." She frowned at the jukebox. "And while you're at it, tell her you're the one who played that dang song so she doesn't lock herself in Butch's office for the rest of the night."

Natalie purposely took her time making her way to the bar. When she arrived, Mac was pouring a whiskey on the rocks into a tumbler in front of Coop.

"Let me know if you want something to eat," Mac said before heading to the other end of the bar to help another customer.

She slid onto the stool next to Coop. "Whiskey, huh? You sure it's okay to drink after this morning's ER visit?" She picked up his glass and took a sip, watching him over the rim as the grain and smoky flavors passed over her tongue and burned their way down her throat.

"Are you working part-time as a nurse when you're not waiting tables, Beals?" He took the glass when she held it out to him. His focus dipped to her mouth as he sipped from the tumbler.

She examined his face. Weary lines fanned out from his gray eyes. Stubble coated his jaw. His hair stuck up in shark fins. "Vacation is hard on you, Coop. You need to go back to Deadwood before you end up in a full body cast."

"Why?" He set his drink down. "You plan on roughing me up before I leave on Friday, Nurse Natalie?"

She laced her fingers on the bar and tipped her head to the side, pretending to give it serious thought. "I believe I'll start with some mild torture, locking you in my private stocks for a rough round of whipping."

He scoffed. "That's foreplay, not torture."

"After that," she continued, "I think a good stretch on the rack is in order while I find your ticklish spots with a peacock feather."

"Peacock feathers are passé." He took another sip of whiskey and then nudged it toward her. "How about using one of those long, iridescent green quetzal feathers that the Aztec and Maya revered?"

"I'll take your suggestion into consideration." She lifted the glass, swirling the amber liquid and ice. "For a grand finale, I'll lock you into a shrew's fiddle and make you read some of Shakespeare's love sonnets."

"Shrew's fiddle? Wasn't that a form of punishment for bickering women?"

"Sure, but I'm thinking it will work on a stubborn man just as well." She took another sip of his drink, setting the glass down in front of him.

He watched her lick her lower lip, his eyes darkening. "Love sonnets are overrated."

"You have a preference for romantic reading?"

"Yep. *The Gunsmithing Bible 100th Edition* is sexy as hell."

She laughed, leaning her head against his shoulder, giving in to her need to touch him while still keeping her hands to herself. "I don't think I can compete with a book about guns."

"You're wrong," he said after she sat upright again. He took another drink, his gaze smoldering as he set down the glass between them. "Especially if you're naked."

Poof! A circuit overloaded in Natalie's brain, blowing a fuse. It took her a couple of blinks to replace the fuse. In the meantime, all of the reasons she'd avoided making a visit to his camper this afternoon circled through her mind.

Great galoots! What was she thinking, trying to out-flirt Coop? What was next in her Amazing Acts of Stupidity sideshow? Juggling lit sticks of dynamite?

"You're an ace flirter, Coop," she said with a brittle smile, patting his arm. "You won that round, hands down."

His brow tightened.

"If I didn't know your history," she added, grabbing the whiskey glass, "I'd have swooned into your arms right then and there." She swallowed the last of his drink, handed the tumbler to him, and stood.

"Natalie," he said, setting the glass on the bar.

She held up her hand, stopping him. She needed to put some space between them before he kissed her and fried her whole damned electrical panel. "I need to go."

"Where?"

To find an extinguisher. Her unmentionables were on fire.

"The nearest nunnery would probably be best."

Coop caught her arm, holding her in place. "I'm not playing games with you tonight."

"Then what are you doing?"

Before he could answer, Butch joined them on the other side of the bar. "How you feeling, Coop?"

Coop let go of Natalie's arm, catching her hand instead and holding tight.

She looked down at their entwined hands. He was breaking her rule about holding hands in public. Then again, last night she'd been willing to have sex on the back patio with him, blasting her sabbatical vow to smithereens.

Criminy, Kate wasn't the only one flirting with bouts of insanity.

"Like I was used for target practice this morning," Coop answered Butch.

"Dick Webber called me this afternoon. He wants to pay for

your ER visit and offered up his new mixer as a peace offering."

Coop chuckled. "Tell him I know it was an accident and not to worry about the bill."

"And the mixer?"

"I don't need his mixer. I'm between houses at the moment. I'd rather have his Remington shotgun."

"You'll have to pry that antique out of his cold dead hands." Butch took a drink from his glass of soda pop. "Did you change the bandages like the nurse told you?"

"No."

"I can help you with that," Natalie offered before her brain realized what her big mouth had done.

Coop scowled. "I don't need a nurse."

She wrinkled her nose at him. "You could certainly use someone to remove that rectal thermometer."

Butch laughed.

Coop tried to hold a straight face, but his grin surfaced. "Fine, Beals. You're hired—for the bandages."

Mac joined them, inquiring about Coop's injuries. After that, the conversation moved to cars. Natalie left to collect money from one of her tables. Her hand stayed warm from Coop's touch long after she'd pulled free of his grip.

An hour later, the bar had a smattering of customers left, including Coop. Kate had given up on her quest to expose the killer for the night, keying in some Fleetwood Mac hits on the jukebox. Claire was working behind the bar with Mac while Butch sat next to Coop, picking his brain about being a small town detective.

"You should take him home," Kate told Natalie as they cleared a table.

"Butch? He's your problem."

"Funny girl you are not. I'm talking about your cop."

"He's not *my* cop."

"If you say so, but he's tired and winces every time he moves."

Kate was right. Natalie had noticed the signs of Coop's pain, too.

"I think he's waiting for you, though," Kate said, taking the tray of dirty drink glasses from Natalie.

It had been a long time since a guy waited for her. "But I need to help clean up."

"Butch, Mac, and I have this, and Claire already cleaned the kitchen. The rest is a breeze. Take Coop back to the RV park. He needs some rest."

"Can I leave my pickup in the lot overnight?"

"Give me your keys. Butch and I will drop it off at the General Store on our way out of here and leave the keys behind the counter."

Natalie handed them off. "Thanks."

Kate sniffed, leaning closer. "You smell like a drunken floozy. Take a shower before you try to sex him up."

"Shhh. I'm not going to sex anyone up," Natalie said under her breath.

"Of course you're not," Kate said, clearly full of disbelief.

"You're the one who stumbled into me and spilled the pitcher of beer down my front." Luckily, Natalie had caught Kate before she hit the floor along with the beer pitcher. "You need to wear safer shoes, preggo. No more slippery-soled boots."

"For the hundredth time, I apologize about the beer and I promise not to wear boots to work anymore. Happy? Now get out of here before I dump the next pitcher over your head."

"Don't even try it, spaz-o-matic." Natalie took off her waitress apron and stuffed it partway down the back of Kate's pants, making her cousin squeal.

She joined the group at the bar. "I'm tired," Natalie said when there was a break in the conversation. "Kate says I can leave for the night." She waited for Coop to make eye contact with her. "You ready to go? I have bandages to change while you snarl and bark at me."

"Sure." He finished off the glass of whiskey he'd been nursing for the last hour and stood, his movements stiff.

"Don't let him close enough to bite," Claire said, grinning wide. "He'll chew through your chastity belt."

"That's it, Slugger." Mac looped his arms around Claire from behind. "You're coming with me." He carried her off through the batwing doors.

Natalie waited for Coop by the door, not offering to help with his coat because she knew it would only make him growl at her again.

With a wave good-bye to Kate and Butch, she followed Coop out to his uncle's pickup.

"Let me drive. I've had less to drink than you." She held out her hand for the keys.

He shrugged and handed them off, opening the driver's side door for her. He rounded the front of the pickup, joining her in the cab as she started the engine.

"What are you doing, Natalie?"

She turned onto the road leading to the park, the headlights illuminating the cholla cacti and tumbleweeds lining the ditch. "Taking you back to the RV park so I can practice my bandaging skills."

"I don't need a nurse."

Natalie didn't feel like butting heads with him, so she came at him sideways. "Where are you sleeping tonight?"

For a few seconds, he didn't answer. "On the couch in the fifth wheel."

She made a buzzing sound. "Wrong answer."

"Okay. Where am I sleeping tonight?"

A glance in his direction found him watching her. "On the queen-sized bed in my grandfather's Winnebago."

He focused out the windshield.

The tires thump-thumped over the tar strips lining the asphalt. "City of New Orleans" played on the radio, Willie Nelson crooning in the dark. Natalie nudged the vents so they didn't blow her way. She was plenty warm just being alone with Coop, no help required from Harvey's rig.

"Am I sleeping there alone?" Coop asked.

Well, that was the big-money question, wasn't it?

Natalie had been waffling on that very subject all day, and frankly she was tired of her brain's incessant yammering about doing the right thing. She wanted Coop in her bed. Decision made. Brain overruled. Jury dismissed.

"That depends," she said.

"On what?"

"I want to help with your bandages and make sure you're on the mend."

He growled under his breath. "I don't want pity sex."

"Good, because I'm not giving out pity sex, you bozo."

"Then what is it?"

She sighed. "Damn it, Coop. Don't interrogate me. Just let me try to fix you tonight."

"Fix me how?"

She frowned as they rolled over the bridge into the RV park. "Do I have to spell it out?"

"Yes, because the last time we talked about 'us' while we were both sober, you just wanted to be friends."

Yes, she had.

She drove down the RV park's gravel drive in silence, parking next to Harvey's fifth wheel.

She killed the engine and turned to Coop. "S-E-X. That's how I spell it. Plain and simple, no strings attached, no pity involved, just hot, wet, and wild sex." She chewed her lower lip. "Although we'll have to keep it somewhat quiet because my aunt is in the next camper over. She might be drunk, though, so we don't have to be church mice."

He stared at her in the semi-darkness, saying nothing.

Whispers of uncertainty started to trickle into her head.

"Listen, Coop, I've wanted you since that night at the Purple Door Saloon years ago. There's no denying it. And you drove all of the way to Arizona to hook up with me, so let's stop analyzing this and just do it."

He sighed. "Nope. Not like this."

Heat crept up her neck, humiliation constricting her chest. "What do you mean, 'not like this'?"

"I didn't drive to Arizona for a hookup, Natalie."

"Then what are you doing down here? Why are you kissing me in the dark and flirting with me in the light?"

"I told you why."

"No, you didn't. Not really. How about you spell a word or two for me this time? A full sentence from you on the subject would be mind-bending."

He cursed.

"What's wrong, Coop? You don't like playing the spelling game?"

His hand snaked across the cab, hauling her close. "Spell this, damn it," he whispered and kissed her hard, his mouth punishing, his hold rigid. She didn't fight him. She didn't want to. This was what she'd wanted from him for years—to feel him lose his grip on that steely control because of her.

Natalie sank into him with a moan.

His kiss softened, deepened, slowed. His hand cupped the back of her head, his fingers entwining in her hair and holding her still as his tongue rubbed along hers and then pulled back, teasing her to follow.

She did, first with her tongue, and then with her body, only the dang steering wheel wouldn't allow her much movement.

"Coop," she panted when his mouth left hers.

"You taste like beer," he said, licking and sucking on her neck. He chuckled deep in his chest. "I wanted to taste the whiskey on your lips earlier, but this will do."

"Spend the night with me," she said, pulling his face back up to hers. "Please."

He stared into her eyes. "I want more than just plain and simple sex, Natalie."

"Well, I'd offer up my virginity, but you're a few years too late to that party."

"Hold that thought." He opened his door and eased out with a small grunt of pain.

He came around the pickup and opened her door for her, pocketing the keys when she handed them over. Taking her by the hand, he crunched along on the gravel drive next to her as they walked toward Gramps's Winnebago.

A breeze rattled the dry grasses down by Jackrabbit Creek. It was too chilly for frogs or crickets, but the stars glittered in the heavens and Natalie's fingers and toes tingled in anticipation of being alone with Coop again.

"I have one condition," he said as they neared the Winnebago.

"Name it."

"After you finish playing nurse, let me run the show."

She pulled the key to the Winnebago from her pocket. "Will I like this show?"

"If I do it right."

"Well, don't let me get in your way." She unlocked the door.

Same as last night, Coop went in first and made sure there were no boogeymen or diamond killers waiting for her. When he returned to collect her, she joined him inside and locked the door behind her.

They stared at each other for a couple of heartbeats.

Bandages, remember?

"First things first," she said, her voice sounded husky. It probably had something to do with her heart huddling in her throat. "Take off your shirt so I can have a look at the patch job they did on you."

He slid off his coat with a slight wince, allowing her to help with the sleeves. "I'd rather you take off *your* shirt."

She chuckled. "You have to uphold your end of the deal." She moved closer, reaching for the hem of his long-sleeve T-shirt. "Want me to help with this?"

He grabbed her hands, stopping her. "If you help me take off my shirt, Natalie, we're not going to bother with looking at my injuries."

That was a good point. "You're right. I'll just watch."

He pulled off his shirt with only a few curses and a grunt of pain at the end.

Natalie stared at his bare chest, her fingers wanting to explore. The last time she'd seen Coop shirtless had been when he was babysitting Violet to keep her from going to jail. He'd been wearing pants and scars and that was it. Natalie's retinas had nearly melted.

Her gaze lowered to the big swatch of white tape and cotton bandages rounding his side. "Does it hurt bad?"

"It stings. Thankfully, it was only birdshot. What's really driving me nuts is the tape. It keeps sticking to some of the wounds."

"Let's go to the bedroom and take it off then." She led the way, pointing at the bed. "Lie down on your stomach."

Once he did, she climbed on the bed and straddled his hips.

Carefully, she picked a corner of the tape loose. The contours of Coop's back were exaggerated by the low lamplight. She imagined bending down and licking her way up his spine. Delicious chills peppered her arms.

But back to this nursing business. "I'm afraid to pull the tape off," she said.

"Just do it."

"It's going to hurt."

"You can kiss me better later."

She smiled. He was reading her mind.

Blowing out a breath, she went to work on the tape, tugging it off while he grunted in pain. When it was done, she wadded up the bandages and stared down at the display of Dick Webber's shotgun art.

"Jeez, Coop," she whispered. "You poor guy. That blast had to hurt like a sonuvabitch."

"It didn't tickle. You said you wouldn't pity me."

"I said I wouldn't have pity sex with you. This is different."

"How's it look? Any visible infection?"

"Nope. It looks pretty good overall, more like a bad rash than a shotgun blast." The lower corner of his back had taken the brunt of the birdshot, with only a few scattered spots up near his ribcage. "Gramps has more bandages in the bathroom," she started to ease off the bed. "I'll get them."

He grabbed her by the wrist. "No. That tape hurts worse than the birdshot. I'll wear my T-shirt tonight and sleep on my stomach."

"But what about—"

"No." He pushed up onto his elbow, turning carefully. "Now, I held up my end of the bargain. It's your turn."

She looked down at her work shirt, smelling the beer that Kate had spilled on her along with the scent of fried food and grilled meat. Under it all, was a layer of dust and sweat from an afternoon of working on the deck. "I want to go shower first."

"This late?"

"I do it all of the time. It's just across the drive."

He started to move toward the edge of the bed. "I'll walk you there."

"No, stay put. The door to the showers has a lock. I'll be fine."

"Be quick while you're at it."

She nodded, bending and planting a kiss on his lips. Before she changed her mind about showering and just climbed back on top of him, she pulled away, grabbing Ronnie's knee-length terrycloth robe. "Give me twenty minutes and I'll be back smelling fresh and pretty."

"As long as you're naked, I don't care what you smell like." He stretched out on his uninjured side and yawned.

She blew him a kiss. "Get some shut-eye. I promise when I return I'll wake you in a way that you'll never forget."

"Hurry up, woman." He closed his eyes, his boyish grin and the dim lamplight making him look years younger. "I've been waiting a long time for this."

He wasn't the only one.

She closed the bedroom door on her way out, grabbing her shower bag and a razor from the bathroom before heading into the cold dark. She jogged across the drive and locked herself in the shower room. She grabbed the old radio Claire kept in the supply room.

As the water washed over her and golden country oldies played on the radio, she imagined what awaited her back in the Winnebago's bedroom. What did he mean, he wanted to run the show? Her body tightened and ached at the images her mind conjured.

She hurried in the shower, but shaving her legs slowed her down. Coating herself with Ronnie's berry-scented lotion after she'd dried off added extra minutes, too. All the primping would be worth it in the end. Soft, smooth, and sweet smelling was part of her arsenal. She wanted this night to haunt Coop long after the sun came up.

Twenty-five minutes later, she stepped out of the restroom into the desert night. The bright, glowing fireball across the drive made her gasp.

She dropped her shower bag. "Oh, God!"

The front half of Gramps's Winnebago was engulfed in flames. Black smoke roiled out from under the hood. Heat blasted her, like she was bending over a campfire, while the stench of burning plastic and engine grease filled the air.

"Coop!" she yelled.

Chapter Twenty-One

Wednesday, January 2nd
Just after midnight …

Ronnie stepped outside, quietly closing the General Store's door behind her. Grady should be here any minute to pick her up and take her home with him for the night. She stared toward Jackrabbit Junction, searching for headlights.

She tightened her flannel-lined jacket around her, pulling up the collar to keep her neck warm. She could smell Chester's cigar smoke in the fabric—a little sweet, a little acrid, and a little obnoxious; just like the bristle-haired buzzard. The stars were out in abundance, a sparkling dust scattered across the black sky. The cold, dry air made her nose tickle when she took a deep breath. The desert breathed in the darkness, a small breeze stirring the wind chimes at the end of the porch with each exhale.

Was the killer out there? Watching? Waiting for the right moment to strike?

Where was Grady, damn it?

Between a few New Year's disturbances by local yokels and the Tank versus the diamond killer bout, Grady had worked an extra long day. When he'd called to ask where he could find Ronnie, mentioning the need for her in his bed "for safekeeping," she'd told him to go home and get some much-needed rest.

But Grady was stubborn. It was probably one of the traits that helped him reach his sheriff status in the county. He'd wanted her to be part of his so-called rest and had insisted on driving out to pick her up, asking her to be ready for him so he didn't have to get out of his truck.

And who was she to disobey the sheriff of Cholla County when he gave her a direct order?

Headlights shone in the distance coming toward the RV park, growing brighter. She eased back into the shadows in case it wasn't Grady heading her way.

The attempt on Lyle's life had her jumping at shadows more than usual tonight, which was why she'd opted to stay tucked away at Ruby's place with Chester and Harvey instead of working at The Shaft. Ronnie had paired up with Jessica to play euchre, losing to the old boys but beating Manny and her mother, thanks to Deborah's extra dose of self-medication in the cognac form.

Ronnie crossed her arms, blowing out a steaming breath, trying to lessen the knot of anxiety in her chest. As if she didn't have enough worries with Lyle's laundry list of lies and schemes, not to mention the diamond killer threat, Deborah's drinking problem seemed to have gotten worse since the visit from Ronnie's dad. Claire was right—an intervention might be in order sooner rather than later, before their mother passed the point of no return.

If Deborah hadn't already.

The approaching vehicle seemed to be picking up speed the closer it got to the RV park. Ronnie watched it, her heart accelerating, too.

What the hell? Was it some drunk coming back from The Shaft? If they didn't slow down, they were going to take the curve after the bridge too fast and slam into the porch.

The vehicle went airborne when it hit the other side of the bridge, just a little, but still … "Slow down," she whispered, stepping out from the shadows.

Holy shit!

She should run.

She should go back inside.

She should try to stop them somehow before they crashed

. . .

Or maybe just run.

The vehicle rocketed into the RV park, skidding sideways across the gravel drive as it came to a hard stop.

She coughed, waving and blinking through the swirling dust, and saw the Cholla County Sheriff's Department emblem on the side of the white pickup.

The window rolled down.

"Get in!" Grady yelled, the CB mic in his right hand. He pointed out the windshield with it. "Fire!"

For the first time since she'd walked out on the porch, she looked back toward the RV park. Beyond the smattering of nearby campers, she could see an orange glow in the sky.

Fuck!

She opened the door to the General Store. She'd left Chester and Harvey inside drinking beer in the rec room while a western played on the television.

"Chester!" she yelled from the threshold. "Campground fire! Keep Henry in the house! Call Claire!"

Slamming the door, she leapt down the porch stairs and climbed into the cab next to Grady, who was rattling off codes into the CB mic, giving orders for fire crews and backup. He hit the gas while he talked, sending gravel flying as he raced toward the fire.

Ronnie crossed her fingers, hoping it was one of the restroom buildings on fire and not a camper.

When they reached the fire, she covered her mouth. "It's Gramps's Winnebago," she cried through her fingers.

She leaned forward, squinting through the windshield at the sight of somebody pounding on the Winnebago's bedroom window. The woman was wearing a robe that looked like Ronnie's. What was she ...

"Natalie!" Ronnie was out of the truck and running toward her cousin by the time Grady yelled for her to stop.

She didn't listen to him.

"Natalie!" She reached her cousin as the window around the back of the Winnebago shattered. A lamp flew out and crashed to the ground.

Natalie frowned at Ronnie. "Coop was inside sleeping," she explained and raced around the back of the Winnebago in her shower flip-flops.

Ronnie followed her, rounding the camper as a billow of

smoke poured out through the broken window.

Coop draped Gramps's bedspread over the broken windowsill and leaned out the window, coughing. "Get back! This place could blow if the flames hit the propane tank."

Ronnie grabbed Natalie and tugged her back toward the trees lining Jackrabbit Creek. In the meantime, Coop slid out the window legs first, dropping to the ground next to the lamp. His face was lined with pain when he joined them, his shirt missing.

Natalie rushed up to him, framing his smoke-blackened face. "God, Coop! I was afraid you'd passed out from the smoke. Are you okay?" She went on her toes and kissed him, not giving him a chance to answer for several seconds.

When Natalie pulled back, Coop ran his hand through his hair. "I'm lightly toasted, but still in one piece." He frowned at the burning Winnebago. "Natalie, when you said you'd wake me in a way I'd never forget, this was not what I was expecting."

Natalie let out a weird cackling-sob sound and buried her face in Coop's bare chest.

He wrapped his arms around her shoulders and looked over her head at Ronnie. "You two should head back to the General Store to be safe."

"Screw safe," Ronnie said. "We need to evacuate the nearby campers, if they haven't already heard the commotion." She didn't wait for him to agree, jogging back toward Grady's pickup as she peered through the smoke for the sheriff. Where was he?

Halfway there she heard someone call her name. She slowed, looking toward the burning camper. Manny rushed toward her with what looked like a big wrench in his hand.

"You need to move Deborah to safety. She's passed out in our bed."

"What about you?"

"I'm going to unhook the portable propane tank before it blows and lights this whole damned RV park on fire."

"What? No! Manny, that's too dangerous."

"Veronica! *Su madre. Ahora.*" He pushed her toward his Airstream and then raced toward the flames.

Where in the hell was Grady? After one last worried glance toward Manny as he rounded the back of the Winnebago, Ronnie raced around to the door of Manny's Airstream. "Mom!" she called, bursting inside.

Snoring came from the bed in the back. Ronnie found her mother sprawled out on top of the covers still wearing the silver lounge outfit she'd had on while playing cards earlier. One of her red feather slippers was on her foot, the other missing. The camper reeked of stale liquor and even staler cigar smoke.

"Mom, wake up!" She shook her mother by the shoulders. Deborah moaned and rolled away from Ronnie.

The fire next door made several popping sounds, flames crackling louder for a few seconds. Ronnie flinched, her heart performing a drum solo in her ears.

"Damn it, Mom, get up!" Ronnie grabbed her mom by the upper arm and hauled her across the bed and onto her feet.

Deborah swayed, almost dragging Ronnie to the floor with her. "Tired," she mumbled in Ronnie's face.

Ronnie cringed. "Jeez, your breath smells like a trash bin."

Cursing and grumbling, Ronnie dragged her mom to the door, knocking over a shelf full of Vegas knickknacks on the way.

Outside, she heard the sound of a fire truck siren in the distance over the roar of the fire next door. Natalie appeared as Ronnie half-carried her mother over to the gravel drive, lending a hand at getting Deborah spread out on a picnic table in an empty camper slot a safe distance from the burning Winnebago.

Ronnie shoved her hair out of her face. "Where's Grady?"

"Last I saw him, he was helping Manny unhook the propane tank."

She frowned at the fire, the front of the Winnebago no longer visible in the smoke and flames. *Please don't let that tank blow.*

The sight of Grady's pickup spurred her back into action. She started back toward the burning Winnebago.

"Where are you going?" Natalie called, following her.

"I need to move Grady's pickup so the fire truck can get through."

Natalie hopped into the passenger seat as Ronnie started the pickup.

"Where's Coop?" Ronnie asked, shifting into reverse.

"He's moving Chester's rig in case there's an explosion. Manny told him where to find the spare keys."

Chester's Winnebago Brave was no longer parked across the drive from Gramps's camper. Coop must have driven it away from the fire already.

"What happened to Coop's shirt?" Ronnie asked as she backed Grady's pickup next to the picnic table with her mother draped over it.

"Really?" Natalie asked. "You're going to ask about Coop's lack of a shirt after he was nearly burned to death in Gramps's Winnebago?"

Ronnie shrugged. "The question popped into my head."

"It's a long story."

She shifted into park and frowned at Natalie. "It's one shirt. How long can it be?"

"It started in the alley behind the Purple Door Saloon in Deadwood a couple of years ago."

Ah ha. Ronnie glanced down. "Is that why you're wearing my robe and your hair is wet?"

"We didn't have sex."

"Not yet?"

"Something like that."

The bright flashing lights of a fire truck came toward them. A crowd of bystanders in various styles of pajamas had gathered in the shadows, looking like sleepy zombie extras from an old George Romero film.

"We need to do some crowd control," Natalie said, opening her door.

Ronnie pocketed Grady's keys and followed, falling into step beside her cousin. "Any idea what started the fire?"

"No. I was in the shower for about twenty-five minutes. When I came out, the front half of the RV was in flames."

They split up then, keeping the other campers safely back from the smoke and out of the way while the fire truck crew arrived and got busy with their hoses.

A half hour later, the fire was out. Gramps's poor Winnebago looked like a charred, sad relic of days gone by.

Ronnie sat on the picnic table bench next to her sleeping

mother, watching Grady and one of the firefighters walk around what was left of the old RV. The fire truck's diesel engines rattled and growled, drowning out Deborah's drunken snores. The strobe light on the second truck flashed red and white repeatedly, almost hypnotizing with its monotony.

Claire dropped onto the bench next to Ronnie. "I called Gramps." She and Mac had arrived right after the first fire truck had pulled up.

Ronnie blinked away her worries about who might have lit the camper on fire, and if it had been meant to be a death trap for her, or Claire, or both of them. "Is he coming home?"

"He was going to, but I told him not to bother. The mess will be here waiting for him tomorrow." Claire thumbed over her shoulder. "We have a problem."

A gurgling laugh rasped from Ronnie's throat. "We have a plethora of problems. To which are you referring?"

"*Your* mother is an alcoholic."

Ronnie nodded. "It's gotten worse since Dad was here." Her gaze returned to Grady, who was now talking to Coop. Someone had given the guy a T-shirt. Judging by the words *Dirty Gerties* scrawled on the back, she suspected the provider was Chester.

A realization hit her. "Son of bitch!"

"What?" Claire asked.

"I need to borrow some clothes from you. Mine were in the Winnebago." Ronnie didn't have a bunch of money to throw at a new wardrobe right now either, damn it.

"Don't worry. Kate and I have you covered."

"Thanks. Where's Natalie going to sleep?"

"There's the couch in the rec room," Claire said.

"Where am I going to live now?"

"You could move in with Grady."

Ronnie blew out a breath. "I'm not ready for that yet."

"I didn't say you had to marry him."

"Once you move in with someone, there is no moving back out and staying together."

"You want to stop seeing Grady?"

"I didn't say that. I just don't want to rush moving in together. That's something you ease into."

"Now you're starting to sound like me."

Ronnie shoulder-bumped her sister. "You're rubbing off on me. Next I'll start scratching my butt and carrying a monkey wrench around in my pants."

Claire backhanded her shoulder. "What am I? Some ass-scratching ape in your head?"

"More of a well-trained chimpanzee."

"Kiss my monkey butt."

They sat in silence for a while, watching the cops and firemen start the cleanup and investigation work. The shock of what had happened—and what had almost happened—left Ronnie feeling dried up inside.

Across the way, Mac joined Grady and Coop, his arms crossed, a frown lining his face as he looked at the burnt remains of the camper.

A thump on the picnic bench made Ronnie look toward Claire. Katie sat on the other side of her, scowling toward the dead Winnebago.

"This was no accident," Katie said.

"Probably not," Claire agreed.

Ronnie rubbed the back of her neck. "Grady came over a bit ago and told me the fire marshal was going to return in the morning to do a more thorough inspection in the light and try to determine the cause of the fire."

Natalie strolled their way, still clothed in Ronnie's robe, but now wearing a pair of baggy sweatpants along with the flip-flops. "I'm tired," she said, sitting on the edge of the picnic table next to Deborah's head.

"How's Coop?" Katie asked her.

"Alive, but sore. When he slid out the window, he scraped up some of his birdshot wounds."

A chuckle came from Claire. "The guy drives all of the way to Arizona for a girl and instead he gets shot and almost burned to death in one damned day."

Ronnie grimaced. "Poor Coop."

"Did you at least give him some sugar before the fire started?" Katie asked.

"They didn't make it that far." Ronnie answered for Natalie.

"Which may have saved his bacon."

"There's a joke in there about safe sex," Claire muttered. "But I'm too tired to come up with it and Chester isn't here to help."

"Now what?" Katie asked.

"I say we get some sleep." Natalie yawned.

"We can put our heads together in the morning and figure out what this fire means," Ronnie added.

"I already know what it means." Katie stood, the flashing light making it seem like her left eye was twitching.

No, wait! Ronnie looked closer. Katie's cheek actually was twitching, along with her eye.

"Uh oh," Natalie said under her breath, frowning at Katie. She leaned next to Ronnie's ear. "I think Mr. Hyde just arrived to the party."

"This fire means that it's time for us to hunt down a killer," Katie stated, pointing in the air as though she were ordering her troops into action. "We are going to teach that John Denver–loving bastard a lesson about messing with the Morgan sisters!"

Chapter Twenty-Two

*L*ike I told Ronnie and Claire," Kate said to Natalie as she sped past the Welcome to Yuccaville sign without slowing. "I don't need a dang babysitter for this trip. I'm just going to get a pint of mint chocolate chip ice cream for my breakfast and some condiments for The Shaft."

"I hear you, Kate." Natalie glanced over at the speedometer. *Slow down, Speed Racer.* "But I lost at rock-paper-scissors today, so you're stuck with me."

Natalie stifled a yawn. She'd spent the night flipping and flopping on Ruby's couch in the rec room. The romantic romp with Coop that she'd fantasized about in the shower last night had gone up in smoke thanks to the fire.

In the harsh morning light, the sight of Gramps's Winnebago had made Natalie wince. All that was left of the old camper was a charred, partially melted, and stinking mess of plastic, aluminum, and polyester. Another nugget from Gramps's pre-Ruby days had gone the way of tall-pile shag carpet and avocado-colored appliances.

Kate had wanted Claire to cover the burnt remains with a death shroud, aka the big silver tarp that was currently covering several stacks of firewood behind the park's tool shed. But Claire refused, telling Kate the fire marshal would be there soon and he didn't want anyone touching anything until he'd finished with his investigation.

As Ronnie had said last night, her clothes were all trashed. Those that hadn't burned in the fire reeked from the smoke and gases released from the paneling, carpet, and linoleum.

Natalie's clothes were toast, too, but she'd only brought

along a small duffle bag's worth. She just plucked some items from Claire's closet this morning to use instead.

Coop's leather jacket and T-shirt were ruined. He'd shrugged off their loss, happy to escape the burning RV alive. The smoke and flames had reached the bedroom by the time Natalie's pounding on the window had woken him. Without her, he might not have made it. Then again, it was because of her that he was sleeping in the Winnebago when it caught fire. Oh, the irony.

Right before Natalie and Kate had left for Yuccaville, Grady had pulled into the RV park with the fire marshal right behind him. Claire and Mac were inside eating breakfast with Ronnie, who'd crashed in Gramps's and Ruby's bed alone, since Grady had been busy dealing with the post-fire mess for who knew how long last night.

Natalie blinked back to the present. Outside her window, the buildings of Yuccaville whizzed by way too quickly. "How fast are you going, Kate?"

"Slow as an old cow. Do you want to drive?"

"Always."

"Too bad. My car, my speed."

"Gee, Kate. Pregnancy has made you so sweet and loving. Aren't I lucky to be in your presence on this sunny morning?"

Kate blew a raspberry in Natalie's direction, but she did slow down to a speed less cringe-worthy.

"What does Yuccaville have for clothing store options?" Natalie needed a couple of shirts and jeans to make it through the weekend. Maybe a winter coat for the trip north, if they had any in stock down here in the desert.

"A couple of thrift stores, one cute little consignment boutique next to the hospital, and a—"

Kate slammed on the brakes.

Natalie reached for the dashboard. "What are you stopping for?" They were in the middle of the road on the main drag, the next stoplight two more streets ahead.

"I think I saw the diamond killer!" Kate made a hard right onto a side street. She hit the gas, the acceleration pushing Natalie back into the seat.

"Where?" Natalie looked left and right, searching porches

and driveways for … "What am I looking for?"

"That blue car."

"Which blue car?"

"The one that turned right in front of us with a Colorado license plate."

A Colorado … *Hold on!* "What makes you think that driver could be the killer?"

"John Denver, remember? 'Rocky Mountain High'? Colorado? Do I need to sing the whole song to you?"

Natalie glared at her cousin. "You're kidding, right?"

"No."

"Kate, there are a lot of Colorado plates in Arizona. The two states share a famous corner, remember?"

"The guy behind the wheel had blond hair," she added.

"Blond isn't exactly a rare hair color."

Kate pulled up to a stop sign and searched left and right several times. "Shit, we lost him."

Lucky for him. "Can we go get you some ice cream now?" Maybe Kate would get a brain freeze and return to her *sane* setting after the thaw.

"What happened to you, Natalie?" Kate took a left and hit the gas. "You used to be more fun."

"I'm still fun." But Kate was reaching an all-new level of deranged now, which was two tiers of lunacy above and beyond Natalie's threshold most mornings. "I'm just tired."

"That's because you were silly enough to try to sleep on Ruby's couch."

"Where else would I have slept?"

"With Coop."

"He's on a couch in their fifth wheel camper."

Kate shot her a grin that would have made Chester proud. "Yeah, but at least you could have had fun while you *weren't* sleeping there."

"That's a hair-raising smile, Kate. Next you're going to ask me if I want some of the candy that you keep in the back of your old Dodge van."

Truth be told, Natalie had mixed feelings about not joining Coop in his uncle's camper. Not that he'd asked her to, but the longing in his eyes last night when she'd told him she was going to Ruby's place to crash could have easily turned into an invitation if she'd pushed for it.

"So, you're still a sabbatical virgin." Kate giggled. It was an unsettling sound, more of a tittering whinny made by people secured in straitjackets.

Natalie changed the subject. "When's your next baby doctor appointment?"

"I don't want to talk about my— Hey! Do you see that guy?" Kate slowed down, pointing at an older man up ahead with silver-blond long hair tied back in a ponytail. He was walking along the sidewalk using a cane, moving slowly.

"What about him?"

"Tank rammed the killer into his workbench really hard. The killer limped when he ran off, his left side or hip injured."

"Kate, that guy is as old as Gramps."

"There's no age limit to being a killer."

"Yeah, but if you're going to stop and add every guy who uses a cane and has blond hair to your suspect list, you'll have that baby before we make it to the grocery store for your damned mint chocolate chip ice cream."

Kate harrumphed. "Claire's right." She eased back up to the speed limit as she drove by the guy with the cane. "You're too uptight lately. You need to get laid."

It wasn't like Natalie hadn't been willing to do just that the last two nights. It was as if the universe was working against her now, forcing her to keep her sabbatical vow. Was it a sign? Was sex with Coop a colossal mistake? Or was it just another example of her rotten luck when it came to men?

Amazingly, Kate made it to the grocery store without any other ridiculous chases. Natalie followed her cousin across the parking lot, checking her phone for messages on the way through the sliding glass doors.

There was a recent one from Coop: *Where are you?*

She replied: *Yuccaville. Ice cream emergency.*

Coop wrote back quickly: *I have an emergency, too.*

He must have been waiting for her reply.

What's wrong now? Natalie typed.

You're not here. Are you available tonight?

She hesitated, waiting for the universe to weigh in on her decision. The universe remained stubbornly quiet, so she went with her silly heart. *Yes. After I'm done at The Shaft.*

We have a pool game to finish.

She smiled. *Are you looking to get your ass kicked by a girl?*

You're cute when you talk tough. Like a tiny hissing kitten.

Prepare to lose your shorts, Law Dog.

He replied: *Prepare to lose your shirt, kitty cat.*

She stopped next to a display of seedless grapes and green apples, her pulse rate doubling. *Are we still talking about playing pool?*

No. There was a slight pause, and then he added: *But I am talking about playing with you.*

A rush of heat warmed her face and then raced south past her navel. She glanced up to see if anyone had noticed she was on the verge of "sexting" in the produce section of the grocery store and noticed Kate. She was standing frozen at the end of an aisle, her jaw gaping. Then the side of her face was hit by a series of twitches, like lightning strikes on the leading edge of a storm.

Uh oh.

Kate's lips flat-lined, her gunslinger mask sliding into place. All she was missing was a cowboy hat pulled low and a pair of six-shooters on her hips.

"Kate?" Natalie called, lowering her phone.

Her cousin glanced her way. *Killer,* she mouthed and took off up the aisle.

"Leapin' lizards!" Natalie pocketed her phone and jogged after Kate. She turned up the aisle, catching sight of her cousin two-thirds of the way along, bending to scan the various boxes of bandages for sale. What the hell?

On the way to Kate, Natalie veered around a blond guy with a shaggy haircut who was reaching high to grab a big bottle of peroxide from the top shelf. The hem of his faded T-shirt lifted up a couple of inches as he stretched, exposing a white bandage on his side.

The sight of the bandage reminded Natalie of Coop, her brain flashing back to last night before everything went up in flames … including her plans for romancing Coop after she'd taken off his bandages.

Oh, Coop. What were they doing? Sex would only complicate the crap out of their regular lives up in Deadwood. Was a night of pleasure worth upsetting the applecart? The old Natalie would have shouted "Hell, yes," and jumped into the fire with both feet. But months of soul searching had given her a new perspective. Sex was good and fun, but she was in it for the long haul now.

What was Coop looking for from her? She doubted he was the settling-down type of guy. One look at his life made that clear—from his soul-consuming career to his current gypsy lifestyle to the number of scars on his body and the risks they represented. He was another bad boy, clear down to his love of guns and motorcycles, and Natalie's history with men like Coop was littered with pieces of her heart.

But what if she didn't take this opportunity to further explore the depths of this mellower, vacation version of Coop? Would she regret playing it safe? Ten years from now, would she think back and wish she'd jumped into the fire one more time and enjoyed a brief moment in the heat with the one guy who got away, came back, and would probably get away again?

Coop … He filled up her senses, like a storm in the desert, like a …

"Natalie." Kate grabbed her arm in a vice-tight grip, yanking her back to reality. She dragged Natalie to the end of the aisle and around a sale display for vanilla wafers.

"Jeez, Kate. You need to seek help." Natalie pulled her arm free. "This ice cream craving is making you downright mean."

"Natalie, listen." Kate leaned closer, speaking low. "We just passed the diamond killer."

"Oh, sweet Orphan Annie! Not this again."

"He's the real deal. I'd bet your lucky underwear on it." Kate peeked down the aisle they'd come up.

Natalie crossed her arms. "Bet your own underwear. My lucky ones are off limits." Luckily they were still up in Deadwood.

"Crud! He's heading for the cash register."

"Kate, you need to stop this mad—"

"Come on!" She tugged Natalie to the next aisle, peering

down it, and then the next. "There! That's him in the green T-shirt."

Natalie looked down an aisle lined with freezers on one side and chips on the other. Sure enough, standing in line to pay was the peroxide buyer. "Yeah, I know, Kate. I passed him, too. Just for shits and giggles, what makes you think that guy is the one? Did he have a limp?"

"Sort of."

"Please tell me it's not just that his hair is blond."

"Did you notice the bandage on his side?"

"Yeah, so? Coop had one too until I took it off."

"It's the same area."

"What area? Same as Coop's?"

"No, Tank said he slammed into him, ramming the guy's left side into the workbench and some tools, and then there was blood left on the bench."

"There can be several reasons for a blond guy to have a bandage on his side." Such as getting hit with birdshot on the way to an old mine.

"And then there's his belt."

"What about his belt?" Natalie had been too distracted by the bandages to notice his belt … well, the bandages and Coop.

"It has the word 'Calypso' stenciled on it."

"The Greek goddess?"

"Calypso was not a goddess—only a nymph. But I'm talking about John Denver's version, not Homer's." Kate started down the aisle, tugging Natalie along. "And I think I saw the tail of a bull."

Was that some sort of idiom? "I have no idea what that means, Kate."

"In an Mexican article Ronnie found about the probable diamond killer, there was a mention of a tattoo of a bull on his neck. His hair was partially blocking the tattoo, but I'm almost certain that was a tail and not a snake." She stopped at one of the freezers and grabbed a half-gallon of mint chocolate chip ice cream.

Natalie would like to have a closer look at that tattoo before playing judge and jury on the guy. She glanced at the ice cream. "I thought you just wanted a pint for breakfast."

"He was also whistling," Kate told her.

"Whistling what?"

But Natalie had a sinking feeling she knew that answer …
Like a storm in the desert, like a sleepy blue … " 'Annie's Song,' " she
answered her own question. It was the same damned John
Denver tune playing in her head right now. She'd heard his
whistling, too, apparently, but had Coop on the brain at the time.

"Exactly," Kate said, handing Natalie the ice cream. "We
need to catch him before he escapes. Come on!" Kate towed
Natalie toward the cash registers.

Natalie pulled up short at the self-checkout station. "Kate,
hold up. Look at me."

Kate turned. "What?" Her left cheek twitched. Twice.

"You need to stop and take a breath."

"There's no time for that." She dug in her pocket and shoved
some wadded bills toward Natalie. "Here, you pay and I'll follow
him out."

"What? Wait, damn it!" Natalie needed to think this through,
but her brain was still cloudy from too much Winnebago smoke
and not enough caffeine.

Kate leaned closer. "He's paying now. We have no time to
wait. You get the ice cream and I'll get the car. Hurry!"

Sputtering, Natalie watched her cousin rush out the doors.
The guy in the green shirt wasn't far behind her.

Mother humper! Natalie had a feeling this morning's trip to
the store was going to end with another stopover at the county
jail. Maybe she should call Claire now so that she and Ronnie
could be ready with bail money.

"Hey there, sugar." A guy in an orange road crew vest
crowded her from behind. His breath was hot on her neck. His
hand brushed over the back of her jeans. "Are you going to buy
that ice cream or not? I have cold beer here getting warm."

She whirled on the guy, her nerves stretched too tight to put
up with this ass-touching troglodyte crying about his freaking
beer. She nailed him with a nut-shriveling glare. "Take a step
back, bitch!"

Whatever he saw on her face made him recoil. He did as told, taking several steps actually.

That was more like it.

Natalie scanned and bagged the ice cream, fed the machine the money, and then raced outside after the crazy pregnant woman.

* * *

Mornings in the desert were Claire's favorite time of day. The birds sang and tweeted, their whistles and chirps sharp in the cool air. Some of the campers were beginning to stumble outside and warm up in the bright sunshine. The chairs next to her worksite were empty. The old boys must be sleeping still after a late night full of flames and smoke.

Thankfully, nobody had gotten hurt last night besides Coop, and that was only a few scrapes during his escape from the Winnebago. He'd waved off the help of the paramedic who'd arrived with the fire crew in spite of Natalie's attempt to convince him a checkup couldn't hurt.

Gramps had called this morning to let Claire know Ruby and he would be home around noon. They were both relieved that nobody had been hurt. Lucky for him, the RV was insured … although as ancient as it was, he wasn't likely to receive much compensation for it.

A raven cawed at Claire from the top of the cottonwood tree next to the house.

"Don't boss me around," she snapped and grabbed a handful of deck screws, dumping them into her tool belt pouch.

The raven screeched and flew off in a rush, its wings swooshing over her head. She frowned after it. What was that about?

Claire tugged her Mighty Mouse cap lower, scanning the campground and the hills beyond from under the brim. Was someone out there right now watching her? Scaring off birds?

She probably shouldn't be out here alone. Mac had warned her that Grady wanted Ronnie and her babysat at all times, but she was tired of waiting around for an escort to go to work. The deck was right outside the back door. One scream and somebody would come running.

Still, to be safe, she searched the area around the RV park for a glare off a pair of binoculars; an ominous shadow in one of the camper windows; or a sniper draped in desert camouflage with a long-range rifle.

She snorted at the last one. "As if you'd be able to see that, dummy."

"Talking to yourself again?" Mac asked from where he was leaning against the side of the house.

"Where did you come from?" She hadn't heard the back door open.

He pushed off the wall and strolled her way. "I was over talking to Grady about the fire."

"Do they have any idea what caused it yet?"

"It's too soon. The fire marshal is still investigating the scene."

She blew her hair out of her face. "This is bad, Mac."

"It could've been the wiring, Slugger." Catching her by the wrist, he pulled her close. He sniffed around her neck. "Why do you smell like a smoldering Winnebago? I thought you showered this morning."

She pulled back and unbuttoned the top of her flannel jacket, showing him her shirt underneath. "Last night's T-shirt. I figured I'd wear it again since I'm going to get dirty." She frowned toward the back of the RV park where Grady and the fire marshal were probably busy sifting through ashes. "I don't think it's the wiring. Gramps took good care of his Winnebago."

His brow lifted. "You think it was arson?"

She nodded.

"With the intention to take out Ronnie or you?"

"Probably Ronnie, but maybe both of us."

"Why not rig it to blow up if that was the case? Make it a sure thing?"

That was a question she'd pondered as well, not coming up with an answer. "I don't know. But after the two anonymous letters stuck on the windshield, it's clear somebody knew we were using the Winnebago."

He scratched his jaw. "Let's see what the fire marshal comes up with and go from there. In the meantime, I'm here to help you build a deck." He rubbed his hands together. "So, put me to work."

She crossed her arms and stared him up and down. He looked lumberjack hot in his plaid fleece shirt, jeans, and boots. "If you're going to help, you need to take off your shirt. It's a requirement for males working on the jobsite."

"Oh, yeah? You don't make Chester take off his shirt."

"He's not working, only observing." And bossing her around. And telling dirty jokes. And …

"That's called sexual harassment, woman."

She winked. "I was hoping you'd pick up on that."

Mac's gaze narrowed. "That was a wink, right? You're not twitching like Kate now, are you?"

She faked spasms in her shoulder and the left half of her face. "What twitch?"

"Funny, Slugger. Meanwhile, your sister's electricity is flickering in her penthouse."

"It's not just flickering, she's short-circuiting." Claire pointed at the stack of composite boards piled next to the house. "You think a big strong man like you can carry a couple of those boards over here?"

"And then what?"

"We line them up, pre-drill holes, and get to screwing." She wiggled her eyebrows at him.

He laughed. "You've been hanging around Chester way too long."

After he carried a board over and set it on the joists, she handed a drill to him. "You can use Natalie's drill to screw."

He caught her by the coat collar and hauled her close for a hard kiss. "Sweetheart, you know I prefer my own tool for that sort of work."

Claire grinned up at him. "I think I'm going to like working closely with you, McStudly. Especially if you keep getting lippy with me." She kissed him back and then leaned down to grab her leather gloves.

"Speaking of working closely," Mac said, lining up one of the boards. "I need to talk to you."

She glanced up from the drill bit she was changing. "About what?"

"About us." He joined her, standing extra close, and reached into her tool belt pouch. "I need a screw," he explained with a sexy grin.

She glanced down at where his hand was taking its sweet time finding purchase. "You want that screw right now?"

His gaze dipped to her mouth. "As soon as I can get it." He held up one of the deck screws between them.

She batted her eyelashes at him. "Tell me, Mr. Garner. Do you always flirt this much with your co-workers?"

"Only the hot ones sporting a tool belt." He reached up and rubbed his thumb along her jaw. "Claire, I'm going to quit my job."

Claire tried to make his declaration fit into the little flirting game they had going, but she couldn't connect the dots. "I don't get it."

"There's nothing to get. When I return to work next week I'm turning in my resignation."

She took a step back, feeling like she'd been sucker punched. "What? Is this a joke?"

"No joke." He was watching her closely, his hazel gaze cautious. Serious. Intense. "I'll give them two weeks. If they need more time, I'll go up to three, but that's it."

She shook her head slowly. This didn't make sense. "But you love your job. Why would you quit?"

"I used to enjoy the challenges there, but now I've found something that I love more." When she gaped at him, he leaned closer and added in a stage whisper, "I'm talking about you."

Oh, no. Her heart hammered. Her knees felt weak all of a sudden. She dropped onto the loose board he'd lined up across the joists. "You can't quit, Mac."

He sat down next to her. "Why not?"

"Because you … because I … you can't quit." She frowned at him. "Listen, if this is because of us living apart like we have been, I'll move to Tucson with you."

He took her hand, lacing his fingers through hers. "Are you worried about money?"

"Of course not." Money was the farthest thing from her concerns about him quitting his job.

"Then why would you give up your family and this," he held his hand out, indicating the RV park, "for *my* job?"

She looked into his eyes, wanting to be crystal clear about her reason. "Because I want *you* to be happy."

"Who says I can't be happy here?"

She scoffed. "You'll get bored at the campground."

"Then I'll get a job."

"Doing what?"

He shrugged. "I'll figure it out." His gaze held hers. "Are you thinking that I'll smother you if we live together on a more permanent basis?"

She shook her head. "You didn't smother me when we lived together in Tucson."

They'd spent several months living together there before Claire had returned to the RV park where she felt much more in her element. City life fit her like one of those latex S&M outfits— tight in the wrong creases and chafing her in the right ones. Not to mention the drooling problem with the ball gag.

She pulled his hand into her lap. "I just don't understand why you would consider moving *here*? Jackrabbit Junction doesn't have many walls to be built."

He shrugged. "Maybe I'll add one or two around the RV park."

"What if you grow bored out here in the middle of nowhere? Worse yet, what if you grow bored of me?"

"You'll keep things interesting, Slugger. You always do with things like finding hidden treasures, trespassing around loaded shotguns, wearing sexy tight T-shirts, exploring creepy old childhood houses, falling down mine shafts … and did I mention your sexy T-shirts?"

She laughed. "I think we need to go back to Joe's old house."

"No."

"Mac."

"Maybe, but we're waiting until I live here full time."

"Deal."

He searched her face, sobering. "Is there any other reason

you don't want me to quit my job?"

"Like what?"

"Something to do with your fear of commitment? Because if that's worrying you, stop. I'm not going to pressure you into anything more than sleeping with me on a nightly basis."

Oddly enough, none of her previous commitment anxieties were even on her radar. "Committing to sleeping with you every night gives me no qualms whatsoever, Mac."

"Good," he said. "Because having you next to me is one of the things I miss most when we're apart."

The tenderness in his eyes made her want to swing her legs. She shot him a shy smile. "Where are we going to live?"

"I was considering your grandfather's Winnebago for the first few weeks so that we'd have our own space, but that's off the table now. I guess we'll have to sleep in Ruby's spare room until we figure out something else."

"What are you going to do with your house in Tucson?"

"Sell it."

"But you worked so hard on that house." He'd put a lot of sweat equity into making it beautiful, both inside and out.

"We can build another house together."

She lifted his hand, rubbing the back of it against her cheek. Another cloud passed over her sunshiny moment. "What if you realize in six months that you hate living here?"

He smiled as she kissed his knuckles. "Then we can talk about other options. But I'm ninety-nine percent certain that with you here, sweetheart, it's not going to happen."

"But if I wasn't in the picture, you would never—"

"But you *are* in the picture." He pulled their joined hands into his lap, rubbing his thumb over hers. "Claire, I want to do this. For me. For us. You were willing to travel with me for my job if I asked. I'm willing to try this instead for our future."

"You're crazy," she said, her throat tight with emotion.

"No, your sister is crazy. I'm just in love with my aunt's handywoman."

Mac was moving to Jackrabbit Junction. No more sad good-byes, no more worrying about him traveling back and forth from Tucson, no more lonely nights away from him.

"I love you to the moon and back, you know," she said, leaning her head on his shoulder. "Are you sure you're ready to put up with my sisters day and night?"

"Day only. At night it's you and me." He snorted. "And my aunt and cousin. And your grandfather."

"Don't forget my mom and Manny."

He groaned, grimacing up at the sky. "You know what? I think I just changed my mind about quitting."

She laughed. "I'll make it up to you."

He turned to look down at her, lowering his mouth to hers. "Deal." His kiss was slow and soft. Her head spun by the time he pulled away. "It's going to be a long two weeks on the job," he whispered, his lips trailing to her earlobe.

"I'll come back with you and stay until you're all done."

He leaned back, his eyebrows raised. "Really?"

She nodded. "I can pack for you while you're at work."

"Okay. We'll have to get a storage unit in Yuccaville. Rent a moving truck."

She smiled and swung her legs. "I'm so glad you're coming here to stay. I hate saying good-bye to you."

His focus returned to her earlobe, making her shiver with the brush of his lips. "Slugger?"

"Hmmm?"

"I have one more thing to talk to you about," he said in her ear.

Her legs stilled. "What now?"

"How do you feel about buying a bar together?"

Chapter Twenty-Three

Once upon a time, Kate Morgan was sane.

Unfortunately, the times had changed and this morning Natalie was left holding the bag—the bag containing a half-gallon of melting mint chocolate chip ice cream for the pregnant nutter. Meanwhile, she stood outside a grocery store in a rusty old mining town waiting for Crazy Kate to pick her up so they could chase down a serial killer.

How had it come to this?

At least the weather was nice today.

Hey, who invited Polly Positive to the party?

Like a storm in the desert ...

Enough with the John Denver songs!

Where in the hell was Kate?

As if on cue, Kate's Volvo raced up to the sidewalk, scaring a couple of teens who were texting while crossing in front of the store.

Kate's window rolled down. "Hurry up, Natalie! He's leaving the lot."

Ah, hell. They were really going to do this.

"Balls!" Natalie shouted and shook her fist at the blue sky, and then she raced around the front of the car.

Kate didn't even give her time to shut her door before stomping on the gas pedal. She took a right out of the lot and gunned it, rolling through a stop sign.

"You're going to get a ticket if you're not careful," Natalie said, gripping the dashboard.

"You sound like an old woman."

Natalie glared at Kate. The wind rushing in through the

driver's side window was blowing her cousin's hair every which way. Oh, how the sane and rational do fall. "Listen, Crazy Kate, I don't want to die before I get to have sex with Coop. I've been waiting a long time for that man."

"You should have followed him to his camper last night then." Kate shot her a glare. "And don't call me crazy!"

Natalie held up her hands. "Whoa! Okay, sorry, but your left eye is twitching faster than a rabbit's nose after snorting cocaine, and you're chasing down a guy who you think is a serial killer with *what* to capture him? Your enchanting wit?"

Enough was enough. Natalie pulled her cell phone from her pocket.

"What are you doing with that?" Kate rolled through another stop sign.

"I'm going to call Claire and tell her to come get us, because at this rate we're going to end up in Grady's jail cell again."

Kate snatched Natalie's phone away from her.

"Hey! Give that back to me."

Kate threw the phone out her open window while blowing through a third stop sign.

"What the hell!" Natalie turned in her seat, frowning out the back window at the sight of her cellphone lying in the middle of the road. Before she could sputter out another word, a huge pickup with a jacked-up suspension and meaty tires rolled over it.

She whirled on her cousin. "What is wrong with you?!"

"Me? What's wrong with you? Have you lost your nerve? We have the killer right in front of us and you're going to call and tattle to Claire."

"I … you … this is so screwed up." She looked backward again. The stupid monster-truck-wannabe was riding on Kate's ass. "That phone wasn't cheap."

"Phones are replaceable. My sisters aren't. We're going to stop this bastard before he hurts anyone else." Kate glanced in the rearview mirror, doing a double take. "Damn it to Betsy!"

"What now?" Natalie faced fully forward, keeping her eyes on the SUV Kate was tailing.

The killer ran the upcoming stop sign and gunned it, putting distance between them. He must have figured out he was being tailed.

"Deputy Dipshit," Kate said.

"What about him?"

"He's driving that asinine, cave troll–sized penis-inflator behind me."

"Good. Let *him* go catch the diamond killer."

"Ernie is as useless as a screen door on a submarine."

"And what are we? You can't ram that guy with your car, Kate."

"Why not?"

"Because you're pregnant!"

"Shoot, that's right."

The pickup sped up and pulled alongside the left of them. The horn blared. "Stop the car, Morgan!" the deputy yelled out his passenger window. Although he was too high up for Natalie to see him.

Kate flipped him off in reply and hit the gas, racing ahead.

"Christ!" Natalie grabbed the oh-shit handle above her door as Kate raced through another stop sign without even slowing down. "We're going to die today," she said. "My parents are going to be so mad at you for killing me, Kate."

"Relax. We're not going to die." She glared in the rearview mirror. "Though I may seriously maim Deputy Dipshit for screwing up our posse chase."

The SUV in front of them locked up the brakes and took a hard left. The vehicle skidded around the turn.

"Damn it!" Kate said. "He's definitely on to us."

"You think? Or maybe he's trying to get out of the way of the two crazy drivers flying up behind him!"

"I'M NOT CRAZY!" Kate screeched while swerving to the left to cut off Deputy Dipshit as he tried to ride up beside them again.

The big truck came up on their right side instead. "You're under arrest, Kate Morgan!" he yelled out his window.

Kate rolled down Natalie's window. "You're not on duty, Ernie! So shove your stupid arrest up your dumb ass! We're chasing a killer, damn it!"

"Pull over now!" The deputy's face was beet red as he glared down at them from his perch up high. Natalie wouldn't have been surprised to see steam puffing out his ears at that moment.

Kate rolled up Natalie's window and punched the traction control system button. "Hold on," she said as she flew past the road the SUV had turned down. "I saw James Garner do this on *The Rockford Files*."

Natalie gawked at Kate. She searched for her tongue and found it hiding behind her tonsils. "What are you going to do?"

"Lose this asshole." Kate hit the brakes hard, coming to a complete stop in the middle of the road.

Deputy Dipshit swerved, laying on his horn, and shot past them.

Kate shifted into reverse, watching over her shoulder, and gunned it for a couple of seconds.

"Please tell me you're not going to try a Rockford," Natalie said.

"Not try." Kate lifted her foot off the gas, whipping the steering wheel counterclockwise. "Do!"

"Fuck!" Natalie yelled, holding on for dear life as the car spun around in the middle of the road.

Halfway around, Kate shifted back into drive. As soon as the car finished spinning, she turned the wheel the other way and hit the gas, heading back the way they'd come. Then she turned down the road the SUV had taken, returning to the chase.

Natalie held her hand over her heart, making sure the poor thing hadn't flown out the window in the middle of that J-turn. The smell of burning rubber filled the car. "When did you learn how to do that?"

"I told you, I saw Jim Rockford do it years ago on the old TV show and then asked Gramps to show me how. He took me out on a back road in the hills and taught me how to do it with Grandma's old sedan."

Dear Lord! Kate wasn't just crazy. She was certifiably, grade-A, stark raving mad. "You're pregnant!"

"That was nothing. I've hit higher Gs rushing around the store with a shopping cart."

"Kate, I'm too old for this sh—"

"There he goes!" She made another hard left, sending Natalie slamming into her door. "I'm going to cut him off."

"What? How?"

"I know a shortcut." Two tire-skidding turns later, Kate turned into a narrow alley with brick buildings on both sides and slammed on her brakes.

The SUV was coming toward them, playing chicken.

"Please stop, please stop, please stop," Natalie chanted.

The SUV slid to a stop.

"Oh, thank the Maker!"

The driver laid on the horn. Behind him, Deputy Dipshit ramrodded into the alley, blocking the SUV from the other direction.

"We got him!" Kate shifted into park. She grabbed the Taser she'd used on Harvey from her purse, shoved it in the back of her yoga pants, and pushed open her door.

"What are you doing?" Natalie grabbed Kate's arm.

"He's trapped. I need to hit the killer with some volts before he makes a run for it." Kate pulled free and stormed away.

Natalie sat for a second, her pulse still racing from the chase. Now what?

"Son of a bitch!" She shoved open her door and followed her pregnant cousin into battle.

* * *

Ronnie leaned against the sheriff's truck, watching over the hood as Grady conferred with the fire marshal about the blackened Winnebago carcass.

Grady couldn't have gotten more than a blink or two of sleep, although his uniform looked crisp enough and his posture had no slouch to be seen. She was often amazed at his ability to work long, long hours without showing his exhaustion to the world. She, on the other hand, had given up last night, crashing on Gramps's and Ruby's bed after Grady told her he'd be another hour tying up loose ends.

After a quick shower to rinse off the smell of burning Winnebago, Ronnie had slept like the dead. This morning, she'd called Katie before she left home and requested her sister bring her red flare pants and black long-sleeve tunic for Ronnie to borrow for the day. Unfortunately, she had to borrow a pair of underwear and a bra from Claire, neither of which fit her quite right. Or maybe it was the knowledge that she had to come clean with Grady that had her squirming in her sisters' clothes.

While she was getting dressed, Grady had stopped by the General Store to see if Ronnie was around. He'd left a message with Jessica to come find him at the fire scene.

And so here Ronnie stood. His beck-and-call girl.

She stared across the drive at his backside view—long legs, nice ass, narrow waist, strong back, and broad shoulders. He was built to carry the weight of the county's worries. She hated to add to that load, but she needed to spill a few secrets now that Gramps's Winnebago had been added to the growing list of fatalities in the sheriff's jurisdiction.

Grady looked around, as if he could sense her stare. He tipped his hat upon seeing her, his face softening into a small smile. Then the fire marshal showed him something on his red clipboard and Grady's smile faded.

This fire was meant for her. Ronnie was ninety-nine percent sure of it, especially after the note Claire had found yesterday on the RV's windshield.

They should have told Grady about that note, but he'd been working a double shift yesterday. And then the whole Lyle mess had blown up in Ronnie's face, knocking her off course.

She sighed, scanning the RV park. So much could have gone wrong last night. This was her fault. If she weren't here, the Winnebago would still be in one piece and Claire wouldn't be next up on a hit man's list.

She ran her hands through her hair, tired of the guilt gorilla beating her down day after day. She needed to flip things around and get the upper hand on this shit, take back her life.

How many times had she thought that lately?

Too many to count. Cripes!

The problem was, she wasn't sure exactly *what* life she needed to take back. She had been Lyle's high-society wife before coming down to Arizona. Before that, she'd been her mother's puppet, doing everything she was told to do in order to find the "perfect" husband.

Truth be told, Ronnie wasn't sure who she really was anymore. Claire had accused her of returning to her old ways, dressing to please others, adjusting her behavior to fit a perceived mold. And she was right. But how did a tiger change her stripes this late in the game?

Ronnie supposed she could start her journey of self-discovery by focusing on the one part of her life she was sure about in her heart—her family. They knew her true character and accepted her, warts and all. Well, maybe not her mother, but there'd be no moving that mountain anytime soon.

Thinking about her family made her think about Grady's family. She cringed. What if they didn't like her? What if they thought she wasn't good enough for Grady? What if …

"Veronica." Grady's gruff voice interrupted her worries. He joined her at his truck. "How are you doing?" He leaned down and gave her a full, lip-savoring kiss.

"Grady, you're on the clock," she chastised, her cheeks warming. What was he doing, kissing her like that in broad daylight? She nudged her chin toward the fire marshal. "Not to mention you have company."

"Buster knows we're dating."

"The fire marshal's name is Buster?"

Grady nodded. "His grandparents raised him. His real name is Ben, but they were big Buster Keaton fans. The nickname they gave him stuck."

"How does Buster know we're dating?" And why would the fire marshal care about Grady's romantic life?

With a shrug, Grady explained, "Most of the town knows it, and those who don't are too busy with their own lives to give a damn."

He tugged on her sleeve. "You didn't answer me, babe. How are you doing?"

"I'm worried, same as before. This was a direct hit."

One side of his face creased. "We don't know that."

"What are the chances of the Winnebago where I usually sleep catching on fire out of the blue?"

"You usually sleep with me now," he reminded her.

"Officially, though, that burned-up mess was my home." Where was she going to store her stuff now? Where would she sleep on the nights she didn't stay in Grady's bed? Chester had offered her his couch, and while she liked the ornery old goat, that was a little too much of Chester in her daily life.

Then again, what stuff did she need to store? Most of her belongings had burned up in the fire. She was back to square one—homeless and hard up, only this time she didn't have any jewelry to pawn.

"Let's wait to see what Buster figures out before jumping to any conclusions," Grady said, leaning against the front fender.

She frowned toward the charred remains of the camper. "There's something else I need to tell you."

He turned her chin back in his direction. "Does it have anything to do with my sister canvassing Yuccaville, asking business owners to be on the lookout for a guy with a limp?"

She winced. "For the record, that wasn't my idea."

"Let me guess, it was Kate's?"

"And Penny's."

"And what about Aunt Millie and her knitting cronies? How did they get pulled into this?"

Man, he knew everything.

Of course he did. That was his job.

"Millie volunteered. You know how helpful she is."

"I know how much she likes to start trouble."

She shifted under his stare. "I would have told you."

"When?"

"Eventually." She twisted her fingers together. "What I really need to tell you about is another situation."

"Something to do with this?" He thumbed behind him.

She nodded. From the waistband of her pants, she pulled out the two letters that had been left on the Winnebago's windshield and handed them to him.

He opened one and then the other, the lines on his forehead doubling as he read. "Where did these come from?"

"They were under the Winnebago's windshield wiper."

"When?" After she gave him the dates, his scowl deepened further.

"The first one spurred us to form the Prickly Pear Posse."

His head tipped slightly. "The what?"

She went on to explain what they'd been up to behind his back, hugging her arms to her chest as his expression grew more and more stormy.

"Goddamn it, Veronica. When are you going to learn to trust me?"

"I do trust you."

"If you did, you wouldn't have formed this posse behind my back."

She raised her chin, standing tall in the face of his thunder and lightning. "The reason for establishing our posse wasn't due to a lack of trust in your abilities, Sheriff. We did it to form a solid front." When he started to speak, she held up her hand. "You can't be everywhere at once, Grady. You're only human."

"This is a matter for the law to handle."

Her laugh was short and harsh. "If the last year has taught me anything, it's that life does not abide by rules and regulations. Shit happens. Messy shit. Protectors come in all shapes, badge-wearing or not."

He growled, dragging his hand down his face. "You can't just go forming a posse on a whim."

"That's not technically correct. According to Arizona state law, a sheriff can request the aid of a volunteer posse."

His mouth tightened.

"A sheriff can also authorize the posse members to carry firearms," she continued.

"If and only if they have received proper training," he finished for her. "Trust me. I know the law. However, I have neither requested nor authorized a posse."

She shrugged. "Just because you haven't officially requested one doesn't mean we can't form a posse and have it at the ready in case you need us."

He looked over her shoulder, his face rugged and stony. "Damn it. Penny is right."

His sister? "About what?"

His amber gaze returned to her. There was no anger in his eyes this time. Nor any frustration. Something else hovered there.

Something bright and warm that made her heart swell. "I've met my match in you, Veronica Morgan."

She couldn't hold back her smile. After the last few days of angst and humiliation and uncertainty, Grady made her feel strong and confident with one loving look. Maybe she needed to see if Cherry from Dirty Gerties had a Wonder Woman costume she could borrow to surprise Sheriff Hardass some night. Although she'd have to pump up the bra part a little to match Lynda Carter's rack.

"I like your sister even more now," Ronnie told him. "And your aunt."

He scoffed in response. "Of course you would."

"But I love *you*, Grady Harrison."

He caught her hand and raised it to his lips. "Here's to many future battles with you." The heated look in his eyes promised more of where that came from later.

"And to the victor go the spoils," she challenged in return, cupping his bristly cheek.

His chuckle sounded gravelly in his throat. "I do enjoy your 'spoils,' babe."

Ronnie leaned her shoulder against the side of his truck. "They want me to meet your mother," she said, watching for a reaction to her announcement. "How do you feel about that?"

His frown returned, although it was shallow. He shifted, his moves hesitant. Wary maybe. Or was it something else? "I think the better question is, how do *you* feel about that? I've asked you to meet my family before, but you've resisted."

She had. Part of her wanted to continue the resistance, too. If she fell in love with his family like she had Grady, and then he dumped her for someone with less baggage and more sheriff's wife potential, Ronnie would be in a much worse position than her current destitute state.

The radio inside his truck crackled to life. "Calling Sheriff Harrison. Come in, Sheriff."

He cursed and stepped around her, reaching inside the open window. "Harrison here."

"We have a 10-80 involving an off-duty deputy and a Volvo registered to a female named Kathryn Morgan. Backup has been requested in the alley behind the Moose Lodge and the old Stage Stop Grocery building off Butterfield Street. Please advise with instructions for the deputy."

Grady frowned at Ronnie.

"What's a 10-80?" she asked.

"Chase in progress."

"Dang it, Katie! Not again."

He pushed the button. "I'm on my way." He tossed the radio back inside. "Your damned crazy sister," he grumbled and skirted her, rounding the front of the truck.

"It's Butch's fault." Ronnie beat him inside the cab.

He paused on the verge of climbing behind the wheel. "What are you doing?"

"Going with you."

"Veronica, get out of the truck."

"Sheriff, that's my pregnant sister giving your deputy chase. Get your ass behind that wheel and drive."

* * *

Natalie caught up with Kate at the front of the Volvo, grabbing her cousin by the jacket. "Kate! Hold up, for chrissake. We need a plan."

A breeze whipped through the alley, swirling dry leaves and a plastic bag around in a small dust devil and then battering them into the cinderblock wall of one of the buildings.

Deputy Dipshit opened his pickup door and scrambled down out of his behemoth, stumbling when he landed due to the two-foot drop from the running board to the asphalt. "You're under arrest!" he yelled. He reached up inside his pickup. When he stepped back, he was holding a handgun.

The SUV's driver's side window rolled down. The sunlight glinted off the top corner of the windshield, making it hard to see anything more than a dark shape inside.

Natalie pulled Kate behind her, blocking the pregnant loonybird from Deputy Dipshit. She raised her hands. "Everybody calm the fuck down!"

"Freeze, asshole!" Kate yelled, taking aim in the SUV's and

Deputy Dipshit's direction with the Taser gun from under Natalie's raised arm.

Natalie frowned at the Taser gun. Cheese and crackers! Somebody was going to catch lead today.

"Which asshole are you talking to?" she asked Kate. The guy in the SUV or Deputy Dipshit, who was striding their way with his arms wide and swinging like a big dumb ape.

Out of the corner of her eye, Natalie saw something flash inside the SUV. A long rifle barrel eased out the open window.

"Gun!" Natalie stepped back, bodily forcing Kate to do the same.

But the barrel took aim in the other direction.

Deputy Dipshit froze, his eyes widening.

Nothing moved but the dead leaves. The plastic bag scraped along the asphalt.

Natalie's focus dipped to Ernie's handgun. Was he going to raise it and shoot? If he did, she and Kate were at risk of catching some crossfire.

A popping sound broke the silence.

The deputy grabbed his neck. "What did you … ?" He pulled out a red dart. "Kate Morgan, I'm going to … " Ernie's knees gave out. "You stupid … " His eyes rolled back. Then he pitched forward, landing face first on the pavement.

Kate tugged free of Natalie's hold and raced toward the driver's side of the SUV. "Get out of the vehicle now!" she yelled, sounding like she'd recently graduated from the police academy.

"Kate!" Natalie ran after her cousin.

As they reached the SUV's open window, the passenger-side door opened and the guy in the green shirt climbed out.

He closed the door and stared at them through the passenger-side window, sizing them up. Another breeze whooshed through the alley, making his hair stand up in tufts. He may have liked John Denver, but he looked more like Buck Owens.

Kate aimed the Taser, seeming to forget there was a closed passenger-side window between the guy and her. "Tank sends his love, dickweed," she yelled, adding under her breath, "Natalie, go get him."

"With what? My ninja nunchucks?"

Kate huffed. "Distract him while I zap his ass."

"How? My juggling skills are rusty."

The guy took off running toward Ernie's truck with a definite limp.

Kate cursed and ran around the back of the SUV, chasing after him with her Taser leading the way.

"Kate, wait!" Natalie raced to Deputy Dipshit, who was still taking a catnap. She grabbed his gun and sprinted after Kate.

She caught up with her cousin a block away around the front of the building. Kate was holding her side, cursing.

"Are you two okay?" Natalie asked, pointing at Kate's baby bump.

"We're fine. I just got a stupid cramp. I can't run like I used to. You need to go after him. You're way faster and he's moving slow, thanks to that limp." She frowned down at the gun in Natalie's hand. "Where did you get that?"

"From your pal, Ernie. Here." Natalie held the gun out to Kate.

"You keep it."

"Take it and give me your damned Taser." She snatched Kate's Taser gun from her and shoved the handgun in her cousin's hand. "Go back and call 911. We need help."

Natalie took off after the suspect, hoping her cousin didn't have her chasing down an innocent man with a Taser gun.

"To your left!" Kate yelled from behind her.

She followed Kate's instruction, catching a glimpse of a green shirt about a block ahead. Kate was right, the guy wasn't moving very fast. That limp had gotten even worse from when he'd first started out. Tank must have really done some damage.

Natalie cranked up the speed, going into her high school track 100-meter dash mode. Her feet slid around more than usual in the tennis shoes she'd borrowed from Claire, but her legs held strong.

Up ahead, the killer climbed a six-feet tall chain link fence on the left. He was circling the block, Natalie realized, heading back toward his rig ... and Kate.

She reached him as he swung his leg over the fence and dropped to the ground on the other side. He cried out in pain upon landing and stumbled backward, falling on his butt out of reach of the Taser.

Natalie jammed the gun down the back of her pants and locked her fingers high in the chain link, looking for a toehold.

"You and yer sisters shoulda left those diamonds alone," he said in a southern accent. His words erased all doubts in her mind that Kate was right—this was the killer.

She pulled herself up the fence, her fingers finding purchase in between the twisted wires at the top. "You fucked with the wrong family, asshole." She pulled herself higher, her chin cresting the top. "The cops are on their way," she bluffed, hoping Kate had actually called 911.

With a grunt of pain, the killer pushed to his feet and limp-jogged away while holding his side.

"Kate!" she yelled as she started over the top of the fence. "He's coming your way!"

Natalie eased her body over the fence, feeling one of the sharp wire tips slice her skin through her shirt. Then she was over and dropped to the ground. Her knees twanged but held steady. She took off running after the killer, praying her cousin was ready for him because she knew there was no way in hell Kate would be sensible enough to hide somewhere safe until help arrived.

A gunshot rang out from the alleyway up ahead.

"Shit!" Natalie pushed harder.

She rounded the side of the brick building and found herself back in the alley standing opposite Kate. The guy in the green shirt was the monkey in their "middle." He stood half-crouched, clutching his side, warily watching Kate.

Her cousin had Deputy Dipshit's gun pointed at the guy. "Don't move, Mr. Killer." She held the gun steady.

Kate's face, on the other hand, was anything but still. Her left eye twitched along with her cheek.

Hello, Mr. Hyde.

The guy looked behind him for an escape, scowling when he saw Natalie standing there. She raised the Taser gun. "You heard the woman."

The sound of sirens pierced the air. A wave of relief rippled through Natalie. Kate must have made the call for help.

He took a step toward Kate. "What are ya gonna do, bitch?" The guy puffed up his chest, trying to look bigger than he was, playing the intimidation game. Apparently, he'd sized up the two of them and found Kate to be the lesser threat. Dumb mistake. "Do ya know how many whores like you I've gutted?" He laughed, harsh and creepy sounding. "I reckon I'll scalp you first."

"I reckon I'll shoot you first." Kate looked at him down the barrel of Deputy Dipshit's gun. Her cheek twitched.

He cackled, giving Natalie the chills. "You must be the crazy sister."

Boom!

The gun in Kate's hand jerked slightly.

The killer collapsed, holding his leg. A howl of pain echoed through the alley. "Ya shot my fucking knee!"

"Don't call me CRAZY!" Kate yelled back and took a step closer. "That bullet was for what you did to Tank. If you move again, I'm going to shoot you in the dick."

Natalie thought of the poor people this son of a bitch had tortured and killed over the last few months.

She stepped closer.

Kate glanced up at her. "What are you doing?"

Natalie aimed the Taser at the skin on his lower back where his shirt had pulled up. "Making sure he stays put." She squeezed the trigger.

The guy's body shuddered and stretched taut, his eyes rolling back the same as Harvey's had in the back of Kate's car. Then he stilled and seemed to deflate into the asphalt.

The sirens shrilled around them as a county sheriff's truck pulled up behind Kate's car. A Yuccaville cop car blocked off the other end, trapping everyone in between.

"Set the gun on the ground, Kate," Natalie said, following her own advice with the Taser.

"How long do you think we'll be in jail this time?" Kate asked, taking a step away from Deputy Dipshit's gun.

They both raised their arms into the air.

"Until we're little old women."

"Damn. My ice cream is going to melt."

Natalie scoffed. "Who cares about ice cream? I should have gone to Coop's camper with him last night."

"Maybe Detective Cooper will find the idea of conjugal visits sexy."

"Shut up, Kate. I'm mad at you." Natalie watched the law dogs prowl closer and groaned. "Here we go again."

Chapter Twenty-Four

High Noon …

Natalie was done.

Chewed up, spat out, and stepped on.

That was the last time she went on an ice cream run with that pregnant lunatic.

However, they had managed to bring down the diamond killer. For that, Kate and she should receive honorary deputy stars.

Grady had disagreed when Kate mentioned the gold stars idea to him. He'd left the diamond killer in Mississippi's hands and dragged Kate and Natalie back to his office along with Ronnie. For the next couple of hours, he'd chewed the three of them out about the foolishness of their posse idea in between taking their statements and making them write down every single detail Natalie and Kate could remember about their morning.

The poor sheriff's hair had been finger-plowed and re-plowed and then plowed some more by the time he allowed Natalie and Ronnie to go home with Claire, who'd come to collect them. Kate was still with Grady, though. Her high-speed chase—and argument with Deputy Dipshit when the dingleberry finally came to after the killer's tranquilizer had worn off—earned her extra after-the-takedown detention with the sheriff.

When Claire, Natalie, and Ronnie stood to leave, Grady walked them to the door. "Stop scaring the hell out of me, damn it," he said to them as they filed outside. He caught Ronnie's arm and hugged her, whispering something in her ear before sending her off with a tender good-bye kiss.

Ronnie had dropped Claire, Natalie, and the melted ice cream off at the General Store and then headed back to The Shaft to help Butch open since Kate would be detained a little longer.

Rather than follow Claire inside the General Store, Natalie took off along the campground's gravel drive.

"Where are you going?" Claire called from the porch.

"To finish something," she answered.

Big puffy clouds drifted across the deep blue sky, dappling the desert with patches of shade. The birds tweeted and sang about how good life was. A cool breeze carried the fresh scent of a new year with exciting possibilities.

It was a great day not to die.

There was one other thing that would make it an even better day for Natalie.

She headed for a certain fifth wheel camper from South Dakota. The decision she'd made this morning while getting lectured in the sheriff's office propelled her toward the guy lounging under the camper's awning in a chair next to his uncle.

Coop had a magazine with guns on the cover in his hands. Oh, good, deadly weapons porn. That should have him firing from both barrels today. A bottle of lemonade sat on the stand next to him. He looked up as she approached, his expression guarded.

"Howdy," Harvey said with a grin. "You look like you've been peein' on electric fences."

"Well, I should smile," she told Harvey, giving him some of his own medicine. She thumbed behind her. "You need to skedaddle."

"What kind of a how-ya-do is that?"

"You heard me, ol' man." She turned to Coop. "You, in the camper now."

She threaded between them and opened the screen door. Stepping over the threshold, she took a moment to check out the RV, in particular the sofa at the back end that Coop was supposedly using as a bed.

Nope, that wasn't going to cut it.

On the other side of the screen door, she heard Harvey say,

"She's got her horns out. What'd ya do now?"

"Nothing. At least nothing that I can remember."

Oh, for the love of law dogs everywhere! Did she have to spell it out again? Some detective he was.

She pulled off her T-shirt and wadded it up, glancing down to make sure her bra covered her girls for Harvey's sake.

Opening the screen door, she threw the T-shirt at Coop. It hit him in the chest. "Hurry up." She let the screen door *thwap* shut behind her and climbed the steps into the bedroom at the front of the fifth wheel.

A queen bed greeted her. Perfect. Harvey had even made the bed. All that was missing were chocolates on the pillows.

Silence came from outside the camper.

"Well, now *you* should smile, boy," Harvey said, following it with a shout of laughter. "How long am I staying gone, girlie?" he called through the screen door.

"Until I come looking for you," she hollered back. "Now git!" She closed the blinds and took off her shoes and socks.

The sound of footfalls crunching on the gravel faded.

She heard the screen door creak and then click shut.

When she looked up, Coop stood in the bedroom doorway. "You lost something." He held up her shirt.

"Did you lock the door?"

"Yes." His gaze dipped to her bra. "What are you doing, Natalie?"

"Finishing what we started years ago." She unfastened her jeans and wiggled them off her hips, stepping out of them. "Are you up for it?"

He joined her in the room, closing the door behind him and leaning against it. "What brought this on?"

Kate's insanity.

A brush with death.

The need for something more fulfilling in her life.

The realization that she wanted what Coop had to offer.

The understanding that having sex with Coop wouldn't destroy the work she'd done during her sabbatical rebuilding her self-esteem because she was a much stronger person now.

But mostly Kate's insanity.

"I'll explain later." She reached behind her and unhooked her bra, letting it fall to the floor.

Coop's eyes widened. His Adam's apple bobbed. "This isn't how I planned 'us' to happen," he said, his voice thick.

"Outside of birth control, I'm not a big fan of planning." She walked to him and began to unbutton his shirt. "How's your back? Sore?"

He grabbed her hands, stopping her. "Are you drunk?"

"Nope. Cold sober."

"You really want to do this here and now?"

She thought that was obvious. Apparently she needed to be more convincing. She pulled her hands free and slid her fingers up his chest, wrapping her arms around his neck. She pressed against him as she went up on her toes.

"Coop," she whispered, her mouth hovering at his lips. "I want you to make me yours."

"Ah, Natalie." Her name came out sounding gravelly, sexy as hell. He palmed her hips, pulling her closer.

She framed his face and brushed her lips over his, teasing a groan out of him before she delved deeper. He tasted like lemonade—sweet yet tart, with no traces of the past's bitterness to be found in his searing kisses. His tongue met hers, bold and hungry, but then played coy, drawing her even deeper.

He turned, pressing her back against the bedroom door. His tongue chased hers back into her mouth. His hands inched up her sides, his thumbs gliding along the skin at her ribs, hovering, so close.

Impatient after their years apart, she took his hands and lifted them higher. The pads of his thumbs were calloused, making her moan as he brushed over her tender skin. His hips moved against hers in sync with the flirting dance of his tongue, his jeans rubbing her just right.

He tore his mouth from hers, his breathing heavy, winded. His lips trailed a burning path down her neck and between her breasts. He dropped to his knees in front of her. His hands slid down her ribcage, his palms following the curves of her hips.

"Natalie," he said her name again with that same husky voice before circling her navel with his tongue.

She leaned her head back against the door. Was this for real? She had played this scene out in her head so many times.

"You're perfect."

He hooked his fingers in the waistband of her panties and eased them down slowly, like he was unwrapping something fragile. First one side, down over her hip, his mouth kissing a trail along her hipbone. Then the other side. This time his teeth nipped at her skin as the fabric slid away.

Natalie's knees almost buckled. "I bet you say that to all the girls," she joked.

"Only you." He tugged the flimsy material down to her ankles. "You've haunted me ever since that night."

Heat filled her at his words, her ache for him doubling. Then his mouth returned to her skin and she trembled.

"Bewitched me," he said, his lips spurring delicious tickles.

She looked down, watching him make love to her body.

This was Coop. The steely-eyed detective. Scars and all. The rough pads of his fingers scratched over her, giving her chills as he caressed her skin.

"So irresistible." He licked her.

She moaned, her body trembling.

"You're mine," he whispered, his breath hot on her inner thigh.

"Please, Coop." She closed her eyes. "I've wanted you for so long."

There was no more talking after that, not until she cried out his name, her body pulsing from his skilled touches and intimate kisses. She clutched his shoulders, reeling, panting, wanting more.

He moved up her body, his clothes blocking her from feeling the heat of his flesh.

"You're overdressed," she told him, kissing him slowly, with all of her pent-up need. The musky scent of her on his skin made Natalie want to feel him inside of her even more.

"Take my shirt off," he whispered in her ear.

She shoved the shirt off his shoulders. "Now what?"

"My pants."

She reached between them, her fingers sure. Her body hummed, electrified at the thought of what was to come. She shoved his jeans down, her hands dawdling, her fingers exploring through his boxer briefs. "Now what, hot cop?"

He pulled back and stared down at her. "Hot cop?"

"You're hot. And you're a cop." She scraped her nails along his length through the cotton barrier. "Now where were we?"

"You were taking off my clothes."

She slipped her hand inside his waistband, but held back, brushing over him once, but no more. So close, yet not quite … She licked her lips. "What now?"

"Touch me, Natalie." His mouth came down on hers. Hard. Like the rest of him. Her head spun as he wrapped his hand around hers and showed her exactly what he wanted and how.

Oh, Coop … This was the real deal. In the flesh. In her hand. She shoved down his boxer briefs.

"Now," she said, hooking her leg around his thigh to give him more access.

"Not here." He stepped out of his clothes and lifted her, dumping her on the bed. "Here." He prowled across the mattress after her as she backed up to make more room for him, his gray eyes locked onto hers.

She wrapped her legs around him as he hovered over her. She waited, wanting all he had.

But he held back.

"What?" she asked.

"Natalie." He kissed her softly, then pulled back to stare down at her again. "You take my breath away."

Oh, boy! Good-bye, heart. Hello, insatiable pining.

She arched, pushing against him. "Coop, if you don't finish what we've started, I'm going to handcuff you to the bed and torture the living hell out of you."

"Whatever you say, wildcat." He moved against her, sliding inside slowly and surely, all the while watching her.

"You feel so good," she whispered, clutching his arms as he pulled back and then drove forward again, filling her body, heart, and soul. She was in way over her head now.

His focus lowered to her mouth, his eyes darkening. "Christ," he rasped. She felt the goose bumps rise on his arms. "You're so ready for me."

She raised her hips to meet his thrusts. "I've been ready for you for years."

"Kiss me," he demanded, his gaze still on her mouth. "Your lips keep me up at night, aching."

She cupped his cheeks, using her lips to woo him further. As he spun her higher and higher, she showed him how much she wanted him with her mouth and tongue.

He groaned loud … or maybe it was her doing the groaning. She tightened her legs and held on as he pushed her to the edge.

"Oh, God!" She clung to his shoulders, wanting more. "I'm so close."

"Look at me," he ordered in a guttural voice. When she did, he pushed deep. "You're mine, Natalie."

The passion in his eyes sent her sailing over the edge. She cried out, her body clenching around his.

He watched through lowered lashes as she shivered and quaked under him, his jaw clenching while he waited for her to still. Then he drove hard a few more times until his whole body grew rigid, his muscles straining.

He collapsed onto her afterward, his body pressing hers into the mattress, his face buried in her neck.

She ran her fingers over his damp back, skimming his scars, careful not to touch the birdshot wounds.

When his breathing returned to normal he rolled off of her onto his good side, bracing himself up on his elbow. His gray eyes held hers.

She was at a loss for words. He'd just mucked up her sex life when it came to being with anyone else after him. If he decided this would be a one-time event, she might go find Kate's Taser and zap him in the ass. Repeatedly.

"Handcuff me to the bed, huh?" he said, breaking the silence. He reached out and traced her curves. "We can try that sometime, but I want to have a turn at it, too."

She smiled, her heart and brain playing tug-of-war about telling him how amazing he'd been.

Her heart won.

"Wow!" she blurted.

Sheesh. Her heart was a lovesick moron! Leading with it was

a bad idea. "What I meant to say was that you were mind-blowing."

His fingers traveled up to her face, trailing along her jawline. "I've been wanting to lose myself in you for far too long."

"Oh my, Coop." She played coy and fanned herself, pretending to swoon until she ruined it by giggling. "I couldn't have asked for a better fireworks-style ending to my sabbatical."

His fingers trailed south, along the side of her breast, his touch almost tickling. "I thought you said you had a tattoo on your right breast."

"You remember that?" She and Violet had been throwing up a smoke screen that day when Natalie had mentioned a boob tattoo.

"Trust me. When it comes to you, I remember details."

"We were trying to distract you," she explained.

"It worked."

"Well, you hid it well, Detective."

"But you weren't telling tales about the knife-stabbed heart on your left cheek."

How had he seen that in the midst of all of those kisses?

His fingers drifted down over her belly. "Along with this tattoo on your hip. But you'd talked about it being a guy's name."

"I went to the tattoo artist you recommended." Natalie glanced down at the tattoo—a Day of the Dead version of Rosie the Riveter. "The cover-up turned out amazing." She couldn't see even a trace of her ex's name.

"You didn't mention that you'd had it fixed."

She shrugged. "It's been over a month. I was keeping it to myself. It's sort of a celebration of letting go of my fucked-up past and embracing the new sabbatical version of me." She sniffed. "Although you blew my no-sex vow out of the water."

"If it's any consolation, you weren't easy to veer off course." He leaned down and kissed the Rosie tattoo, his lips making her quiver.

"I like the new one. It's sexy. Like you." His focus returned to her face. "What happened today?"

She grimaced at the memory of her wild ride through Yuccaville. "It's complicated."

"Complicated how?"

"Crazy complicated."

One of his eyebrows climbed up his forehead. "You realize that by taking off your shirt in front of my uncle, you're going to be a popular topic during his drunken and non-drunken revelry for months to come, right?"

She chuckled, but then remembered her earlier Yuccaville adventures and sobered. "Kate and I caught the diamond killer this morning."

He pulled back, pushing up onto his hand so he was half-sitting over her. "Are you kidding?"

Natalie licked her lips and let loose about her adventures in Yuccaville with Kate, ending with Grady chewing Kate's and her asses in between picking their brains over and over before releasing Natalie from custody.

When she finished, Coop let out a flood of curses. "You chased a violent serial killer with a damned Taser gun? Are you insane, woman?"

"Probably. It's Kate's fault."

"Oh, really?"

Natalie shrugged. "Mostly, but I couldn't let my pregnant cousin chase down a killer on her own, could I?"

"Is this from going over that fence?" he pointed at the small wound on her side.

"Yeah. Ronnie cleaned it, though, while we were at the cop shop, so it should heal up fine."

Coop let out a frustrated growl and eased down onto his back. "God, woman. I can't believe you."

"Me? You should have seen Kate. She went all Clint Eastwood on the killer, shooting him in the knee when he took a step toward her." Natalie left out the part about the killer calling Kate "crazy" and instigating her wrath. "Grady should hire her to track down criminals."

"You and your cousins are nuts." Coop closed his eyes, pinching the bridge of his nose. "I dread going back to Deadwood."

Natalie stilled. *I don't date local girls* … "Why's that?"

He opened one eye, looking at her. "Because you're going to hook up with Parker like usual and give me daily heart attacks."

Oh, that wasn't so bad.

"Yeah, so?" She pushed up onto her knees and straddled his thighs. "Are you going to rue the day you succumbed to me and my bewitching touch?"

He tucked his arms behind his head, staring up at her with both eyes now. "Rue? No. Although I might regret letting you see how wild I am about you."

She leaned over him, running her lips along the stubble on his jaw. His body hardened under her. "How wild are we talking?"

"More wild than your cousin, Kate." He watched her as she tasted his skin in different spots on her trek south.

"So straitjacket wild, then?" she asked at his hips, peeking up at him.

He groaned as her fingers climbed up his thighs. "Sure."

"Coop." She leaned over him, wetting her lips with intent to do delightful harm.

His gaze lowered to her mouth. "Hmmm?"

"Read me my rights."

His brow wrinkled "What?"

"You heard me." She wrapped her fingers around him. "The Miranda warning. Say it to me."

His eyes darkened. "Are you serious?"

"Yeah, I have this fantasy." She ran her tongue over him, making his body bow under her.

"Tell me." His hands gripped the sheets at his side.

"Tell you what?" She enticed another groan from him.

"About ... your ..." he growled low in his chest. "Fantasy."

"I want to resist you when you're in cop mode and tease you over to the dark side."

His gray eyes held hers for several breaths. Then a grin eased onto his face. "Natalie Beals, you have the right to remain silent," he started.

She bit him below the navel, and then sucked on the tight skin there, leaving her mark on him.

"Anything you say can and will be ..." He paused to gulp as she ran her lips over his hard flesh, following with her tongue. "... Used against you ..." His fists twisted in the sheets.

"Oh, really?" She slid up his chest, teasing, arousing. And she then sank back down, taking him in full. "Use it against me," she taunted.

"Sweet hell." He clamped onto her hips and helped her

move. "Natalie …" He said her name with a gruff intensity that lit her up inside. "Yessss. Just like that, wildcat."

"You're mine, Coop." She claimed him the same as he had her earlier.

That was as far as he made it through the Miranda warning … that time.

* * *

Later that night …

Mac sat on a stool on the customer side of the bar tonight with a local craft beer in his hand. He looked out over The Shaft. If Butch agreed to sell, this would be his future home away from home. No more hot, dusty days toiling under the desert sun. No more late hours working to fill someone else's bank account. No more long, lonely trips back and forth to Tucson.

Would he miss the work he'd done for years? Would running a bar challenge him as his job in the field had?

Change was good, he reminded himself. Life had grown stagnant … until Claire showed up at the RV park and turned his world upside down.

"You ready for another beer?" Gary the bartender was back and serving drinks with a smile after having a couple nights off to enjoy his own holiday fun.

"Thanks, but not yet."

Mac searched for Claire, finding her over by the jukebox talking to Ronnie and Natalie. The three of them were serving drinks tonight, but the crowd was light, allowing more time to hang out at the bar and share laughs—which were plentiful now that the diamond killer had been hauled off by the FBI.

Butch had figured tonight would be quieter due to most folks being back to work, trying to recover from the double wallop of Christmas and New Year's on their wallets and psyches. In lieu of the lower attendance, he'd decided to close early to enjoy a private family celebration after today's excitement. They were an hour away from Butch turning off the Open sign.

Mac took a drink from his glass, tasting a hint of something sweet in the craft beer. Maybe honey? He'd visited a small brewery once, enjoying the science behind beer making. If The Shaft became his new focus, he'd like to explore brewing beer more, dabble with creating his own concoctions. He could test out the results on patrons, fine-tuning with their help.

A rhythmic creak made Mac glance over his shoulder.

Grady's aunt with her dingle-ball accented walker paused behind him. "So, did you see Joe Martino's iron lung?" she asked, her eyes twinkling.

Mac turned and gaped at her. "How do you know about that?"

She winked. "I know a lot about plenty, including a certain pain-in-the-ass deputy." She grabbed something from her purse that was sitting in the basket of her walker and then held her closed fist toward him.

He held his palm out and she dropped something in it. He frowned down at the wrapped butterscotch candy she'd given him.

"I have more," she said. "Stop by the library sometime if you're curious."

The Shaft door opened, framing a familiar face.

When Mac looked back, Grady's aunt was squeaking toward the jukebox. What the hell was that about?

"This seat taken?" Coop pointed at the stool next to Mac.

"It is now." Mac turned back toward the bar.

Coop ordered a whiskey on the rocks from Gary. "Is it nice to be back on this side of the bar again?"

Mac shrugged. "I sort of like it back there."

"You were smooth." Coop tossed some bills on the bar, exchanging them for the tumbler of amber liquid. "A quick draw with drinks, too. Made the customers happy. Makes for good tips."

Mac nodded. How much money would it take to purchase a couple of brew kettles? He'd need to build onto the bar, make a place for the equipment. Luckily, he knew a handywoman with building experience.

"When do you go back to Tucson?" Coop asked.

"Sunday night. Then I'm turning in my resignation."

Coop took a drink. "No shit. Then what?"

"Jackrabbit Junction full time, I guess."

Coop chuckled. "The women around here will scramble your brains."

"It's too late for me. But not you. When do you head back to Deadwood?"

"Friday morning."

"Back to catching the bad guys?"

"Something like that." The detective smiled, downing more of his drink.

Mac took a hit off his beer. Something was different about Coop tonight. His smile came easy, for one thing. But the change went deeper. He couldn't pinpoint how he knew, but maybe it was the vibes rolling off the detective. *Vibes?* Now he was starting to sound like Claire and Jessica. Oh hell, things would only slide further south with him living here full time.

He smiled, too, and tipped his beer again.

But back to Coop.

Judging by the laid-back grin on his face, one would never guess the guy had been shot and nearly burned to death in the last forty-eight hours. Now that he thought about it, though, someone else had been extra happy tonight, singing and dancing as she'd served drinks. He'd attributed it to the diamond killer no longer being a threat, but maybe it was something else.

Or someone else.

Mac turned, looking for Natalie. She was easy to find, because she was making her way toward them. Her eyes were bright, her face glowed, and her focus was locked onto the guy sitting next to him.

Bingo.

He turned back to Coop. "Congratulations."

Coop's brow rose. "On going back to work?"

"On reaching the end of a dry spell."

Natalie joined them, setting her tray on the bar. "No orders, Gary," she said when the bartender looked her way. "I just stopped to visit."

The heated stare that passed between Natalie and Coop confirmed Mac's suspicion.

"I'm guessing that Natalie told you about her and Kate's excitement today in Yuccaville on their way to get ice cream," Mac said, interrupting their steamy moment.

Coop cursed, raising his glass. "They're both crazy."

"Shhhh." Natalie stole Coop's drink from him. "Kate put a bullet in a guy today for using the C-word. You don't need to get shot twice on this trip." She downed the remaining finger or two of whiskey before handing the glass back. "Oops, I stole it all, Detective Cooper. If it makes you feel any better, you can *try* to read me my rights later."

Coop grinned up at her. "I'll do more than try, Beals."

"Yeah, well the road to Hell is paved with good intentions. We'll see how far you make it this time." She patted Mac on the shoulder. "Keep Coop out of trouble. I have big plans for him later and don't need him facing down death again."

She left, heading over to where Ronnie was talking to Grady's sister.

Mac waved to the bartender. "Gary, another whiskey for the sucker sitting next to me, please."

"That obvious, huh?" Coop asked.

"You were staring at her like her picture was pinned up on the locker room wall."

Coop grunted. "I think I'm in serious trouble here."

"I'd disagree if I wasn't busy upending my life to move closer to the troublemaker leading me along by the collar."

When Gary brought another whiskey, Mac tossed out some bills. "This one's on me. Welcome to the family."

"Isn't that jumping the gun a little?"

Mac glanced his way. "You drove over a thousand miles, got shot, nearly burned to death, and then you let her steal your drink. Yet here you still sit, sneaking glances at her when you think nobody is looking."

"When you put it that way—I'm fucked." Coop swirled the amber liquid in his glass, grinning.

"Pretty much."

The door opened and Grady blew in with the cold desert air. He was still in uniform, albeit a very wrinkly one. His stubble-covered jaw had its own five-o'clock shadow. He hung his jacket on the coat rack and took the seat on the other side of Mac.

"Whatever lager is on tap, Gary."

"Pale or dark?"

"The darker the better tonight."

Grady nodded toward Mac and Coop.

"You look like you're one wheel down and dragging the axle," Mac said. "How was your day, Sheriff?"

"Kate's crazy." He thanked Gary for the lager and took several swallows, wiping the foam mustache off with a napkin.

"Careful, Grady," Mac said. "Natalie already warned Coop here about using the C-word tonight. The diamond killer catcher might shoot you next."

"She's a paperwork nightmare. I'm going to lock her up until that baby comes, I swear."

Mac laughed. "So, what's the status on Ronnie and those missing diamonds the FBI wanted to pin on her?"

"The killer isn't talking much, but the FBI found evidence in his vehicle that links him to the last three killings, so they're content that they have their man and that the diamonds he's hunting down aren't the same as those Veronica's ex swiped."

"So she's off the hook?"

"Sort of." Grady pointed over his shoulder toward the pool tables. "But Mississippi is still hanging around, so that means she's not in the clear by much."

Mac had noticed that the FBI agent was playing pool again tonight. "Is he here because of Lyle's accident in prison or is something new going on?"

"According to Mississippi, he's been told to keep an eye out for a new problem. Oddly enough, trouble is coming again in the form of someone looking for Lyle's diamonds." Grady shook his head. "I'd laugh at the irony if it wasn't Veronica waiting for the hammer to fall."

"Here we go again," Mac said.

At least Claire wasn't in the crosshairs this time. He felt for Grady. The last month had been full of sleepless nights. Maybe the sheriff was used to that level of stress for breakfast, lunch, and dinner, but Mac was not. Quitting and moving to Jackrabbit Junction was kids' play in comparison.

"How's your deputy?" Coop asked, adding, "Natalie told me about her morning chase with Kate."

"Well, he's up and moving, but he's pissed off."

Mac took a drink of beer. "Because he was shot with a tranquilizer dart?"

"Because Kate used his gun while he was tranquilized to shoot the killer. In his eyes, she stole his thunder and embarrassed him at the same time."

"Did he know that he had the killer trapped in the alley?" Mac asked.

Grady shook his head. "And that fact has him even grumpier than usual. He's accusing Kate of leading him into a trap."

Coop smirked. "We have a detective like him up in Deadwood."

"What do you do about him?" Mac asked.

"There's not much I can do besides grind my teeth while he's around." Coop smirked again. "Although Natalie's best friend does give him a solid dose of shit. As much as Parker drives me to drink, I do love to watch her sink her teeth into the detective's ass."

"Maybe I should send my deputy up to help you out, since you have experience with pains in the ass."

Coop scoffed. "No thanks. I'm full up on sons of bitches." He took a sip of whiskey.

"What's going to happen to the diamonds the killer was here to collect?" Mac asked.

"I handed them off to the FBI. I talked to Juan Moreno, a friend of mine at the local paper today. He's writing an article that with any luck will get picked up by the newspapers and television stations in Tucson and Phoenix—and farther maybe. In it, I state that the diamonds are now in the FBI's possession."

"In other words, leave us alone," Mac said.

"Exactly."

Butch pushed through the batwing doors, stepping behind the bar. He joined them, turning their trio into a quartet. "What have we here? Pretty maids all in a row?" He focused on Grady. "Except for this one. He looks like he's been hit in the face with a wet squirrel."

"It's your damned fault, Carter. You had to go and get your woman pregnant in *my* county."

Butch laughed. "I will remind you that Veronica is the one who kept the damned diamonds." He pointed at Mac. "And Claire found them under the camper. So this is your women's fault. Kate merely fixed the problem for them."

Coop chuckled. "Your three hens make quite a trio."

Thumbing toward the Deadwood detective, Mac said, "This guy thinks he's free and clear of all this because Natalie doesn't live here. He doesn't realize that the 'wild and crazy' trait is genetic."

Grady leaned forward. "How's that sabbatical treating you, Coop?"

"You're behind the times," Mac told the sheriff.

"What's that mean?" Grady looked to Butch.

"Coop scored a hat trick," Butch answered.

"Really? An old, decrepit, shot-up cop like him?" Grady grinned at the detective. "That's impressive stamina."

Coop's brow pinched as he stared at Butch. "How do you know that?"

Butch crossed his arms. "Kate pumped Natalie for answers earlier. To Natalie's credit, she tried to fend Kate off, but my bad mama jama is a real badger when she gets her teeth into something."

"Tell me about it," Grady said with a growl. "Speaking of Kate, where is she?"

"Hiding from you."

The sheriff's gaze tightened. "What did she do now?"

"Nothing. She just doesn't want to talk to you any more today."

"That's rich." Grady took a drink. "Just tell me this. Do you have her contained?"

"She's working in the kitchen tonight."

"And later?"

Butch winked at Grady. "I'll keep her busy at home."

"Good. I could use some sleep."

"You might want to tell Ronnie that. She needs a bunk now that her grandpa's camper burned down."

"Tell me what?" Ronnie said from behind Grady.

Grady turned, his gaze traveling up over the Pink Panther T-shirt Mac recognized as one of Claire's. "You're a sight for bloodshot eyes, Veronica."

"That's what all of the drunks around here tell me." She jested and kissed his cheek. "Are you done for the night, Sheriff Hardass?"

He nodded, shooting Butch a scowl. "Until Carter lets Kate loose again."

"Good." She squeezed up next to Grady, sliding her arm across his shoulders. "Your sister and I have a bet going."

"Penny's here?" At Ronnie's nod, his head tipped to the side, looking toward the pool tables. "Is she harassing Mississippi again?"

She leaned into Grady's side, rubbing her thumb over his jaw. "Not yet, but the night's young."

"What's the bet?" Mac asked.

"Penny doesn't think Grady can beat Katie's record on the video game in back. But I think he's a better shot than my little sister."

Grady snorted. "The gun sights on those video games are usually off."

Ronnie trailed her finger down the side of the sheriff's neck. "So, you're saying Penny is right? You can't beat a pregnant girl?"

"Kate is an ace shot." Butch's expression radiated pride. "Her grandfather trained her years ago. She can outshoot me at the range."

Grady cursed. "Why does the craziest person in this bar being an ace shooter *not* make me feel warm and fuzzy?"

"I'll tell you what, Sheriff Hardass," Ronnie said. "You come over and win the bet for me and I'll make you feel extra warm and fuzzy later."

Grady looked at Mac. "Did she just offer what I think she offered?"

Mac shrugged. "She is a salty bar wench."

Ronnie backhanded Mac's shoulder. "Watch it, Garner, or I'll move in with Claire and you once you're settled in."

"It'll be tight in Aunt Ruby's spare room."

"I'll plant myself right between you and my sister."

"Nice, Ronnie," Claire said from behind Mac, wrapping her arms around him. "But you can't have the middle. You kick," she reminded Ronnie. "We'll put Mac in the middle."

Grady stood, offering Claire his stool. "Have a seat. I have a record to break. 'Warm and fuzzy' is on my list of must-haves for a good night's sleep."

Claire took Grady's seat, watching Ronnie lead him toward the other side of The Shaft. She turned back to Mac. "Warm and fuzzy, huh? Poor Grady, Ronnie must not have shaved her legs again."

Butch laughed. "After the week Grady's had, I have a feeling hairy legs wouldn't put a dent in Ronnie's mojo."

Mac was still frowning about sharing a living space with Ronnie. The three of them had tried that once before and he'd ended up working all of the overtime he could muster rather than go home to Claire's sister.

"She's joking about living with us again, right?"

"I hope so." Claire leaned forward, giving Coop two thumbs-up. "I heard about your hat trick, law dog. Way to smash that sabbatical of Natalie's into the boards."

Coop cursed and took a big swig from his glass.

Mac patted Claire's arm. "Slugger, men don't really want to be congratulated about sex by their girlfriend's family—especially the womenfolk."

She wrinkled her nose. "You think that was too personal for the detective?"

"Talking about the details of Natalie's sex life is probably too personal for all of us."

"Well, he is sleeping with my cousin." She leaned forward again. "If you're going to continue to fornicate with Natalie, you need to learn a few ground rules."

"I thought you ladies didn't cotton to rules," Coop shot back, his gaze challenging.

"He has a good point," Mac told Claire.

She nodded. "You're right, Coop, we don't. Never mind. Throw Natalie over your shoulder and have your way with her. Just be careful how you treat her, or we'll sic Crazy Kate on you."

Coop chuckled.

Claire didn't. She took Mac's hand, squeezing it. "Coop thinks I'm joking."

Mac leaned forward, stealing a kiss. "He'll learn."

Patsy Cline's version of "Crazy" started playing on the jukebox. Claire smiled into his eyes and stole a kiss back.

"Who's playing that damned song?!" Kate yelled out from the order window.

Claire looked toward the kitchen. "Where's my order, Kate?" She palmed Mac's glass of beer. "May I?"

He nodded, watching her lick a little bit of foam off her upper lip. *Damn!*

"Get back here and make it yourself," Kate hollered.

"That's some shitty line cook you hired," Claire said to Butch. She stood and turned back to Mac. "Did you ask Butch yet?"

He shook his head.

"Did you change your mind?"

He shook his head again.

"Me either. Talk to Butch." She gave him one more kiss, tasting like his beer, and then strode through the batwing doors.

"Talk to me about what?" Butch asked.

Mac finished his beer. "I'm quitting my job and moving to Jackrabbit Junction."

"No shit?" At Mac's nod, Butch poured another glass of beer and set it on the counter in front of Mac and then refilled Coop's glass. "Congratulations. This one is on the house."

He held out his own glass of beer for a toast. The three of them clinked glasses and drank to Mac's announcement.

Natalie called for Coop, waving for him to join her at the pool table.

"Excuse me, gentlemen." He stood, his drink in hand. "I need to go get schooled at pool by a hot babe."

After Coop left, Mac took another drink and went for it. "Here's the thing," he said to Butch. "I need something to do day in and day out after I move here or I'll drive Claire nuts. You would like to spend your time fixing up classic cars, and Kate's having a baby." Mac laced his fingers together on the bar. "Claire and I have a solution. We'd like you to consider letting us buy The Shaft from you. If you're game to sell, I need numbers to take to my accountant in Tucson next week so I can start lining up the money."

Butch rubbed his jaw, his brows wrinkled in the middle. "You and Claire want to buy The Shaft?"

"Yes."

"Together?"

Mac nodded.

"That sounds like a serious case of 'commitment' from Claire," Butch said, his forehead smoothing out.

"You don't say?" Mac couldn't hold in his grin. He'd found a way to skirt Claire's issue with exchanging vows while still tying their futures together for years to come.

Next up, a house in both of their names.

"Well played, Garner." Butch toasted to Mac again.

"So, what do you say? You want to sell The Shaft?"

Butch's smile reached his ears. "Hell, yes!"

Chapter Twenty-Five

Friday, January 4th

K ate's crazy," Claire told Natalie and then tugged her Mighty Mouse hat down lower on her head.

She pulled a small handful of screws from her tool belt pouch and stuck them to the magnet on her drill. The railing and deck steps were coming along smoothly. At this rate, Natalie and she would be wrapping things up by tomorrow, which would leave Sunday morning free before Mac and she headed to Tucson later that day to pack him up for good.

Claire smiled at the idea of Mac sleeping next to her every night, eating breakfast with her, building a new life together here in the desert. Things were about to get busy around here, and just in time for birding season, too. She'd have to figure out how to balance her time at the RV park and The Shaft. Ronnie and Jessica were going to need to step up to help more. Too bad Natalie was heading back north. They could use her help around here. What was Natalie's brother up to these days? She hadn't seen Luke in years. She wondered if he needed a job.

Natalie looked up from the electrical box she was installing under the edge of the deck. "You say Kate's crazy as if that's news to me. I'm the one who ended up on a deadly race to chase down a serial killer because of her insanity."

Claire scoffed. "Quit your crying, baby. You didn't even have a gun pointed at you at any time during your so-called deadly race."

"I'm not getting into a pissing contest with you today about who's suffered more from your sister's bouts of insanity." Natalie set her wire-crimping tool on the edge of the deck. "So, why are you calling Kate crazy now?"

"Careful using that C-word," Chester called from his supervisor's chair. "I saw Porn Star's Volvo pull up around front a few minutes ago."

"Remember, Coop's not here anymore to take the bullets fer you two," Harvey added.

Claire looked at Natalie to see her reaction to Harvey's words. It was hard to tell if her cousin was frowning about Coop's absence, Kate's craziness, or the deck's wiring situation. Maybe it was all three.

"So the detective headed north this morning?" Claire asked, fishing.

"Yep." Natalie nudged her chin toward Coop's uncle. "Since Harvey wanted to stick around a little longer to hang out with Chester the Molester, I let Coop drive my pickup home. I'll ride back with Harvey early next week."

"For the record," Chester said, cracking a beer. "I only molest the ladies who sexually proposition me first."

"It's self-defense," Harvey agreed with a snicker. "Speakin' of sex—"

"Nobody was," Natalie cut in.

"Now that yer lovin' man is gone, I'm takin' my bed back tonight. You can have the couch."

"Fine," Natalie said, her cheeks a little pinker than they'd been a moment ago.

"I need my beauty rest," Harvey continued.

"Okay," Natalie said, her frown and blush now mixing.

"And you two lovebugs had that bed squeakin' last night like a windmill needin' oil. I was gettin' seasick from all of the rockin' and rollin' comin' from the front end of the camper."

"Jeepers creepers, Harvey!" Natalie scowled at Coop's uncle. "I gave you ear plugs."

Harvey's smile widened until both of his gold teeth shone. "I couldn't hear anything fun with 'em in."

Natalie grumbled something under her breath about filling Harvey's backside with birdshot next time.

"You kicked a poor old man out of his bed?" Claire joined in the teasing, laughing at Natalie's glare.

"Fer two nights in a row, even," Harvey bellyached.

"We didn't kick you out," Natalie said. "And your nephew paid you per night, remember?"

Chester hooted. "Now that's using your noggin to make some quick cash."

"Sex pays," Harvey added with a nod.

"When are you and Mac taking off?" Natalie asked Claire, changing the subject.

"Sunday." Claire secured a piece of the railing to one of the deck posts she and Mac had installed yesterday while Natalie was out hiking with Coop. The two lovebugs had spent their last day together playing instead of working. "Between you and me and Mac, we'll have this deck done by tomorrow, I'm thinking."

"If not, Gramps and I can finish the last bit Sunday afternoon," Natalie said. "Chester and Harvey are going to help me with cleanup, aren't you, boys?"

"Don't be getting too rambunctious now," Chester said.

"Ya need to come to Deadwood sometime," Harvey told Chester. "We could stir up plenty of trouble in the Hills if ya get tired of bird watchin' down here."

"Let's make it so." Chester held up his beer, clinking cans with Harvey.

Natalie groaned. "The last thing Deadwood needs is you two coyotes hunting trouble together."

The back door opened and Ronnie stepped out on the new deck. She wore a pair of Kate's yoga pants and a faded yellow Dancing Winnebagos RV Park T-shirt.

"Natalie," she said, walking over to where Natalie was working on the junction box. "Katie wanted me to tell you that the drugstore in Yuccaville left a message on her phone about that camera film you guys turned in last week. They weren't able to develop the film. Something about it looked like it'd been overexposed."

"That was the film you found in the old electric box under the deck?" Claire asked.

Natalie nodded. "One and the same."

"Dang. I was hoping there would be some interesting

pictures on the roll."

Ronnie scoffed. "You trying to stir up trouble again?"

"You're one to talk."

"I can't control the shit Lyle keeps getting me into."

"I'm not talking about *your* ex. I'm talking about Grady's."

Ronnie crossed her arms. "What about Elizabeth? What have you heard? That bitch better not be bringing Grady lunch anymore."

"Kate said you're challenging her to some fight."

"What? I haven't even seen Grady's ex since that night Katie gave her a good soaking at The Shaft."

"You think there'll be bikinis and mud involved?" Chester asked, grinning at Coop's uncle.

"It ain't worth watchin' otherwise," Harvey replied.

Claire threatened the two clowns with her drill before turning back to Ronnie. "Ask Kate about it. I'm just repeating what she told me last night."

"Why would you believe Katie? Her marbles are scattered far and wide over the desert floor."

Claire grinned at Natalie. "I told you Kate is crazy."

"Yeah, but you didn't specify why. The range of possibilities is vast when it comes to your little sister these days."

"Are you selling tickets for this fight?" Chester asked.

"There isn't going to be a fight," Ronnie told him. "But if there were, you'd be in my corner giving me pointers, not in the stands."

Chester winked at her. "I'll wear bells, Rocky." He leaned over to Harvey. "Ronnie is one hell of a scrapper."

"I think Natalie and Claire have me beat," Ronnie told them. She sat on the edge of the porch next to where Claire was installing the railing. "Are Mac and you really buying The Shaft?"

"That's the plan."

"Are you going to need a bookkeeper?"

"Yep, and a waitress. Maybe something else before it's all said and done, too." Claire stuck a screw on the end of her drill bit. "Don't think for a minute that you're getting out of working your ass off when Butch is no longer the owner. Besides, Kate's a short-timer with that baby coming this spring."

"What am I?" Kate asked, stepping out onto the deck with a bowl of ice cream in her hand.

"*Not* crazy," Chester said and pulled two cigars out from his shirt pocket, offering one to Harvey.

"You're a kiss ass, Chester," Claire said to the wiseacre.

Kate smiled. "Thank you, Chester, but I'm still not naming my first child after you."

"Worth a shot," he muttered around the cigar, fishing his lighter out of his cargo pants.

Claire glanced at Ronnie. "You'll have a job as long as you want one. A place to live is another story, though. Ruby's place is going to be tight. You sure you wouldn't rather bunk with Grady than Jessica?"

She sighed, nodding. "I can't move in with Grady."

"Why not?" Kate sat next to Ronnie at the edge of the deck. She spooned mint chocolate chip ice cream into her mouth. "Does he have cop cooties?"

"Cute. You act more and more like Natalie every day."

"Lucky her." Natalie stuck her tongue out at Ronnie.

"What's your problem with living with Grady?" Claire asked. "You sleep at his place most nights now."

"That's different." Ronnie chewed on her lower lip. "Moving in together is big. Seems too fast. Besides, I need to make sure I'm not just clinging to him because he makes a nice and stable buoy while I'm weathering Lyle's shit storms."

"You think you're just using him?" Kate asked.

Ronnie shrugged. "Most likely not, but I want to be sure. He deserves a good woman. I'm not certain where I land on that scale."

"You're not using him," Natalie said, her focus on the circuit box.

"How do you know?" Kate took another spoonful of ice cream.

"Because that's Claire's and my style, not Ronnie's."

"Hey!" Claire said, aiming a mock glare at her cousin.

"Even so," Ronnie said. "If I move in with Grady, there's no turning back. I can't move out without it being a big problem."

"She's trying to keep an escape hatch open," Chester said,

blowing out a cloud of smoke.

Harvey grunted. "Makes sense. I always like to know there's a way out, in case ya get wasps in yer outhouse."

Claire was wary of outhouse wasps herself. "Did you tell Grady any of this stuff when he offered his place?"

"Of course not. I said I wanted to think about it."

"Chicken shit," Kate said. "Life's more fun if you just dive in, clothes and all."

"I don't have any clothes," Ronnie said. "Or anything else for that matter, thanks to the Winnebago fire."

"You're like a phoenix rising from the ashes," Chester said, waxing poetically as he puffed on his cigar. "Father Time will quell all doubts."

"Who are you and what have you done with Chester?" Claire asked.

"I've been reading a book of quotes someone left in the latrine. I'm going to use some of the tear-jerking ones on the women around here to see if that softens 'em up."

Harvey snickered. "So long as they don't *soften* you up, too, if ya get my meanin'."

"If they do, I'll just swallow another pocket rocket pill." Chester hooted and took another puff from his cigar.

"Don't listen to Kate," Natalie said to Ronnie. "She'll drag you into the middle of a gunfight and hand you a measly Taser gun."

Kate laughed loud enough to scare off a pair of scrub jays. "What a ride this last week has been." Then she sobered too quickly for Claire's comfort. "We have a problem, you guys."

"What now?" Claire lowered her drill, her gut tightening.

"It's about Gramps's Winnebago," she said in a low voice, frowning back at the house.

"If you're worrying about Gramps and Ruby hearing you, they are in Yuccaville getting groceries now that you've been banned from making grocery runs by the rest of us."

"What about the Winnebago?" Natalie asked, her tone tight. She must still be pissed about Coop almost becoming a crispy critter that night.

"I know who started the fire."

"What? How?" Ronnie asked. "Grady said the fire marshal hasn't given his official report yet on how the fire was started."

"I figured it was the diamond killer," Claire added.

"Who?" Natalie pressed.

Kate grimaced. "Mom."

"What?!" Claire and Ronnie said in unison.

"Aunt Deborah did it?" Natalie sounded winded.

Chester leaned forward. "You're kidding."

Kate laced her fingers together on her lap. "Mom called me last night in tears. She said that she'd been drinking too much again the night of the fire. She'd been angry at Dad."

"That hair of the dog is dangerous stuff," Harvey said.

"Angry about what now?" Claire asked. "The divorce is long over."

"Dad told her that he's going to start visiting us more and wanted her to try to put their differences aside so he can have his daughters back in his life." She frowned. "Mom told me she remembers going to the bathroom with one of Manny's cigars. He doesn't like it when she smokes, so she sneaks them."

"Oh, no," Claire said.

"Oh, yeah. On her way back to bed, she tossed the cigar toward Gramps's Winnebago. She can't remember running it under water like she usually does when she's sober." Kate looked toward Natalie. "You must have been in the shower while she was in the restroom sneaking the cigar. Did you smell it when you stepped outside?"

Natalie shook her head. "All I could smell was the burning Winnebago."

"Shit," Ronnie said.

"She could have killed Coop," Natalie growled.

"Not to mention burned up the damned campground," Claire said. If the wind had been blowing harder and the guys hadn't moved those propane tanks, the whole park could have been flattened.

Kate nodded. "She knows how bad this is."

"What's she going to do about it?" Ronnie asked.

"She said she talked to Manny. He asked her to consider checking herself into a rehab clinic in Tucson. He's researched a couple and is willing to join her there if she needs him." Kate shrugged. "She agreed."

"Good," Claire said. "This has gone on long enough."

"She said as much," Kate said. "She also mentioned needing to work on her anger issues with both Dad and Grandma."

"Do we believe her?" Ronnie asked. "How do we know she'll follow through and not slide back into another glass of cognac?"

Claire wanted to believe her mom, but … "She'll have to prove she means it."

Kate nodded. "I told her that. I also said that she's made life rough for all of us, including Gramps. She needs to get help or go back home to Rapid City and drink herself into the grave there, because we don't want to watch her self-destruct if she's not willing to try to turn her life around."

"Wow," Natalie said, her face lined. "That must have been a hard conversation."

"It was." Kate took another bite of ice cream. "The excessive drinking has to stop, though. Alcohol will not fix Mom's problems. She has to take the first step. The rest of us can help, but initially it's up to her."

"Gramps is going to be pissed about his Winnebago," Ronnie said.

"If Deborah gets help," Chester spoke up, "your grandfather will forgive her. He's been worried. I can see it whenever she's playing cards with us, drinking like a fish. Ford watches her a lot, all scowls and snarls."

"Gramps always scowls," Claire joked.

"Yeah, but this is different. It's more of a worried-about-his-kid sort of scowl."

"There's something else," Kate said. "Something I have to show you guys, but it has nothing to do with Mom."

"What now?" Claire asked.

Kate extracted an envelope from inside her jacket. "I found this on Claire's Jeep last night at The Shaft when I took out the trash."

"What were you doing taking out the trash?" Claire said. "You know Butch doesn't like you doing that."

"I'm pregnant, not deathly ill. Valentine needs to loosen up, give me a little more rein."

"I don't know about that," Natalie jested. "I'm all for keeping you locked up until that baby pops out."

"Keep it up, hussy, and I'll draw a Fu Manchu mustache on your face with permanent marker while you're sleeping."

Harvey snickered. "I'd listen to her," he told Natalie. "She looks like she'd stomp a mudhole in yer guts if you crossed her wrong."

Ronnie took the envelope from Kate and opened it, pulling out a piece of paper. Her face paled. "Fuck." She looked up at Claire. "Turns out the diamond killer wasn't the one leaving us the cryptic notes." She held out the paper for Claire to read.

The author used cut-out magazine letters again:

I'm coming for you.

"Son of a cockroach." Claire looked at Ronnie. "You think this has something to do with Lyle's mess?"

Natalie joined them, reading the letter. "Why would it be on the Jeep windshield if that were the case?"

"Because Ronnie doesn't have a vehicle," Chester said.

"It's Elizabeth, I'll bet," Ronnie said, her upper lip wrinkled. "That bitch doesn't know when to stop."

"You did take her man," Natalie said.

Ronnie's chin jutted. "Grady is *my* man."

"It's not Elizabeth," Kate said, taking another bite of ice cream. She pointed her spoon at Claire. "It's not related to Lyle's crap either."

"Oh, yeah, Sherlock? Who do you think is behind this?"

Kate's left eye twitched. Twice. "Deputy Dipshit."

"What?" Natalie scoffed.

"Why would Ernie do this?" Claire asked. "He could lose his job."

"Katie, you're just pissed at the deputy for the shit he said about you to Grady the day you took down the diamond killer with his gun."

"I'm telling you guys, Ernie's the one." Kate's eye twitched again. "The Prickly Pear Posse will ride again!" she crowed. She took another bite of ice cream. "We need to get posse jackets."

"Kate," Claire started.

Kate scrambled to her feet. "This time we're taking down Deputy Dipshit for good!" With a nod, as if both the Dr. Jekyll and Mr. Hyde version agreed with that last statement, Kate turned and went back into the house, slamming the door behind her.

"Oh, crud," Ronnie said. "Grady is going to be pissed she's going after his deputy."

Claire looked over at Natalie. "I told you, Kate's crazy."

Natalie ran a hand down her face. "You guys are going to get into so much trouble with the law dogs."

Harvey whooped. "You know what, Chester? I like it down here in Jackrabbit Junction." He rubbed his hands together. "This place is excitin'!"

The End ... for now

Author's Note: I hiked to Fort Bowie National Historic Site with my husband and children a few years ago in the early spring and fell in love with it. If you ever have the chance to visit the old fort, it's worth the time and hike. However, my daughter will tell you to wear good hiking shoes (and socks!), carry a lot of water, and watch out for rattlesnakes.

About the Author

Ann Charles is a *USA Today* bestselling author who writes award-winning mysteries that are splashed with humor, paranormal, romance, and whatever else she feels like throwing into the mix. When she is not dabbling in fiction, arm-wrestling with her children, attempting to seduce her husband, or arguing with her sassy cats, she is daydreaming of lounging poolside at a fancy resort with a bottle of tequila in one hand and a great book in the other.

Connect with Me Online

Facebook (Personal Page):
http://www.facebook.com/ann.charles.author

Facebook (Author Page):
http://www.facebook.com/pages/Ann-Charles/37302789804?ref=share

Twitter (as Ann W. Charles):
http://twitter.com/AnnWCharles

Ann Charles Website:
http://www.anncharles.com

More Books by Ann

Books in the Deadwood Mystery Series

WINNER of the 2010 Daphne du Maurier Award for Excellence in Mystery/Suspense

WINNER of the 2011 Romance Writers of America® Golden Heart Award for Best Novel with Strong Romantic Elements

Welcome to Deadwood—the Ann Charles version. The world I have created is a blend of present day and past, of fiction and non-fiction. What's real and what isn't is for you to determine as the series develops, the characters evolve, and I write the stories line by line. I will tell you one thing about the series—it's going to run on for quite a while, and Violet Parker will have to hang on and persevere through the crazy adventures I have planned for her. Poor, poor Violet. It's a good thing she has a lot of gumption to keep her going!

Short Stories from Ann's
Deadwood Mystery Series

The Deadwood Shorts collection includes short stories featuring the characters of the Deadwood Mystery series. Each tale not only explains more of Violet's history, but also gives a little history of the other characters you know and love from the series. Rather than filling the main novels in the series with these short side stories, I've put them into a growing Deadwood Shorts collection for more reading fun.

The Deadwood Undertaker Series
Life at the Coffin Joint

Deadwood (late 1876) ... A rowdy and reckless undertaker's delight. What better place for a killer to blend in?

Enter undertaker Clementine Johanssen, tall and deadly with a hot temper and short fuse, hired to clean up Deadwood's dead ... and the "other" problem. She's hell-bent on poking, sticking, or stabbing anyone that steps out of line.

But when a couple Santa Fe sidewinders ride into town searching for their missing uncle, they land neck deep in lethal gunplay, nasty cutthroats, and endless stinkin' snow. Their search leads them to throw in with Clementine to hunt for a common enemy.

What they find chills them all to the bone and sends them on an adventure they'll never forget.

From the bestselling, multiple award-winning, humorous Deadwood Mystery series comes a new herd of tales set in the same Deadwood stomping grounds, only back in the days when the Old West town was young.

The Dig Site Mystery Series

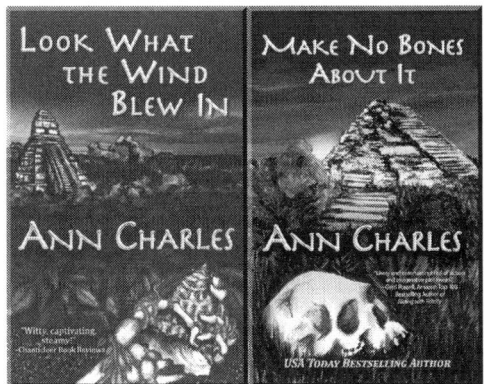

Welcome to the jungle—the steamy Maya jungle that is, filled with ancient ruins, deadly secrets, and quirky characters. Quint Parker, the renowned photojournalist (and lousy amateur detective), is in for a whirlwind of adventure and suspense as he and archaeologist Dr. Angélica García get tangled up in mysteries from the past and present in exotic dig sites. Loaded with action and laughs, along with all sorts of steamy heat, these two will keep you sweating along with them as they do their best to make it out of the jungle alive in every book.

Made in the USA
Columbia, SC
13 July 2019